VANISHING POINT

Danielle Ramsay is a proud Scot living in a small seaside town in the North East of England. Always a storyteller, it was only after initially following an academic career lecturing in literature that she found her place in life and began to write creatively full time. After much hard graft her work was shortlisted for the CWA Debut Dagger in 2009. Always on the go, always passionate in what she is doing, Danielle fills her days with horse-riding, running and murder by proxy.

Vanishing Point is her second novel. Her first, *Broken Silence*, is also published by Avon.

By the same author

Broken Silence

DANIELLE RAMSAY

Vanishing Point

AVON

AVON

A division of HarperCollins*Publishers*
77–85 Fulham Palace Road,
London W6 8JB

www.harpercollins.co.uk

A Paperback Original 2012
1

First published in Great Britain by
HarperCollins*Publishers* 2012

Copyright © Danielle Ramsay 2012

Danielle Ramsay asserts the moral right to
be identified as the author of this work

A catalogue record for this book is
available from the British Library

ISBN-13: 978-1-84756-233-3

Set in Minion by Palimpsest Book Production Limited,
Falkirk, Stirlingshire

Printed and bound in Great Britain

MIX
Paper from
responsible sources
FSC˘ C007454

FSC™ is a non-profit international organisation established to promote
the responsible management of the world's forests. Products carrying the
FSC label are independently certified to assure consumers that they come
from forests that are managed to meet the social, economic and
ecological needs of present and future generations,
and other controlled sources.

Find out more about HarperCollins and the environment at
www.harpercollins.co.uk/green

Acknowledgements

I would first like to thank all my family and friends. Especially Francesca, Charlotte, Gabriel and Ruby, who are without a doubt my inspiration. I extend the same gratitude to Jordan, Nathan and Lily Turnbull – thank you for being there. Thanks to Elaine and Pete Wilson for their constant encouragement and kindness – I am indebted to you. Thanks also to Dr Lynne Johnston and David Kenny for their invaluable advice. Thanks to Paul and Jacqui Treweek, and Suzanne Forsten for their endless support. And to Keith and Michelle Murphy for keeping me sane.

I am eternally grateful, and always will be, to my literary agent, Jenny Brown. Thank you for believing and still believing in me.

Thanks also, to all at Avon, Harper Collins, for being such a fantastic team, and in particular to Keshini and Helen. Finally, so much credit and heartfelt thanks go to my editor Caroline Hogg for all her patience and hard work in bringing this book about – thank you for persisting with me and for being such a visionary.

For Re – you know why.

Chapter One

Friday: 2:40am

'*Kales vaikas!*'
  '*Gaukite sušikti kekše!*'
  'Oh God . . . no . . .' she muttered.

She didn't hear the foghorn in the distance, or feel the wet sea fret as it wrapped itself around her thin, cold body. All she felt was fear.

She turned and ran as hard as she could up the dark street, away from the glow of the main road where she'd managed to jump out the car.

She could hear them continue to shout in what sounded like Russian followed by the roar of a car's engine. She knew it was them. They wouldn't give up until they caught her. She knew too much. Had seen too much for them to let her disappear.

Suddenly a hazy white glow appeared at the top of the dark street as a car turned down it, heading towards her.

Seeing her chance she ran as fast as she could towards the blinding glare of the approaching vehicle, grazing her bare feet against the jagged, uneven pavements. She suddenly tripped over the kerb and fell, landing heavily on her hands and knees on the road.

'Fuck!' she cried out.

She staggered up, her long dark hair clinging in damp clumps to her waxen, terrified face. Ignoring her bleeding knees, she lunged into the middle of the road, right in front of the oncoming car.

Skidding, the car slammed on its brakes, just missing her.

'Help me, please . . . help . . .'

Furious, the driver punched his horn to get her out of the way.

'Please . . .'

Visibly pissed off, the driver blasted the horn again.

Desperate, she ran round to the passenger door and tried to open it.

The door was locked. She started pounding at the window.

The driver, a dark-haired man in his late thirties, looked at her with contempt.

'Please . . .' she begged. 'You've got to help me . . . please . . . They're going to hurt me . . .'

'Piss off home, you drunken cow!' he said in disgust as he looked at her.

Her face was covered in a sheen of cold sweat as smudged black eyeliner and mascara trailed down her cheeks. Her short, strapless black dress was ripped halfway down the side, immodestly showing the scanty black lacy bra and thong underneath.

'No, you can't leave me here! They'll kill me!' she begged.

'Too right I can, you slapper!'

He put his foot to the floor, threw the gear stick into first and took off, tyres screeching as he did so.

'No . . . God . . . no . . .'

Feeling sick she watched the car speed away. She didn't know what to do or where to run. All she knew was that if she didn't hide, if they found her . . . She didn't want to think about what would happen next.

She had to keep moving. And fast.

She turned and started running, following the direction the car had come from, hoping that she would find someone. Anyone who could help her.

Then she heard them turn into the street. Their footsteps pounding hard against the road, gaining on her. They were fast. Faster than her.

'*Stop jūs sušikti apskretėlė!*'

She didn't know what he was saying but she instantly recognised the voice and it caused her stomach to tighten with fear.

She stopped, paralysed.

Despite her instinct to run, she turned around.

He was standing less than twenty feet away. Six foot tall, if not more, wearing a designer black suit, an open-necked white shirt. Beside him, his muscle-bound brother. Virtually identical in height, build and dress. Both dark-skinned, covered in stubble that crept up their necks and across their prominent jawlines and cheek bones. Their hair was the same length as the stubble on their faces; coarse, thick and black. Their eyes just as dark with a hard, menacing edge.

Unable to move, she watched as a car idled up the street, coming to a stop behind the two men.

'*Ateiti cia kale!*'

'No . . . please . . .'

'*Ateik čia apskretėlė. Dabar!*' his brother barked, gesturing for her to come to him.

She shook her head as tears started to trail down her face. She didn't need to understand the words to know what he wanted. He wanted her.

'No . . . no . . .'

'Fucking bitch!' he cursed in a heavy accent as he strode over to her.

'Help me! Someone! Help me!' she screamed.

He grabbed her aggressively from behind. Yanking her head back by her long dark hair as his other leather-gloved hand silenced her. She struggled, unable to breathe as his hand covered her mouth and nose.

'*Sustabdyti!*' he ordered, snapping her head back as punishment.

She stopped fighting him.

'Good girl,' he muttered.

He then forced her over to the idling black Mercedes with blackened windows. The rear passenger window buzzed down to reveal a man in his early forties, tanned with short blond hair and piercingly blue cold eyes.

He momentarily held her terrified gaze, enjoying her fear.

The man put his right hand out the window and gently touched her cheek. His gold signet ring with the emblem 'N' catching her skin.

She winced, noticing that his smallest finger was deformed. Half a gnarled stump remained where the finger had been chopped off.

Terrified, she stared into the man's eyes.

A delicate smile played at the corner of his lips.

He then nodded at the man restraining her.

'Please . . . please . . . let me go . . . I won't talk . . .' she begged.

He ignored her.

She watched with sickening realisation as the dark tinted window buzzed up.

Her captor suddenly relaxed his grip on her.

'Good. You're learning . . .' he whispered hoarsely, brushing his lips against her cold, glistening cheek.

The pungent smell of strong, stale tobacco lingered on his sour breath.

His hands gently encircled her throat.

'No . . . no . . . please?' she implored as she looked at the other brother.

He stared at her, unmoved, with eyes that had seen it all before.

She tried to prise the gloved hands from her neck.

His grip tightened.

Terrified, she struggled, clawing and scratching at his large hands.

Grunting with satisfaction he squeezed even harder.

She frantically tore with bloodied, broken nails as her lungs began to burn.

Ten seconds later she felt hot urine trickle down her legs as the fight started to leave her body.

'Sssh, little bird . . .' he moaned gutturally as she began to spasm.

He picked up her eight-stone body, threw her over his shoulder and carried her to the rear of the waiting black Mercedes. He released the boot and stared in admiration at the immaculate thick black plastic-lined interior. Without effort he dumped her into the prepared space. Smiling, he pulled out a ten-inch serrated knife from inside his coat and gently caressed the gleaming blade against the faint pulse in her neck and then slowly ran the tip down towards her full, pert breasts.

'Later,' he muttered in a heavy Eastern European accent before slamming the boot of the car shut.

He then looked around the shadowy street checking to see whether anyone was about. Nobody. The street was in darkness. He expected as much. It was after two-thirty in the morning. But he knew they had been lucky. This time.

Chapter Two

Moaning, she lifted her aching head up off the cold tiled floor. It was dark, too dark to make anything out. The acrid stench of urine filled her nostrils. In the background, the razor-sharp noise of dripping water echoed again and again.

She tried to remember what had happened but her head hurt too much. It felt heavy and foggy. It took her a couple of moments to realise that she was cold, very cold, and another few more before she became aware that she was naked. An overwhelming sense of panic started to build. She couldn't figure out where she was or how she had gotten there.

All she knew was that she was hurting. Really hurting.

She tried to swallow and gagged, forcing saliva and blood to dribble out the corners of her mouth. She attempted to gulp back the thick, metallic taste in her mouth but found herself choking. She knew something was wrong as blood continued to pool at the back of her throat.

Panicking, she staggered to her feet, causing a searing white burst of pain in her abdomen. She instinctively placed her hands over her stomach and felt a warm stickiness. She

7

ran her fingers across the gnarled slash realising that it ran from hip to hip. Horrified, she slipped on the wet floor, falling backwards.

The only noise emanating from her mouth was a gurgling splutter as she continued to choke.

Suddenly the door was kicked open and harsh light from the hallway flooded the men's urinals.

'Fucking hell!' muttered a male voice as he took in the carnage in front of him.

'Get Madley! And I mean now!' he shouted as he ran over to her thrashing body.

He knelt down beside her and gently moved her into the recovery position, ignoring her moans of agony as he turned her. She suddenly began convulsing. With two fingers he started to pull out the blackened blood clots which were choking her.

It was then he realised where the blood was coming from.

Her tongue had been cut out.

His eyes dropped to her mutilated left breast. Scorched deep into her skin was a four-inch 'N'. On the other breast, the word 'PIG' was cut into it. He then noticed that the pool of blood he was kneeling in was coming from the deep slash running across her stomach.

He had recognised her immediately as the copper who had been in earlier.

She had come looking for trouble. And it seemed that it had found her.

She was now passing in and out of consciousness. It was bad enough having a mutilated copper found in Madley's club, let alone a dead one.

She didn't have much time. Blood was continuing to ebb from the knife wound across her abdomen.

He turned towards the corridor.

'Get Madley. Fucking get Madley!' he yelled as he looked around for something, anything to stem the flow of blood. He quickly took his shirt off and pressed it hard against her slashed stomach.

'Shit! Shit!' he muttered as he waited for instructions.

He couldn't figure out what was taking Gibbs so long. All he had to do was ask Madley what he wanted done. He needed to know whether they had to dump her somewhere.

Then he heard the screech of approaching sirens. It was too late. Some bastard had set Madley up. Whoever had done this to her had made sure Madley had no time to clean up and get rid of her before the cops turned up.

'Fuck it!' he cursed, agitated.

He was worried. Madley was in trouble. And this was just the start.

Chapter Three

Jack Brady watched as the blood-red sun continued to rise, blazing from the depths of the North Sea horizon. In the background Mazzy Star played, soulful and unobtrusive.

The calm was disturbed by the buzz of his phone. He stretched over for his BlackBerry. The copper in him told him it was bad news.

'DI Brady,' he answered quietly.

He listened.

'Conrad?'

Brady sat forward. 'Run that by me again.'

'Christ!' Brady let the shocking words sink in.

'Yeah . . . yes, I hear you, Conrad,' Brady answered. 'Yeah . . . I'll be ready . . . No . . . you're not interrupting anything . . .'

He thought about the previous night. After a couple of pints in the Fat Ox watching the band, Damaged Goods, he had left. Not knowing where he was heading, only that he didn't want to go back to an empty five-bedroomed house. Somehow he had ended up down at the Blue Lagoon nightclub.

10

And that was what had led him to spend the early hours sitting waiting for her call. Waiting for an explanation of why she was back in the North East. Why she hadn't told him, hadn't warned him. After all, the last time he had seen her was over a year ago. But DC Simone Henderson, his ex-junior colleague, was back. The problem was, she had been more than a colleague. He had regrettably spent a drunken night with her which had resulted in the end of his marriage. Ironically both Claudia, his wife, and DC Simone Henderson ended up transferring as far away from him as possible.

He had spotted her standing at the bar laughing with two men. Her black hair had shone in the dim light.

Brady had stood there, shocked. Not believing that she was actually there. It didn't make any sense. She worked for the Met now, so why would she be back in the North East, let alone in the Blue Lagoon of all places?

He was about to go over. But in one move she flirtatiously tilted her head back and, laughing at whatever had been said to her by one of the men, turned and caught Brady's eye.

Her smile froze. Something in her eyes told him to disappear. And fast. She clearly didn't want him there.

Then, acting as if she didn't know him, she turned her attention back to the two men.

Brady could see that they had money: their sharp black suits and sharply cut hair said as much.

Resisting the urge to go over, Brady did as she had intimated and quietly slipped out. He had then returned home and took up his vigil by the first-floor bay window, watching the black, unforgiving sea, waiting for her to call. He had played with the idea of ringing her. He still had her number. But he had fought the compulsion; this was her call.

Seeing her last night had uncomfortably awakened emotions that he had tried to suppress when she had suddenly put in for a transfer. She had literally disappeared from his life, refusing to answer any of his calls or emails. Finally, he got the message. But all he had wanted to do was to apologise for forcing her to leave the Northumbrian force.

'Sir?' questioned Conrad, interrupting his thoughts.

'I'll see you shortly,' Brady replied.

'Yes, sir,' Conrad answered.

He'd only told Brady part of it. What was left unsaid had to be told face to face. The station was reeling from the news. But Conrad knew the news would hit Brady the hardest out of the lot of them.

*

Not a lot had happened to Jack Brady in the last six months. In fact to be fair, not a lot had happened in Whitley Bay; a small seaside resort in the North East of England. Overall, targets had been met and crime figures appeared to be at an all-time low. But Brady knew it was the calm before the storm. Police budgets were being slashed to the bone by the government. The thought of having to tackle the same inevitable crimes of second and third generations who had known nothing but a life of living on shoestring benefits was not one Brady relished. Especially armed with little more than a pencil sharpener and a box of staples.

Brady still had the same hard-nosed boss, Detective Chief Inspector Gates, and the same obtuse, career-chasing sidekick, Detective Sergeant Harry Conrad. And he still had the same old job as Detective Inspector. Simply put, he wasn't the kind to get promoted. Not after everything he'd been through. Shot in the thigh, too close to his balls for comfort during an undercover drugs bust that had gone wrong. And then there was his affair with DC Simone Henderson.

But he was still a hell of a lot better off than his long-standing friend and now ex-colleague, Detective Inspector Jimmy Matthews. Jimmy'd found himself locked inside Durham Prison, with the very scum he had risked his neck – and at times his career – to put away. Scum who would gut a copper on the inside as soon as look at him, which was why he was in a segregated unit sharing his time with the worst sex offenders imaginable. As far as Brady knew, no one from the job had been to see Matthews; he was a bent copper who had seriously been on the take and in doing so had sold out. Even Brady had not been to see him, despite repeated requests from Matthews. He still didn't have the stomach to look Matthews in the eye after what he had done.

Showered and changed, Brady slugged back what was left of his black coffee. He picked up his car keys off the granite worktop as he wondered exactly what had washed up onto the shores of Whitley Bay beach. Or to be more precise, exactly who had floated to the surface of the cold, grey murky waters of the North Sea.

Chapter Four

Brady bent under the police cordon and started making his way down the promenade steps looking for what his guts were already telling him was going to be trouble.

It was clear enough where he was heading; it wasn't difficult to spot uniform on the sectioned-off beach below him. Not to mention the grim-faced SOCOs dressed in black pants and black polo shirts who were methodically working along the beach and lower promenade. As expected, they had created a wide circle around the crime scene, photographing and documenting everything and anything that might have some relevance to the investigation. Directly below him, a tight inner circle was in force, stringently controlled by SOCOs clad head to foot in white, who were painstakingly moving in and out of a large white forensics tent.

Brady caught sight of Conrad.

His deputy's erect, stiff figure stood out from the crowd; for all the right reasons. Unlike Brady, he had the makings of a Chief Superintendent and soon enough it would be Conrad kicking Brady around. They were the antithesis of one another. Brady was six foot two and lean with muscle, whereas Conrad was a few inches shorter with a heavier, muscular frame. Conrad was invariably clean-shaven, regardless of the hour, with neatly cropped and gelled blond hair. Brady didn't know how he did it, but he always looked impeccable in his array of suits, shirts and silk ties and tan brogues. Brady was all too aware that his own clothes – t-shirt, battered black jacket and matching skinny trousers and heavy black leather Caterpillar boots – made him stand out against Conrad's typical CID traditional, conformist image. Not that Brady didn't look smart, but his look was unconventional for a copper to say the least.

Brady nodded in response as the young, clean-cut figure of Conrad approached him.

'Sir,' greeted Conrad.

'Conrad,' Brady replied. 'So what exactly do we have?'

'Better you see this for yourself,' replied Conrad, deciding it would be easier than explaining what they had found. Or more to the point, what they still had to find.

*

'Bloody hell!' muttered Brady as he held a gloved hand over his nose.

The overpowering stench hit him hard as soon as he entered the tent.

Without even taking into consideration what was left of the body, the smell emanating from it was bad enough to make him want to retch his guts up. The fact that the body had been washed ashore on one of the warmest mornings of the year so far wouldn't have helped.

He was doing his best not to react to what was lying in front of him. He clenched his hands in an attempt to stop his guts curdling as he grimly stared down at the victim.

Conrad swallowed hard, trying not to breathe as he watched Brady crouch down.

Brady let out a low moan as his leg twinged again. It had been nearly a year since he had been shot in the thigh but the pain remained as a constant reminder of that night. They still hadn't got the person or persons responsible, though Brady had a fairly good idea who was behind it. Which was one of the reasons that Gates now had him on a tight leash. The DCI didn't want Brady causing trouble, particularly where Mayor Macmillan was concerned. Brady had been watching Macmillan for some time now. A man whose morals, principals and politics stood about four hundred yards to the right of Genghis Khan. And this was a man who had made powerful friends as a Conservative councillor and now Mayor of North Tyneside.

On the surface Mayor Macmillan was everything his brother, Ronnie Macmillan, wasn't and that was exactly how Mayor Macmillan wanted it. He wanted no one making the connection. Brady had often moaned to Rubenfeld, a hardened, heavy drinking local hack, about the injustice of Macmillan's dark past not making it onto the front pages of the local papers – to say nothing of his drug-selling gangster brother and prostitute of a sister.

'Money, Jack!' Rubenfeld said scornfully before knocking back yet another whiskey chaser paid for as usual by Brady. 'Bloody money is what it's all about! It can buy you anything! Including friends in high places.'

Brady accepted, as had Rubenfeld, that Macmillan was very good at what he did: lying. He was a politician after all. He had removed himself so far from his past life that no one would believe that he was the same Macmillan who had been raised in Blyth with a criminal for a brother who now lived in the deeply entrenched crime world of Wallsend.

'You alright, sir?' asked Conrad.

'Yeah,' muttered Brady, putting Macmillan to the back of his mind.

He held a gloved hand over his nose and mouth as he moved in closer to what was left of the victim's neck. Flies had already started to gorge on the brutally hacked wound where bone and flesh ended in a jagged formation.

'Some kind of serrated weapon was used to . . .' he faltered, unable to state the obvious.

He turned and looked up at Conrad.

'So where's the head?'

'I don't know, sir. This was all that was washed up. The beach has been thoroughly searched, but nothing's turned up.'

'Here's hoping for our sakes it does. Without a head it makes it damned difficult to identify her.'

'They're going through missing persons reports back at the station, sir,' answered Conrad.

Brady raised a questioning eyebrow. 'Damned hard to know whether we do or don't have a match considering all that's left of her, don't you think?'

Brady knew that without a victimology, figuring out the modus operandi would be virtually impossible. To understand why she had been murdered, they needed her identity. Her family. Her friends. Her life story.

'No identity, no murderer,' Brady resignedly muttered.

He looked at Conrad.

'You know what doesn't rest easy with me?'

Conrad shook his head.

'Whoever did this wanted her found. They wanted her

to wash up on Whitley Bay beach. If she'd been dumped far enough out at sea then she wouldn't have floated to the surface. Add in the fact that it's easy enough to weigh a body down so it permanently disappears.'

Brady was worried. Something about this didn't feel right. 'Why did they want her found?'

'I don't know, sir,' shrugged Conrad.

Brady turned back to the body. 'See the bruising on both her arms? Someone's held her down. There's finger marks on the upper part of her arms but also around her wrists . . .' Brady paused as he stared at what was left of the victim's hands.

'We've searched, but again, nothing,' informed Conrad.

Brady carefully picked up the victim's left hand and closely inspected the stubs of flesh and bone where her fingers should have been.

'They've been cleanly cut off. Different to the neck. Probably garden pruners.'

It was becoming more apparent that whoever had murdered her knew exactly what they were doing; without the victim's fingers or head it was impossible to positively identify her. Unless, Brady mused, she had some other identifiable traits on her body; that and a missing person's report to match. Otherwise, Gates had tossed a dead case his way. Brady's gut feeling told him that Gates knew this case was sunk as soon as the headless body had floated to the surface.

'No clothes, no jewellery, no plastic. No formal identification. Her fingers and head hacked off . . .'

He suddenly realised something was wrong. Her breasts looked unnatural. The skin looked too stretched, too taut. He carefully lifted one of her large breasts and looked at the skin underneath.

'Sir?' Conrad, asked, curious.

'Fake, Conrad. See the scar tissue underneath where she was opened up to insert the breast implants?'

He was well aware of the statistics when it came to young women and anorexia and wondered if the victim was another casualty of society's body fascism.

Brady let his eyes drift slowly down to her flat navel and then further to her perfectly smooth, waxed groin. Yet another testament to the ubiquitous influence of the porn industry; that and the fake breasts, he mused.

'We don't deliver on this one, Conrad, Gates will make damned sure that by the end of the year I'll be begging for my P45.'

Brady shook his head. There was no way he would be able to cope stuck behind a desk for another six months. He'd go stir crazy; even the threat of being demoted to uniform and walking the drug-ridden streets of Blyth was better than pushing pens for the rest of his days.

He sighed heavily as he questioned his chances of solving this murder. His guts kicked off, telling him it didn't look promising.

'Let's take a look at her back and see if there's any identifiable marks,' suggested Brady.

'Are you sure, sir?'

'Ainsworth's finished with her, Conrad, so moving her now won't make any difference.'

Conrad wasn't so sure. He knew that Ainsworth, the head SOCO, had a ferocious temper and hated anyone messing with his crime scene. But he kept quiet, accepting that Brady knew what he was doing. He watched as Brady carefully rolled the body onto its stomach.

The victim's back and legs were covered in bruises. Brady

had expected as much, but there was something else which took him by surprise.

'Look at this,' he muttered to Conrad as he pointed out the distinctive mark at the bottom of her spine.

Conrad nodded, puzzled.

'What do you think it is?' Brady asked as he gently touched the newly puckered, burnt flesh with a white latex gloved finger, lightly tracing the shape of the mark. It was two inches in diameter and seemed to be a scorpion. Below it were the bold letters, 'MD'.

'I don't know, sir. It doesn't look like anything I've seen before.'

Brady took out his BlackBerry and photographed the burnt flesh.

He didn't like what was coming to mind and knew that Gates would like it even less.

He stood up and turned to Conrad.

'Let's see what Wolfe has to say. He is carrying out the autopsy?'

'I believe so, sir.'

'Good, that's something then.'

They were going to need all the help they could get with this case. And he trusted Wolfe. He was a cantankerous old bugger who drank too much, but he knew his job. He was the best Home Office pathologist the force had ever had, and they'd had a few. Even Chief Superintendent O'Donnell was aware of Wolfe's foibles, but since he was the best pathologist around, everyone turned a blind eye.

'Come on, let's get out of here. I think we could both do with some fresh air.'

Chapter Five

'So why didn't the DCI ring me himself?' Brady quizzed once they were outside.

He already knew that something wasn't right.

'He's busy,' Conrad replied uneasily.

Brady raised his eyebrows.

'He's dealing with another incident that happened last night,' answered Conrad.

'What? Involving Madley's nightclub?' asked Brady.

'Yes, sir.'

That came as no surprise to Brady. He had noted the police tape sealing off the premises and the two uniforms stationed by the entrance as he had crossed the road heading for the beach that morning, and had assumed it was another early morning drugs raid. The nightclub belonged to Martin Madley, reputed to be the boss of the local mafia. Not that the police could ever finger Madley. It was rumoured that his main business was drugs. But right now Madley was the least of Brady's concerns. He'd leave that to Gates.

'Sir,' Conrad said, trying his best to hide the apprehension in his voice. He was acutely aware that Brady still didn't have any idea about what had happened in Madley's nightclub. 'We need to talk . . . before we go back to the station.'

'Can it wait?' said Brady distractedly.

He had only one thing on his mind right now and that was the mark burnt into the victim's flesh. There was one person he needed to talk to and he needed to do it immediately.

Conrad didn't answer him but his expression was enough for Brady to know something was troubling him.

'Meet me back at the station. Then we'll talk,' assured Brady. 'Just let me sort this out first. Alright?'

'Yes, sir. But I need to speak with you as soon as you get back.'

'Yeah, no problem. Just give me five minutes,' Brady replied absent-mindedly. The last thing he wanted to do was make that call, but he had no choice.

Conrad nodded, realising that now perhaps wasn't the best time. Not that there was a right time for what he had to tell Brady.

He reluctantly turned and walked across the beach back to the steps leading up to the lower promenade. He shoved his hands deep in his trouser pockets as he tried to figure out how to handle the fact that Brady still didn't have a clue. The problem was, Conrad didn't know how Brady would handle the news. He didn't want to be the one to tell him, but perversely, he would rather it came from him than someone back at the station. In particular, someone like DI Adamson, who would take great relish in throwing it in Brady's face.

Conrad decided the best thing to do was get back to the station and wait for Brady. He had no choice.

*

Brady watched Conrad leave. He had a bad feeling about that look in Conrad's eyes. It couldn't be good news.

But it would have to wait. Right now he had bigger problems to worry about.

He needed to make that call. And then he'd have to face the rest of the team back at the station. All hell would have broken loose there. It wasn't every day that a girl's body washed up on the shores of Whitley Bay. Never mind a headless one.

He hoped to God that somewhere, someone would be missing the victim. The problem he had was finding that someone. The odds at this moment were stacked high against her.

Brady sighed heavily he searched his jacket for his pouch of Golden Virginia tobacco. He then took a sheet of Rizla paper and placed some tobacco in the paper with a filter before delicately rolling it tight. He lit it with trembling fingers as he closed his eyes and allowed the smoke to clear the decaying, sickening air from his lungs. He inhaled deeply a couple more times until it was enough to quell the desire to retch. He had tried to give up smoking and had failed, swapping chemical-filled cigarettes for roll-ups. It was an easy cop out. Too easy.

He cast his eyes up at the sky. The day was already changing. The angry, crimson ball of sun was nowhere to be seen, blanketed instead by the heavy, mournful, gunmetal-grey clouds rolling in off the horizon.

It was an all too familiar sky. The North East of England was well known for its continuous grey drizzle, regardless of the seasons. The only difference was the temperature. Brady found he was either freezing his bollocks off during the winter months when the Arctic winds whipped in from the North Sea, bringing snow and treacherous plummeting sub-zero temperatures, or sweating during the humid summer months. But hot or freezing cold, there always seemed to be grey drizzle. Regardless, Brady loved the place. It was in his blood. He knew that no matter what, he'd never leave the North East.

Brady took his BlackBerry out. He needed to make a call. One that he didn't want to make.

He scrolled through the names listed until he came to the one he wanted. Reluctantly he pressed call and then waited. And waited. And waited until she eventually picked up.

'For God's sake! It's not even seven o'clock on a Saturday morning! This better be good!' finally answered a familiar voice.

Brady could hear a man's deep voice in the background asking who was on the phone. A man's voice that Brady recognised.

'Who do you think would call at this time?' came the muffled answer as she covered the mouthpiece.

'Claudia?' interrupted Brady, trying to control his voice.

He had heard the rumours but hadn't wanted to believe them. Now he had no choice.

'This is work,' he stated. 'Nothing else.'

He heard her sigh heavily. 'Go on . . .'

'A girl's headless body has washed up onto Whitley Bay beach.'

'Alright . . . but what's that got to do with me? You know my job profile. I deal with sex trafficking victims, Jack. Remember?'

'I know,' answered Brady, taken aback by the coldness in her voice. 'But this isn't just any murder victim. She has some odd markings at the base of her spine.'

'Go on.'

'Well . . . there's a scorpion and below that two initials: MD. But these aren't tattoos, the marks look as if they've been burnt on to her skin. As if . . .' Brady faltered as Claudia quickly cut in.

'She's been branded,' interrupted Claudia.

Brady waited.

'Can you send me the photos of the markings?' she finally asked.

'Sure, I'll send it to your mobile after this call,' answered Brady, relieved that she was interested.

But he was no fool. This was work, and this was exactly the kind of thing that Claudia was involved in.

Branding was about registering ownership in the dark world of sex trafficking and sex slavery. And given that Claudia was involved with one of the first projects in the UK where the police and the Home Office worked in conjunction to free imprisoned women and occasionally children – mainly illegal immigrants – from brothels and houses where they were held hostage as sex slaves, he needed to know whether she recognised the brand left on the body.

Once the women were freed by the specialist police team, Claudia then worked hand in hand with the Poppy Project who offered the victims support and accommodation, providing specialist legal back-up to secure the illegally trafficked women rights to stay in the country. Claudia had told Brady enough tragic accounts of young women freed from sex slavery only to be forcibly sent back to their country of origin, straight back into the hands of the organised criminals who enslaved them in the first place.

'If this is what I think it is, then this could mean she's not the only one . . .'

'I know,' muttered Brady.

'I hope for our sake that you're wrong, Jack.'

Brady didn't reply.

In the background a male voice complained about her taking too long.

Brady shoved his hand deep into his pocket and tightly gripped the only object he carried with him everywhere. He could feel the cold metal of his wedding ring digging into the palm of his hand as he thought about the implications of the mark on the victim. And more significantly, the implications of the man who was now sharing his ex-wife's bed.

'Send me the photo and I'll start making enquiries my end, alright?' Claudia instructed.

'Yeah . . . thanks,' muttered Brady.

'Jack? You do know if this girl has been trafficked and imprisoned then you've got a problem on your hands?'

'I know . . .'

'Because the question is, why would someone kill her? These women can sell for something like £3,000 to £4,000, if not more. And her earning potential makes her a valuable commodity. And don't forget how much money these women can make in one day. So why murder her?'

This was what was worrying Brady. Sex trafficking and sex slavery were growing international crimes; ones that had a stronghold in the UK. He knew the statistics. Claudia had brought her work home often enough for him to be keenly aware of the worrying exponential growth in sex slavery. Girls ranging from as young as eleven up to twenty-five were trafficked from all over Eastern Europe, across the fractured borders of Russia, smuggled through Afghanistan, and even brought in from as far afield as Thailand and China.

Brady shut his eyes as he massaged his forehead with his other hand. This was exactly what he didn't want. A body turning up connected to sex trafficking. Not in Whitley Bay of all places. After all, this was just a small seaside resort in the North East of England where organised crime of this level didn't exist. If it had been a major European capital then Brady would have been more ready to accept such a premise. Even Newcastle he could understand, but not Whitley Bay.

'Unless . . . unless she was being made an example of?' Claudia questioned, interrupting his thoughts.

'Meaning?'

'All I know is what I've heard from the women we've managed to free. But there are some horrendous stories of coercion and blackmail, Jack.'

'Check out the markings for me first, yeah?'

He didn't want to acknowledge that this problem had landed on his doorstep. But he couldn't ignore what Claudia was suggesting. He had the same gut feeling that someone wanted to make a very public statement with this girl's body.

Admittedly, Whitley Bay had a reputation for stag and hen parties and binge drinking. But that was a world removed from organised sex trafficking and sex slavery. Brady thought back to Matthews' allegations against Madley and Mayor Macmillan. He had been adamant that between them they had a highly profitable sex trafficking and slavery operation. But Brady had put his crazy accusations down to the ramblings of a cornered man who, about to lose everything he had worked for, had decided to bring down as many people with him as he could. Brady would be the first to admit that there was something about Mayor

Macmillan that didn't sit easy with him. But even he had to concede that sex trafficking was a stretch too far. And as for Matthews' claims against the local mafia figure, Madley, who was rumoured to be involved in drugs and other such lucrative enterprises, Brady couldn't take it seriously. Sex trafficking was something that he knew Madley wouldn't touch. Regardless.

'Let me worry about why she's been murdered once we know for certain that she's been branded.'

Claudia's only response to Brady's words was to let out a heavy sigh.

Before he had a chance to say anything else she disconnected the call.

All he could do now was send her the photograph. He watched his phone to make sure that the image had definitely been sent. Satisfied, he put his phone in his jacket.

Now he had to wait. And pray to God that his hunch about the victim being a sex slave was wrong.

Chapter Six

Brady steadied himself before opening the doors to the station. He wasn't sure why he had been handed this investigation. By rights it should have been Adamson called in; lately, he had been Gates' first choice when it came to anything decent. Whereas Brady was just being thrown the rubbish murders.

So why this one, he mused? And where the hell was Adamson? It wasn't like that weasel not to sink his teeth into such a high profile crime. Once the press got their greedy, grasping claws into this story, the seaside town of Whitley Bay would make national headlines.

He sighed heavily, accepting that maybe he was starting to get paranoid. The past six months behind a desk would do that to any copper, let alone him.

The air in the building was still rancid. Regardless of how often Nora, the station's cleaner, swabbed down the Victorian green-tiled hallway, there was always an acrid, lingering dampness that resiliently clung to the walls and floor. That and the stale smell of old piss from one too many drunken louts dragged in to sleep it off in the cells.

The building was old and decrepit. But Brady felt at ease inside its cold, flaking walls and winding, maze-like corridors. His office, with its high, rattling windows and bulky, rust-stained, leaking radiators, felt more comfortable to him than his own home. Which wasn't surprising given that over the years he had spent most of his waking life at the station. More so now that he couldn't stomach going home to nothing.

Brady went through the second set of double doors and was greeted by the scraggy, wizened face of the desk sergeant, Charlie Turner. He was a short, rotund, balding man in his early fifties.

'I better warn you, Jack, all hell's breaking loose here,' Turner greeted as he raised his white spidery eyebrows. It made no difference; his small dark eyes were still hidden beneath his sagging, crumpled eyelids.

'Tell me about it.'

'So you heard about the stabbing then? Christ! How bad can things get, eh?'

Brady frowned. Apart from Conrad, he hadn't caught up with anyone yet.

'What stabbing?'

'You don't know, do you?' Turner replied worriedly. 'It explains why the DCI has been desperate to talk to you. You do turn your phone on, don't you, Jack? Because he's been chasing my hide for the past hour wanting to know as soon as you turn up! And Conrad's been hanging around waiting for you. I convinced him to get me a coffee just to get him out from under my feet.'

Automatically Brady reached for his phone.

He had forgotten to turn it off silent mode. He'd missed three calls; two from DCI Gates and one from Dr Amelia Jenkins.

Jenkins was the police shrink who, a year ago, had spent

the first six weeks after Brady had been shot in the thigh trying to sort his head out. He had insisted all he needed was a couple of bottles of Scotch and a divorce lawyer but she had wanted to try the more professional method. In the end she gave up. She was into the 'talking cure' – which had become a problem given Brady's refusal to talk.

But why she would be calling him at 7:30am was anyone's guess. He hadn't seen her since the last investigation they had worked on together, which was over six months ago. Amelia worked with the force as a forensic psychologist. But for some reason she opted out and had turned to practising clinical psychology instead. Brady presumed something had shaken her to her core. Which was why he was so surprised both that Gates had asked her to be part of the investigation and that Amelia had agreed. He knew that Gates had worked with Amelia when she had been a forensic psychologist, which meant he knew she was good. That, and he trusted her, which was why Brady presumed he had requested her assistance.

'The DCI is out for blood given that one of our own was attacked early this morning in Madley's nightclub,' continued Turner.

Brady realised now why Turner was so agitated.

'Who?' Brady asked, realising he had been sat behind his desk for too damned long. Once news this crucial would have reached him immediately. Now he was so out of the circuit that it took the watchdog Turner to fill him in on the night's events.

Then he remembered Conrad. This was obviously what he had wanted to tell him.

'I'm sorry, Jack . . . I don't know how to tell you this . . .' Turner uncomfortably began.

'Who, Charlie? Who was attacked?' asked Brady, starting to feel uneasy.

'Henderson,' Turner quietly replied.

Brady felt as if he had just been punched in the guts. He couldn't breathe. He leaned forward, resting his hands on the reception desk to steady himself. His head was spinning. All he could think was that it *couldn't* be her. She wasn't the Henderson Turner was talking about. It had to be someone else. But he already knew it was. After all, he had seen her with his own eyes in Madley's nightclub. And he had turned and left. Left her alone with two men who, for all he knew, were responsible for . . . He couldn't bring himself to think about it.

Brady raised his head and looked at Turner's concerned face, searching for some sign that he had got it wrong.

'Simone?' Brady mumbled, his dark brown eyes begging Turner to tell him he was mistaken.

Turner nodded sadly, unable to repeat her name.

'What happened to her?' Brady whispered hoarsely, trying with all his might to ignore the panic that had taken hold of him.

'That's it. We don't know,' Turner answered quietly. He dropped his gaze, unable to look Brady in the eye. 'An anonymous emergency call came through shortly after 3am this morning locating an injured DC locked in the gents' toilets in the Blue Lagoon . . .'

'And?' pushed Brady, already fearing the worst.

Brady now understood why uniform had been stationed outside Madley's nightclub and the reason the double glass doors into the premises had been sealed off with blue incident tape.

32

Turner shook his head, still unable to look Brady in the eye.

'She was found naked . . . whoever had left her there had . . .' Turner faltered, not wanting to say.

'What? What did they do to her?' Brady hissed, clenching his fists hard, fearing the worst.

'Someone took a knife to her stomach and sliced her open . . . and cut out her tongue.'

'God no . . .' He felt as if he was going to throw up. 'Is she? Is she still . . .' Brady couldn't bring himself to ask the obvious question.

'She's in a critical condition, Jack. As far as I know she's still in surgery.'

Brady numbly nodded as he dragged a trembling hand through his hair. He was trying his hardest to keep his head together.

'Why wasn't I called in for this, Charlie?' he eventually asked.

Turner shook his head.

'You know better than me,' he reluctantly answered.

'What do you mean?' Brady asked as shock turned to desperation. 'Surely Gates will need everyone he can get to work on this?'

'I know, I know, bonnie lad,' sympathetically agreed Turner.

'Why would that stop Gates from letting me work on finding out who . . . who did this to her?' Brady asked, already knowing the answer.

'Even you can understand why Gates doesn't want you involved. Especially now he's got Claudia back working for the force again. She may not be a duty solicitor here any more, but she's doing a fine job with that sex trafficking project of hers in Newcastle. A lot of really good PR's coming out of that for Northumbria Police and that's down to her,' explained Turner gently.

Brady said nothing.

Turner shook his head. 'Come on, Jack. You know Gates was furious with you when she suddenly left for London. And then the next thing, there was Simone requesting an immediate transfer out of here. I'm surprised you didn't end up in uniform.'

Brady knew that Gates had a soft spot for Claudia. Who didn't? When Claudia suddenly quit the North East, Gates had found it difficult to replace her. She was damned good at her job and sorely missed by everyone; including Brady.

'You've got too much invested, Jack. Sooner or later it clouds the judgement.'

'Gates? Where is he?' demanded Brady.

'He's in the first-floor conference room. It's set up as an Incident Room. You should still find him there,' Turner replied. 'But if I was you I'd stay out of the way for now. Let him deal with the briefing on Simone's attempted murder and then talk to him afterwards. The last person they're going to want walking into that room is you.'

Brady ignored Turner and started to make his way to the first floor.

'Jack?' Turner called after him. 'Watch yourself, will you? Gates is out to crucify someone and, given your track record with him lately, you want to make sure it's not you.'

'Thanks,' muttered Brady. 'I'll keep that in mind.'

Brady suddenly halted and turned back. 'Charlie?'

Turner looked at him.

'Who's heading the investigation? Into Simone?'

Brady knew the answer from his silence.

'Adamson?'

Turner nodded. Brady had expected as much.

'Jack? Don't do anything stupid,' warned Turner.

In all the years he had known Brady, Turner had never seen him react to news this way. Then again, he couldn't blame him. This was personal to Brady: he had worked closely – too closely some would say – with DC Simone Henderson. And that's what was troubling Turner.

Brady forced himself to meet Turner's concerned gaze.

'Like what?' he asked, trying to keep his voice steady.

Turner resignedly shook his head. 'I don't know, bonnie lad. But that's what worries me.'

Chapter Seven

Brady took a deep breath before entering the first-floor conference room. He had to get himself together. He would be no use to anyone in this state. Especially Simone. He did his best to sneak in. The room was filled with over twenty coppers; a mixture of uniform and CID all crammed in together. The atmosphere was electric. One of their own had been targeted. And this wasn't some random attack. This was a brutal attempted murder. Brady scanned the room, recognising most of the faces. At least half of them had been called in from other area commands, but Brady knew most from the Sophie Washington murder investigation six months back.

Brady worked his way to the back of the room. His eyes automatically scanned the whiteboard next to Gates who was addressing the room. He held his breath as he took in the photograph of the blackened crimson clotted mess around Simone's open mouth, an all too vivid contrast against the clean shiny white incident board.

Brady's eyes then uncomfortably moved across to the images of the nightclub's gents' blood-stained floor. With gut-wrenching clarity, he registered that the blood was Simone's.

Why the Blue Lagoon?

He didn't like the answer that kept coming to mind. When she had been stationed at Whitley Bay, she, like the rest of them, would end up having a late night drink in Madley's club. He remembered that she had seemed too interested in Madley and his whereabouts. When Brady had challenged her, she confided that she had heard that Madley's nightclub was being used as a front. Brady had laughed it off, telling the over-zealous rookie that every resident in Whitley Bay knew that, never mind the police. He had updated her on Madley's drug-dealing reputation and that to date he had never been caught. But Simone wasn't interested in Madley's drug activities. She had claimed that it was something bigger than that, involving someone more dangerous than Madley. Brady had tried to get more from her, but despite being a rookie she was savvy enough not to hand over everything she knew to a commanding officer who would then take the credit for all her undercover observations.

Brady continued to stare at the photographs, despite feeling sickened by the images. He couldn't shake the idea that if he had gone over to her last night then she wouldn't be fighting for her life.

Gates' voice suddenly caught his attention.

'I've just received an update from the hospital and . . . it isn't good. Simone's out of theatre now, but she's still not regained consciousness. She's lost a lot of blood and there was significant internal damage. More than they expected, which has caused some complications. She's in ICU right now, so all we can do is pray that she pulls through.'

The room was tense.

Gates had everyone's attention; especially Brady's.

He was roughly Brady's height and build, despite being ten years older. Gates' muscular, toned body was a testament to the hours he put in at the gym. Everything about him was regimented and controlled. Even his aggressively receding dark hair was cropped short, unashamedly exposing his baldness.

Brady wanted to walk. Anywhere was better than being stood there. But he was unable to move. His gaze obsessively returned to the large whiteboard. He tried to focus on the clumps of frenetic scrawl, recognising it as Gates' handwriting. Anything was better than looking at the gruesome photos of Simone's injuries or the crime scene.

He suddenly felt someone staring at him. He turned and caught Amelia Jenkins' eye. She was sitting at the front of the room observing everyone. Brady expected no less from her; after all she was the police psychologist.

As if conscious of his gaze, Amelia adjusted her skirt. She shot him a concerned look and then turned her attention back to Gates.

Brady forced his attention back to the Detective Chief Inspector, who was still speaking.

'I know that every one of you will give one hundred and ten percent to this case and, given the circumstances, I would expect no less.'

Gates then turned to Adamson and gravely nodded.

Brady watched as Gates sat down and Adamson stepped forward. He couldn't help but notice Adamson's arrogant expression. This was exactly what he was born to do; exert his power. Brady waited while he made the most of the situation.

Adamson straightened his thick, dark burgundy tie as

he cleared his throat, allowing the tension in the room to build. The air soon became electric as the team waited for Adamson to speak.

Eventually he nodded, acutely aware that he had them. 'The assailant knew exactly what they were doing when they cut her – otherwise Simone Henderson would already be dead. The incision that was made across her abdomen was carried out by a skilled hand. The knife missed the inferior and superior vena cava which saved her life as these branch out into the femoral artery and vein. If he'd cut any of these major vessels then she would have bled to death in a matter of seconds. The heart pumps about eight litres a minute and given the average adult roughly has four to five litres . . . well I'm sure you can do the maths. The question we need to ask is why did they want to risk her being found alive?'

Brady was too aware that the room was silent, a few heads shaking. The same thought would be going through everyone's mind – that even though Simone Henderson was found alive, she'd been left in a condition which guaranteed she would never talk. These were hardened officers used to dealing with the worst possible crime. But this was different. This was one of their own.

'We know from the forensic evidence that . . .' Adamson cleared his throat as he looked back at the gruesome images '. . . that Simone was attacked at another location and then dumped in the toilets.'

Adamson shook his head at the gravity of the attack but Brady couldn't help but get the feeling that he was loving every minute of this. All eyes on him. Everyone waiting for his next word.

'You can see that her left breast was also burnt during

the attack. And the word 'PIG' slashed across the other breast. We've run the image through our national database but no matches have come back.'

Brady looked at the image of Simone's burnt left breast. He could make out the raised mark of the letter 'N' that had been burnt deep into the flesh.

Two victims on the same night. Both branded; flesh burnt. Both found yards away from one another. One in a nightclub, savagely cut up, and another headless, washed up on a beach. But even Brady had to admit to himself that the burnt 'N' on Simone's breast bore no similarity to the branding of the scorpion and the letters 'MD' found on the murder victim.

'We know from the nightclub's security tape that Simone was with two men,' Adamson paused and pointed to the whiteboard. 'This is the best image we have of them. As you can see, there's not a lot to go on. But we're hoping that the bar staff who were on duty last night will be able to help us with a photofit.'

Brady looked at the grainy freeze-framed images. Adamson was right, all you could make out was that they were both dark with short hair. Nothing more. Brady had replayed the scene of Simone with the two men over and over again in his head but he still couldn't come up with anything that would be of any use. His problem was that he hadn't seen their faces – they had both had their backs to him. If he had, then he would have had no qualms in sharing it with the investigating team, despite Adamson.

Nothing had been mentioned of Brady's presence in the nightclub. He would have known by now if they had caught him on the club's surveillance camera. But Brady had come in through the back door of the club used by Madley and his men. Brady knew there was no camera covering that door. Madley was too clever for that. He ran his affairs from his first floor office above the nightclub and liked the assurance that he could come and go unnoticed. And that included his business associates. The last thing they or Madley wanted was footage that could fall into the wrong hands – especially the police's.

It was from there that he had spotted Simone standing at the bar with the two men. She had turned and caught his eye and in that one look had said enough. So he had left. The only person who had known he had been there was Simone. And now she was . . . Brady couldn't bring himself to think about the consequences of him turning and discreetly leaving.

'Simone left at approximately 1am and then two hours later we get a tip-off call from an unregistered mobile to say she's been attacked and left in the gents' at the Blue Lagoon . . .'

Brady looked at Adamson.

Adamson paused. For effect. Brady was sure of that.

Brady narrowed his dark brown eyes as he watched Adamson, knowing what was coming next.

'The very same nightclub owned by Martin Madley. A local businessman who, we have been led to believe from certain sources, is connected to drug dealing. But as of yet, this is something we haven't been able to prove. Whether Simone's attack has anything to do with Madley is some-thing we have yet to determine.'

Brady was certain that Madley had nothing to do with Simone's attack. This wasn't his style. In all the years he had known Madley he had never hurt a woman, let alone a copper. Aside from that, he was too clever to leave one of his victims in his own nightclub. Brady couldn't figure it out. All he knew was that his gut feeling was telling him that Madley had been set up. Someone was sending him a very clear message. But who and why were questions that only Madley could answer.

'We have already taken a statement from Martin Madley and he has a watertight alibi proving that he was nowhere near his nightclub last night.'

Brady looked at Adamson's expression which clearly showed that he didn't believe Madley.

'We also have Simone's blood results back and there are strong traces of Rohypnol. Whoever did this to Simone knew exactly what they had in mind.'

Rohypnol was effective at wiping the victim's memory and removing their inhibitions. Brady had dealt with numerous rapes where the victim's only memory was of drinking in a pub or nightclub and then coming to the next morning, completely unaware of what had happened over the past four to even twenty-four hours.

'It's crucial we find the identity of the caller,' Adamson continued. 'We're releasing the tape at the press conference later and seeing what results we get. Hopefully, someone will recognise the caller's voice.'

Brady watched as Adamson caught Amelia's eye. Brady couldn't help but notice that something passed between them.

'This is all we have to go on,' Adamson said. 'But someone out there will know him.' He turned to press play on the emergency call.

'A female police officer is locked in the gents' toilets in the Blue Lagoon nightclub . . . If you don't get there in the next few minutes she will bleed to death.' The voice was low and muffled, as if the caller was holding a gloved hand over his mouth. But there was no question that there were traces of an accent; a Geordie accent.

'Sir? Can you elaborate? Can you give us your name and address? Sir?' The phone line clicked dead.

Brady inwardly recoiled. He clenched his hands as he steadied himself.

No . . . It can't be . . .

He could feel himself starting to sweat as his mind raced.

It's not possible . . .

Brady closed his eyes as he tried to block out what he was thinking.

The voice, despite being distorted, sounded like someone from his past. Someone who had been very close to him. Brady quickly discounted the possibility as being *too* incredible.

It was just a distorted Geordie male voice. One that no doubt sounded like any number of men in the North East.

He breathed out and opened his eyes, only to meet Amelia's inquisitive look.

He quickly composed himself and focused on Adamson.

'We've gone through the surveillance footage in the Blue Lagoon from the point that she left with the two men she was seen with, up until when she was discovered attacked in the nightclub. But how she ended up in the gents' is beyond us. There's nothing on the security tapes. Forensics are currently examining the toilets to see whether it was possible that she was brought back in through the window in there which faces out on to the back of the premises.'

Adamson stopped and looked around.

'All we have to go on is the anonymous caller and these two men seen with Simone two hours before she was discovered. It's crucial we find these men and the male caller. As you can see, we've got our work cut out. But it's our job to find out who did this to her and why.'

The room bristled with agitation. Everyone more than eager to get started.

'Thank you, DI Adamson,' said Gates, resuming command. He stood and deliberated as he looked around the tense room. 'I don't need to add that this isn't just any ordinary investigation. I'm sure there's a lot of you here who remember Simone for the hardworking, capable officer—'

Suddenly Gates' voice stopped. Something or someone had caught his attention.

Gates' dark brown eyes were now unnervingly fixed on Brady. They belied the cold, detached intelligence of a man who would never allow himself to be compromised.

Brady waited for Gates to address him. He was dressed in his typical black uniform with gold braid, as befitted a man of his rank. Brady looked at the heavily etched lines on Gates' hard face; a testimony to his dedication to the job. His skin was covered in harsh, pitted acne scars, some partially hidden by a permanent five o'clock shadow, but there all the same. Irritably Gates pulled the cuffs of his expensive white shirt down past his black uniform as he glared at Brady.

'Can I help you, Jack?'

Brady tensed. He now realised that he had made a mistake coming in. What had he been looking for? He didn't know. But the last thing he wanted was disapproving glances from colleagues who had heard the rumours about his relationship with the victim.

But worse than that, he was certain he had recognised the

caller's voice, despite the attempt at disguising it. He cleared his throat, aware that the entire room was watching him.

'I was just waiting until the briefing ended so I could have a word, sir,' Brady answered, inwardly cursing.

'My office in ten minutes.'

'Yes, sir,' Brady answered.

'If that's all, you can leave,' Gates ordered. 'I'm sure you've got enough work to do.'

Brady caught the mocking stare of DI Robert Adamson who was clearly enjoying his downfall. Brady held his breath as Gates shot him a cold, penetrating glare before he turned to Adamson and quietly muttered something. Adamson nodded in response as he shot Brady a dismissive look.

Brady turned and left the room, feeling more certain than ever that his career was shot to hell.

More so, if he was right about the identity of the caller.

Chapter Eight

Brady walked downstairs and careered straight into DS Tom Harvey.

'Bloody hell, Jack! You look like shit,' Harvey confided.

Brady just looked at him. He didn't need Harvey pointing out the obvious.

'Are you OK? What with . . .' Harvey mumbled, realising that he'd obviously heard.

Brady nodded as he ran his right hand through his hair. He was trying his best to keep his head together. 'Yeah,' he muttered. 'Just . . . you know? It's hard to believe that anyone would want to . . . to hurt her like that . . .'

Harvey simply nodded, at a loss for what to say.

Brady had known Harvey for years. They went way back to the early days where they both had worked long hard shifts followed by equally long sessions over too many pints. Harvey was a good copper and a long-standing friend. And most importantly, he was someone Brady could trust.

Brady had gone on to get promoted to DI whereas Harvey had stayed as a DS. The fact that Brady was now his boss had never come between them. Harvey was more than happy with his role and had no intention of furthering his career. He liked the job too much to get involved with the politics that came naturally with a more senior role. Not that Brady could blame him. If Brady had known how the politics of the role got in the way of the job itself, he wasn't so sure that he would have ever taken on the role of DI.

Brady shook his head as he met Harvey's eyes. 'The worst thing is I wouldn't trust Adamson to wipe his own arse never mind head something as crucial as this . . .'

'I know,' agreed Harvey. 'He's one fuck-up if ever I've met one. He'll screw up big-time, Jack. Just wait.'

'The problem is I don't want to be proved right about him with this case. Christ, this is Simone we're talking about.'

'I know . . .' Harvey mumbled awkwardly.

Brady looked at Harvey, realising he wasn't the only one who had been deeply affected by what had happened to her.

'There's nothing we can do, Jack. How about we get started on this investigation and leave Adamson and his team to find out who's responsible for attacking Simone?'

Brady's mute reaction told Harvey he didn't agree.

'Jack?' warned Harvey, recognising the look on his face. 'Leave it, will you?'

'Tell the others I want to hold a briefing at 1pm, will you?' ordered Brady, changing the subject.

Brady needed time before the briefing. He had too many questions that needed answering first.

'Where?' asked Harvey.

'I'll tell you that after I've talked to Gates. I need to see what kind of resources he's allocating us, which includes where we can set up the Incident Room.'

Harvey nodded, relieved that Brady was now thinking about the murder investigation.

'And, Tom? I want a list of every girl that's been reported missing over the past year between the age of sixteen and thirty.'

'Why the past year and not more recent reports?' Harvey asked, puzzled.

'Just trust me, will you?' replied Brady. 'And make it a national search. I have a feeling that this is bigger than the North East.'

'You seriously want us to search through all that data?'

'That's what I said,' answered Brady. 'And given the fact I want that information ready for the briefing you better get a move on.'

'You're the boss,' accepted Harvey as he turned and started to make his way up the stairs to the first-floor computer room. He turned and looked back at Brady. 'Despite the fact I think Adamson's a fool he will get whoever did this to Simone.'

Brady looked as unconvinced as Harvey sounded.

'Look, regardless of Adamson, his team will,' Harvey continued. 'I know most of them and I can guarantee that not one of them will rest until they catch whoever's responsible. And when they do, God help him!'

Brady didn't argue with Harvey.

The last thing he was going to do was tell Harvey that he would be making enquiries of his own into who could have done this to her. And he was certain he'd get to the bastard responsible before Adamson got even close.

*

'What do you think you are playing at?' demanded Gates as he sat down.

'Sir?' Brady asked.

His boss's attitude came as no surprise. He'd been expecting to get it in the neck.

'Walking into that briefing when you did.'

'I didn't realise that it was off-bounds, sir.'

'Christ, Jack, do I have to spell it out for you?'

Brady didn't answer.

'Don't mess with me,' warned Gates.

He sighed heavily as he deliberated what to say next. Leaning forward, he rested his elbows on his desk and clasped his hands together as he looked Brady in the eye.

'Look, I understand this must be difficult for you,' Gates said, choosing his words carefully. 'It's hard enough for the rest of us.'

Brady didn't reply.

'But I want to make myself perfectly clear. You are to go nowhere near this investigation. Understand?'

'Yes, sir,' replied Brady coolly.

'DI Adamson is in charge of the Henderson investigation. You have your own investigation to deal with and I can't have you compromising that because you're not giving it your undivided attention.'

Brady watched as the DCI sat back in his chair. He looked agitated and Brady knew the reason why. Gates didn't trust him not to get involved.

'You've got your usual team; I wish I could give you more but unfortunately that's all I can offer you under the circumstances.'

Brady nodded. He expected as much. But he was relieved that at least he had his old team. They were good, but whether they could pull off this investigation with such limited resources was highly questionable.

'And you can have Room 201 on the second floor as an Incident Room. It's one of the largest on that floor.'

Brady made the mistake of slightly reacting to the demotion. Ordinarily a murder investigation such as this one would have been given priority and the large room on the first floor would have been used. But that had been assigned to Adamson. And under the circumstances, Brady couldn't object. He of all people wanted Simone's attackers found and if that meant Adamson being assigned the best room and resources available so be it.

'If I had my way I would have offloaded this murder investigation onto another area command. We're already stretched as it is with Henderson's attack. But no one wants to touch it. And I can't say I blame them considering how little we have to go on. Who wants to have an unsolved murder case on their books affecting their damned targets?'

Gates was making it perfectly clear that he expected Brady to deliver on the case. Brady refrained from stating the obvious – that his boss was asking the impossible.

'So far we have the best target record this year. Don't blow it!'

'Yes, sir,' replied Brady dutifully, not feeling that optimistic.

Gates looked at Brady expectantly. 'Well, Detective Inspector? What are you waiting for? From where I'm sitting you've got a lot of work cut out for you.'

Brady stood up.

'And just to be totally clear, Adamson's investigation is off limits,' the DCI repeated.

'Yes, sir,' replied Brady before heading for the door.

'And, Jack?'

Brady turned back to face him.

'Do you know what Simone Henderson was doing in Madley's nightclub last night? Let alone back in the North East?'

'No, but I wish I did, sir,' replied Brady.

Gates deliberated for a moment and then nodded.

He watched Brady as he walked out of his office, hoping that he did as he was instructed and left the Henderson investigation alone. His personal relationship with Simone Henderson made him a liability and Gates wasn't prepared to have him screw up under his watch.

Chapter Nine

Brady walked out of Gates' office and straight into Amelia Jenkins.

'Sorry, I didn't see you there,' he apologised.

'We need to talk,' suggested Amelia.

'Look, I wish I could but I'm really busy,' replied Brady.

He couldn't believe his luck. It couldn't have happened at a worse time.

He could see from her expression that Amelia wasn't buying it. He dropped his gaze, finding himself staring uncomfortably at the ground.

Dr Amelia Jenkins had a way of getting to him. She had a knack of looking too deeply into his eyes and searching for the truth. That was partly why he had never looked directly at her when they had had their shrink sessions a year ago. And at this precise moment the last person he wanted knowing that he was vulnerable – dangerously so – was Amelia. He had too much to lose. The last thing he wanted was to unravel in front of her; he needed to keep his wits about him. Especially after the emergency call he had heard. He was certain he recognised the voice. That alone was enough to send him over the edge.

'I understand that. But given the circumstances, I thought you might want to off-load?' Amelia ventured gently.

It had been six months since he had last talked to her. Then she had been assigned by DCI Gates to work with him on the murder investigation of a local fifteen-year-old girl.

Brady didn't respond.

'Jack? Listen, I know what happened between you and DC Henderson. Remember the counselling sessions we had after you had been shot?'

Brady slowly raised his head and looked at her. Of course he remembered the sessions. That was the very reason he didn't want to talk to her now.

Before he knew it he was looking into her almond-shaped dark brown eyes. They were filled with genuine concern.

Brady's problem was he didn't like to talk. Especially about personal matters. Whatever he was feeling about the fact his ex-colleague was lying mutilated in Rake Lane Hospital was personal. Which meant it was off-limits. Way off-limits. He had his own way of dealing with his feelings.

His reply was straight to the point.

'Amelia, I'm sorry. I just can't . . .' he muttered.

He turned and started to walk down the corridor.

'Jack? Please?' she called out, regardless of the two officers walking down the corridor towards her. He gave no sign he had even heard her. Amelia sighed heavily and quickly walked after him, her heels clicking irritably against the wooden floor.

'Jack?' she called again as she caught up with him.

Brady continued walking. He had somewhere to go and the last thing he needed was any distractions.

She grabbed him by the arm, forcing him to turn and face her.

He looked at her and waited.

'Look, I know this must be really hard for you. Alright? I'm here if you need me, that's all. I . . . I want to help . . .'

Brady looked at her. He wasn't sure exactly what kind of help she was offering. And more worryingly, he didn't know whether DCI Gates had put her up to this to get the ammunition he needed to get Brady signed off as unfit for work because of personal reasons.

'Look, I really appreciate your concern, But I'm alright. I've just got a lot to deal with right now. I'm sure you heard about the murder victim found washed up on Whitley Bay beach this morning?'

'Yes, I heard,' answered Amelia as she searched his face. 'Actually, I asked DCI Gates if I could be assigned to your case. Given what I know, it sounds like you could do with some help profiling the victim's murderer.'

Brady looked at her, surprised. Then he swiftly composed himself, unsure of what game was being played.

'Thanks,' he replied. 'But if I'm honest I'd rather you were working with Adamson. They need your kind of expertise to find whoever has done this to Simone. But I appreciate the offer.'

Before Amelia had a chance to answer he walked away.

He hated himself for the reaction his words had elicited. For a brief moment she had looked hurt. Then she had composed herself and nodded coolly with an air of professional detachment. A look that he recognised from his time with her as his shrink.

*

Brady slammed his office door shut and walked over to his desk. He was angry with himself. Angry that he had shut Amelia out. He'd already done that once before when the investigation they had worked on together had ended. He had promised her a drink with the rest of the team and found himself bailing. Unable to let anyone get close; especially someone like her. So he had left when she had turned up. He knew that she wouldn't wait around for him to sort his act out. Why would she? Amelia had everything going for her. She was only in her early thirties, with a career that was going somewhere – and fast. Add to that, that she had that fatal combination of intelligence and uniqueness about her.

He sighed heavily as he sat down at his desk. He had to focus. He didn't have the time or luxury to wonder about what ifs where Amelia was concerned. His life was already too complicated.

He needed to make a call.

'It's me,' Brady said.

'I've been expecting a call.' The voice was controlled, with an air of menace.

'We need to talk,' stated Brady.

'Usual place?'

'Yeah, give me a couple of hours or so. There's a few matters I need to sort out first.'

Brady hung up.

He needed questions answering about what exactly had happened in the Blue Lagoon last night and there was only one person who could tell him.

His phone began to buzz. He looked down at it.

Matthews.

'Damn!' he cursed. This was the last thing he needed.

'What? Haven't I already said I'm not interested?' Brady answered, his voice heavy with a guttural Geordie inflection.

'Jack? Come on, pal. This is ridiculous. What can I say to convince you that I just got caught up? And before I realised it, I was way in over my head. Don't you think I wish I could change what's happened? For fuck's sake, my life is hell in here.'

'Yeah? My heart bleeds,' answered Brady.

'Fuck you! Don't you think I've suffered enough? I've lost everything . . . My wife, my daughter and . . . and my career.'

'You lost your career as a copper the day you started taking backhanders, Jimmy.'

'Come on, Jack. It's not that simple and you know it,' replied Matthews.

'Isn't it?'

'Don't start getting all moral with me. There's a few things in here I've found out about you. Information that I'm sure the DSI would be interested in hearing.'

'Yeah?' questioned Brady, trying to sound calm despite feeling as if he'd been punched in the stomach.

'Don't mess with me,' snapped Matthews. 'You know exactly what and who I'm talking about!'

'Like what?' he pushed, not wanting to hear it but knowing he had no choice.

'It concerns your old man. Let's say he's been saying some things that concern you and Madley.'

Brady slowly breathed in as he tried to figure out what the hell to do. He knew what Matthews was referring to and the last thing he wanted was Gates finding out. If he did, then it wouldn't be the streets of Blyth he'd be working – he'd be banged up alongside Jimmy Matthews. Let alone if Adamson got wind of it. He didn't like Adamson and he definitely didn't trust him. Brady needed to make sure that his tracks were covered. Out of desperation he had asked Madley to help him out. He'd needed a problem from his past to disappear; for good. And it had. Whether Madley had sorted it, or it was coincidence, Brady had never asked. He was just relieved that the shabby old drunk claiming to be his old man had been taken care of, no questions asked.

'Alright, I'll come visit. But I can't say exactly when,' replied Brady, trying his best to keep the panic out of his voice. 'All hell's broken loose here. We've got two major investigations running concurrently.'

'I know,' interrupted Matthews. 'Another reason why I need to talk to you.'

'How the hell do you know?'

'You shouldn't concern yourself with that, Jack. You should be more concerned with how quickly you can get here. And when you come, bring me 200 grams of Golden Virginia.'

'You don't smoke,' stated Brady.

'I do now,' replied Matthews with an edge of desperation.

Brady wasn't sure whether Matthews wanted the tobacco for himself or as a trade with other inmates to keep himself in one piece. But that wasn't his concern. Matthews had brought whatever hell he was living in on himself.

'Come on, Jimmy, how am I meant to bring that through?' asked Brady.

'You'll figure it out. Call it payment.'

'You shit,' muttered Brady.

'Yeah? We're the same you and I, Jack. Don't forget it.'

Before Brady had a chance to respond the line had gone dead.

'Damn it!' he cursed as he looked up and stared up at the dusty grey slats of daylight stabbing through the off-white Venetian blinds.

He was wondering whether Matthews was bluffing or whether he actually had some information on the two investigations. Whatever it was, Brady had no choice but to make a visit. After all, Matthews had him firmly by the balls. Whatever he was holding over him regarding his old man could be enough to destroy him once and for all.

Brady breathed out.

A loud rap on the door broke him from his thoughts.

'Yeah?'

The door swung open and Conrad walked in carrying a black coffee and a bacon stottie from the basement canteen.

'Thought you might need some breakfast, sir.'

'Thanks, Conrad,' replied Brady, though he knew he wouldn't be capable of keeping anything down right now.

Conrad carefully cleared a space on Brady's cluttered desk. He then looked at his boss trying to gauge his mood.

'I'm sorry, sir . . .' he began uncomfortably.

Brady stopped him.

'You tried to tell me. I should have listened, Conrad. I'm the one who should be apologising.'

Conrad mutely nodded, relieved.

Brady picked up his coffee and took a slow, deliberate drink.

'Sir, Wolfe is carrying out the victim's autopsy now,' Conrad offered, filling in the awkward silence.

'Is Adamson still questioning the barman from the Blue Lagoon?' Brady asked, ignoring what Conrad had said.

He needed to talk to the barman about the two men who had left with Simone. The two men Brady had seen drinking with her.

'Sir?' Conrad questioned.

'Simple question, Harry. Yes or no?' demanded Brady agitatedly.

'No, sir. I saw Amelia a minute ago and she said that Adamson had let him go. They've got a photofit of the two men which helps, given how blurred the images of them are on the nightclub's surveillance tape.'

'Has Adamson sent it over to Jed to get him to digitally enhance the security tape images?' Brady asked.

Jed was the force's computer forensic analyst. And he was the best, if not the only, one in the field. A shrinking budget now saw Jed overloaded with too many cases. But given the seriousness of the crime against one of their own, Brady was certain that Jed would prioritise this job.

'As far as I am aware, sir,' Conrad replied, uneasy with Brady's line of questioning. They had their own murder investigation to be working on rather than obsessing about Adamson's.

Brady nodded, relieved. Jed would send him a copy of the enhanced images, he was certain of that. 'If Adamson finds the emergency caller on CCTV footage, I want to know. Understand?'

'How, sir? Adamson won't let me anywhere near the investigation,' Conrad pointed out.

'Amelia,' stated Brady simply. 'She's on Adamson's team. You're good friends: I'm sure she'll keep you updated.'

Conrad wasn't convinced, but he let it go. It was pointless arguing with Brady. More so given Brady's personal attachment to the case; it was clear that he wouldn't be able to persuade him otherwise. Conrad decided to keep quiet. It would be dangerous to tell his boss to let Adamson just get on with the case instead of Brady torturing himself with updates related to Henderson's attack.

'I reckon we should keep Kenny and Daniels out of trouble by getting them to go over every bit of CCTV footage caught last night down on the Promenade and the surrounding streets.'

'Won't Adamson think that we're interfering in his case?' suggested Conrad.

'Can't see how. Not when we're working on finding anything we can connect to our murder victim being dumped on the beach directly opposite the Blue Lagoon. Do you?'

'But wasn't she washed up? Dumped at sea?'

'Says who? As far as I'm concerned I need Daniels and Kenny looking at that CCTV footage for any unusual activity.'

Brady's mind was on the anonymous 999 caller. He desperately needed to know if the man had been caught on CCTV footage. Only then would he know if his fear about the caller's identity was true.

'Sir?' Conrad said tentatively. 'Tell me this isn't connected to Simone Henderson. Because we've already got our hands full with our own investigation.'

He had been worried that this would happen. That as soon as his boss heard about what had happened to Simone Henderson that he would go all out to apprehend whoever had done this to her. Regardless of the consequences.

Brady looked at Conrad's worried expression.

'No, like I said, I want to cover all possibilities with our case,' calmly reassured Brady. 'Now we've got that sorted, get your jacket. We need to be somewhere, which means rescheduling the briefing for 2pm.'

Conrad didn't move.

'Come on, Conrad. We haven't got all day,' stated Brady as he stood up.

'Sir? I'm sorry . . . about Simone.'

Brady nodded.

'I know you are,' he answered. 'So am I.'

Chapter Ten

'Left here.' The sudden instruction from Brady came halfway through a conversation on his BlackBerry. 'No, not you!' His attention returned to the person on the other end of the line. 'I'm talking to Conrad. Listen, I'll call you later. Alright?'

'Bloody hell, Jack!' replied Rubenfeld. 'This won't wait.'

'That's the same line you've been threatening me for years. Give me a couple of hours and I'll get back to you and then we'll meet? Call you later,' concluded Brady, not giving the hardened hack a chance to argue.

'I said left,' repeated Brady, relighting his cigarette.

'Sir?' Conrad asked as he turned to Brady.

'What?' asked Brady as he dragged on his cigarette.

'Do you think this is a good idea?'

'It is if I want to find out what's happened to our murder victim.'

'As long as you remember that's why we're here, sir,' warned Conrad as he pulled into Rake Lane Hospital.

'Drop me off at the emergency entrance. Then meet me at the morgue,' Brady instructed, ignoring Conrad's comment.

Conrad didn't reply.

Instead, his steel-grey eyes looked straight ahead as he did as he was told and parked by the emergency entrance. His strong jaw remained firmly set as he watched Brady get out, throwing what was left of his cigarette butt to the ground.

Conrad noticed that the ground was covered in cigarette butts. Smoked by either patients driven to distraction by their prognosis, or their equally worried relatives.

He watched Brady stride towards the entrance. He knew exactly where he was heading. And that was straight for trouble. He didn't trust Brady to let it go. He decided to park the car and then follow him. The problem was, he knew exactly where he would go – and it wouldn't be the morgue.

Without looking back at Conrad or the car, Brady made his way through the addicts who were standing, regardless of the smoking ban now in place on the hospital grounds, shivering in dressing gowns and slippers, with tubes attached to their arms and portable oxygen tanks or morphine drips.

Desperate wasn't the word.

Brady walked straight over to the reception desk and flashed his ID badge at the receptionist.

'Here to see Simone Henderson,' Brady said.

The receptionist nodded at Brady before keying the name into the hospital's database.

'ICU, Ward 7, Room 2,' she replied when she found her.

Grateful, Brady nodded.

Before he turned away the receptionist stopped him.

She conspiratorially bent forward.

'I think you should know that two men were in first thing this morning asking if they could see her. I thought it was suspicious at the time since she's under police protection and they obviously weren't officers.'

'What did they look like? The two men?' Brady asked.

'Maybe late twenties, early thirties? Dark, good-looking. Well-built. And they had a funny accent like they were foreign. Definitely not from around here.'

Brady accepted that anyone who didn't have a Geordie accent was seen as being foreign in North Tyneside.

'I thought they were lawyers or something . . . you know? Both wearing suits. Expensive-looking. Looked like they had money.'

He nodded, thinking back to the two men he had seen talking to Simone in the Blue Lagoon. They could easily have fitted the receptionist's description. But as for their accent, Brady didn't get close enough to hear whether they were locals, or to clearly see their features.

'Was there anything about them that stood out? Something they said, maybe? Or even a distinguishing mark?'

'There was something that struck me as odd . . .'

Brady nodded for her to elaborate.

'One of them had a large platinum signet ring on the third finger of his right hand.'

'Why did that strike you as odd?' quizzed Brady.

'Because when they turned to leave I realised that they were both wearing them. One of them had his hand in his pocket you see. Then his phone rang. And when he took it out I saw that he was wearing an identical ring. And on the same finger.'

'What did the rings look like?'

'It was the letter "N". But it was all fancy, inset with diamonds. And the backdrop to the letter had what looked like Latin writing on it. They looked expensive, you know?'

'You've got a good eye,' Brady said. 'Ever thought about becoming a copper?'

She laughed. 'Divorced and single,' she explained. 'Force of habit, checking out whether a man's married or not. First thing I look for now is a wedding ring, or the tell-tale sign that it's been temporarily removed. Been stung in the past you see.'

Brady shoved his hand in his pocket and gripped the silver wedding ring he kept on him at all times. He couldn't manage to let go of it, despite the undeniable fact that Claudia had taken up with another man. DCI James M. Davidson was a muscle-bound, ex-military Ross Kemp look-alike, who had swaggered into the Armed Response Unit on the back of his hands-on combat experience in Iraq and Afghanistan.

Not that Brady would take that away from him. It took balls to risk your life in a war reminiscent of Vietnam. In other words, a war against fundamentalist insurgents who used dirty, guerrilla warfare against the enemy. But, regardless of his heroism, Davidson was still an arrogant, tall, good-looking, dangerously charming player, who had war stories that mere mortal men would kill for.

And that was Brady's problem. He didn't want Claudia to be played. But he wasn't in a position to say anything, given his own history with her.

'Thanks for your help,' Brady said.

He stopped and turned back.

'What did you say to them when they asked to see her?'

'I said only immediate family could visit,' she answered. 'But what was odd was their reaction. They didn't say a word. Just walked straight back out.'

Brady nodded. He expected as much. They had got all the information they had needed. Whether or not Simone Henderson was still alive.

'Where's the security camera?' asked Brady.

The receptionist pointed at the camera discreetly placed on the ceiling behind the reception area. Perfectly positioned to capture whoever came in and out the hospital main entrance.

Brady would need the footage from earlier that morning to see whether the two men who had come in were the same ones he'd seen with Simone hours before she was brutally attacked.

Somehow he would have to get Amelia to request it. Nobody would question her authority. After all, she was working on the investigation as a forensic psychologist. Her job was to come up with a profile of the attacker.

He knew that he couldn't get any of his team to do it. Inevitably word would get back to Adamson and then Gates. Brady knew that that letter 'N' wasn't just coincidence. What it meant he didn't know but he sure as hell was going to find out why it had been burnt into Simone Henderson's breast.

'Thanks,' he said to the receptionist before turning and heading down the maze-like corridor.

The only thing on his mind now was Simone.

Regardless of what Conrad had said in the car, he needed to see her.

Chapter Eleven

Brady pressed the intercom button for the security doors leading into the Intensive Care Unit.

'Detective Inspector Brady to see Simone Henderson,' Brady said into the intercom, trying to keep his voice level.

The door buzzed open and Brady walked through into the sterile, white hall and headed for the nurses' desk at the end.

'Simone Henderson? DI Brady,' he added as he flashed his ID at the young Filipino nurse.

She nodded distractedly as an alarm from one of the patients' machines went off.

'Down there, Room 2. On your left,' she instructed before hurriedly walking off in the direction of the alarm.

Brady turned and walked past the ward of male and female patients. Most of an age, attached to bleeping machines that monitored their every breath and heart-beat. Brady looked straight ahead, not wanting to witness the loss of humility that came with old age. Craggy, parched mouths hanging open, with skin peeling off from their tongues due to lack of hydration and eyes either tightly shut against their situation or open, staring ahead with a watery, glazed look.

Brady hated hospitals. Hated the smell, the noise and the fact that death morbidly clung to every patient, silently waiting.

Brady didn't need to be told which room. The uniform outside was obvious enough. Brady approached the door of the private room, noting that the blinds on the window looking into the room were closed. Immediately, he knew it was a bad sign.

'Sir?' PC Smith asked uncomfortably.

Brady could see in his eyes that Smith, along with everyone else, knew that he was the reason Simone Henderson had transferred out of Whitley Bay.

Brady looked at him. He was twenty-three, if that.

'I'm here to see Simone Henderson.'

'I'm sorry, sir, I've been instructed not to allow you in,' the PC answered nervously.

'Who by?' demanded Brady as he edged towards PC Smith, forcing him to strategically place his six-foot-four, rugby-playing bulk between Brady and the door.

'DI Adamson, sir,' explained PC Smith, his cheeks reddening.

Brady noted that Smith was another Conrad in the making. Smart appearance, short, cropped blond hair, bright, boyish blue eyes and clean-shaven. But more importantly, Smith had that look of integrity about him.

'Is he here?'

'That's not the point, sir.'

'I only want a minute, Smith. That's all. I just need to see that she's OK.'

PC Smith uncomfortably stared straight ahead past Brady, refusing to make eye contact.

'I can't do that, sir. I have my orders.'

'Fuck your orders!'

Smith fixed his stare on the wall ahead of him, clearly desperate for someone to intervene.

'One minute is all I'm asking for, nothing more,' attempted Brady, too aware that getting angry with Smith wouldn't get him anywhere.

'I wish I could, sir, but her father's here. And he'll be back shortly. He's only gone to fetch a coffee from the cafeteria.'

'One minute. You can leave the door open and warn me when he returns.'

PC Smith frowned, torn between doing his job and loyalty to Brady. He'd worked on an investigation headed by Brady nine months back and had seen what a dedicated copper Brady was at heart.

After a beat, Smith shook his head resignedly.

'One minute, sir,' he said. 'But if anyone finds out . . .'

'No one will,' assured Brady. 'Thanks, Smith.'

PC Smith turned and opened the door to allow Brady in.

Nothing could have prepared Brady for what greeted him.

DC Simone Henderson lay unconscious. From what he could tell she had been heavily sedated. Various other wires were attached below her paper-thin hospital gown, recording her heartbeat with irritable regularity. Intravenous tubes wormed their way into her lifeless arms.

Brady stood, unable to move towards her. Her face was unrecognisable from that of the woman he had seen the night before. Brady clenched his fists as he played the 'what if' game. What if he had gone over to her? Maybe she wouldn't be lying in a hospital bed fighting for her life.

Brady didn't need a doctor to tell him that she was in a bad way. The ghostly, sickly greyish pallor that clung resiliently to her skin scared the hell out of him. He didn't know whether to go over to her and try his damnedest to shake her out of the shadowy underworld she now inhabited. He wanted to shout her name out loud enough to bring her back. To remind her that she didn't belong where she was, that she needed to return to the living. He needed her to regain consciousness so he could find out who had done this to her. So he could hunt them down and make them suffer the way she had been made to suffer.

He struggled to hold her name at the back of his throat, knowing that if he uttered it out loud it would only be heard as a painful, primeval, anguished sob.

He forced himself to walk towards the bed. Each step feeling as if he was walking barefoot on broken glass.

He reached her side and waited. Willing her to feel his presence.

She didn't move.

He bent over her waxen, taut face, gently brushing her long, damp hair away from her cold, translucent skin.

'I'll get them, Simone . . . whoever did this to you . . . I'll get them . . . .'

He couldn't help but notice how young and fragile she looked. And yet, there was something about her which suggested she was too old for this world. She had seen too much and was done with this life.

Brady breathed in and tried to get his head together.

He didn't have time to reflect. He had work to do.

Hand trembling, knowing that what he was doing was breaking every rule in the book, he pulled back the tape

70

holding the gauze padding covering her left breast. He knew he shouldn't be interfering with the dressing but he needed to see for himself the four-inch letter 'N' burnt into her flesh.

He forced himself to look. He willed himself not to react as he took in the gnarled, weeping, open wound. He took out his phone, the reason he was there, and photographed the letter 'N'.

Satisfied with the image, he carefully replaced the dressing and turned away, feeling disgusted with himself. He fought back the overwhelming tumult of emotions coursing through his body.

He pulled himself together. Now wasn't the time to get emotional. He owed Simone more than that. It was simple: he had a job to do and that had to be his main focus. Breathing slowly he gave her one last look before turning and walking out.

'Sir,' greeted PC Smith, relieved when Brady joined him in the hall.

'Thanks, I owe you one,' Brady said.

But he couldn't bring himself to look at him. He didn't want the junior copper to see the pain etched across his face. Or the shame he felt at what he had just done.

He turned and walked away, head bent down as he sent Claudia the photograph accompanied by an explanatory text.

He watched as the signal ebbed and then surged, until the photo finally disappeared, along with the message.

'DI Brady? Jack Brady? You bastard!'

Brady turned and before he had a chance to react he felt a hard blow to his face knocking him against the wall.

Another landed and before he knew it he was down on the floor.

'I'll kill you!' threatened the assailant.

Brady scrambled to his feet while trying to get away from the punches and kicks that his attacker was relentlessly delivering.

The last thing Brady could do was retaliate, despite the blows and kicks being delivered in his direction.

After all, this was Simone Henderson's father.

And at five foot eight with a stocky, pit-bull build and thick, brutish arms that kept coming, he was a serious contender. His bald, shaven head glistened with sweat as he did everything he could to kill Brady.

Suddenly PC Smith was there trying to pull Frank Henderson back.

'You son of a bitch! How dare you show your face here!' panted the fifty-something man as he flailed around against PC Smith, trying to land as many blows and kicks as possible on Brady. 'Do you know what those bastards have done to her? To my little girl? Do you? It's all your fault!'

Brady backed away from him, trying to avoid the frenzied punches.

Suddenly the security doors buzzed.

Conrad walked through. It took him a moment to take stock of the situation. He'd expected to find Brady here. Which was why he had come to the ICU first before going as instructed to the morgue. But what he hadn't expected was to find Brady on the floor with Simone Henderson's father's boots violently kicking his face and body while PC Smith did his best to hold him back.

Without a second's hesitation Conrad ran over and

forcibly restrained Simone's father. Between them, PC Smith and Conrad somehow managed to hold him long enough for Brady to get some distance and get to his feet.

Brady looked at Conrad's face, which was flushed as he fought to control Simone Henderson's father. He was relieved that his deputy hadn't followed his orders and was too aware that this wasn't the first time he had stepped in and saved Brady's neck.

Bent over, gasping for breath as he held his ribs, Brady backed away from his struggling assailant who was still intent on finishing the job. Catching his breath in deep shallow gasps he raised his head to meet Henderson's hate-filled eyes. From that one look of absolute fury and disgust Brady realised that this man held him responsible for the fact that his only child was lying in intensive care, heavily sedated after too many hours on an operating table, not knowing whether she would even pull through.

'If you've been in her room, I'll kill you! You hear?' shouted Frank Henderson as Conrad pinned his arms behind his back.

'I wanted to but Smith there wouldn't let me in,' hoarsely panted Brady, still winded from the blows he'd taken.

'You stay away from her!'

'For what it's worth, I'm sorry . . .'

'You think I believe that? It was you, you bastard, that made her transfer to the Met. Left me and her mother because of you. Her mother was dying of cancer, did you know that? Did you? That's what you did to us. Forced our only child to run as far away as possible from the North East,' yelled Henderson as he continued to struggle like a man possessed against Smith and Conrad.

Conrad's face was now burning red with the exertion of

holding him back. Even Smith was clearly struggling to restrain him.

Still clutching his right side, Brady turned to leave before Henderson's sheer hatred of him overpowered both men holding him back.

'I'm sorry,' muttered Brady. 'You'll never know how much.'

'And so you should be. If it hadn't been for you she wouldn't have come back here. I want to know what happened. I want to know how you could let her get hurt.'

Brady stopped. He turned round, confused.

'I don't understand. I haven't seen Simone since she transferred from Northumbria a year ago.'

Henderson stared hard at Brady. It was evident that he didn't believe him.

'Then why did she tell her flatmate that she had to talk to you? That she had some unfinished business?'

Brady looked at Conrad who looked equally puzzled.

'She never contacted me,' Brady replied, shaking his head.

'So you tell me why her flatmate said that she was coming up here on leave to see you.'

Brady stared at Henderson, not understanding what he was saying.

'Maybe you got it wrong,' suggested Brady carefully.

'I got it wrong, did I? I didn't find out that she was in the North East until your lot showed up on my door. You tell me why she didn't want me to know she was here?'

Brady couldn't answer him.

'I'll tell you, shall I? Because she knew how I felt about

you. If I'd known she was coming up to see you I would have done everything in my power to stop her!'

'She didn't arrange to meet me,' Brady answered quietly but firmly.

It was the wrong answer. Henderson lunged forward, fighting Conrad and Smith with renewed vigour.

Conrad, breathless and scarlet-faced, shot Brady a look which told him to disappear, and fast, before he lost control of Henderson.

Dejectedly Brady turned and limped out of the ICU, feeling as if he had just had the worst kicking of his life. And the worst part was, he knew he deserved it.

Chapter Twelve

Brady held onto the washbasin.

He was still shaking from the attack.

But it wasn't the blows that had got to him.

He turned the cold tap on and splashed himself with water. Face drenched, he looked up at his reflection in the mirror.

He looked like shit.

Wincing, he straightened up and lifted his t-shirt. His light olive-coloured skin was starting to discolour into mottled purple patches spreading across the side of his right ribcage. He gently ran his fingers over the bruising which led down to his abdomen.

He let go of his t-shirt. Bending over the washbasin again, he drenched his face, groaning with the exertion.

But no matter how hard he tried he couldn't get rid of the image of what they had done to Simone.

He was very aware that word would get back to Gates. Brady could deny having seen Simone. He knew that Smith wouldn't say a word. But there was no way he could deny the run-in with the victim's father. Nor could he explain why Frank Henderson believed his daughter had returned to the North East because of Brady. It didn't make sense. He hadn't talked to her in over a year. Nothing. And then suddenly, she's back up here lying critically wounded in the ICU.

He narrowed his eyes as he looked at the damage. Nothing was broken. His left cheek was split open. Frank Henderson had also landed a lucky blow above his left eyebrow, resulting in another open gash. Blood trickled down into his eye.

He bent down and doused himself in more cold water in a bid to get rid of the blood. He didn't have time to go and get the cuts stitched. Not that he would have done. He'd had a lot worse than this and had lived to tell the tale.

He raised his head up and slowly breathed out. His head was throbbing. He ran his hand over his scalp for any tell-tale damage. Nothing. Apart from the raised four-inch scar at the back of his head where his father had taken a baseball bat to him when he was eight years old. All he remembered was hearing the swoosh of air as the baseball bat had swung towards him. He'd felt it connect with his skull before everything went black.

When he had come round, it wasn't to concerned medics. He had found himself lying on grime-encrusted bare floorboards, in a pool of his own blood. He had awoken to the terrified eyes of his younger brother Nick, four years old, huddled in a foetal position on the piss-stained mattress dumped on the floor in the corner of the room they slept in.

The room was empty of furniture, apart from the old, torn, flea-infested mattress. There was no wardrobe or drawers in the bedroom; there was no need. The only clothes Brady and his brother owned were the ones on their backs. Everything went on his father buying his next pint and pack of tabs. Resulting in them living in squalor with little or no comforts, despite his mother's best intentions.

Their father being imprisoned was the best thing that had ever happened to Brady and Nick. Being dumped around the North East in countless foster homes was luxury compared to their brutal start to life.

Brady stared at his reflection, fingers touching the gnarled scar at the back of his head as he remembered the price he had had to pay to get away from his father.

The same night that his father had taken a baseball bat to him, breaking not only three ribs and his right arm, but also splitting open his skull, he had then turned on his mother.

Brady was acutely aware that if she hadn't intervened when she had, he would have been the one that was later found dead.

That was why, when he came to, the first thing he saw was Nick's wide, petrified eyes watching, huddled in the corner like a wild animal. The second thing he registered was his mother's screams as his father 'taught her some respect'.

Brady blinked back. His eyes stinging with fresh, salty pain.

He reminded himself that it might have taken years, but his father had finally been made to pay.

Yet, it still didn't ease the pain of witnessing your own mother being beaten and raped in front of you.

When his father had momentarily stopped, leaving the room, his mother had whispered to him to get up and run.

'Take Nick, Jacky, and run. Don't stop. Understand? No matter what, don't you stop, Jacky. Now go! *GO!*' she had urged, knowing that her husband was coming back to finish what he had started.

Brady did exactly what he was told. He knew, as she did, what would happen if he didn't.

He never saw his mother again. Well, he never saw her alive again.

Brady had pulled out the court case records and autopsy report a few years back, thinking it would give him some kind of resolution. It hadn't. The crime scene photographs brought to life his worst nightmares.

When he had taken his mother at her word and run, his father had returned to stab her over twenty times. Her face was so mutilated from the frenzied knife attack that the only way she could be identified was through her dental records.

Brady let go of the old wound and gripped the sides of the washbasin, steadying himself as he forced himself to come back to the present.

To Simone.

Brady desperately needed to talk to Madley. Whatever was going on had to have something to do with him.

A gutted and mutilated copper being dumped in Madley's toilets wasn't an everyday occurrence. This was a warning to Madley. The question was why?

He leaned over the sink and splashed his face one more time. He needed to clean himself up. He looked bad enough with the purple and black bruising and cuts, without the blood.

His phone suddenly vibrated in his pocket.

He took it out: Conrad. A sudden reminder that he had a case of his own to work on.

But he couldn't shake the feeling that somehow the two cases were connected.

Chapter Thirteen

Brady shivered involuntarily.

Unlike Wolfe, he didn't have the stomach for this. He was grateful that he'd left the bacon stottie that Conrad had brought him earlier, certain he wouldn't be able to keep it down.

Brady glanced at Conrad who was stood next to him, grim-faced, lips tightly sealed in nothing less than a grimace.

Not that Brady could blame him. It wasn't just being witness to the autopsy that was clearly disturbing Conrad. That in itself was bad enough. It was having to be in the same room as Wolfe. For some reason he and Wolfe didn't quite see eye to eye. And Brady knew for a fact that Wolfe didn't appreciate Conrad watching him work.

Brady had suggested that Conrad wait in the cafeteria, which unbeknown to the public was located right next to the morgue. But Conrad had refused. He didn't have to say it, but Brady knew he didn't trust leaving him on his own while Simone Henderson's father was still on the premises. Rake Lane might have been a huge, sprawling maze of a hospital but Conrad clearly believed that it wasn't large enough to keep Brady away from trouble.

Brady looked down at the dissected body, wishing he

was anywhere rather than in front of a mortuary slab looking at a body that resembled a Damien Hirst piece of art. His face hurt like hell and his ribs burnt every time he breathed. But he didn't have time to feel sorry for himself.

'You don't look so grand. You want Harold to fetch you the bucket, laddie?' Wolfe said mockingly, as he looked across at Brady.

Despite having lived in the North East for the past thirty years, Wolfe's Edinburgh roots had never left him. His soft, well-educated Scottish lilt was a constant reminder that he was originally from north of the border.

Brady swallowed hard and shook his head, avoiding Conrad's concerned look.

The 'sick bucket' was always on stand-by for new coppers or for the particularly gruesome autopsies, where the bodies had been left to fester for weeks, allowing insidious, eye-watering bodily gases to build.

'No . . . I'm fine.'

'Aye, I can see that!' Wolfe said with a wheezy laugh.

Wolfe suddenly went from a wheezy gurgle of laughter to struggling to breathe. Brady watched as the pathologist bent over as he tried to free up some air in his lungs. Despite suffering from asthma, and having carried out countless autopsies on lung and throat cancer patients, Wolfe was still a hardened smoker. His twenty a day was seen by him as moderate. As was his daily couple of lunch-time pints.

'You want to cut back,' Brady advised, concerned by his old friend's sudden loss of colour from his face and his bluing lips.

'I *have* cut back . . . I used to smoke forty a day . . . didn't I?' panted Wolfe, still bent over. 'Aye, and it's no doing me any harm!' wheezed Wolfe, still managing a wry smile.

Brady watched as he pulled out his blue Becotide inhaler and breathed in four long puffs to open up his airways.

Finally, he straightened up. He frowned at Brady's look of concern.

'It's not me you should be worried about, Jack. Take a look in the mirror. You look worse than half the stiffs we get in here.'

Brady unconsciously touched the open wound above his eye.

'I can put a couple of stitches in that for you?' Wolfe offered.

Brady shook his head. 'Thanks, but no thanks,' Brady replied. 'You've got your work cut out as it is.'

'Well, laddie, it's your funeral when DCI Gates clocks you,' Wolfe replied, disgruntled. The look of disapproval on his face was aimed directly at Conrad. As if for some reason Conrad was responsible for the condition of his boss's face.

Wolfe dropped his gaze back to the work at hand. He was dressed in a white surgeon's gown and skull hat with white rubber boots which had a yellow stripe down the back with his name, Dr A. Wolfe, written in black ink. On his small, but long-fingered, delicate hands he wore white latex gloves.

To anyone's eye he looked like a surgeon. The difference was, his patients couldn't be saved.

Brady winced as he looked at the gutted insides of the victim. Her ribs had been forced apart and her organs had been removed leaving behind a scene of bloody carnage.

A pool of black blood swilled around in what was left of the empty carcass.

'You sure you don't need the bucket?' queried Wolfe.

He had an uncanny knack of knowing when someone was going to puke.

'No, just aching a bit. That's all,' Brady said.

'This isn't like you, Jack. Normally you'd take someone down before they even had a chance to look at you,' Wolfe wheezed.

Brady held his breath as he tried not to react. Wolfe had performed most of the autopsy, which accounted for the disconcerting smell emanating from the systematically butchered body. The internal organs still had to be replaced back into the chest before the deep Y-shaped incision which worked from the shoulders down to the groin could be stitched up and the body could be stitched back together. But first the internal organs would have to be individually weighed and documented. The slightest detail noted.

Brady looked across at Harold, the anatomical pathology technician. Not that Wolfe ever used him. Harold's job was mainly to stand around and watch as Wolfe cut up and investigated every unusual detail on whatever stiff Harold had removed from one of the thirty body refrigerators in the hospital. Harold was a tall, gaunt-looking young man with long reddish-blonde hair tied back in a ponytail and a long red goatee beard plaited in two strips.

'What have you found?' asked Brady as he walked round to Wolfe.

He was busy examining the victim's internal reproductive organs which were still in situ.

'The victim wasn't pregnant at the time of death but she

84

had had an abortion within the last month I'd say,' replied Wolfe.

'Both her fallopian tubes and ovaries are scarred by severe endometriosis. As is the uterus which also shows evidence of extreme trauma. So I'm surprised she was able to get pregnant given the scar tissue. But you see here?' Wolfe said, pointing. 'There is an area of haemorrhage on the anterior surface of the cervix where it joins the body of the uterus. This haemorrhagic area measures approximately two centimetres and there is also a tear in the cervix measuring three centimetres in length.'

Brady stared at the mutilated body, wondering what kind of short life she had lived.

'See this scarring on the cervix here?' questioned Wolfe as he looked up at Brady.

Brady nodded.

'Caused by an abortion – a bad one at that. She would have had extensive bleeding afterwards. Still evidence of haemorrhaging pooling by the cervix, as I already pointed out. In all honesty I'm surprised she survived. I've had autopsies where women have died from botched abortion jobs like this one. She would never have been able to have children after that.'

Brady looked closely at the scarring from the botched abortion. It was bad. Even to his untrained eye.

'And you see this trauma here?' Wolfe pointed out.

'These internal and external wounds were carried out when she was alive and are indicative of her being raped. Gang-raped and violently might I add to cause that kind of damage.'

Brady looked across and caught Conrad's eye. He looked equally as uncomfortable with the finding.

'When you get the autopsy report you'll see that I've established numerous finger marks on her lower and upper legs and her hips and back from where she has been forcibly held down. I've checked them and there is a consistency which shows that three different people held her down.'

'What about any traces of DNA evidence? Sperm? Pubic hair?' Brady asked.

'Bleach has been inserted into her vagina and rectum, no doubt to cover the DNA evidence. But it appears that they wore protection as I've found nothing. And then we have to add in that she's been in the sea for approximately two hours.'

Brady sighed. He had been hoping that Wolfe would have been able to find some trace of forensic evidence left behind.

'What about the victim's age?'

'Approximately 16 to 18 years of age; body length 65 inches and weight 90 pounds which suggests she's malnourished.'

Wolfe paused.

Brady followed his gaze to the sagging flaps of skin that had once been her breasts.

'As you can see the victim had breast implants which I have removed. The serial number on the implants might be of some use to you,' Wolfe said. 'Harold will give you a copy of it.'

'At least that's something,' Brady conceded as he caught Conrad's eye.

Brady didn't know whether Conrad's silence was because he was fighting the urge to puke, or whether he was keeping quiet to avoid Wolfe's acerbic tongue.

But he looked as hopeful as Brady felt at the possibility of being able to identify the victim from the serial number.

'Cause of death?' asked Brady.

'Well . . . this is the interesting part. You would think asphyxiation because of the damage to her neck externally and internally,' Wolfe explained as he pointed to the mottled bruising around what was left of her neck. 'But that wasn't the cause of death. She was strangled but whoever did this stopped before she actually asphyxiated. The hyoid bone, the thyroid and the cricoid cartilages are fractured, and there is pulmonary edema, with froth in the trachea and bronchi. The lungs are bulky, crepitant and over-distended and there is right ventricular dilatation. But . . .' Wolfe paused, 'the damage isn't significant enough for her to have suffocated.'

Brady nodded.

'Cause of death was definitely cardio-respiratory arrest due to shock,' added Wolfe.

'Was she alive when they started to decapitate her?' asked Brady, hoping that for her sake that wasn't the case.

He saw Conrad shift uncomfortably at the question.

Wolfe shook his head.

'No. There's no defensive knife wounds which is what you'd expect if she had been conscious. And if she had been alive when they decapitated her, the blood loss would have been extreme. The carotid arteries on either side of the neck are the major arteries that pump blood to the head and then there are the jugular veins which return the blood back to the heart. If she was alive when these were cut, she would have died within seventeen seconds from blood loss. And believe me that would be one grue-some crime scene. But as you can see from the pool of blood that's still left in the body's cavity this wasn't the case. She was definitely deceased before she was decapitated. Whether she was shot in the head or received a blow to the head which caused cardio-respiratory arrest, I can't say.'

Brady nodded, relieved.

'The knife that was used?' Brady asked.

'Ten-inch stainless steel hunting-survival knife with a five-and-a-half-inch large serrated spine capable of easily cutting through bone. I'd say the handle was also steel with a knurled handgrip as there's no traces of fabric or any other material on the neck wound.'

Brady nodded as he wondered what kind of person carried such a knife.

'Finally,' Wolfe began. 'The burn mark of the scorpion and the letters "MD" are intriguing. Reminiscent of cattle branding. And from the condition of the wound, I'd say it's only two days old.'

'How long do you think she's been dead?' Brady questioned, not wanting to think about the implications of a branded victim.

'I'd say she'd been dead for about three hours before she was found on the beach,' Wolfe answered. 'Time of death was approximately 1am, or thereabouts.'

'She looks in a bad way for just three hours,' Brady suggested as he looked at the swollen and discoloured body in front of him.

He caught Conrad's puzzled expression, which told him he was equally surprised.

Wolfe gave Brady a withering look.

Brady remembered that there was one thing with Wolfe that you couldn't do and that was question his skill.

'I'm certain. From the body's rate of cooling and the degree of rigor mortis and the partially undigested food in her stomach, she had been dead for three hours before she was discovered.'

'The tide was coming in at 1am. So, whoever dumped her in the water must have known that she would be washed up onto the beach.' Brady shook his head as he considered the implications.

'Which means that they wanted her to be found, laddie,' Wolfe noted.

Brady looked at the body, wondering why she had been gang-raped then murdered. And crucially why her murderers wanted the body found.

'The head . . .' began Brady. 'Makes identification damned difficult without it or her fingers. Why would someone go to those lengths to make sure she can't be identified and then want her body found?'

'*Mortui vivos docent,*' Wolfe simply replied.

He nodded at Brady's puzzled expression.

'Latin for,' he paused for effect, 'the dead teach the living.'

Chapter Fourteen

Brady checked his watch. It was nearly 12pm. He was running late.

He had someone to see connected to Simone's attack. Whether he would glean anything was another matter, but he felt compelled to follow it through. But first, he needed to get a hold of Amelia back at the station. He needed her to do him a favour. Whether she would was questionable, but he had no option but to ask.

'As fast as you can, Conrad,' instructed Brady.

He was on edge at the thought of what lay ahead of him. And the prospect of walking back into the station wearing the brunt of Frank Henderson's fists wasn't helping.

Conrad simply nodded as he reversed his new dark silver sports Saab Phoenix out of the hospital parking space, all too aware that Brady was holding a take-out black coffee from the hospital cafeteria. He didn't want coffee spilt all over the new interior, or his highly-strung boss.

Brady took a slug of lukewarm, weak black coffee. He forced it down, despite its bitter, burnt taste.

'Would you believe this is worse than the station cafeteria's coffee?'

'I did warn you, sir. Which was the reason I didn't want

one,' replied Conrad as he slowly pulled his car out of the hospital grounds.

The muscles in Conrad's jaw were knotted as he concentrated on the busy traffic ahead. That and the call he had received while he had waited in the car when Brady had gone off to get some coffee.

'Christ, Conrad . . .' muttered Brady as he shook his head.

'Sir?'

'What do we have? An unidentified, decapitated victim whose head is still missing, aged between sixteen and eighteen, savagely gang-raped, then murdered and dumped in the sea with the intention of her body washing up on the shores of Whitley Bay beach,' Brady said, sighing. 'And then there's the markings burnt onto her body which suggest . . .' he faltered.

'Sex trafficking, sir?' suggested Conrad.

Brady turned and looked at him, mildly surprised.

'What makes you say that?'

'Just that the letters "MD" and the scorpion seem like an ownership mark, sir.'

Brady wearily nodded. 'And that's exactly what's worrying me, Conrad. You tell me what sex traffickers would be doing in Whitley Bay of all places?'

'I don't know, sir,' answered Conrad, as much at a loss as his boss.

'That's the problem, Conrad, neither do I,' replied Brady. 'In all the years I've been stationed at Whitley Bay I've never come across a crime of this nature. I really hope we're wrong.'

From the tense expression on Conrad's face he obviously felt the same way.

Brady took another mouthful of the bitter coffee. He was still waiting for Claudia to get back to him regarding the markings found on the victim. He knew better than to chase her up. He had no choice but to wait for her call. If the victim was a sex slave, then Claudia was right – she wouldn't be the only one.

'I've heard that Adamson's out to cause trouble for us,' Conrad began tentatively.

'Don't you mean he's out to cause trouble for me? Nothing new there then, Conrad.'

Conrad shook his head. This was serious and he needed his boss to know just how serious.

'Frank Henderson has made an official complaint about you, sir. And Adamson is demanding to know why we were in the ICU. That, and why Simone Henderson's flatmate claimed she was coming up to the North East to see you in connection with an old case you both worked on.'

Brady felt his stomach knot. What exactly had Simone got involved in, and why had she brought his name into it?

'Adamson can go fuck himself,' muttered Brady darkly.

'Rest assured, one day it will happen, sir,' replied Conrad dryly.

Brady turned and looked at Conrad, surprised by the hardness in his voice. Conrad never had a bad word to say about anyone, especially a colleague. But Adamson was a different case entirely. Conrad had spent his first two years of training at Headquarters in Ponteland with Adamson and so knew him of old. After they'd both passed, Conrad swore never to work with the man again. Brady had never asked Conrad exactly what Adamson had done to elicit such an uncharacteristic reaction from his deputy and Conrad had never volunteered one.

Conrad was the kind of guy you wanted around. He was level-headed, reliable with an unerring sense of fairness. Add to that his unquestionable sense of loyalty where Brady was concerned, and the fact that he knew when to keep his mouth shut, and he was invaluable. Without Conrad by his side, Brady didn't know what he would do. Ironic given how much flak he gave DCI Gates when he had first assigned Conrad to him, never mind the hard time he'd given Conrad for being the poor, unfortunate sod appointed as his sidekick.

Brady took another slug of the unpalatable black coffee as he thought about what Conrad had just said. He'd heard rumours about Adamson. Ones that didn't rest easy with him.

'You know you could press charges against Frank Henderson, sir? After all, he did assault you,' Conrad pointed out. 'And it might counteract the complaint he's made against you.'

Brady looked out the passenger window and shook his head. He couldn't bring himself to press charges when he felt that the punches were deserved. He just had to make sure he kept out of Adamson's way.

He caught a glance of his reflection in the wing mirror. He face was a mess, which explained why he hurt like hell. The cut above his swollen eye looked nasty and his ribs still burnt every time he breathed. But he didn't have the time or inclination to get himself checked over. There was still too much work to do; and part of that involved Simone's attack.

He rummaged in his jacket pocket for some painkillers. Finding some, he popped a couple in his mouth and washed them down with a swig of coffee. He grimaced at the bitter aftertaste.

'Any updates while you were waiting for me?' he asked abruptly.

'We've got a local teenage girl whose parents have just rung the station to file a missing persons report.'

'How long's she been missing?' Brady questioned as he turned to Conrad.

'That's all I know, sir,' answered Conrad. 'Harvey and Kodovesky are dealing with it though.'

Brady nodded. Given the number of teenagers who disappeared for a couple of days after an argument with their parents, it wasn't worth getting excited about. Most would eventually return home. But unfortunately there were always the few cases where the missing teenager never resurfaced, swallowed up in one of the large cities by prostitution, or worse.

Brady leaned his head back against the headrest and wearily massaged his forehead.

'Problem, sir?' queried Conrad.

'I'm not sure,' answered Brady honestly.

Conrad looked over at him. It was clear from his dark, pensive expression that his boss had no intention of sharing whatever it was that was bothering him.

Brady's silence troubled Conrad. He hadn't spoken about whether he had actually seen Simone Henderson in the ICU. But Conrad knew better than to ask.

*

Conrad parked up outside the station. Brady got out the car without waiting for him. He took out his BlackBerry as he walked towards the station and scrolled down his list of contacts until he came to Amelia Jenkins. He pressed call.

'Amelia?' Brady said.

Before she had a chance to say anything Brady quickly cut in. 'Where are you?'

'I'm heading to the cafeteria for lunch,' answered Amelia, surprised by his directness.

'Good, I'll meet you there in a few minutes.'

He hung up before she had a chance to object.

'I'm going to grab some lunch from the basement. Do you want anything?' Brady asked as Conrad caught up.

Conrad's expression was enough to let Brady know he was still feeling queasy from the autopsy.

'Thanks, but I'm fine, sir,' answered Conrad.

'Alright, you check with Harvey and Kodovesky exactly what they have on this missing girl.'

Brady didn't wait for an answer as he walked in through the double doors of the station. Neither did he give Turner, the desk sergeant, a chance to ask what had happened to his face. He'd leave the damage limitation to Conrad.

Chapter Fifteen

Brady kept his head down, avoiding the quizzical looks as he made his way through the lunchtime crowd towards Amelia. The last thing he wanted was questions about his beaten-up face. Then again, he accepted, he'd be surprised if news hadn't already got around.

He headed for the cracked, red laminated, sixties-style table under the wrought iron barred window where Amelia was sitting with her back to him and the rest of the cafeteria. She was easy to spot with her black razor-cut bob. That, and the fact she was the only one sitting alone.

'I take it you heard,' she greeted him coolly, not looking up from her phone.

There was an edge to her voice. Exasperation . . . irritability? Brady wasn't sure. He accepted that maybe it was both.

He pulled out a chair and sat down next to her, waiting until she'd finished whatever message she was sending.

'Oh my God, Jack? What happened to you?' she said, her voice betraying her as she looked up and saw his face.

'It's nothing,' Brady answered lamely.

'Have you had that cut above your eye checked out?' she asked, frowning. 'It looks really nasty . . .'

'It'll be fine. Don't worry about it,' replied Brady, embarrassed by her concern.

He looked away, pretending to be distracted by the noise around him, unable to hold her questioning gaze.

To Brady's relief her phone suddenly buzzed, diverting her attention from him.

Amelia picked it up and read the message.

He watched, surprised, as she chewed the corner of her red lips while she contemplated the content. He wondered whether the text was from some boyfriend and was surprised by the pang of jealousy he felt at the thought.

'Sorry about that,' Amelia said, as she turned the phone onto silent without replying.

'Go ahead, answer it,' offered Brady.

'No. It's not important,' she lied.

He looked at her. He didn't know what it was about Amelia that made him feel so nervous when he was around her.

'You were asking if I'd heard?' Brady reminded, wanting to break whatever it was that was going on between them. 'Heard what?'

A flicker of disappointment registered on Amelia's face. She nodded, suddenly resuming a detached and professional air.

'Gates is furious with you,' she pointedly stated.

'Tell me something new,' replied Brady laconically.

'This isn't funny, Jack,' Amelia snapped, clearly frustrated by his response. 'Adamson went straight to him and lodged a complaint about you – to add to the one from Frank Henderson.'

'I take it Frank Henderson has been talking to Adamson then?'

'You could say that,' answered Amelia.

Brady didn't say anything.

'Jack, why didn't you just stay away? Why go looking for trouble?'

'What if I was to say that I think the murder investigation I'm working on is connected with Simone Henderson's attack?'

'How?' questioned Amelia, intrigued.

'That's what I'm trying to figure out. And that's why I needed to talk to you.'

'I'm listening . . .' she said as she sat back, folded her arms and waited.

Brady bent forward and lowered his voice, not wanting anyone around to overhear.

'I haven't got time now because I've got to be somewhere. But I promise I'll fill you in later. In the meantime, I need you to do something for me. If I had any other choice, believe me I wouldn't ask . . .'

'Go on,' she instructed with an edge of cynicism.

'What I need is the surveillance footage for this morning's shift covering the main reception area at Rake Lane,' Brady explained. 'And . . . I need your help to get it.'

'Why me?' she asked, frowning.

'Because I can't and you can. You're part of the investigation into Simone Henderson's attack which ultimately gives you the authority I don't have to request it.'

Amelia reached for her cappuccino and slowly took a sip as she thought it over.

She placed the cup back in the saucer and looked him in the eye. 'Tell me why I should do that for you?'

'We've got one headless girl in the morgue who was gang-raped and sodomised before being murdered. Then we have one of our own coppers in ICU. What connects them is the fact they've both been branded.'

Amelia gaped at him. 'Run that by me again?' she asked quietly, trying to hide her surprise.

Brady edged forward in his seat towards her.

'Both victims have been branded. Simone has the letter "N" burnt onto her breast and the girl in the morgue has the letters "MD" with a scorpion above branded at the base of her spine.'

'If you think there's a connection—' began Amelia, starting to shake her head.

'I know there's a connection. Don't ask me how I know, I just know.'

'What? A hunch? Is that it?' questioned Amelia with an edge of scepticism.

'It's enough to worry me,' Brady replied, sighing heavily.

She didn't reply. From the troubled look on her face Brady could see that she was weighing up the enormity of what he was asking her to do.

He nervously dragged his hand back through his hair as he waited for her to respond.

Eventually she looked him in the eye.

'You've got to take this to Adamson. If you don't then you'll be seen as withholding evidence. If Gates finds out he'll crucify you.'

'Like you said, it's just a hunch. For the time being I want to keep this between you and me. Get me that surveillance footage and I'll have a clearer idea as to whether or not I actually have something concrete.'

She remained unmoved.

'Please, Amelia. Believe me, if I had any other choice . . .' Brady's voice trailed off. He didn't know what else to say to convince her. She didn't owe him anything. And he was acutely aware of that fact. Until today they hadn't seen each other in over six months and then only in a professional capacity. She had hinted that she wanted more, but he had backed away, unable to move on after Claudia.

'You know what you're asking me to do, don't you?' asked Amelia, raising her head.

'I'm desperate . . .'

She lightly sighed. 'Alright, I'll do it. Only because I'd hate to see you do something that will mean you end up losing your job once and for all.'

'Thanks.'

'Don't thank me, thank Conrad. He rang me earlier. He's the one who convinced me to help you. He's a good man, Jack. You're lucky to have him on your side.'

'Yeah, I know. What did he say?'

'Enough,' answered Amelia.

Brady didn't say anything.

'Do not screw up and involve me,'

'Thank you, Amelia. I owe you one,' Brady replied, relieved.

'This is against my better judgement, Jack. And I'm not doing this as your colleague, I'm doing this because I care about what happens to you. Even if you don't.'

Amelia held his eye as she waited for a response.

But typically, Brady didn't say a word. Instead he uncomfortably broke away from her gaze.

She knew why. She'd read the files from his childhood and knew better than anyone why he couldn't deal with emotion. Why, when offered the chance of something good, he would inevitably end up running from it for fear of destroying it. But there was something about him, a vulner-ability that meant she couldn't resist wanting to help him. Despite her better judgement.

'Amelia, I . . . I . . .' began Brady.

But Amelia was already gathering up her bag and phone.

'Save it, Jack. For when you actually mean it,' she said as she stood up to leave.

Before he had a chance to say anything she was already walking away.

*

Brady made his way back to his office. He was cursing his stupidity at leaving his car keys on his desk. He needed to be somewhere and fast. And the last place he wanted to be was wandering around the station when Adamson was looking for blood: his blood.

He grabbed his keys off the desk as someone knocked on the door.

'Yeah?' Brady called out distractedly.

Conrad walked in.

'Sir?' Conrad greeted, surprised that Brady looked as if he was going somewhere.

'I've got a meeting to go to, Conrad,' answered Brady. 'This won't take long, will it?'

'You wanted an update on the missing girl, sir.'

'What have you got?'

'I've just spoken to Harvey, sir.'

Brady sighed as he agitatedly ran his hand through his hair. 'Can it wait?'

'You might want to hear this,' replied Conrad.

Brady sat down.

'Does she fit the body type?' he asked, cutting to the chase.

'Yes, sir.'

'Go on,' he instructed, aware that he was going to be late. And the person he was meeting wouldn't hang around.

'Well, she's been missing since Thursday morning, sir,' answered Conrad. 'Didn't turn up at school.'

'So why wait until now to report her missing?'

'Harvey said her parents weren't overly concerned until they saw the news this morning about our murder victim. Panicked them. They tried calling her mobile, but she's not answering.'

'Where did they think she's been since Thursday? I mean, this is Saturday for Christ's sake.'

'Parents believed that she'd been staying at a friend's house. It seems her younger sister's been covering for her. The missing girl's called Melissa Ryecroft and unbeknown to her parents she was allegedly approached by a model agency scout on her Facebook wall last Sunday. Said he could get her in front of a top model agency in London if she was prepared to move fast. Said he'd arrange a meeting with them which was supposed to have been scheduled for 10am Friday. He also said he'd meet her in London on the Thursday. All of this was arranged without her parents' knowledge. They had no idea about this model agency or scout. As I said, they believed she was staying over at a girl-friend's house. They had no idea what she was getting involved in.'

Brady looked sceptically at Conrad.

'And they haven't heard from her since she left for London on Thursday?'

Conrad nodded. 'The model agency scout doesn't exist

either. But the model agency he said he's booked in with does exist. However, when Harvey contacted them they hadn't heard of Melissa and had no meeting booked with either her or some model scout. Seems it was a scam, sir. Models 1 agency said they don't work with external model scouts. They did say this isn't unusual and that there's a lot of people out there scamming money from wannabe models.'

Brady had a bad feeling that this wasn't about scamming Melissa Ryecroft out of her own money. It was about making money out of her body; and not as a model.

'Any distinguishing features, or marks on her body?' Brady asked.

'Same height and body type. And she's also had a breast augmentation job.'

'How old is she?'

'Sixteen and currently studying at Tynemouth King's School in their lower sixth form.'

'Sixteen with fake breasts? How the hell did she pay for those and get legal consent?'

He couldn't believe the way society was evolving. Reality TV like *The X Factor* commanded more votes than any government election ever could. People were more than happy to be anaesthetised by TV programmes about reality TV stars rather than face the bigger issues in the real world.

'King's is a private school, sir. Means her parents have money. They gave their consent and paid for the breast augmentation as a sixteenth birthday present. Took her abroad on holiday to Budapest allegedly.'

'What the fuck is the world coming to, Conrad, when parents teach their daughters that all their self-worth is tied up in looking like a bloody porn star?'

'Parents said she wanted to be a model, sir. Like Jordan, or should I say Katie Price,' answered Conrad uncomfortably.

'What happened to kids growing up wanting to be a doctor or a lawyer? Tell me, Conrad, when did being a topless model or a lap dancer become a girl's ultimate goal in life?'

Conrad didn't reply.

He knew there was nothing he could say that would snap his boss out of his diatribe about Western society's ills. He was also well aware that the young, headless woman lying cut open in the morgue had deeply affected Brady. As had Simone Henderson's attack.

Brady sighed as he stood up, trying not to wince as a searing pain in his ribs kicked off.

'I need a copy of the parents' statement on my desk by the time I get back,' he ordered, clutching his car keys.

'Don't you just want me to drive you?' asked Conrad. 'You don't look so good, sir.'

'I'm fine, Conrad. Just some bruising, that's all.'

Conrad clearly didn't believe him.

'Look, it's better if you're not involved,' replied Brady uneasily.

He wasn't good at lying; especially where Conrad was concerned.

'Sir?'

Brady couldn't look him in the eye. Instead he turned and walked to the door. He opened it and waited for Conrad.

His deputy didn't move. Brady realised he was clearly waiting for an explanation.

'Trust me on this, will you? Anyway, I need you to trace

this serial number taken from the victim's silicone implants,' Brady said, offering the piece of paper that Harold, Wolfe's assistant, had given him.

'Why?'

'It could identify our victim. And I want that information before I talk to the missing girl's parents. Saves us all a lot of time.'

Conrad reluctantly walked over to him and took the paper.

'Sir, look . . . we've got the briefing in less than an hour.'

Brady agitatedly rubbed his hand over the coarse stubble on his chin. He felt cornered. But he knew he had no choice. He had to go.

'This won't take long. I'll be back to handle the briefing. Just tell the team the meeting's been pushed back until 3pm. It gives you time to set up the Incident Room and run a check on that serial number for me. I need to know for certain if the victim is or isn't the Ryecrofts' missing daughter before the briefing, Conrad.'

'Sir?' objected Conrad. 'What happens if I need to contact you?'

'To you, and you alone, I have my mobile. If anyone asks, tell them I'm at lunch,' ordered Brady as he left the office.

Conrad watched him leave. He had a bad feeling that Brady was independently working on a connection with Simone Henderson's investigation.

Conrad looked at the paper he had inadvertently crumpled up in his fist. He had work to do and decided that, knowing Brady, he was right: it was better that he didn't know. All he could do was exactly what Brady had asked – cover for him until he got back.

Chapter Sixteen

Brady parked up and got out of his black 1978 Ford Granada 2.8i Ghia. He looked across at St Mary's Lighthouse. It looked serene, ghostly even; crumbling white against a backdrop of muted grey and black clouds rolling in from the horizon. The lighthouse had once been a beacon of light shining across the cold, battering North Sea, stretching out as far as the naked eye could see, until it reached a vanishing point.

When he was a kid, he and Martin Madley would skip school, jump on the Metro to Whitley Bay and then walk the length of the beach and over the rocks to get to St Mary's Lighthouse. With his brother Nick in tow they would spend tireless days wading in the rock pools, exploring St Mary's Island.

St Mary's was now a major tourist attraction for the small seaside resort. It was a leisurely stroll down from Feathers caravan site; still a popular destination with the Scots for their annual fortnight holiday, just as it had been since the fifties. The two council-owned car parks at St Mary's were positioned to take in the breathtaking curve of beach and cliffs that was Whitley Bay. Brady looked at the beach stretched out ahead. This place was in his blood.

No matter how much he fought it, he knew he was tied to it. That regardless, he'd never be able to leave.

He watched as early afternoon dog walkers and joggers dominated the white, unblemished sands while birds scavenged the promenades fighting over the previous night's curried chips, charitably dumped by passing drunks stumbling home.

Brady locked his car and walked over to the grassy bank, breathing in the salty, fresh air. He headed along the path towards the second car park opposite the lighthouse, looking for Madley. He wasn't there. But Paulie Knickerbocker's ice-cream van was there waiting for the weekend trade. Brady slowly walked over, aware that his leg was starting to play up again.

He grimly nodded at the thirty-something, smart-looking, dark-haired, second generation Italian hanging out of the hatch watching him with interest.

Paulie nodded at Brady taking in the damage to his face. But he knew not to ask.

'What is it with you coppers? Always on my back, eh? What? Am I illegally trading now?' laughed Paulie Knickerbocker. 'Believe me, officer, the only white stuff I'm selling to kids is ice-cream!'

Brady didn't laugh. That was enough for Paulie to know something was wrong.

'Have you seen Martin?' Brady asked, getting straight to the point.

Paulie frowned. His large, deep black Italian eyes were questioning.

'Why?'

Brady had known Paulie since St Joseph's Primary School. As had Madley.

When word had got out amongst the kids that his parents were Italian and ran the ice-cream vans parked up in all weathers outside St Mary's Lighthouse, Tynemouth Sands and Tynemouth Priory, the nickname 'Knickerbocker' came about. And for some reason it had stuck, regardless of the years and Paulie's two Italian restaurants which were known by his family name, Antonelli.

These restaurants were hugely successful, both located along North Shields quayside. The original was known as 'Antonelli's' and the second one as 'Antonelli's 2'. Brady had heard that there was going to be another Antonelli's opening up in Whitley Bay. The food was good quality Italian, accompanied by simple wine or Peroni. The key to Paulie's success was not being greedy: he never over-charged his customers, making sure that a good night out could still be a cheap night out. It meant his customers came back again and again, to the extent that it was so busy that they couldn't guarantee you a table.

Brady knew why Paulie still covered the odd weekend shift in the ice-cream van – he owned a family business, which was over-run with squabbling Italian relatives and inevitably high tempers. That, and the fact that he was also a talented amateur photographer. Something he kept quiet. But he would use a still, brooding afternoon like this one to build on his black and white landscape portfolio, the best of which could be seen on the walls of his restaurants.

And running two restaurants and the family ice-cream business wasn't all Paulie was known for: he was also the local fence. The vans and the restaurants acted as the ideal cover for such an operation. Paulie had contacts that Brady could only dream of and was always Brady's first unofficial line of enquiry when a violent burglary had taken place.

Paulie had a strong sense of moral duty which generously extended beyond family and friends. He was happy to fence stolen goods as long as no unnecessary violence was exacted during the robbery. Brady had often laughed about the irony of being a fence with a conscience, but Paulie didn't see the incongruity of it. His attitude was that you should always act civilised, regardless of what you did for a living. Brady put Paulie's morality down to being raised a devout Roman Catholic, combined with growing up in the Ridges, where the brutal reality of surviving the streets meant that, at times, Catholic morals had to be temporarily put on hold.

'This is nothing to do with work, Paulie,' Brady explained, aware that there was an edge to Paulie's voice. 'It's personal.'

He realised that Paulie had obviously heard about the copper who had been mutilated. Who hadn't? He had listened to Metro Radio in the car on the way from the station and it had been the only topic of conversation. He had even turned over to BBC Radio Newcastle's Jonathan Miles morning show only to be confronted by the same discussions. The attack had also reached the national news – given its gruesome nature, Brady wasn't surprised.

But as for the body washed up on the beach, for some reason it wasn't quite hitting the headlines Brady had expected. It had been overshadowed by the human interest story of a beautiful young copper at the start of an exceptional career in the Met who had been brutally knifed and unceremoniously dumped, left with her tongue cut out to slowly bleed to death. If it hadn't been for the anonymous emergency call and the bartender that found her, then they could have been dealing with a murder enquiry.

Brady knew that her photo would already have been

uploaded onto Sky and BBC 24-hour news. Simone was young, attractive and talented, and the tragedy of what had happened to her, and the speculation as to why, would sell the news over and over again.

The difference between Simone Henderson and the story of the headless body was that she was still fighting for her life and they could get a background story; unlike the unidentified girl lying butchered in the morgue.

Paulie handed Brady a polystyrene cup of black coffee. 'You look like you need this.'

'Thanks,' accepted Brady. He reached in his pocket for change.

Paulie shook his head. 'Do me a favour, will you?'

'What?' asked Brady as he took a mouthful of strong Italian coffee.

'Watch yourself, Jack. There's shit happening here that you haven't got a clue about. New people are turning up, trying to take over. Things are changing . . . Fucking bastards coming in from London, Europe, all thinking they can throw their weight around . . .' Paulie faltered.

Brady turned and followed his gaze as a car sidled round into the car park.

'Look out for him, will you?' Paulie asked as he stared at the new black Bentley saloon. Its registration plate read 'MAD 1'.

Brady turned and shot Paulie a quizzical look. If there was one person who didn't need protecting, it was Martin Madley.

'Word is some bastard is trying to take him down,' Paulie explained.

Brady looked at Madley's new Bentley. Gibbs, his driver who doubled as his henchman, depending on what mood

Madley was in, was behind the steering wheel. Once a professional boxer, the 6′4″, forty-five-year-old African Caribbean was still an imposing sight, with the physique of a brick shithouse. His thick, knotted, black dreads, interwoven with strands of silver, now hung down to his shoulders. He looked at Brady and flashed him a menacing smile, making the most of the new diamond set in his left front tooth.

Gibbs didn't trust Brady and he made no apology in letting him know it. Not that Brady could blame him; he was a copper after all. Behind Gibbs' black Oakleys, Brady knew his eyes would be cold and predatory.

Beside Gibbs sat a weaselly, sharp-nosed, beady-eyed character. He stared at Brady, refusing to back down. From past experience, Brady knew always to be wary of the thin, sinewy, on-the-edge, wiry types. They were the ones who would have a knife in your neck before you knew it. His small, darting, bloodshot eyes told Brady there was trouble. Brady didn't need to look at him to know that. The fact that Madley had hired him was evidence enough.

'Fuck,' muttered Brady under his breath, unsure of what he was getting into here.

He waited as Gibbs got out of the car and walked to the back passenger door to open it.

A few seconds later, Madley stepped out. He looked composed and dignified in his black Armani sunglasses and black Armani suit. His brown hair was neat as always, but his tanned sharp features and menacing eyes spoke of a cut-throat malevolence. Madley was Brady's age, a few inches shorter at 5′10″, with a smaller frame. However, Brady had witnessed Madley fight and knew that he could take down even his own man, Gibbs.

Madley liked to look good. His tastes were expensive, compensating for a childhood of desperate poverty. He wore no jewellery apart from an expensive watch, which cost more than Brady's annual salary. After sharing a childhood in the war-torn streets of the Ridges, they had both chosen a life of crime: Brady fighting it, Madley living it – and clearly profiting from it.

Brady watched with interest as Madley's new henchman got out of the Bentley. He strutted behind Madley, making a point of adjusting his cheap black version of Madley's suit for Brady's benefit. Underneath the Burton suit jacket Brady caught a glimpse of exactly what it was Weasel Face wanted Brady to see. A bulging shoulder holster with a Glock 31 semi-automatic pistol resting underneath the jacket. Brady was under no illusion: the manoeuvre was intentional. And the Glock 31 would be loaded.

Madley nodded at Brady as he approached him.

'Brought in someone new,' he said in a smooth, refined voice; the hardened Geordie edge of his childhood years long gone.

'I can see,' answered Brady as he glanced towards Weasel Face.

Madley turned to his new employee. 'Wait for me in the car.'

'Are you sure, boss?' questioned the wiry man in a thick Cockney accent as he gave Brady a distrustful glance.

Madley shot him a look.

It was enough for Weasel Face to turn back to the car.

Something wasn't right if Madley had been forced to hire some trigger from the East End. It was now obvious to Brady that the dumping of Simone Henderson's mutilated body in his nightclub was no accident.

It was a warning. They wanted her blood on Madley's hands. The question was why?

'What's going on, Martin?'

'Maybe you should tell me,' replied Madley as he studied Brady's swollen, cut face.

Brady ignored the question.

'I got a call from Jimmy Matthews this morning,' he said, changing the subject.

Madley looked at him. Brady could see that behind the dark sunglasses his eyes had suspiciously narrowed.

'Go on,' Madley instructed.

'He reckons he's got something on me. Wants me to go in and talk to him. I think it's connected to—'

'Go visit him,' interrupted Madley, cutting Brady off.

'The last person I want to visit behind bars is Jimmy,' objected Brady.

'Then that's your choice. But right now Jimmy Matthews isn't my main concern.'

Brady was about to ask what he meant but Madley's expression was enough to silence him. He had met Madley on the assumption that they needed to find out exactly what kind of damaging information Matthews could have got hold of, and how to silence him.

Brady's eyes dropped to Madley's right hand. He noticed that Madley was holding a package.

'I've kept this back from that shit Adamson. So this is between you and me, Jack,' Madley said as he handed the brown envelope over. 'Understand?'

Brady nodded. 'What is it?'

But he already knew. It was the surveillance footage from the Blue Lagoon, Madley's nightclub. He realised that Madley must have replaced some crucial footage on the tape. Brady

113

knew that Madley was paranoid about covering his tracks and it came as no surprise that he had the expertise or had someone close to him who could alter his security tapes if the need ever arose.

'Better you see for yourself.'

'What did you do?' he asked.

'Copied it and then replaced the previous Friday night's footage after the club had closed. So when your lot got there, the surveillance camera shows nothing unusual. You owe me for this, Jack.'

'Why? What has this got to do with me?'

Brady was worried. But he made a point of not letting Madley know.

'Everything.'

Brady looked at Madley's face. He realised that he was deadly serious.

'Who is on the tape?' asked Brady.

'Watch it,' answered Madley, his expression dark and menacing. 'No one fucks with me, Jack. No one.'

'Who are you talking about?' asked Brady as he tried to keep his voice steady.

'Someone we both know well . . . too well.'

'Is this to do with Matthews? Is that the reason he's demanding to see me?' asked Brady.

Madley laughed. It was a cold, hard-edged response. 'Like I said, he's the least of my concerns right now. This isn't Matthews' style. He hasn't got the balls.'

'For Christ's sake, Martin, stop playing games. Just tell me.'

Madley shook his head. 'Better you see this for yourself. But I'm not the only one who's being fucked over here. You don't sort this then it's not only my reputation that's ruined, it's your career.'

Brady kept quiet. He had no idea who Madley was talking about. The only person who came to mind who would have a score to settle with them both was Jimmy Matthews. And he was locked up in a secure unit for his own protection. Besides, Madley was right. Matthews could be an evil fucker, but even he didn't have the balls to be involved in something of this magnitude.

'Here,' said Madley, thrusting a piece of paper at Brady. 'I think you'll need to talk to Johnny Slaughter once you've watched the tape.'

Brady reluctantly took the paper with the number on it.

'Sort it. Or . . .' Madley let the sentence hang.

'I'll sort it,' Brady said.

But he didn't know exactly what it was he was sorting.

He knew Madley wouldn't go to the police. He'd already proven that. And he had known Madley too long and knew that he wasn't prone to hyperbole. If he said it could destroy Brady's career then he was under no illusions; that's exactly what it could do.

Chapter Seventeen

Brady unlocked his car door and got in. He reached across to the passenger floor for his laptop. He paused, not really wanting to go through with it. But he had no choice.

Madley had given him no choice.

He ripped open the package and took out the unmarked DVD. He laid it on his knee as he rolled a tab. He needed one to steady his nerves.

His phone started to vibrate in his jacket pocket.

'Christ!' he cursed, startled. He decided to ignore it.

He shakily lit the cigarette and inhaled deeply. His dark brown eyes narrowed as he looked out the windscreen at the winding bay that was Whitley Bay. In the distance he could just make out the row of Indian, Italian and pizza restaurants and takeouts that littered the stretch of road facing the sea. In between them sat Madley's nightclub, the Blue Lagoon, and next door, the Royal Hotel. As he did so he unconsciously tightened his grip on the package.

When he was ready, he pushed the DVD into the laptop and waited.

The image went from black to a grainy grey empty corridor. Brady fast-forwarded. Then he saw it. A blurry, tall male figure with cropped, short hair carrying something over his shoulder. Something bulky wrapped in what looked to be black plastic, like a bin liner.

Then Brady saw it. A hand fell from out of the plastic wrapping.

Brady exhaled, knowing that it had to be Simone's.

He watched as the figure went into the gents'. At least a minute or more went by before the man exited again.

Brady noted that he was wearing a G-Star Raw camouflage jacket. He knew it was G-Star Raw because he recognised the distinctive style.

But he was at a loss. He didn't recognise the figure. None of this was making any sense.

The tall, well-built figure headed down the corridor, passing the camera. As he did so, Brady caught sight of a blurred image of his face.

He sat for a moment, staring at the face. Not fully registering who he was staring at.

Then it hit him. It was all the confirmation he needed that he was right about the voice on the 999 call. Cold dread took hold of him. Then sheer panic.

Brady squeezed his eyes shut, willing the image of the face to disappear.

He shallowly breathed out, trying to slow his racing heart down. Steadying himself, he opened his eyes hoping that he had been wrong. He had to be wrong.

But as he stared at the evidence in front of him he realised that everything he had believed in, worked for, had suddenly evaporated. Replaced by an inconceivable fact: he knew the attacker.

His past had come back to haunt him.

'No!' shouted Brady as he hit the dashboard in pure rage.

Brady didn't need Jed to digitally enhance the image. He

already knew who it was – the three-inch scar down the left cheek was a dead giveaway. Then there was the jawline, the nose, those eyes. All unmistakable.

He was going to throw up.

Brady quickly opened the car door and bent over and retched. Acrid black coffee hit the ground, burning the back of his throat on its way out. He retched again and again until there was nothing but bile forcing its way up from his empty stomach. He slowly breathed in deeply, trying to steady himself, but the foul, decaying stench that hung in the air was only adding to the urge to retch again. Brady put the rancid smell down to the slurry from the agricultural fields behind the car park being carried over on the slight coastal breeze.

He could hear his phone vibrating as he clung onto the car door with his head hanging over the ground.

'This can't be happening. Please God this can't be happening . . .' Brady said to himself. Again and again and again.

A car slowly drove past, the elderly driver and passenger watching him. They stopped and waited, not sure if he needed help.

Brady realised he must have looked as bad as he felt.

It was enough to bring him to his senses. He pulled himself up and slammed the car door shut.

Brady sat and stared blankly out the windscreen. Minutes went past as he sat there, not seeing the horizon or the North Sea. All he could see was that scar running down the left cheek of the man who had dumped Simone Henderson in the gents'. Every muscle in his body, every sinew was taut. Every nerve on edge; waiting. Not knowing what to think, let alone what to do. All he felt was blinding panic.

Brady could feel himself starting to hyperventilate. His breathing was coming in short, rapid bursts just as it had done when he'd finally come round in hospital to the knowledge that someone had tried to blow his balls off and that his wife had walked out on him.

He tried to focus on steadying his breathing. Remembering the technique Amelia had taught him in the hospital to control the panic attacks he had suffered after realising he had lost Claudia for good. He had explained the panic attacks away as a result of being shot and reliving the memory of hearing the handgun go off and simultaneously feeling the impact of the bullet. Amelia had never said as much, but she had known that he wasn't suffering from post-traumatic stress from being shot. It was the shock of being left by the only person he had loved. Claudia was the one person he had opened up to and he never meant to hurt her, let alone drive her away.

Brady put his head back against the headrest and closed his eyes, trying to breathe slowly. But the face he had recognised on the tape kept tormenting him. He couldn't shut it out.

He had to watch it again. Just in case he had made a mistake. In case Madley had made a mistake. It couldn't be him. It just couldn't.

Brady pressed play and then paused the DVD on the close-up of the figure's face. But there it was, the three-inch, gnarled scar down his left cheek.

Brady stared at the image desperately trying to convince himself he was mistaken. But the longer he stared, the more certain he became that it really was him.

He looked at his phone. With shaking hands he started to key in a mobile number. He knew it from memory. He

119

had never stored it in the phone just in case it fell into the wrong hands.

'Come on!' shouted Brady when he keyed in the wrong number.

His hands were shaking uncontrollably. He tried to breathe slowly, deliberately, in an attempt to steady his nerves. He keyed the numbers in again and pressed call.

He listened as the phone rang and rang.

'Pick up. . . . pick up!' urged Brady.

Eventually it cut to an automated voicemail. He disconnected the call and started keying in a London landline number.

He waited. The dial tone was dead. The phone had obviously been disconnected.

'No . . . no . . .' he muttered, his hands trembling as he cut the dead tone.

He didn't know what to do next. It took him a minute to realise that he had no choice but to follow Madley's advice.

He took out the piece of paper that Madley had given him. On it a mobile phone number was scribbled.

Brady keyed it into his phone and waited.

'What?' came the sharp answer.

'Johnny?' answered Brady. 'It's Brady . . . Jack Brady.'

'What the hell do you want?' Slaughter demanded. 'And who gave you my fucking number?' His hoarse voice had a heavy, thick East London accent. It was a voice that carried with it an air of sinister threat.

Slaughter didn't want anyone getting close to him and used his brother, Billy, as a front man. There was a good reason why Billy was known amongst his friends and enemies as 'Slash'. Anyone who came into contact with Billy never again crossed Johnny Slaughter.

'Madley gave it to me,' answered Brady.

He was certain there wouldn't be any ramifications for Madley. He knew Slaughter and Madley looked out for one another. Madley took care of business if Slaughter ever needed it in the North East and the same applied with Slaughter in London.

'And why the fuck would he do that?'

Brady steeled himself. 'I need to know where Nick is.'

'And how would *I* know where he is?'

'Madley reckoned you'd know. That's why he gave me your number. He's in trouble, Johnny. Serious trouble and I need to find him before the police get him . . . or worse.'

'Are you having a laugh or what?'

'You know what I mean, Johnny. I wouldn't ask if this wasn't serious.'

'You should keep a better eye on him. You being a copper an' all!'

'I can't get hold of him. He's not answering his mobile and his landline's been disconnected.'

'Doesn't surprise me. He's no doubt on the run!'

'From who? You?'

'If he knows what's good for him, he will be! Nick stopped working for me a month back. Got involved with those Eastern European bastards who are coming over here and taking all our bloody money!'

It didn't sound like Nick. At least, not the Nick he knew.

'Are you sure?' questioned Brady.

'Too right I am. I saw him myself at Heathrow with two Eastern European Lithuaks!'

'What was he doing?' demanded Brady, knowing he wasn't going to like the answer.

'What do you think he was doing?'

'I don't know . . .' pushed Brady.

'Trading in goods is what. Him and his new Lithuak mates. Presumably waiting for what they've paid for to come off the plane and then they start trading with the other Lithuak shits who hang around there. Just come back from Spain and I run straight into your Judas of a brother. Bloody didn't know where to look!'

'Are they dealing in drugs?' Brady asked.

He was silently hoping that was what the answer was going to be.

'What didn't you hear? I said he was in with some Lithuaks! Do you reckon they're moral like us? Hell no! They're evil shits. Dirty money is what they deal in. They bring in girls. Eastern European girls from back home, and they sell the poor buggers for the highest price as soon as they're through customs.'

'Shit!' muttered Brady.

'Yeah, that's one word for it. I wouldn't touch that trade if my life depended on it. I've got standards. And sadly, I thought Nick had too!'

With that, Johnny Slaughter hung up, leaving Brady worried. The last person he wanted hunting Nick down was Billy 'Slash' Slaughter.

He decided to call Nick again. He had no choice but to leave a voicemail.

He waited while the phone connected. It rang and rang before cutting to voicemail.

'Nick? What the fuck are you doing? Call me, as soon as you get this. I'll help you, OK? Whatever it takes, Nick, I'll get you out of this . . .'

Brady stopped. He didn't know what else to say so he hung up.

How he was going to help him, he didn't know. But he was certain about one thing – he'd cross the line to save his brother. Regardless of his career. And that included not letting Madley's new boy use him as target practice, nor giving Billy Slash-Slaughter the chance to redesign his face.

Chapter Eighteen

Brady thought long and hard about ringing Madley.

But he had no other option.

'Martin?'

'What did you find out?' Madley asked, getting straight to the point.

'Slaughter said that Nick stopped working for him a month back. That he's got involved with some Eastern European guys.'

'Did he give you any names?'

Brady noticed he didn't sound surprised.

Either Madley had already talked to Slaughter about Nick or . . . he was holding back on him.

Brady hoped it wasn't the latter.

'No . . . called them Lithuaks though.'

'Means nothing,' Madley replied.

Brady couldn't ignore the fact that there was an edge to Madley's voice.

'Martin?'

'What?'

'You'd tell me if something was wrong, yeah?'

'You're a fucking copper, Jack! Or have you forgotten that? A copper whose brother has just tried to stitch me up.'

Brady kept his mouth shut. He couldn't deny it.

'Do you know how long that wanker Adamson questioned me for this morning? Two fucking hours! Two hours out of my life! If it hadn't been for Rogers turning up, I reckon the wanker would have tried to nail the fucking copper's attack on me!'

Madley was more than furious.

Brady knew he had to act fast and find Nick before he did.

'Do you know how much that stunt cost me?' Before Brady could answer, Madley told him. 'Too fucking much!'

Brady knew Rogers was one of the best lawyers in the North East, which was why Madley employed him.

'You find him, you hear? And you make him talk. Make him talk before I get my hands on him. Understand?'

'Tell me something, who wants you out, Madley?' asked Brady.

'Why don't you stick with what you do for a living and leave me to get on with what I do?' Madley said quietly, with an air of threat.

'It's a little bit late for that, don't you think, given one of ours is caught up in the middle of it?' replied Brady.

He waited for a response.

Nothing.

'Listen to me, Martin, Adamson won't let this go. Paulie reckons you've got competition, that someone's leaning on you. If that's the case do you want Adamson sticking you with a copper's brutal mutilation? Because I promise you, that's exactly what's going to happen unless you talk to me.'

Brady listened as the line went dead.

Madley's silence said it all. The problem was, he wasn't

going to make it easy for Brady. He'd have to do some work to find out exactly who wanted Madley out, and why.

He dragged his hand back through his hair, catching his reflection in the rear view mirror. He looked like he'd had the crap beaten out of him. Which he had.

Then something caught his eye. Something on the back seat.

It was a black bin liner.

Brady quickly spun round.

He suddenly realised that there was something wrong. There was a heavy, foul smell in the air. He had initially thought it was coming from outside the car. He now realised it was coming from the black bin liner behind him.

Chapter Nineteen

He yanked open the door and retched. The contents in the black bin liner gave him no choice.

His stomach kept heaving, even though there was nothing there to force out. Once he was certain that he wasn't going to retch again, he shut the car door.

He had to get his head together. He needed to make a call. At the end of the day he was still a copper. He had no choice but to call in the SOCOs. It was a crime scene. There was a victim. And if Nick was involved . . . Well, he'd deal with that later.

He should have parked the car where he could see it. Not that he would have ever expected someone to break into his car and leave behind a black bin liner filled with human remains.

Picking up his phone he saw he had two missed calls. One from Conrad and one from Claudia.

He scrolled through his phone until he found the number he needed. He pressed call and waited. He needed to talk to the head SOCO.

'Ainsworth? It's Jack.'

'This has to be serious for you to be calling me,' Ainsworth replied.

Brady steeled himself.

'It is . . .'

'Spit it out then, lad. I haven't got all day!'

'Evidence was left in my car.'

'What evidence?' questioned Ainsworth.

'A black bin liner containing what I believe to be the murder victim's head and . . . a note . . .'

'Bloody hell!' spluttered Ainsworth.

'Ainsworth? Can we keep this between me and you for now? Just until I can figure out what's going on?'

'I'll tell you what's going on, lad, someone's fucking with you. And that someone is serious.'

'Tell me something new,' muttered Brady as he looked up at the dark, overcast sky.

'Right, where the bloody hell is your car?' demanded Ainsworth.

'At St Mary's Lighthouse,' answered Brady.

'What the fuck are you doing there?'

'You don't want to know,' answered Brady.

'Aye, knowing you, Jack, you'll be right about that. Alright, we'll be there soon.'

'Thanks.' Brady hung up then scrolled down his phone-book and found Wolfe's number. He pressed call.

'What's your problem?' answered Wolfe.

'The head's turned up,' answered Brady.

'That was bloody quick work, laddie,' answered Wolfe. 'Where was it?' he questioned, realising from Brady's silence that he was being serious.

'In my car,' replied Brady.

'Oh shit,' wheezed Wolfe.

Brady sighed heavily. 'Are you still at the morgue?'

'Where else would I be?'

'The pub?' replied Brady.

'Aye, but not in the middle of the afternoon, Jack.'

'Ainsworth will have it sent over as soon as he's finished,' Brady replied before disconnecting the call.

He got out the car, slamming the door shut. He resisted the urge to start kicking it. Pounding it with all the pent-up fury he felt towards his brother. He wanted to destroy it. Destroy everything and anything that connected Brady to Nick.

The car had been bought as a project, one that he and Nick had worked on. Nick had a gift. He had always been able to fix things ever since he was a young child. He had a knack of making something out of nothing, which was exactly what he had done with the car. It had been a shell when they had bought it ten years ago, but Nick had spent months working on it on the odd weekends, patiently rebuilding it to beyond its former glory.

That was before Nick's work started to get in the way and he moved to London permanently. He had said it was for more lucrative jobs, but Brady knew better. He was basically keeping out of Brady's way. The last thing Nick wanted was for his choice of profession to sabotage Brady's career as a copper. Or for his brother to be the one to nick him, should it come to that. Brady knew exactly what Nick did for a living; but he never asked questions. Nick hired himself out as a bodyguard; at least that's what he had told Brady. At 6´3˝, muscle-bound but lithe, with intelligent, calculating green eyes and cropped dark blonde hair, and a thick, three-inch scar down his left cheek, he was never short of work. Or money.

The loyalty between them was unquestionable.

Brady had always made sure that he took his father's sadistic and drunken beatings instead of Nick. He had protected Nick at all costs, even to the detriment of his mother's life. If it hadn't been for Nick, Brady would never have left his mother to die at his father's hands. But instead he had done as his mother had begged, taken his younger brother and hidden him from his father's murderous rage.

And Nick had been worth protecting.

So why would Nick, his own brother, turn on him? Let alone get involved in something so sick, so wrong?

Brady stared at the car, his watering eyes burning with pain as he fought the tumult of emotions that were threatening to break him. He wanted to get a can of petrol and throw it over the car and torch it in a bid to exorcise himself of the agonising betrayal he felt. But he couldn't. It was part of a crime scene. One that involved him in too many ways.

He took the DVD which he had removed from the laptop and thrust it into the inner pocket of his jacket. The last person he wanted getting their hands on this evidence was Adamson.

Despite what he felt, he still couldn't believe that his brother was capable of such a heinous crime. Not against Madley and definitely not against him. Above all, he wouldn't be part of something that would abuse and terrorise a woman like that. It was unthinkable.

He turned away from the car unable to look at it. Unable to accept that here he was still protecting Nick. He was putting his career on the line and for what?

But he knew the answer. Nick was all he had now. And

until he had spoken to him, Brady refused to believe, despite the evidence in his pocket, that his own brother could be involved in such a sickening crime against a female copper. Let alone one who meant so much to him personally.

Chapter Twenty

Brady drew heavily on his cigarette as he thought about the evidence on the surveillance tape Madley had given him.

He watched as Conrad hit the traffic lights where the amusements had once been on the sea front opposite the Spanish City Dome. He automatically glanced in the wing mirror to make sure they weren't being followed. Or more to the point, *he* wasn't.

He'd left his car being examined forensically by Ainsworth's team. He had no choice. Hopefully he'd get it back by the end of the day.

He was worried about explaining all this to Gates. The reason he had been at the lighthouse was because he was meeting with Madley – a suspect in Adamson's books when it came to Simone Henderson's attack. And one alleged to be a local drugs baron, although that was still an unsubstantiated claim.

'The serial number, sir,' Conrad began. 'Sir?' he repeated when Brady didn't reply.

Brady distractedly turned to Conrad, unable to rid himself of the gruesome image of the victim's head in the black bin liner.

'Sorry?'

His mind was racing.

There had been a note in the black bin liner. A note which made it quite clear that it was no accident that a severed head had been left in Brady's car. He hadn't told Conrad about the note. He had simply handed it over to Ainsworth to be forensically examined. He needed time to figure out exactly what the note meant before sharing it with Conrad and the rest of the team.

'The serial number you gave me, sir,' explained Conrad. 'It seems that every silicone implant has a serial code which is registered with the clinic where they are surgically inserted. The silicone implants removed from the murder victim are registered with a cosmetic surgery clinic named Virenyos in Budapest, sir.'

Brady thought about the sixteen-year-old girl who had been reported missing earlier.

'Did they have the patient's name registered with the serial number?'

'No, sir. Seems they have too high a turnover to keep all the records. They keep records for up to two months after the surgical procedure and then they delete them. I think it's more to do with patients suing them for malpractice once they get back to the UK and realise that cheap surgery combined with a holiday comes at a price. You reckon it could be the missing girl, sir?' Conrad asked.

'We can't rule out coincidence. But all the same, she did have a breast job carried out at a clinic in Budapest.'

Brady took out his phone. He needed to get Harvey on this straight away.

'Tom?' Brady asked.

133

'Fuck me, Jack! How the bloody hell did you end up with the victim's missing head in your bloody car, eh?' quizzed Harvey.

Brady's silence was enough.

'Well, at least it's saved us a job hunting up and down the coastline looking for it,' Harvey continued, filling in the awkward gap.

'That's if it's her,' Brady coolly pointed out.

'Yeah . . . let's not get a*head* of ourselves, eh?' replied Harvey, unable to help himself.

Brady didn't laugh.

He knew that in all likelihood it would belong to the girl lying in one of the thirty body refrigerators in Rake Lane Hospital's morgue. The girl whose body had been sadistically raped, sodomised and then murdered.

'Conrad's traced the serial number from the silicone implants found in the victim's breasts to a clinic called Virenyos in Budapest. We need to see if they match with the missing girl so I need the details of the clinic and the serial number of the silicone implants from her parents. But under no circumstances let them know what we've found.'

'Conrad's already informed us. So I went ahead and requested the clinic details and serial number from the parents,' answered Harvey.

'Thanks, Tom.'

Brady sighed as he disconnected the call, relieved that Harvey was already onto it.

'Gates wants to know when you're holding a press call, sir,' Conrad informed him.

Brady momentarily took his eyes off the wing mirror and shot Conrad an incredulous look.

'Not exactly looking my best right now,' replied Brady.

Conrad didn't respond.

'You did put the briefing back?' asked Brady. It was already nearly 3pm, which was when the briefing was supposed to take place.

'Yes, sir,' Conrad replied. 'I pushed it back by an hour given the circumstances.'

'Good,' muttered Brady. It gave him some time to get his head sorted and make a couple of calls.

'Oh, and sir, Claudia, your ex-wife—' Conrad began.

'I know who Claudia is, Conrad!'

Brady nervously rubbed the dark, emerging stubble on his face as he checked the wing mirror again.

Conrad refrained from saying anything. Instead he focused on the traffic lights, waiting for them to change.

'I'm sorry, Conrad,' apologised Brady as Conrad slowly pulled away. 'I've just got a lot on my mind right now.'

His deputy nodded,

'I understand sir,' he answered simply.

'Claudia then?' Brady asked.

'She's waiting in your office for you,' Conrad nodded. 'Seems she has some information.'

'Do you know what it's about?' asked Brady.

Conrad shook his head. 'No sir, she wouldn't say.'

*

Conrad pulled into a rare parking space opposite the station.

Brady waited until he had turned off the engine before slowly getting out the car. He still felt shaken. His head

135

and ribs still hurt and he couldn't get rid of the stench of decomposing flesh from his nostrils. He knew the smell would be clinging to his skin. And he could feel the decay emanating from his pores.

'Conrad, do me a favour will you? Go and tell Claudia I'll be with her directly.'

'Yes, sir,' answered Conrad as he locked his car.

He turned expectantly to Brady, surprised he wasn't making a move towards the station.

'I just need five minutes on my own to clear my head,' Brady explained.

Conrad gave him a questioning look.

'Get Harvey to leave a copy of the missing girl's parents' statement on my desk for me. Just in case the clinic and silicone details match.'

'Yes, sir,' answered Conrad.

Brady watched as he walked across the road and up the stairs into Whitley Bay Police Station. Conrad turned and looked back at him briefly before going through the heavy, wooden double doors.

Brady was the first to admit that at this precise moment he didn't look too good. His face told a recent story of having had the shit kicked out of him. He was temporarily vehicle-less while forensics treated his car as a crime scene and he was withholding evidence in his jacket pocket that fingered his brother Nick for the attempted murder of a copper.

In those early, blurred months over countless bottles of Scotch, Brady remembered talking to Nick about the reason his wife had left him. But he was certain he wouldn't have mentioned Simone by name. Or had he? He wasn't sure about anything any more.

The only thing he was certain about was the fact that he needed to find Nick before someone else did.

He took out his phone.

Trina McGuire was Nick's girlfriend of old. And apart from Brady and Madley, she was the only other connection Nick had with the North East.

He scrolled down his list of numbers. He knew he had her in there somewhere. He'd had to call her enough times in connection with her wayward son, Shane McGuire. Trina was a lap dancer at the Hole in Wallsend. A place that only the hardened locals would dare visit.

Brady found her number. He pressed call and waited.

'Yeah?' croaked a sleepy voice.

'Trina? It's Jack,' answered Brady.

'Oh fuck! What's he been up to now, eh? I swear I'll drown him in the Tyne if he's been stealing booze again!'

Brady cleared his throat.

'No, Trina, this has got nothing to do with Shane.'

'Then why the hell are you calling me at 2:47pm on a Saturday afternoon when I just crawled into bed a few hours ago?'

Brady realised that she must have had a busy night at work. Despite the recession, the sex trade was still going strong.

'It's Nick,' Brady answered. 'He's back in the North East.'

'So? What that's got to do with me, DI Brady?'

'I need to get in touch with him.'

'Hadaway and shite, will you? Do what most people do, give him a call!'

'He's gone to ground. And I was hoping he might have got in touch with you.'

Trina was silent.

Brady knew her silence meant that she knew something. She was a woman of many words; too many at times.

'No . . .'

'Come on, Trina.'

Silence again.

'What is it? What do you know?'

'Nothing. Alright? I know nothing!'

'Don't make me put out a call to get Shane lifted. Maybe he'll be a bit more forthcoming. Last time I heard he was dealing in coke.'

'You bastard! I could never figure out how you could be Nick's brother. At least he's got principles!'

Brady didn't answer her. Once he would have agreed that you couldn't meet a man with more honour and principles than his brother.

'Look, Trina . . . please. I'm desperate . . .'

'Listen to me, Jack Brady, you stay well away from me and my Shane. Understand?

With that Trina McGuire hung up.

He tried to call her again. The phone rang and then it cut off. He tried a third and fourth time to no avail. She was making it very clear that she had no intention of talking to him.

Brady wearily sighed.

He looked up and down the street. He had every right to be paranoid. Someone was playing with him. Once he was satisfied that no one had followed him, or was watching him, he walked across the road to the station. His biggest fear was that someone had a hold over Nick. That he was being coerced into doing whatever it was he was involved in. Trina was right. Nick had principles. More principles than he himself did.

So he knew that Nick couldn't have harmed Simone. But then, questioned Brady, troubled, why was it that he'd been caught on Madley's nightclub surveillance camera carrying her body, wrapped up in black plastic, into the gents' toilets five minutes before an anonymous call was made to the emergency services?

And despite the attempt at disguising the voice, Brady had recognised it. He had denied it, of course. Argued with himself that it could be anyone with a North East accent. Brady assumed Madley, like himself, had recognised Nick's voice when Adamson had played him the 999 call. But Madley, being Madley, obviously hadn't reacted.

That didn't mean he was protecting Nick. No, Madley was protecting Brady. At least for the time being. Madley wanted Brady to find out exactly what Nick was involved in and why. So Madley could sort it his way without police involvement.

Brady knew that Carl, the one-eyed Mancunian barman who had found Simone Henderson's body in the gents', had sent for Madley. Immediately. Carl always looked out for Madley. His loyalty was sealed when Madley had got even on his behalf with the bastard who had punched him in the face with a car key. All because he thought Carl had short-changed him at the bar. Madley had taken the bloke into the cellar and had both his arms broken at the elbow by Gibbs. Effectively making sure he couldn't even wipe his own arse, let alone take someone's eye out again.

Carl owed Madley and would do anything he asked. Including discreetly removing the copper from the nightclub and making her someone else's headache. The last thing Madley wanted was a copper turning up gutted and mutilated in his nightclub. It wasn't good for business and it wasn't good for his reputation. Madley didn't want his competitors, always hungry for the next big job, to know that he'd been set up.

But Nick hadn't given Carl, or Madley, time to sort it.

The emergency call had come in before Carl had a chance to get Madley. Before he knew it the police had covered the place.

Brady sighed heavily as he walked up the stairs to the station doors. Unsurprisingly, his head was pounding from repeatedly going over everything and getting nowhere.

Before he realised it, he had walked straight into DI Robert Adamson coming out through the wooden doors of the station.

'You're the last person I would expect to see here after the stunt you pulled at the hospital!' Adamson thickly greeted.

Brady shot him a dark look before pushing past.

'I take it you haven't seen DCI Gates yet?'

'What particular aspect of the star sign "prat" were you born under?' Brady muttered.

'What did you say?' demanded Adamson.

Brady turned back and stared at him.

'I'm going to make sure that you get kicked off the force,' snarled Adamson. 'Just wait until the DCI gets a good look at your face. Go on, tell me how you're going to hold a press call for that washed-up murder of yours? Eh? Not exactly going to instil public confidence in the police if you go about looking like some thug from the Ridges. Oh, I forgot – that's exactly what you are!'

'Fuck off!' replied Brady, turning away.

'Say that to my face, you wanker!' shouted Adamson.

Brady clenched his fists and forced himself to walk through the double doors. Otherwise he would end up doing something he would later regret.

Chapter Twenty-One

Brady walked past reception and the desk sergeant and through the door that led into the station.

Still pissed off by his run-in with Adamson, he didn't see Amelia coming round the corner.

'I'm sorry,' he quickly apologised. 'I didn't mean to . . .'

'What? Walk straight into me?' replied Amelia irritably. 'Second time today.'

She bent down and picked up the folder of notes she was carrying.

'Here, let me help,' offered Brady, bending down. He winced slightly as his bruised ribs objected.

Amelia heard him moan and looked up from the scattered notes she was hurriedly gathering up off the floor to see Brady uncomfortably crouching down, clutching his right side.

'Christ, Jack!' Amelia said. 'You need to get seen by a doctor.'

'I'm fine,' lied Brady. 'Honest.'

She gave him a hard, unimpressed look before she resumed picking up the sheets of paper.

'Tell me why I should jeopardise my job so you can run around like some Dirty Harry crusader? What, are you above the law now?' she asked, refusing to look up.

142

Brady frowned, unsure why she was so angry.

'I don't understand.'

'Think about it!'

Brady suddenly realised that she was talking about the hospital security tapes that he had asked her to get for him. So much had happened he had forgotten what he'd asked her to do – ultimately compromise her job and the investigation she was working on for him.

'I'm sorry . . .' he replied lamely, not knowing what else to say.

'In future, Jack, stick to the rules,' Amelia said coldly. 'You have your case to work on, and Adamson and I have ours.'

Finished, she abruptly stood up.

Trying not to wince, Brady also slowly straightened up.

'You'll find what you wanted on your desk. But don't ever expect me to do something like this for you again. It might surprise you, but I don't want to lose my job.'

'Amelia . . . I didn't—'

'Save it for when you actually mean it,' Amelia interrupted.

Brady didn't say anything. He knew that whatever he said wouldn't be enough.

'Remember, I do work at Rake Lane Hospital as well,' Amelia continued. 'And I hear things. Like you going into a patient's room when it has clearly been made off-bounds to you. Then you have a fight with her father. You were in the ICU! The patients there are lucky if they make it through the next couple of hours, without a copper having a brawl with a victim's father. When will you grow up?'

'It wasn't like that,' Brady lamely replied.

'What was it like, then?' questioned Amelia, folding her

arms. 'I'm intrigued. Because I'm sure your version of events will be dramatically different from everyone else's.'

Brady frowned as he dragged a hand through his hair, pulling it back from his face. He had no idea why she was so mad at him.

'I'm sorry, Amelia. Honestly, I am.'

'I hope it's worth it, Jack.'

Brady shook his head, confused.

'Being able to crack the case on your own before the others. Because from the way Gates is acting you may as well pack up your things and go home now. Just so you know, Adamson has a copy of the same surveillance footage.'

Brady visibly reacted – Amelia would have got the same response if she had slapped him.

'Adamson is heading this investigation. Don't you think he needs every bit of information and evidence he can get? I was curious about what it was that you wanted so badly. So I talked to the receptionist and she told me what she told you. It wasn't hard to find them on the surveillance tape once I knew who I was looking for.'

Brady didn't say anything. He couldn't. He was still trying to get his head around the fact that she had taken this information to Adamson.

'You compromised my loyalty and . . . and after what I saw on the tape I had no choice.'

Brady looked away, unable to look Amelia in the eye.

'What's really going on, Jack? Why wouldn't you want Adamson to see something as significant as that?'

'It was just a hunch . . . that was all. Remember, I still haven't seen the tape.'

'Bullshit!' retorted Amelia. 'What? Two men just so

144

happen to walk in to Rake Lane Hospital by chance and ask at reception about the condition of a copper who has been brutally attacked. Jack, no one could have known about this, don't you get that? When they turned up, the news still hadn't been released to the press. Only we knew about it. No one on the outside did, which means they were involved in her attack. Maybe they turned up because they thought they'd left her for dead. Now they'll be worried about whether she'll talk.'

Amelia suddenly realised what she'd said. But it was too late.

The look in Brady's eyes told her that her words had cut him.

She knew, as they all did, that Simone Henderson would never talk again.

'Look, if there had been any way of withholding the tape I would have done. But it's too crucial to the investigation,' explained Amelia.

'I understand that you had no other option,' answered Brady. 'And I'm sorry for putting you in such a position,' he added quietly.

Amelia looked up at him. Something about the wounded look in his eyes at the mention of Simone Henderson's condition had got to her.

She didn't know what it was about Jack Brady. He was the only person who could make her feel this way. He worried her. It was rare to see him look so vulnerable.

Something about him at this moment told Amelia that he was in trouble.

She watched as he dragged a nervous hand through his long, dark brown hair again. Pulling it back from his handsomely rugged, albeit beaten-up, face.

'I promise it won't happen again,' assured Brady as he made a move to leave.

Amelia placed a hand on his arm, stopping him.

She made sure no one else could hear before she spoke. 'I also got the security tape for the hospital grounds. There's something there that you need to see. I haven't handed the grounds CCTV footage to Adamson yet. And he hasn't asked for it. But he will. Once he's had a look at the surveillance tape of the two men talking to the receptionist he'll be on to it. You haven't got long before he requests it.'

'Thanks, Amelia . . .' Brady said falteringly.

Without another word he turned and left.

*

Brady ran along the first-floor corridor, ignoring the pain in his side. He turned the corner, and continued until he reached his office. He didn't have much time.

Whatever was on that security tape, Adamson now had access to it.

He reached his office door. It was unlocked.

Had Amelia got someone to unlock his door? Or had it already been unlocked? He couldn't shake the feeling of paranoia he'd had ever since he found the victim's head, along with the note, in the rear of his car.

Then he remembered that Conrad had said Claudia was waiting for him in his office.

He prepared himself before walking in. He wasn't in the right frame of mind for a face-to-face meeting with Claudia. The only thing on his mind was watching that DVD before Adamson.

He opened the door and breathed a sigh of relief when he saw that the room was empty.

On the table sat an envelope.

He picked it up and ripped open the seal.

It was a DVD accompanied with a note: *You know where I am if you need me. A.*

Brady crumpled the note up and threw it into his waste paper bin. There was nothing Amelia could do to help him. In fact, no one could help him right now.

He sat down behind his desk and opened up his Apple Mac laptop.

He shoved the DVD in and waited for it to load.

He could feel his heart starting to pound.

The DVD started playing. Fuzzy images from inside the reception area kicked into life. Patients, visitors and staff entered and left through the revolving doors by the reception area. He watched and waited.

Then he saw them.

Two well-dressed men made their way through the revolving hospital doors straight to reception.

He narrowed his eyes as he tried to get a clearer image of the two men. It was impossible. All he could make out was that they were tall, well built, with short, cropped dark hair and in their late twenties to early thirties. But what he could see was a glint of white gold on one of their hands: the third finger, right hand. Any identifiable trait at this point was crucial.

He thought immediately of Jed, the force's computer forensic expert. He'd have to call in a favour. He had no choice. Jed was the only person he knew who had the ability to digitally enhance the image of the two men's faces and the rings.

Brady watched as the men spoke to the receptionist before leaving through the revolving glass doors. He waited, wondering exactly what it was that Amelia had seen.

Nothing happened.

He saw himself come into the reception area. Talk with the receptionist and then leave, heading off towards the ICU. He fast-forwarded until he saw himself return. This time looking the worse for wear. Clothes dishevelled, face bleeding.

He watched as his figure walked out the main entrance.

Then a glitch appeared in the tape as it seemed to jump. Brady didn't understand why. Then he realised. It was the CCTV footage from the hospital grounds.

He waited, curious as to what it was that had caught Amelia's attention. Then he saw it. A black Mercedes dropping the two men he was after off at reception. The car idled for a second and then pulled away.

Brady tried to get a closer look at the driver's face, but it was obscured by an ambulance.

He fast-forwarded again, watching as the men entered the hospital and then reappeared. They then walked over to the car park. The black Mercedes with tinted windows was parked close to the main reception.

Brady continued to fast-forward the tape until he recognised Conrad's car pulling up outside the emergency entrance. He watched himself jump out, slam the door and walk inside. At the same time, he saw the driver of the Mercedes get out and casually lean against the car. There was no mistaking it: he was watching Brady. Then his attention turned to Conrad's Saab.

Brady's stomach knotted. He was being watched. That

was what Amelia had seen. Without needing to watch the rest of the CCTV footage, he knew what was coming next. He fast-forwarded once more, feeling sick.

Just as he thought. When Conrad had driven out the hospital grounds they were being followed. It wasn't obvious. They were two cars behind. But they were being tailed all the same.

He rewound, realising he had missed something: the driver. The driver who had been leaning against the car watching both him walking into the hospital and then Conrad parked up in the Saab.

He found what he wanted and then froze the DVD.

The driver of the Mercedes was tall, 6′3″ with cropped hair and a G-Star Raw military-style jacket.

There was no mistaking it. The driver was the same guy captured on surveillance camera in Madley's nightclub.

It was Nick.

Brady rewound the DVD until he could get a freeze-frame of the partial image of the Mercedes' licence plate. He could barely make out the letters 'LT' in the blue square on the left-hand side of the plate and the first two letters of the plate which were 'AV'. But that was it.

He quickly opened up a browser on his laptop and Googled 'LT' to find the nationality of the car and its occupants.

It took seconds before it uploaded. 'LT' stood for Lithuania: the car's country of origin.

He felt as if he had been side-punched. He had been hoping against the odds that Madley had been wrong about Nick.

But the evidence was damning.

Brady thought back to Johnny Slaughter, who had said

his brother was now working for the 'Lithuaks'. He couldn't shake the memory of Johnny's words:

'Nick stopped working for me a month back. Got involved with those Eastern European bastards who are coming over here and taking all our bloody money!'

Brady took out his BlackBerry.

He looked at his hands and realised they were shaking.

He needed a drink. There wasn't a time in his life when he needed one more than at this precise moment.

Hands still trembling, he reached down and opened the drawer of his desk.

He kept a bottle of single malt Scotch for emergencies. And in his books, this wasn't just an emergency; it was a fucking write-off.

How was he going to explain *this* to Gates?

He picked up his red and white Che Guevara mug. Still trembling, he poured himself a liberal measure. He cupped the mug in two hands, not trusting himself to hold it steady, and took a much needed, burning gulp. He then leaned back and sighed, staring darkly at the grey stabbing light squeezing through his dusty Venetian blinds.

He needed a minute to clear his head and figure out what he was going to do.

The only thing he was certain of was that he needed to keep some distance between himself and Gates until he knew exactly how he was going to play it.

First, he needed to call Jed.

He picked up his BlackBerry again. Hands slightly steadier: it seemed his emergency Scotch was already working.

He pressed call and waited.

'Yeah, Jed here,' came the reply.

'Hi Jed, it's Jack,' answered Brady.

'Hey, Jack. Good to hear from you. What's up?' Jed asked.

My back against the wall, that's what, thought Brady. But he kept it inside his head.

'Not much. Just the usual crap, you know?' he replied, trying to make his voice sound as relaxed as possible.

'Tell me about it, Jack. I'm wading knee-deep in shit here! But do they give me a bigger budget so I can employ more people? Do they hell. Resources have been slashed again and they now expect me to do the job of ten people in half the time,' complained Jed.

Brady breathed in.

In all the time he had known Jed, there was never a good time to ask him to do some work. Never mind asking him to do the impossible for nothing more than 'I owe you one'.

Brady's silence said it all to Jed.

'Alright, spit it out. What exactly do you need me to do?'

Brady massaged his forehead, trying to ease the pressure that had been building all day.

'How'd you guess?'

'Like, the silence. I know you too well!'

'Alright, here's the score. I've got a couple of blurred surveillance tape images that I need digitally enhancing so I can try and get an ID on a couple of suspects. Two men, dressed in suits at reception at roughly 8:10am. I need close-ups of their faces and a close-up of what I think is a white platinum ring that both are wearing on their right hands, third finger. Same suspects leave and wait in the car park. They have a black Mercedes with what I believe is a Lithuanian licence plate. I need you to digitally enhance the licence plate to be certain I'm right. I also need a close-up of the driver who gets out the car at one point.'

'Is it connected to what happened to that young DC?'

'Could be,' Brady said simply.

'Alright. Email it to me and I'll see what I can do.' He paused then asked suddenly, 'Is this the same footage at the hospital that Adamson sent over?'

'Adamson's already sent it?' questioned Brady feeling sick.

He'd clearly underestimated Adamson.

'Yeah, he sent me this material over ten minutes ago.'

'You haven't given him anything yet, have you?' Brady asked

'No . . . haven't worked on it yet.'

'Stall him for me, will you? I just need some time.'

'If it wasn't you, Jack, you know what the answer would be . . .'

'I know, Jed. But if this wasn't so important I wouldn't be asking you.'

'Alright. But I can't hold Adamson off for long. You know that.'

'I know. Thanks, mate.'

Brady listened to the dull tone of silence.

He breathed out. It had been harder than he had imagined asking Jed to cross the line.

Brady had to be certain that Nick was the driver.

Until he had indisputable evidence in front of his eyes, he was still clinging onto a sliver of hope that it was all some horrendous coincidence.

Chapter Twenty-Two

He opened the file left by Harvey on his desk.

It was already 3:47pm. The briefing was now supposed to be going ahead at 4:00pm. But due to recent circumstances it had been postponed. Again, mused Brady with frustration. But this had to be done. Given the fact that the Ryecrofts had suddenly turned up at the station wanting answers, he had to familiarise himself with the report on the missing girl.

Despite a desperate search, the serial numbers for their daughter's breast implants couldn't be found. Neither could the paperwork and receipts for the operation. The Ryecrofts weren't sure whether their daughter had taken them with her or placed them for safe-keeping somewhere. Or even if they had been thrown out by accident. All they knew was that the police wanted the serial implant numbers for a reason. And that a murder victim had washed up on the shores of Whitley Bay. Consequently, Brady couldn't blame the Ryecrofts for refusing to sit around waiting at home for further news about their missing daughter. Brady reckoned he would have done the same if he had been in their situation.

He looked at the photograph of Melissa Ryecroft.

He picked it up, studying it.

He stared at her face, searching for a similarity.

Long brown hair, large, dark brown eyes.

The problem was, he couldn't tell.

The damage to the murder victim's severed head had completely disfigured the face. The extent of the knife wounds and . . .

Brady stopped.

It was unthinkable what they had done to her.

It was something that Brady had never before witnessed in all his years as a copper.

He looked back down at the photograph.

There was no denying it. Melissa Ryecroft had the same body type as the murder victim.

Brady thought of her father sitting waiting for him downstairs.

How could he tell him that the murder victim had had all her teeth removed? As a consequence, this ruled out the option of using Melissa Ryecroft's dental records as a form of ID, which given the circumstances would have been preferable.

Instead he would need Melissa Ryecroft's parents to ID what was left of the body.

He picked up the notes in the file that accompanied the photograph. He needed to make sure he knew everything there was to know about the missing girl before interviewing her parents.

*

Brady made his way to the interview room.

He knocked on the interview door before walking in.

154

Kodovesky gave him a surprised look, reminding Brady that his face was a mess.

'Go on, take a coffee break. Conrad will be here in a minute,' suggested Brady.

The young DC looked like she needed some fresh air. He couldn't blame her. The air in the small room was stale and claustrophobic.

Brady stretched his hand out towards Brian Ryecroft first, then Michelle Ryecroft and finally, their eleven-year-old daughter, Lucy.

'DI Jack Brady,' he introduced, aware that the cuts and bruises on his face weren't exactly the best look for a Detective Inspector.

Brian Ryecroft nodded at him. He was too lost in grief and anguish to pay much attention to Brady's run-in with a brick wall.

Brady realised that Melissa Ryecroft was very much her father's daughter. They had the same handsome, perfectly shaped face. Strong, but with precise symmetry. They were both dark: dark hair, eyes and skin with a slight tanned hue to it. They had a look about them which spoke of Italian ancestry.

Ryecroft's jowly jaw was locked and his full lips were downturned. His receding black hair was peppered with silver strands. More silver than black, thought Brady. What would have been a neat, orderly haircut was now all over the place from where he had obviously dragged a nervous hand repeatedly through it. His brown, heavily bagged eyes were filled with pained acceptance. A pragmatic, cold reality had kicked in. His daughter had been gone since Thursday morning; it was now Saturday afternoon after 4:13pm.

The time jarred with Brady. He was running over. Things

were starting to get away from him. If he wasn't careful he would lose the plot.

It was clear to Brady that this was a man in his mid to late fifties who loved his daughters. Spoiled them, as much as he spoiled his forty-something wife.

Ryecroft had his own business in construction. A self-made man who had made good. Brady imagined the women in his life played him like a fiddle. Not one of them would be wanting for anything. Which explained why his missing sixteen-year-old daughter attended a private school in Tynemouth, sporting her fake breasts amongst other material possessions.

'I . . . I . . .' Ryecroft broke down. Tears streamed down his jowly, lined face as he dropped his head, unable to look at Brady.

A knock at the door broke the awkward moment.

Conrad walked in.

'Sir,' he greeted when he saw Brady sitting across the table from the Ryecrofts.

Tactfully pretending not to pick up on Ryecroft's breakdown, Conrad placed a steaming black coffee in front of him.

'Two sugars, sir,' Conrad said.

He turned to Michelle Ryecroft, whose red-rimmed blue eyes watched Conrad for a sign. Any sign of hope from the outside world, instead of the hell that she was living in the interview room.

'White tea, two sweeteners,' Conrad said. His steel-grey eyes were filled with sympathy, his voice filled with professionalism. Finally, he placed the chilled can of Coke Zero down in front of Lucy Ryecroft. He shot her a warm, gentle smile before pulling a chair out and sitting down beside his boss.

156

Lucy Ryecroft uttered a weak, 'Thanks.'

Her eyes weren't only the same colour blue as her mother. They were also just as red-rimmed and puffy from crying. Her pubescent skin was patchy with red blotches and trails of black smudged mascara. Her blonde highlighted hair had been scraped back into an aggressive, angry ponytail.

It looked to Brady's eye as if she was trying her hardest to get back to being a kid again. No GHD straighteners had been used that morning. Nor had foundation with eyeliner and lipgloss. Instead, she was wearing a baggy Hollister t-shirt, her scrawny arms covered in bruises and nail indentations where she had gripped them so hard that she'd broken the skin.

The painful, troubled adult world was now too dangerous and dark for her to want to cross over into. After all, her older sister who had tried to grow up too fast, too hard, had disappeared.

And the one unspoken question, the elephant in the room, was whether the headless girl washed up on the beach was Melissa Ryecroft.

Brady swallowed hard.

He had some painful questions to ask.

First, one had to be directed at the person who held herself responsible for Melissa's disappearance: her younger sister.

'Lucy?' Brady gently began.

She dragged her red, bloodshot eyes up to Brady's. They shone with a mixture of fear and self-loathing.

'I've got to say that from what I've read of your state-ment, you've really been a great help. But . . .' Brady paused, gauging her reaction.

The girl looked like a rabbit caught in headlights.

'You say that Melissa got on a train to London, early Thursday evening. Yes?'

Lucy nodded.

It didn't go unmissed by Brady that she had bitten her bottom lip hard, causing blood to trickle out.

'Here,' Brady offered as he handed her a tissue from the box beside him.

She didn't understand.

'Your lip,' Brady gently said.

'Oh . . . thanks,' she mumbled as she tasted the blood.

'What I don't understand is, if she had left on the 5:30pm train to King's Cross, why update her Facebook page shortly beforehand, saying the exact opposite?'

Lucy looked at Brady, startled.

She obviously hadn't realised that the first thing Brady got Harvey to do when the Ryecrofts had reported her as missing was check out her Facebook page. And to see whether she blogged or used Twitter.

'Did she get on the train or was she met by someone?'

Tears started to flow down the young girl's face.

She looked nervously from her mother and then to her father's anguished face.

'She made me promise not to tell,' whispered Lucy.

It was barely loud enough for Brady to hear.

He noticed the Ryecrofts tense at their daughter's admission.

'Oh my God . . . Lucy? What? What didn't you tell us?' questioned Michelle Ryecroft, her voice shaking.

Brian Ryecroft's eyes flashed with a sudden anger.

Brady looked at them, wishing they weren't in on the interview. But Lucy Ryecroft was a minor; he had no choice. He could have a social worker here with her, but her parents had refused. Wanting to be present. Not wanting to let another child disappear from their sight.

'She . . . she was flying down to London.'

Brady nodded.

He already suspected that was the case. He had just had a look at her Facebook page.

Melissa had updated her wall from her mobile stating that she was flying first class, all expenses paid, accompanied by her agent for a meeting at Models 1 agency.

Powerful stuff, thought Brady. Especially for a sixteen-year-old kid.

'They said first class,' Lucy whispered. 'That they were paying. All she had to do was turn up with her passport and an overnight bag . . .'

'Was she just supposed to be staying the night?' Brady asked.

Lucy nodded, head down. Eyes fixed on her small, delicate hands.

'So, when was she supposed to return?'

'About 5ish yesterday. To make it look as if she had been at school all day . . .'

Brady frowned.

'She told Mum and Dad that she was staying over at Libby's house to revise. She said they'd be up late studying so it was better that she stayed the night and that they'd then go to school together the next day.'

Brady looked at Brian and Michelle Ryecroft. Their expressions told Brady that this was exactly what had happened; their eldest daughter had played them.

'Why did she tell you all this, Lucy?' questioned Brady.

It seemed odd that Melissa would go to so much trouble hiding this from her parents to then tell her younger sister.

159

It didn't add up.

'She'd gone to get a shower last weekend. It was Sunday night I think and I . . . I had gone into her bedroom and . . . checked out what she was up to on her computer. The page was still up and it was on her Facebook page. Some guy had written on her wall that she was stunning. Real model material. He asked her to email him her contact details and he'd start talking to people in London to arrange a meeting and a photo shoot. All at his expense. He suggested that if she was up for it, he could get her in front of them on Friday. Yesterday . . .'

'Do you remember his name?'

Lucy shook her head.

'No . . . before I could read any more Melissa had suddenly come back in. She'd forgotten something.'

Brady tried not to show his disappointment. A name would have been good. But then again he mused, whoever this bastard was, he definitely wouldn't be using his real name.

Harvey and Kodovesky had gone through her Facebook account and no such message was on her wall. Brady presumed she must have taken it down. Worried perhaps, that one of her friends might mention it to their parents, out of teenage jealousy and spite. Brady imagined that a good-looking girl like Melissa would have her fair share of envious admirers.

'What made you decide to sneak in to her bedroom?' asked Brady.

A look briefly crossed Lucy's face which spoke of a history of sibling rivalry. She then shrugged.

'You know? Like, there was something different about her . . .'

'Go on,' prompted Brady gently.

'She was . . . more arrogant than usual,' Lucy said as she shot her father a nervous glance.

Brady noticed Michelle Ryecroft squeezing Lucy's arm in support.

Brian Ryecroft on the other hand looked agitated. But he kept his mouth firmly shut. Even though it was clear that he didn't agree with his younger daughter's perception of her older sister.

'She also kept saying things like, she wouldn't be finishing sixth form because she was going to move to London soon. That she was going to be a model. That . . . that there were people, important people who believed in her. Said that she had something special. That they could make her famous, like. You know? A supermodel like Gisele Bundchen or Kate Moss or something? Stupid stuff like that. That . . . that she might then move to Europe . . .'

'Did she have a boyfriend?' Brady asked, realising that a girl Melissa's age wouldn't be making such grand plans on her own.

'No,' answered Brian Ryecroft quickly.

Too quickly for Brady.

Ryecroft looked across at his wife for backup.

She shook her head but Brady couldn't help noticing the tears welling up in her eyes again.

He thought back to Wolfe's autopsy findings. The victim had had an abortion as recently as a month ago. An abortion that hadn't gone as planned.

'But surely she must have had one. Beautiful girl like Melissa, I imagine she must have had lots of boys chasing her.'

'What about Marijuis?' Lucy asked innocently, as she turned to her mother.

Michelle Ryecroft's face clearly told her daughter to keep quiet.

'Who's Marijuis?' asked Brady, throwing a sideways glance at Conrad, who looked as surprised and as intrigued as Brady.

The statement that Brady and Conrad had both independently read had stated quite clearly that Melissa Ryecroft did not have a boyfriend. Boyfriends were always the first in line for questioning in a murder investigation. As were the parents. But only a fool would think that either her mother or, more likely according to the statistics, her father, were involved in their daughter's disappearance. And horrific murder. If it was indeed her body that had washed up on Whitley Bay beach.

Both parents were clearly beside themselves with grief and anguish at what might have happened to their daughter. And at this point, Brady could honestly say that Brian Ryecroft didn't seem capable of harming his daughter, let alone carrying out the heinous crimes committed on the decapitated murder victim lying in the hospital morgue.

'We don't know, alright?' snapped Brian Ryecroft suddenly, taking Brady by surprise.

Brady looked at him.

'I'm sorry, all I'm trying to do is establish some facts that could help us find your daughter,' apologised Brady.

It was clear that Melissa *had* had a boyfriend. Ryecroft's reaction was too telling. And the anger in his voice told Brady that this boyfriend had hurt his little girl.

'That's if you haven't already found her,' replied Brian Ryecroft as his eyes started to water.

'Well . . . the reason for this line of questioning is to

establish whether the girl we have at Rake Lane Hospital is in fact Melissa. Rather than take you straight there for identification purposes.'

Brian Ryecroft bent his head forward, resting it in his large, trembling hands.

'I know . . . I'm sorry . . . I . . . just want my baby back . . . I just want Melissa . . .' he choked.

'Dad?' questioned Lucy, scared.

Brady had no choice but to continue. It wouldn't matter if he stopped the interview. Questions would still have to be answered. Whether it was now or later.

'Who was Marijuis?' he asked, ignoring Brian Ryecroft's breakdown.

'He . . . he was Melissa's boyfriend,' whispered Lucy as she nervously looked at her father. 'Mum and Dad didn't know until . . . until it was too late . . .'

'Do you have any contact details for him?' asked Brady, looking directly at Lucy's mother.

Michelle Ryecroft shook her head as her pale, long-fingered hand fluttered nervously around her throat.

'We believe Melissa met him in Budapest when she went on holiday for her sixteenth birthday with a group of girls last November.'

'What, for the breast augmentation operation?' asked Brady.

'No . . . that . . . that came after. She came home with this crazy idea that she wanted larger breasts. And she had checked everything out. The clinic in Budapest, the cost . . . everything.'

'Who gave her the idea?' asked Brady.

Michelle Ryecroft looked over at her husband. His head still hung down in defeat, but his large hands were now resting on the edge of the desk clenched so hard his knuckles were white.

'It . . . it was that Marijuis . . . the man she met on holiday.'

'Man?' questioned Brady as Brian Ryecroft's knuckles clenched even tighter.

'When Melissa eventually told us he was twenty-eight that's when we . . . we tried to stop her contacting him.'

'Bastard!' cursed Ryecroft.

'Brian!' hissed his wife.

'Well . . . what other word would you use to describe him? Apart from paedo!'

Michelle Ryecroft didn't answer him. Nor did she disagree.

'How were they communicating?' asked Brady.

'Texting . . . or phone calls,' answered Michelle Ryecroft.

'On her BlackBerry?' asked Brady, realising he would have to get Harvey to chase up her call details dating back from last November.

Michelle Ryecroft nodded.

'So why let her go back for the breast augmentation surgery?'

Michelle Ryecroft thought about it.

'Because she talked about nothing else. She wanted it as a Christmas present. Had this idea that she wanted to be a model. And to be one, she needed to have larger breasts . . . you know what it's like . . .' she explained apologetically.

Brian Ryecroft shook his head.

'We . . . we made her promise that if we paid for the operation she would never see Marijuis again. And . . . and she agreed.'

Lucy shifted uncomfortably in her seat.

'Oh Lucy . . . no . . . Tell me you didn't know that Melissa was still seeing him?'

Lucy nodded, too scared to speak.

Brian Ryecroft's head suddenly lifted, spinning round to face his eleven-year-old daughter. The look on his face was pure rage.

'Lucy?' gently questioned Brady as he leaned forward.

'I . . . used to look at her BlackBerry, like. When she'd leave it lying around. I'd . . . I'd just play around on it . . .'

'Look at her messages maybe?' asked Brady.

'Something like that. There were all these messages there . . . 'cos that's all she ever did was text. And they were mainly from someone named "Mandy". It was obvious it was him, you know? And his English was lousy which is how I knew.'

'You sure it wasn't just text speak?'

She nervously looked at him and shook her head.

'I think I know bad English like, from text speak.'

She then dropped her eyes and began fidgeting with the ringpull on the Coke can.

'Go on,' Brady encouraged.

She took another tentative sip of Coke as she thought about it.

She then nodded, putting down the drink before apprehensively looking at Brady.

'She told me that she was going with him to London. That he was the one who had contacted the model scout because he believed in her. He arranged it all. Gave the scout her details and . . . you know the rest.'

'Do you know have any idea who it was who put this message on Melissa's Facebook page about the model agency, Lucy?'

Lucy numbly shook her head.

'No . . . I have no idea . . .'

Brady watched her as she looked away, tears filling her eyes.

'What did she promise you to make you keep all this a secret?'

Lucy looked back at Brady, weighing up whether she should say.

'She said that I could have her Superdry jacket and . . . and her BlackBerry.'

'You've got her phone?' asked Brady.

'No, I got the jacket before she left and she promised me her phone when she got back on Friday afternoon . . . She . . . she said that Marijuis was buying her an iPhone 4S for agreeing to go to the meeting in London,' replied Lucy, biting her lip again.

The realisation that her sister hadn't returned was hitting her hard.

'Lucy? Why didn't you say? Why didn't you tell us any of this?' questioned Michelle Ryecroft, her face ashen.

'I . . . I . . . promised Melissa . . .' mumbled Lucy. 'I . . . I just thought she'd got delayed coming back from London . . . The last thing I was going to do was have her think I was a snitch . . .'

'Was the name of the clinic in Budapest Virenyos by any chance?' Brady turned to Michelle Ryecroft.

He didn't need her to answer; the reaction on her face was enough.

'How? How did you know . . .' she asked before her face crumpled with realisation.

Brady decided not to ask whether her daughter had had an abortion. They had already gone through enough. If

Melissa had, he was certain that she would never have told her parents. The internal scarring on her body was telling enough in itself.

*

'Sir?' Brady said, stopping Brian Ryecroft before he left the interview room.

He turned and nodded at Conrad to close the door behind him.

Brady had chosen to wait until his wife and daughter had left before having a word with Ryecroft.

Brian Ryecroft eyed Brady suspiciously.

Brady swallowed. His throat was dry. The words were difficult to speak.

'I've arranged for a family liaison officer to take you to Rake Lane Hospital, sir,' began Brady, unable to bring himself to say the word 'morgue'.

Ryecroft shook his head.

'There's no need. I have my car outside. I'd rather drive.'

'I recommend that your wife drives your daughter home and you and the liaison officer go ahead without them,' Brady suggested.

'Why?' asked Ryecroft. 'What haven't you told us?' he demanded as he searched Brady's face.

'The body we have. . . . the woman we need you to ID . . . is . . .'

'Go on.'

'She's in a really bad way, sir. I just don't think it would be wise for your wife to be there.'

'How bad?'

'Her head has been removed . . .' Brady began.

He knew that this small detail had been withheld from the press. Too gruesome to be released for public consumption, Gates had decided.

'Sir?'

Ryecroft looked at Brady, his eyes filled with emotion as he tried to fight back the tears.

His face was ashen as he tried to make sense of what Brady had just told him.

'Do you think . . . do you think it's my daughter? Honestly? Do you really think it's her?' asked Ryecroft.

Brady looked away. He couldn't stare at the agony that was etched across Ryecroft's face.

Suddenly Ryecroft grabbed hold of Brady, forcefully pinning him against the wall.

'For fuck's sake! Tell me!' he spat.

Brady had no choice but to look him in the eyes.

He reluctantly nodded.

'I wish I could say I wasn't sure. But . . . there are a lot of similarities between your missing daughter and the body.'

'What the hell do you mean, similarities? You've got a photograph of her surely? You must be able to tell?'

'That's the problem, sir, the damage to her face is so extensive that it's difficult to say. But the hair and body type match, as do the brown eyes . . . and . . .' Brady looked Ryecroft in the eye.

He had already had word back from Wolfe before the interview that the head matched the body. No question.

'But . . . the autopsy shows that the victim had had an abortion about a month ago . . .'

Brady watched as the realisation hit Ryecroft.

In that moment Brady knew that Ryecroft was certain it was his daughter lying in the morgue.

Ryecroft stared at Brady as he absorbed this final, damning fact. He shook his head. 'Whatever you do don't tell my wife. She didn't know that . . . that Melissa was pregnant. She needed money to go private. So she came to me and asked. I wouldn't give her the money until she told me why. But she promised me it had nothing to do with that bastard Marijuis. . . . she promised me. . . . she promised . . . All she wanted was to be a model . . . that's all she wanted . . .' he mumbled.

'Did you personally take her to a private clinic?' asked Brady.

Ryecroft looked at Brady, surprised by the question.

'No . . . I . . . she said she would take care of it if I gave her the money. That she was too embarrassed as it was . . . She told her mother she was staying at her friend's for the weekend a month back and I presumed that's when . . .' he shook his head. 'I asked when she came back on the Monday and she just said she didn't want to talk about it.'

Brady wasn't sure what Melissa had spent her father's money on, but it definitely wasn't a private clinic.

'So, you didn't know where she went for the abortion?'

Ryecroft shook his head, ashamed at his answer.

Brady caught Ryecroft as his body suddenly collapsed forward sobbing with anguish at what he had just been told. Until then he had been holding out that it was just coincidence. That she'd turn up unharmed and life would automatically go back to normal.

Brady held him and waited for the man to compose himself.

Conrad opened the door and looked at Brady.

Brady shook his head, signalling to Conrad to give them a few more minutes.

Conrad understood and discreetly closed the door.

Brady continued to hold Ryecroft as his bulky frame convulsed with agonising sobs.

Brady had had a gut feeling that Ryecroft hadn't been as forthcoming as he could have been during the interview. There were a few moments when Ryecroft had over-reacted, or had got angry. Too angry. And he had seemed too adamant that his daughter didn't have a boyfriend. And that she had never had one.

Even a fool wouldn't believe that of a girl who holidays abroad for her sixteenth birthday with her girlfriends independently of her parents. Throw into the mix the breast augmentation job. This girl was clearly way ahead of her sixteen years.

Brady could imagine that Ryecroft and his eldest daughter were close enough for her to have managed to borrow money from him to get an abortion done privately. She wouldn't have gone to her mother; that much was clear. She was a daddy's girl. And she knew how to work it. And Ryecroft obviously adored her. He was no different from most parents today. When it came to their children, it was easier to pay their way out of trouble. And the trouble here was this Eastern European man named Marijuis.

And whether that was his real name was debatable.

Ryecroft suddenly straightened up. 'I'm sorry . . .' he mumbled, embarrassed.

He went over to the table and picked up a fistful of tissues from the box that had been put there intentionally.

'It's perfectly understandable, sir,' replied Brady quietly as Ryecroft roughly dried his face.

Brian Ryecroft had to go out looking strong. He needed to have his head together. For the sake of his wife and his youngest daughter. They were all he had now. And he would be damned if he'd let anything happen to them. What had happened to Melissa was his fault. He knew that. And he would live with that knowledge until the day he died.

He was relieved that they hadn't witnessed his breakdown. He breathed in deeply as he composed himself, making a promise to himself that it wouldn't happen again. No matter what.

'Thank you, DI Brady. I would like to be taken to Rake Lane now if you don't mind. Get this over with,' Ryecroft stated.

Brady nodded.

'Of course, sir. Our family liaison officer is already waiting for you.'

Brady knew it wasn't worth asking Ryecroft why he'd withheld information. He was suffering enough as it was without Brady adding to it.

And anyway, the worst was yet to come, thought Brady.

Brady hadn't told him the cause of death.

He was still waiting on Wolfe's call to confirm his suspicion. And until then, he couldn't release that information.

Not even to Brian Ryecroft.

No matter how much Brady wanted to prepare him for the horror of what some maniac had done to his daughter, he couldn't.

Chapter Twenty-Three

'Conrad, get Harvey and Kodovesky to check out flights on Thursday from Newcastle to either Heathrow or Stansted,' ordered Brady as he and Conrad walked along the corridor. 'I need to know whether Melissa Ryecroft was booked on a flight and if so, who was booked next to her. And crucially, who made the booking.'

'Yes, sir. What about CCTV footage of the airport and the grounds?'

Brady nodded.

Conrad seemed to be thinking what he was thinking. That she hadn't got on any plane to London. That much was clear. Brady's gut feeling was telling him that someone picked her up from the airport. And he was certain that this twenty-eight-year-old Eastern European – or perhaps Romanian – boyfriend going by the name of 'Marijuis' was involved in Melissa Ryecroft's disappearance. Brady wouldn't have been surprised if he had been behind the Facebook message offering her the false promise of a meeting with a top London model agency.

But they had to check out all possibilities.

'And make sure we get a copy of all numbers logged to and from her phone ASAP, will you?' ordered Brady.

'Yes, sir,' replied Conrad.

'We should have had those by now,' muttered Brady distractedly. 'And tell Daniels and Kenny not to bother continuing going through the CCTV footage last night down on the Promenade.'

Conrad shot him a questioning look.

'They're going to have their hands full going through the footage at the airport,' said Brady.

His mind was preoccupied with the surveillance footage that Jed was currently digitally enhancing for him. He was struggling to focus on the work at hand. All he could keep thinking about was Nick and who and what he was involved in. He didn't need any CCTV footage of the anonymous 999 caller to know that it had been Nick. He had more damning evidence.

'Conrad, can you make sure we've got everything together for the briefing? Chase up Ainsworth if you have to for the crime scene photographs of the head.'

Conrad's steel-grey eyes narrowed at the prospect of asking Ainsworth for anything, let alone telling him his job.

Brady reached his office door. He paused before entering.

'And, Conrad, tell him I need images of the note and any forensic information they have,' instructed Brady.

'Sir?' questioned Conrad, puzzled.

Brady still hadn't told anyone about the note. There was only himself and Ainsworth's team who knew about it. He still hadn't quite figured what it meant and why it had been left for him.

The obvious came to mind. But until he had more evidence he didn't want to accept who could be behind the murder of the girl, and who had left him the note along with the victim's head.

For all Brady knew, they could be two separate crimes. But he seriously doubted it.

He looked at Conrad. He was waiting for Brady to explain himself.

Brady shook his head.

'Let me fill you in at the briefing, Conrad. There's a couple of things I need to check out first,' Brady said feeling guilty that he was holding something as crucial as this back. 'Trust me here. I just need a bit more time,' added Brady.

'Yes, sir,' answered Conrad, knowing better than to ask his boss what exactly was going on.

'And ask Ainsworth when he's releasing my car, will you?' Conrad nodded.

'Thanks,' replied Brady.

He turned and walked into his office, closing the door behind him.

He breathed in deeply, relieved to be alone.

Jed had tried calling him while he'd been in the interview room with the Ryecrofts. He had left a message telling Brady he'd emailed the information he'd asked for.

Brady steeled himself as he went to his desk and sat down. He opened his laptop.

There it was: an email with attachments from Jed.

Hands shaking, Brady opened up the attachment and downloaded the freeze-framed digitally enhanced photographs.

He breathed out a sigh of relief. The photograph of the driver was still grainy and poor quality. The features were blurred. It would be difficult for Adamson's team to put the image out to the public and hope for anyone to identify the driver.

But Brady knew it was definitely Nick. There was no

mistaking it. He would recognise his face anywhere. Just as he had recognised his face on the security tape Madley had given him of Nick walking out of the gents' in the Blue Lagoon.

The question was, who was he working for and why?

Brady knew two things: Nick would never cross someone close to him. That included Madley. Like Brady, Nick had never forgotten his allegiance to Madley. Growing up in the war-torn Ridges did that to you. Madley was his friend, as much as he was Brady's. Admittedly, Nick's contact with Madley was infrequent given the fact he had left the North East, but he still made a point of seeing him whenever he returned. And, just as Trina McGuire had said, Nick had morals. He was a man of principle. A man who Brady was certain would never touch something as heinous as sex trafficking.

Brady breathed deeply, trying his damnedest to keep himself together as he moved onto the next set of images.

They were freeze-framed close-ups of the two men who had gone to Rake Lane's reception desk asking about Simone Henderson.

They were good-looking men, albeit dark and dangerous. From what Brady could make out, they looked like brothers, in their late twenties to early thirties. They both shared the same dark eyes and straight nose, and their chiselled cheekbones were identical. Both had coarse black stubble that blended in with the brutally short number one haircuts they sported. There was definitely no doubt in Brady's mind that they were the men he had seen on the CCTV footage wearing the rings.

Brady jumped onto the next photograph.

He sighed heavily.

He was right. Jed had digitally enhanced the partial CCTV image of the licence plate. There was no mistaking the car's country of origin was Lithuania.

He moved onto the next image.

An enlarged photograph of the platinum signet ring with the letter 'N' as an emblem.

It was similar to the 'N' branded on Simone.

And identical to the 'N' signed on the note he had received earlier.

The note left with the head in his car.

Signed was the wrong word, mused Brady: it had been embossed onto the paper.

In blood.

Brady jumped from photograph still to photograph still. One thing he was aware of was their ethnicity. Their dark looks and olive skin suggested an Eastern European background. Not only that, thought Brady, they both looked ex-military. The expensive black pinstriped Yves Saint Laurent suits couldn't disguise the fact that there was a menacing air about them. No amount of money could disguise that.

'Who the hell are you involved with?' Brady said aloud. 'And why are you involving me?'

He moved onto the photograph of the black Mercedes driver.

There was no doubting it.

The same man in Madley's nightclub was also the driver of the black Merc.

'Nick?' questioned Brady as he looked at the blurred, grainy image of his brother's taut, expressionless face.

But there was a determination about him. A coldness that Brady didn't recognise.

No one on the force knew Brady had a brother. It was something he had kept quiet. He hadn't even discussed Nick with Claudia. She knew he existed. But that was as far as it went. She had never met him. Nor had she ever seen a photograph of him.

As far as Claudia was concerned, Brady had lost touch with his brother when they had been placed in separate foster homes as young children.

Brady had made a point of never talking about his past. Claudia had accepted this without any questions. She knew that his mother had died a brutal death. And that his father had served time in Durham Gaol for the murder.

Reading the court records had been enough for Claudia. She knew not to ask any more. Nick's name had come up, but Claudia had resisted questioning Brady.

There were no photographs of Nick. None had been taken of him or Brady as children. And if they had, they had been permanently lost when they had been shunted from one foster home to another. And as an adult, Nick had refused to have his photograph taken. As far as Brady could tell, Nick lived off the grid. Nothing tied him to the state. No bank accounts, no mortgage, no council tax, no electoral vote.

Nothing.

If Nick had a passport and driving licence, Brady was certain they would be fake; he knew that the right kind of money could buy you anything. Including a new identity.

Brady stared at the close-up of Nick. No one would recognise him as Brady's brother – apart from Madley. And no amount of data cross-referencing would bring him up. He just didn't exist in the police database. Hadn't ever been caught. He was too clever for that, thought Brady.

And he had never got involved with serious organised crime.

Until now.

Brady was desperately clinging onto the fact that someone had a hold over Nick. That they had him by the balls and he had no choice. Brady studied Nick's watchful, intelligent eyes as they looked over in the direction of the hospital emergency doors.

He was waiting for me, noted Brady.

Why?

To follow me and leave a severed head and note in my car.

It was a cold, unwanted answer. But it was a fact that Brady couldn't dispute.

Brady's guts had told him it was a warning.

The question was, did it come from his brother?

The words on the note came to mind.

Cut from newsprint and glued on. Apart from the signed 'N' which had been imprinted in blood. And if Brady was right, it was from the platinum signet ring on the Eastern European's right hand.

He took out his BlackBerry phone and looked at the photograph he'd taken of the note.

A loud rap at the door made him jump.

'Yeah?' shouted Brady, abruptly closing his laptop.

Conrad walked in.

'The family liaison officer has taken Mr Ryecroft to the morgue to ID the body, sir' he said. 'We should know for definite in the next half an hour whether it's Melissa Ryecroft.'

'Good,' replied Brady, relieved it bought him time. 'Anything else?'

178

'Ainsworth said your car will be ready when it's ready.'

Brady sighed heavily.

'His words, not mine, sir,' explained Conrad apologetically.

Brady nodded. He'd expected such a response from Ainsworth. Especially if Conrad was doing the asking. Brady didn't know what it was about Conrad that riled Ainsworth so much, but the cantankerous old bugger treated Conrad the way he treated uniform. And to say he treated uniform like a bunch of incapable idiots was putting it mildly.

'I've just seen the pictures of the head, sir, and . . . the note . . .'

Brady looked at Conrad, waiting for him to say something.

He didn't.

'If that's all . . .' Brady said.

Conrad didn't move.

Brady realised that he looked uneasy. His face was a little too strained, his jaw too tight; even for Conrad.

'What does it mean, sir?' asked Conrad worriedly.

'I wish I knew . . .' muttered Brady.

He nervously dragged his hand through his hair, desperate not to have this conversation.

Conrad looked at his boss. He looked a mess. And it wasn't just that he'd been beaten up by Frank Henderson. There was something else wrong. Conrad could see it in his eyes.

'Sir?' tentatively began Conrad, not knowing how to say what he was thinking. 'Do you think it was a threat?'

It hadn't even occurred to Brady. Instead, he'd thought Nick was sending him a warning. But for his own good.

Now Brady considered Conrad's question.

Could Nick be working for someone who wanted to hurt Brady? But why would his own brother be doing this to him? Brady didn't have the answer and that worried him.

And if Brady was to go by the look on Conrad's face, then he should be worried.

Brady could picture the smudged black words as if the note was right in front of him:

KEEP YOUR HEAD JACK OR YOU COULD BE NEXT – 'N'

'Who's "N", sir?' asked Conrad.

Brady sat silent. He couldn't answer Conrad's question. He wasn't even sure if he had the right answer anyway. Brady shrugged as he looked up at his deputy.

'Your guess is as good as mine, Conrad,' answered Brady.

Chapter Twenty-Four

Brady picked up his jacket from the back of his chair just as his phone started to vibrate.

He grabbed the phone, recognising the number immediately.

He knew he had no choice but to take it. He looked at Conrad's concerned face.

'One minute, yeah?' Brady said. 'I'll be straight up after this call.'

He waited until Conrad had left.

'Yeah?' he quickly answered.

'Figured out who's playing games with you then?'

'Fuck you!' answered Brady.

He didn't have time for Matthews' games.

'Sounds like you haven't,' stated Matthews sourly.

'Don't you have better things to do with your time than hassle me?' demanded Brady.

'What do you think? Banged up in here with the worst shits possible. Constantly watching my back so I don't end up in a fucking morgue . . .'

'Look, Jimmy, I haven't got time for this,' Brady pointed out.

'What happened to you visiting me? Didn't I say I had something that might interest you?'

'You know the score better than anyone! I can't come and see you because everyone here thinks you're some bent ex-copper on the take. Now if I visit you, what does that make me look like?' answered Brady. 'Add in the fact that I have my hands full here with a murder investigation.'

He was started to lose his patience with Matthews. He had bigger problems to contend with than whatever it was Matthews thought he had over Brady.

'Your worst nightmare is just beginning, Jack. And being seen talking to me is nothing compared to what's going to happen if you don't get your arse over here and find out what I have to tell you.'

'Why can't you just say it now? Save me a hell of a lot of trouble. Especially considering I'm heading a murder investigation here. I haven't got time to shit let alone take a couple of hours out to visit you.'

'If you don't make the time that'll be the least of your worries,' warned Matthews.

'Says who?'

'How about your old man who you and that shit Madley set up?'

'I don't know what the fuck you're talking about,' answered Brady.

He clenched his right fist tight as he waited for Matthews' response.

'Fuck you do. And so does Ronnie Macmillan,' answered Matthews.

'What do you mean?' questioned Brady as his heart started to beat faster.

'Let's say I saw him and his boys here making a special visit to see your "Da". Remember him, Jack? Or did you think he'd been got rid of like that fucking tramp that Madley had torched to death?'

Brady was speechless.

His heart wasn't racing now. It had stopped.

'I . . . I don't know what you're talking about,' answered Brady.

'Fuck you do! Anyway, get your arse in here first thing tomorrow and don't forget my fucking baccy!'

With that Matthews hung up.

Brady stood still. He couldn't move.

Madley, he thought. He needed to talk to Madley.

Brady pressed Madley's number.

'Yeah, Martin . . . it's me. We've got a problem . . .' Brady began.

*

Brady had no idea why Ronnie Macmillan would want to talk to his old man. But it was clear there was trouble coming his way. Or should he say, even more trouble.

Ronnie Macmillan was trouble of the nastiest sort. The kind of trouble that Brady could do without.

Brady wearily sighed.

He knew he should go and visit Matthews but he didn't have the time. The day was running away from him and he still hadn't held the briefing.

Brady put his jacket on and left his office, locking the door behind him.

He didn't trust anyone.

And after the day he'd had, who could blame him?

Chapter Twenty-Five

Brady attempted to run up the stairs to the second floor but failed miserably. His leg was now giving him so much jip, coupled with the pain from his bruised ribs, that he found himself limping. He paused for a moment, wincing as he bent down to massage the old wound, waiting for the agonising spasm to cease.

Too many months behind a desk, he mused. Six months of paper-pushing to suddenly being thrown a case of this magnitude was taking its toll. Both physically and mentally.

He had a briefing to hold and he was late. Add in that the briefing had already been put back by too many crucial hours.

He forced himself to make the final steps up to the second floor, cursing inwardly at the debilitating burst of pain. He desperately needed some more painkillers. But first, he had a briefing to give.

He limped along the corridor, heading for what had been assigned as the team's Incident Room.

As he reached the room his phone vibrated.

'Brady,' he answered.

Three words hit him.

'It's her, sir,' stated the liaison officer who had accompanied Brian Ryecroft to ID the body.

Brady paused, digesting the news.

He could hear the agitated mumbling of his team from behind the closed door. Every so often the name 'Simone' was thrown in, swiftly followed by 'bastards!' It was clear that tempers were frayed. People were on edge. Angry at what had happened to one of their own. Scared even, that whoever did it might strike again. Worst case scenario, they could have a cop killer on their hands.

'He's certain?' demanded Brady.

Given the condition of the body, he had to ask.

'Yes, sir. No question.'

Brady couldn't imagine the pain that Brian Ryecroft would be feeling after seeing the horror of what had happened to his daughter.

'Tell Mr Ryecroft I'm really sorry for his loss, will you?' replied Brady, knowing that his words would carry little comfort.

'Of course, sir.'

Brady disconnected the call and steeled himself before facing his team. This radically changed the investigation. Instead of some unidentified body they now had the victim's name.

Steadying himself Brady opened the door and walked in. The first person to catch his eye was Claudia.

'Sir, can I have a quick word before you start?' Conrad asked before his boss had a chance to question Claudia's presence.

Brady nodded, aware that Claudia was watching him. Closely; too closely.

Then he realised why. He looked as if he'd had the crap kicked out of him; which he had.

Brady walked back out, followed by Conrad who shut the door discreetly behind them.

'What is she doing in there?'

'She's got some information about the branding found on the murder victim, sir,' answered Conrad.

Brady narrowed his eyes.

'What exactly has she got?'

'She hasn't said, sir. She's saving it for the briefing.'

'I don't think so, Conrad. She has no jurisdiction here.'

Admittedly he had asked her to look into the branding marks found on the victim's body, but he hadn't expected her to turn up at the briefing without talking to him first.

'She seems to think she does,' Conrad replied uncomfortably.

'Yeah? Well, let's see about that, shall we?'

Before Brady opened the door, he looked at Conrad.

'While I have a word with her can you let the team know that the body's been positively identified as sixteen-year-old Melissa Ryecroft?'

Conrad looked mildly shaken. But he quickly composed himself.

'Yes, sir.'

He looked the way Brady had felt when he heard those fateful words.

Conrad waited for his boss to make a move but Brady looked distracted. His face dark, troubled.

In all the time he had worked with him, Conrad had never seen Brady look so on edge. It was too easy to dismiss it as a reaction to Simone Henderson's attack and the gruesome murder case which, if not solved, could have dire ramifications for them all; in particular Brady. But Conrad knew there was more to it. Exactly what, he couldn't say, but he had known Brady too long and had too much respect for him not to be concerned about what it was that was affecting him so badly.

Conrad followed Brady as he suddenly turned and walked into the Incident Room.

'Claudia?' Brady said, addressing his ex-wife as he entered the room.

Conrad kept his head down, avoiding Claudia's questioning look as he walked over to the large conference table.

Claudia looked from Conrad to Brady.

'Yes?' she questioned, her vivacious green eyes trying to gauge what was going on between the two men.

'Can we have a word?'

'Of course,' she answered.

Brady detected a slight hesitation in her voice.

He watched as she collected her thoughts. She irritably swept her long, curly red hair back from her face as she stood up, aware that he was watching her. As was the rest of the room.

Not surprisingly she was smartly dressed.

She had always worn clothes that commanded respect from men; she used to be a lawyer and was damned good at it.

She walked across the room towards him with an air of control. But Brady could tell that something was troubling her. He knew her too well.

Brady walked out into the corridor and waited until she had closed the door.

'Why are you here?' he said bluntly, annoyed that she

hadn't had the courtesy to ask his permission first, before making herself a part of his team.

'It might surprise you that I'm actually here to help you with this investigation. Be grateful – it's my day off.'

'Really? Then maybe you've got better things to do than sitting in on my briefing.'

'Believe me I do. But right now my only concern is helping you with this girl's murder. Not wasting time arguing.'

Brady didn't look convinced.

'Have you seen yourself?' she questioned, scathingly taking in the damage to his face.

'What exactly do you have?' demanded Brady, cutting straight to the point.

'A typical Jack Brady response. Always dodging the bullet!'

'I'm serious, Claudia, why are you here?'

She crossed her arms and looked at him.

'I have information that could be invaluable to the investigation.'

'And?' Brady asked. 'It still doesn't explain why you're sat in there. Surely a phone call would have been as good?'

He was mad with her. And he was mad at himself because here he was still letting her get to him. But ironically, he was relieved to have her there, despite how he was coming across.

'I did try calling you. Maybe you should check your messages. And then I sat waiting in your office for over half an hour.'

'I got caught up,' replied Brady edgily.

With everything that had happened since he got back to the station he had simply forgotten to contact her. A foolish oversight, given the information he needed from her.

'I have better things to do than wait around for you to show. And whether you like it or not, right now you need my expertise,' she pointed out with an edge of irritation to her voice.

'I'm sorry, alright?' Brady said quietly.

He knew he desperately needed her assistance on this case.

She gave a slight nod. Her way of accepting his apology.

'I'm here now so why don't you tell me exactly what it is you've found out?' he asked, trying to defuse the situation.

'I'll brief you in the meeting with the rest of the team. I've already discussed my findings with DCI Gates and he's agreed that I now need to be part of this investigation.'

Before Brady had a chance to remind her of who exactly was in charge she quickly moved on.

'I did some research on the photograph you sent me of the letter "N" burnt into Simone Henderson's breast.' Claudia stated. She looked up at his darkening expression. 'Don't worry, this is between you and me. Luckily for you I talked to Conrad first before my meeting with DCI Gates otherwise he'd be wanting to know why you've been covertly working on DI Adamson's case and not your own murder investigation.'

Brady didn't answer. But the look on his face was enough for her to know that he was all too aware he was crossing the line.

She wasn't sure why, but she hoped for his sake he wasn't on some personal crusade.

'I've cross-referenced the image with every possible case of branding we know of, but nothing. It's a dead-end.'

Brady tried to hide his disappointment.

'I'm sorry, Jack. For her, that is – I'm sorry I couldn't be of more help.'

Brady nodded. He checked the time. It was 5:15pm and time was running out. 'Alright, let's get on with the briefing so we can see exactly what you have for us regarding Melissa Ryecroft's murder.'

'Melissa Ryecroft?' questioned Claudia.

'Like I said, let's get on with the briefing,' instructed Brady.

She was now part of his team and he had no choice but to treat her accordingly.

Claudia hesitated.

'There's something I still need to discuss with you . . .' she said hesitantly. 'It's . . . personal . . .'

Her eyes were serious and that worried Brady. But right now he had a team of people sitting around doing nothing. He could hear them, their voices getting louder. They'd waited long enough, he decided. If it was personal, then standing here wasn't the right place for whatever it was she wanted to talk about.

'My office, after the briefing,' he ordered as he turned to open the door.

'Jack?'

He turned and looked at her. She was clearly agitated.

'This is important . . . it's personal . . .' she faltered.

'Not now – later,' Brady insisted, his tone final.

'You're the boss,' she said, shaking her head as she watched him walk away.

She took a moment to compose herself before turning and following Brady back into the Incident Room.

Chapter Twenty-Six

Brady had to give Conrad his due. His deputy had done his best to dress it up. But the room was what it was: a dumping ground for unsolved cases from years ago. Overflowing filing cabinets filled with local crime cases spanning fifty years dominated one wall. Cardboard boxes with ongoing murder cases sat on top of the metallic grey cabinets. The cases were still classed as open, even though the murders had happened decades ago.

There was only a handful of people sitting at the table, strategically positioned in the centre of the room. This was his team. If that was the right word. He had no idea how they were going to manage to solve a major murder case with only these resources.

Brady studied Harvey, the oldest member of his team. He wasn't the kind of Detective Sergeant to waste time with small talk. Unmarried and in his mid-forties, he made the best of his average, stocky appearance. A smart, dark grey M&S suit with a burgundy shirt and matching tie. His light brown hair was cropped short in an attempt to minimise the flecks of grey. His square jaw was severely shaven with telling razor nicks.

Brady's gaze drifted over to DC Kodovesky who was

sitting next to him; the youngest member of his team and Harvey's partner. They made a good team, a fact that still surprised him.

Kodovesky kept herself to herself. Unlike Harvey, she didn't socialise with the other coppers. She came in, did the job and then went home. Always the first one in and the last one home. Brady admired her dedication and determination. She knew where she wanted to be, which was sitting behind the DCI's desk. Her long black hair was harshly pulled back in a tight ponytail. Her clothes were professional yet practical: a light grey wool polo neck with dark grey trousers and low-heeled black boots. In all the time she had been stationed at Whitley Bay, Brady had never known Kodovesky to wear make-up. Not that she needed it.

She had an air of cool detachment about her which Brady assumed she needed for the job. She was a woman in her late twenties trying to make a career for herself in a male-dominated police force. Consequently she had more to prove than her colleagues.

Brady's eyes glanced over at Conrad, sitting opposite Kodovesky. He was very much the male version of Kodovesky, but with a few years on.

Daniels and Kenny were the other two DCs who made up the team. Both in their early thirties. Unlike Conrad and Kodovesky, they weren't graduates. Nor were they focused on fast-tracking.

Daniels was well-built at 5′11″ – a testament to the long hours he put in at the gym. Good looking in a hard way, with his hair shaved so close to his scalp that you could only just make out that his hair was sandy blond. He had hazel eyes that were normally filled with mirth and a strong, determined, clean-shaven jawline.

He and Kenny were inseparable: best mates on the job, best mates off. Kenny was tall at 6′4″, with short, curly dark brown hair. His face with his deep set, small, mischievous, darting brown eyes was already heavily lined. Brady had lost count of the amount of times he had to get Kenny to tone down his role as the team's stand-up comic. But Brady knew it was Kenny's way of dealing with the dark world they were paid to investigate. Being a copper suited Kenny, there was no disputing that fact.

As it did all of them.

As Brady observed them all he was keenly aware that no one was speaking. The air was tense.

DC Kenny and DC Daniels sat motionless. Both averting their eyes from Brady's penetrating gaze.

As were DS Harvey and DC Kodovesky.

Even Conrad was studying his hands.

Brady knew that their minds were elsewhere.

The critical condition of Simone Henderson was affecting everyone. That, and the fact that, given a choice they would all rather be working on finding her attacker. Not stuck here, forced to deal with another brutal crime investigation. As it was, whether it due to unspoken loyalty to Brady or a deep, intrinsic dislike of DI Adamson, this was Brady's investigative team. Demoralised and preoccupied.

Brady unintentionally caught Claudia's eye. She was the only one looking straight at him. And if he wasn't mistaken, she looked worried. Worried about him.

Maybe it was the open cuts to his cheek and above his eyebrow that had got to her. But Brady seriously doubted that. He was certain it would be connected to her earlier meeting with DCI Gates. Brady knew that Gates wouldn't take the incident at the hospital with Frank Henderson lightly. Especially since both Frank Henderson and Adamson had made a formal complaint against him.

Brady rubbed the coarse dark stubble on his chin as he thought about the job at hand.

'Harvey, Kodovesky. You two have the details on the victim who we now know has been identified as the missing sixteen-year-old girl, Melissa Ryecroft. How about you update us?'

'Right,' began Harvey as he stood up and walked over to the whiteboard.

Harvey cleared his throat and looked around his colleagues.

Brady waited. He knew what was coming next.

Harvey pointed to the photographs of the decapitated head that Ainsworth had sent through.

'Wolfe has confirmed that the decapitated head left in DI Brady's car does in fact belong to the victim, who we now know has been positively identified as Melissa Ryecroft, a local girl.'

Around the table there were a few murmurs at the gruesome sight of the victim's head.

'As you can see, Melissa Ryecroft was partially strangled and then a captive bolt pistol was placed in the centre of her forehead and fired,' stated Harvey. 'In between that . . . well . . . you can all see what they did to her after she was dead. Presumably, this was to make it difficult to identify the victim.'

Brady looked at the rigid faces around the room. The only one whose expression never altered was Kodovesky. She sat expressionless, not allowing the photographic carnage on the whiteboard to penetrate.

'For those of you who aren't familiar with captive bolt

pistols, they're a device used for stunning animals prior to slaughter. Also known as a cattle gun.'

Harvey had everyone transfixed.

This was a new kind of crime. Or at least that's what Brady thought. But the inquisitive look on Claudia's face told him this was something she'd already come across in her sex trafficking work.

'The point of it is to stun the animal into unconsciousness, enabling the slaughter house to hang it up and slit its throat, so it bleeds to death.'

Claudia nodded.

She then tucked a long, stray red curl behind her ear before politely interrupting.

'I've come across this before but I never thought I'd see a case of it being used on a victim here in the North East. Let alone Whitley Bay. Having said that, this isn't as atypical as you might think. It's becoming a growing trend amongst a certain clientele in the sex slavery business.'

Brady looked at her questioningly.

She held his gaze for a second too long before turning back to the room.

'However, the use of penetrating captive bolts, which if I'm right is exactly what has been used on the victim, Melissa Ryecroft, has been discontinued in commercial situations in order to minimise the risk of transmission of disease. Sometimes it causes the brain tissue to actually go into the bloodstream of the animal, contaminating other tissue with bovine spongiform encephalopathy,' Claudia explained. Realising she had lost them, she added, 'To you and me, that's BSE, otherwise more commonly known as mad cow disease.'

Harvey looked at her with candid surprise.

Conrad didn't.

It was clear to Brady that Claudia and Conrad had already discussed the case while he had been busy in his office.

'Claudia's right. The captive bolt pistol used on the victim . . .' Harvey paused as he directed them to the hole in the centre of the victim's head '. . . is a stunner. It uses a pointed bolt propelled by a blank cartridge. The bolt penetrates the skull of the animal, or in the case here, the victim's head. It enters the cranium and damages the cerebrum and part of the cerebellum. The damage to the brain tissue here was catastrophic.'

He stopped and cleared his throat, disgusted with the thought of what had been done to the victim.

'She would have lost consciousness pretty much immediately, as it destroyed the brain matter in her skull. But crucially, and this is the point of the captive bolt pistol, it left her brain stem intact.'

'But she's dead, right? So what does it matter if the brain stem's intact?' asked Daniels as he looked from Harvey to his partner Kenny.

Kenny shrugged.

'Don't look at me, mate. Biology was never my strong point!' Kenny pointed out.

'Is that why you don't know your arse from your elbow?' quizzed Daniels, giving him a wry smile.

'If you two bloody paid attention then you might learn something, you boneheads!' commented Harvey.

Kenny and Daniels refrained from saying something.

Brady dismissed what on the surface appeared to be insensitive camaraderie, aware that this was the men's way of dealing with the horror of what had happened to the victim.

'That's precisely why it's been used on the victim. It had

the same effect as it does on cattle. Leaving the brain stem intact allows the heart to continue beating, so the animal bleeds to death.'

Claudia looked across at Kenny and Daniels, clearly unimpressed with their cavalier attitude.

'You want to know the reason a captive bolt stunner was used on this sixteen-year-old girl?' Claudia questioned as she stared at them.

'To kill her?' bluntly answered Daniels as Kenny nudged him under the table.

'The whole point is that she dies two minutes later. During that time she gets fucked. Mind you, given what I've heard about you two, that's probably a minute and half longer than you'd need,' Claudia said pointedly, as her eyes flashed emerald green.

Claudia's eyes could change from a tranquil bluish-green to a passionate emerald green in a split second. Brady recognised the sign, unlike Kenny and Daniels. And was more than relieved it was them on the receiving end.

Brady sat forward.

He caught Claudia's eye. It was enough.

He then shot Kenny and Daniels a look which told them they deserved as much for fucking around.

'Tom, did Wolfe's autopsy report show the victim to have been raped and sodomised in the leadup to her death?' Brady asked, backing up Claudia's statement.

Harvey nodded, not wanting to get caught in the firing line.

'That's one word for it,' he said uncomfortably, as he caught Brady's eye.

Harvey knew Claudia of old. Both in a professional capacity when she had worked as the Duty Solicitor at the station, but also in a personal role, when she had been married to Brady. And something Kenny and Daniels didn't know but were about to find out, was that Claudia didn't suffer fools gladly.

Claudia looked at Harvey and then turned to Daniels and Kenny, not finished with them yet.

'While her body contorts and convulses, while she lies there unconscious with half her brain tissue blown away, men will pay a great deal of money to have the ultimate fuck. The ultimate fuck being . . . fucking a woman and making it the very last thing she'll ever feel.'

In one sentence she wiped the boyish smirks off Daniels and Kenny's faces.

Nobody said a word.

Harvey dropped his gaze to the floor, clearly finding the reality of how the victim had died distasteful.

The atmosphere in the room was tense and suffocating.

Every man in the room wished they were anywhere else at this precise moment than sitting here with the glaring evidence of the level of depravity some men would reach to get their kicks.

Men were bastards. Brady couldn't dispute it. The evidence was plastered in front of them on the whiteboard.

Brady looked at Kenny and Daniels who were squirming with discomfort at having made light of the situation. And then at Harvey and Conrad.

But *these* men weren't the bastards here, Brady reminded himself.

And Claudia knew that. As did Kodovesky.

These were the men who would spend thankless, sleepless hours hunting down and apprehending the sick bastards who gave mankind a bad name.

Harvey was the first to break the awkward silence.

'The cartridge used had 3 grains – that's about 190mg of gunpowder, giving the velocity of the bolt 55 metres per second.'

Claudia nodded at Harvey. She then looked at the rest of the team.

'What is frightening here is that this penchant for paying for sex with a girl while she's dying is a growing phenomenon,' Claudia explained.

She looked up at the countless, brutal images of the victim, deliberating for a moment.

'What we're dealing with is a new breed of sex crime,' concluded Claudia.

No one said a word. Not even Brady.

All of them were lost in the horror of what was before them.

Chapter Twenty-Seven

'You might be wondering why I'm here, apart from to make you feel like shit,' Claudia said, looking directly at Kenny and Daniels.

She then shot them a wry smile.

Her objective hadn't been to alienate or humiliate them, it had been simply to wake them up to the seriousness of the situation.

'This is what I do,' she said, with a note of sadness as she cast her eyes up at the photographs of the victim laid bare and naked for all to see.

'I deal in shit like that,' she said, trying to keep her voice level. 'My job is to find these women – sometimes girls as young as eleven – before it's too late. Before they end up on your desk either as missing persons or, at worst, murder victims. I'm here because I can help you find the men who did this to her. I help you and you help me by catching the perpetrators and making sure they never do this to another girl again.'

Claudia turned and stared at the team, clearly worried.

'Because I guarantee, she isn't the first. And unless you apprehend the group of men responsible, she won't be the last.'

Brady shot her a questioning look.

'Can you expand?'

'My team, which I co-head with DCI Davidson, have spent the last few months trying to get information on an international, elitist group who call themselves "The Nietzschean Brotherhood". We initially got intelligence from Scotland Yard about this group when we first set up the sex trafficking unit in Newcastle.'

'I've never heard of them,' Brady replied.

From the puzzled looks on the faces around the table, he wasn't the only one who hadn't heard of the Nietzschean Brotherhood. However, Brady *had* heard of Friedrich Nietzsche, a nineteenth-century German philosopher. And he presumed the name of the group was no coincidence, given the Nietzschean Brotherhood's quest for the ultimate power – to take another person's life while climaxing.

'I wouldn't expect you to have heard of them,' Claudia began. 'They are a covert organisation who are the most difficult group we've ever come across to infiltrate. SOCA set up a unit twelve months ago to break into this group without much success.

'Firstly, they communicate through encrypted chat rooms and websites. Secondly, these men are wealthy. They can buy whatever they want, including a girl's life. Our informant has said that a year's membership costs £100,000. Now that's membership only. That doesn't buy you the girl of your choice. What they do have is an exquisite catalogue of girls ranging from ten to twenty-five years old. Whatever creed or nationality you want, they deal in it. And from the evidence on the victim here,' Claudia pointed to Melissa Ryecroft's severed head, 'I'd say the Nietzschean Brotherhood is spreading out from London.'

'How do you know it's not just some kind of copycat killing then?' interrupted Harvey.

'We don't know for certain. But from the way she's been sadistically raped and sodomised by a group of men, I'd say it's in keeping with previous murders. Especially the use of the captive bolt pistol.'

She looked around the room. It was uncomfortably silent.

'The Nietzschean Brothers have their own unique take on life. As I'm sure you can guess by their name, we presume they have been inspired by the philosopher, Friedrich Nietzsche, whose idea of the "superman" is what this brotherhood appears to be emulating. Nietzsche wanted to challenge the ingrained values of society, especially the Church's indoctrination of ideas about good and evil, believing they hamper human potential. The rejection of God could give us "superman" – a man who would trust his own sense of good and evil and not some Christian doctrine. In 1900 Nietzsche declared the death of God, leading to outright nihilism . . .' Claudia paused, realising that she had lost her audience.

Brady gave her a look which told her to move it along.

'Nihilism is the belief that nothing has any inherent importance and that life lacks purpose. If God is dead, then nothing remains to which man can cling and orient himself by. He can effectively do what he wants as long as he doesn't get caught.'

Brady noted that Claudia had lost Kenny and Daniels five minutes ago.

'That's all very interesting, I'm sure,' interrupted Brady. 'But what has a group of nihilistic blokes got to do with this investigation?' he asked.

'Everything,' answered Claudia.

'Go on,' said Brady, intrigued by the conviction in her voice.

But he was already starting to do the maths himself.

The platinum signet rings that he'd seen the Eastern European men wearing had the letter 'N' as the emblem.

The note left in Brady's car alongside the victim's severed head had been signed with the 'N' emblem, matching the freeze-framed, digitally enhanced image of the ring's emblem that Jed had sent him.

He then thought of the 'N' branded on Simone Henderson's left breast.

Had Simone come across something to do with the Nietzschean Brotherhood? Is that what had brought up to the North East?

He wanted to run some of these ideas past Claudia to see what she thought. Also, given that Simone Henderson's investigation was off-limits for him, he'd have to tread carefully.

'Well . . .' began Claudia. 'Two things.'

She stood up and walked over to the whiteboard.

'You don't mind, do you?' she asked Brady.

'Be my guest,' he replied, noting that she didn't give him much choice.

Brady nodded at Harvey to step down.

Harvey shot a questioning look at Brady. As did Kodovesky.

Brady discreetly gestured for them to let Claudia talk.

Claudia looked at the whiteboard which was also a smart board.

Brady watched as she touched icons at the bottom left-hand corner of the screen, bringing up multiple images of the branding found on Melissa Ryecroft's body.

'As you can see here, the two letters "MD" positioned below the scorpion are roughly three inches in diameter. This branding exists in the livestock trade of course, but also in the sex slavery world. It's about ownership, as I'm sure you have realised.'

She paused as she uploaded new photographs of other female victims onto the whiteboard.

'These ten female sex victims you can see here have all been branded with the same mark as your murder victim,' Claudia pointed out. 'I've seen these letters "MD" and the scorpion marking on five victims from the South as well as ten allegedly trafficked girls brought to the North East and made to work in the sex trade. We carried out a raid on the Dock pub down by the quayside in Newcastle. The seedier end, not the refurbished part.'

Brady nodded. He knew exactly where it was – had been dragged down that way a couple of times by the lads. It wasn't a savoury place. It was down the dark end by the Tyne Bridge where hookers stood about in doorways tabbing or injecting, depending on their habit. And once they'd had their fix, they would be ducking and peering as the cars slowly drove down. Money for their next fix their only concern.

Claudia continued. 'The place was raided because we'd had reports that the lap dancing girls there were offering an extensive range of sexual services in a couple of the back rooms. That, and they were being held against their will. One of the punters had become concerned when one of the girls disappeared. His favourite girl. She told him her name was Edita Aginatas and that she was from a Lithuanian village. He couldn't remember the name of the village, only that it began with "R". He started asking too many

204

questions about where she'd gone and ended up badly beaten on his way home from the pub one night. Reckoned it was one of the men in charge of the girls: had an Eastern European accent like them. Punter reported the attack, which is why we went in. But by the time we got there we found that the girls had been moved.'

She turned and looked at the room, her face expressionless.

'We presume that when the punter kicked up a fuss about the missing girl, they got nervous and relocated the group. It happens.'

Brady noticed a hint of regret in her voice.

Regret that they hadn't got there sooner.

'That wasn't that long ago. Last Saturday night to be precise,' she said, shaking her head. 'But the information we got from the punter is that all ten girls were branded with this identical mark. So I'd suggest that the victim you have here, Melissa Ryecroft, was either bought or lured by the men that ran the operation at the Dock pub and are presumably running it at some other premises.'

'Where is she now? The girl who the punter reported missing. Did you find her?' asked Brady, leaning forward.

'No . . . we did run a check on the name. We found out that Edita Aginatas is in fact a seventeen year old from a Lithuanian village by the name of Raseiniai.'

Claudia suddenly put her photograph on the whiteboard.

'Now listed as missing. The punter did say that she hadn't been branded like the others with the letters "MD" below the scorpion. Why that was, we have no idea. Maybe they were planning on selling her on and so didn't brand her, we're not sure.'

Claudia tentatively bit her lip as she looked at the photograph of the girl.

The missing teenager had long dark hair tied up at the back. Her dark brown eyes smiled at the camera. Her tanned skin glistened in what must have been the summer sun. She had a carefree beauty about her.

But something about her reminded Brady of someone.

He realised it was Melissa Ryecroft.

'Lithuanian, you said?' Brady questioned, his mind racing.

He thought of the two Eastern European looking brothers and the Lithuanian licence plate on the black Mercedes his brother was driving.

Johnny Slaughter's words had also got under his skin, making him uneasy.

'Lithuaks', Johnny Slaughter had said. 'Lithuaks' who dealt in sex trafficking.

'Yes, definitely Lithuanian,' answered Claudia. She caught his eye, curious as to what was going through his mind.

'I believe these initials belong to the two Eastern European brothers who are running this operation,' continued Claudia.

'Eastern European?' questioned Brady.

Claudia nodded. 'Yes. Edita Aginatas had told this punter that one of them was her boyfriend. He was Lithuanian also. They'd met allegedly in Vilnius, the capital of Lithuania, and he had persuaded her to come over to the UK. She flew into London a few months ago, flight paid for by him. When she landed, he was waiting . . . with his brother. They took her passport and took her to an undisclosed house in London where she was raped and beaten by both men, until she acquiesced.'

Claudia noticed the confusion on Daniels' face.

'They rape and beat these girls to break their spirits. Sometimes it takes a couple of days to break them, for others it can take up to a week. Then they get put to work, maybe servicing up to twenty punters a day, working a fifteen-hour day.'

'Why don't they escape then or go to the police?' asked Daniels.

'They're threatened that if they run, or tell any of the punters what's really going on, then they'll be punished. Or worse, a family member back home will get hurt. They're also watched twenty-four-seven by these men. They're valuable commodities that can earn these men tens of thousands of pounds.'

Daniels looked taken aback.

Brady had to remind himself that the kid was working in Whitley Bay, not London or Paris or Frankfurt. This was a small seaside resort that relied on stag and hen parties to keep the pubs and clubs afloat. Or more to the point, to keep North Tyneside Council in revenue.

'Brothers? You said the two Eastern European men were brothers?' questioned Brady.

Claudia nodded.

'That's all the information we got. No names, nothing. Just that the men were Lithuanian and were brothers. Evil by all accounts,' she added.

'Why did they move her up here from London? And the other girls, I presume they were moved as well?' asked Brady.

'Maybe they've relocated here because it was starting to get too difficult for them in the South. They could be getting squeezed out. Or it could simply be that they're expanding.

207

I don't know. All I know is that they brought this girl up with them along with the others. But this is the first time we've come across this type of branding up here in the North East. So they're new to the area.'

'Did you get a description of the brothers, apart from the fact that they're Eastern European?' asked Brady.

Claudia shook her head.

'The girl was too scared to tell the punter. Thought they might kill him if he found out too much. And she was scared they would harm her for talking.'

Brady nodded, disappointed.

'Two rules when you're a sex slave. Never say no to a punter, regardless of what they want. And rule number two, you don't talk. Nothing personal about your old life or who's pimping you.' Claudia paused as she looked around the room. 'Sorry. Wish I had more to give . . .'

'You've told us a lot more than we expected,' assured Brady.

He sat back and thought over what she had told them. His eyes were automatically drawn to the images of the sex slaves on the whiteboard whose whereabouts were unknown.

Brady leaned forward, turning his attention back to Claudia. 'You said the punter was attacked? Who attacked him? Did he give you a description of them?'

Claudia shook her head. 'No, it was dark and the attacker was wearing a hoodie under his leather jacket. Had it pulled right over his head, partially covering his face. The punter reckoned he was tall, about 6'2" and well-built. As if he went to the gym. He also reckoned he had an Eastern European accent.'

'I see,' muttered Brady. 'Can we talk to this punter?' He

realised he could have some information that could help the investigation.

Claudia shook her head. 'No . . . last Sunday evening, the night after we'd raided the Dock, his first-floor council flat in Elswick was firebombed. The front door was the only way in and out and it had been locked from the outside. He was barricaded in. I don't know if you remember it on the news? It made national headlines.'

Brady nodded, as did everyone else. They had heard about it.

A single man in his early fifties had burnt to death, unable to get out the front door. Even if he hadn't been locked in, he would have had to run through the petrol that had been poured through the letterbox and set alight. And then there was the Molotov cocktail they'd thrown in for good measure.

What the hell were they up against, Brady mused as he looked at Claudia.

He wondered if she knew more than she was telling him. If she was holding something back. Something connected to Simone Henderson. But what?

And as for the Eastern European brothers, he wondered whether they were the same men that Nick was working for and perhaps, as Claudia had suggested, the same men connected to Melissa Ryecroft's murder. Brady didn't want to think about the part Simone Henderson had played in all of this. Whatever she had found out had cost her more than she could ever have anticipated.

His biggest problem now was keeping Adamson in the dark as much as possible. He needed to get to Nick first. Talk to him before he brought these men down. He still couldn't believe that his own brother could be involved in

organised crime of this nature. And until he had confirmation from him and him alone, Brady still held onto the
belief that Nick was being forced to do this against his will.
That these men had some hold over Nick.

He looked at the photograph of the missing Lithuanian
girl, Edita Aginatas. He had a gut feeling that she had
suffered the same fate as Melissa Ryecroft. And what of the
other girls that had been relocated?

The odds of finding them were heavily stacked against
them.

Chapter Twenty-Eight

'So, what have these European brothers and the sex business they're now believed to be operating here in the North East got to do with "The Nietzschean Brotherhood"?' Brady asked.

Claudia nodded at him. 'That was my next point. The note left with the victim's head in your car,' she said, bringing up an enlarged image of the note. 'It's been signed with the letter "N". Unfortunately, no forensic evidence was found on the note. Whoever left it was very careful not to leave any traces behind.'

Brady nodded, dreading what might be coming next.

'From the source we have regarding the Nietzschean Brotherhood they wear a crest ring or a signet ring with the "N" emblem. Just like the "N" on the note here.'

Brady did his utmost not to react.

'So you think someone from this Brotherhood followed me and dumped the victim's head and a note in my car?' he said calmly.

Her look said it all.

'Why?' asked Brady.

There was a heavy, pregnant silence in the room.

'Can we discuss this in private?' Claudia replied.

Brady frowned. This was obviously what she had wanted to talk about earlier.

He looked from Claudia to Conrad.

Conrad dropped his eyes.

He obviously knew what it was that Claudia was holding back.

Brady cursed under his breath, feeling very much left out of the loop. But it was his own fault. He had chosen not to listen to her. She had tried to tell him and he had insisted on starting the briefing regardless.

'Look, Jack, this organisation is not to be messed with . . . These are powerful men who so far have eluded justice.'

Brady didn't say a word.

Instead he looked at the brutal images of Melissa Ryecroft's tortured body.

He then looked back at Claudia.

'I don't give a damn how rich or powerful this group is, no one has the right to rape, sodomise and torture a young girl,' Brady said, his expression darkening as his voice slipped into a thick Geordie accent. 'And I for one will not be threatened or scared away by anyone. So you tell your informant, whoever he is, that they can go fuck themselves.'

Claudia looked at Brady, her eyes burning a vivid emerald green.

'Highly commendable, I'm sure, Jack,' she said after some deliberation. 'As for our informant . . .' Claudia turned back to the whiteboard and brought up a new image.

A slender, tall, bleached-blonde-haired girl was unceremoniously laid out on an autopsy slab.

Brady looked at her. Her spiky, short punkish hair was discoloured a dirty rust colour: blood. The damage was as brutal as Melissa Ryecroft's, if not worse. Apart from not having a hole through her head. Her body was covered in what appeared to be cigarette burns. But he wasn't sure. He then caught sight of the autopsy photographs of the victim's genitalia; damning evidence that she had been brutally gang-raped.

Brady turned away, sickened to his core.

'Katya is her name. That's the only detail we have. That and she said she was Russian. We tried tracing her with what few details we had, but nothing . . .' She pointed at the murder victim. 'Unless you're psychic it would be difficult to talk to her,' Claudia said, as she looked at Brady.

'She was a nineteen-year-old Russian girl. Beautiful, model material. Brought over to London by a sex trafficker and bought by two men in the Brotherhood. She lived long enough to tell the Met officers who got there what we now know . . . The hotel she'd been taken to was in the West End of London. Old school money. A fellow guest had heard screams coming from the hotel room and had thought that she was some high-class hooker. He'd evidently seen her being led in by two well-dressed men. Heard her accent and knew that she was Russian. Room got raided and there she was tortured and bleeding to death on the bed. The two men torturing her had received a warning from someone that there had been a complaint made to the hotel staff and that the police were being called. They left before they had the opportunity to put the captive bolt pistol to her head. You see, Katya told us that one of the men had pulled out what looked like a black pistol and had put it to her head saying, and I quote: "This will be the best and last fuck of your life."'

Claudia paused for a moment. 'From her description the weapon put to her head matches a captive bolt pistol.'

She brought up a photograph.

To Brady's eye it looked like a black hand pistol, but the end of the barrel was thicker, chunkier.

'Forensics found DNA evidence on her body and in the room. Hair samples, fingerprints . . . but they don't match with anything we have on the database. We've cross-referenced the DNA evidence with agencies in Europe and America. Nothing . . .' Claudia's voice trailed off. 'But the victim did say that the man who pulled out the pistol was right-handed and on his hand he was wearing a platinum signet ring on the third finger.'

This jarred with Brady.

'What about security camera footage?' asked Brady, keen to see what these men looked like.

'The hotel doesn't have surveillance cameras. Guests don't like it. Their attitude is they pay too much money to be spied on. And no one remembers the men coming in with the Russian girl. And, all transactions were paid in advance online by a stolen credit card. So no trail. The only eyewitness we had was the guest next door who reported the screams.'

She looked Brady straight in the eye, anticipating his next question. 'He was found dead the following morning. Two weeks ago to be precise. Gunshot wound to the head. Armed robbery, held up at gunpoint a street away from the hotel, coincidentally before the police got a statement from him. Too coincidental if you ask me.'

Brady absorbed the enormity of what had just been said. They were just an under-funded, under-staffed murder team in a small seaside resort. This wasn't a major European capital and yet here they were, dealing with what effectively could be an international criminal organisation.

'Have you shared the details of Melissa Ryecroft's murder with SOCA?'

Claudia shook her head.

'Not yet.'

Brady breathed a sigh of relief. The last thing he wanted was them coming here to take over his investigation. He needed time to figure this out. More so for Nick's sake.

'Thanks, you've given us some invaluable information there,' replied Brady.

Claudia looked at him, not quite able to gauge his comment.

Brady looked around the room. The atmosphere serious, the faces grim.

They were all thinking what Brady was thinking.

Had Simone Henderson been targeted by this group? It seemed likely given the mark left on her left breast.

And was Brady their next target?

Brady thought back to Frank Henderson's words when he attacked him in the ICU. That Simone had come back up to the North East because of Brady. What if they thought that she had talked to Brady before they got to her? And crucially, what exactly did Simone know about the Nietzschean Brotherhood?

Chapter Twenty-Nine

'Alright,' said Brady clearing his throat.

He poured himself a glass of water and took a much-needed gulp.

This was the last place he wanted to be right now. He needed to have a word with Claudia; in his office. He needed whatever the other information was that Claudia couldn't share with the team.

The investigation had changed. It was much bigger than a murdered girl. This was connected to Simone Henderson and . . .

Brady couldn't think straight.

He realised he had to wind up the briefing as quickly as possible. There was too much at stake. He didn't even know if he was still going to be in charge of the Ryecroft investigation given the fact it could now be connected to Adamson's case. Add to that, it now seemed that Brady was being targeted.

He looked around the room.

'This is what we know. The victim, Melissa Ryecroft was a sixteen-year-old student who attended King's School, a private school in Tynemouth. She was in the lower sixth, studying four A Levels . . .' Brady's voice momentarily trailed off.

He realised that what she had been studying was pointless now.

He took a deep breath before continuing. 'We know that last November she went to Budapest on holiday with her friends for her sixteenth birthday. There, we are led to believe, she met a twenty-eight-year-old man known only as "Marijuis" to us. Her parents asked her to stop communicating with the man but it seems that she continued, without their knowledge. She returned to Budapest to a clinic to have a breast augmentation operation accompanied by her father, Brian Ryecroft, who signed the consent form and paid for the plastic surgery.'

After re-reading the Ryecrofts' earlier statements he had a clearer understanding of Brian Ryecroft's guilt. After all, the man had taken her back to Budapest for a breast enhancement operation and, by his own admission, he spent most of the time in the hotel bar, believing that in the days before the scheduled operation his daughter was in her hotel room watching TV and on her laptop. But Brady was sure that she wouldn't have been alone in her room. He was certain that her boyfriend Marijuis would have been keeping her company.

Brady had read the logged calls and it was clear that on her second visit to Budapest she had been receiving calls from another unregistered mobile also located in Budapest.

'We've got the call log details through from her mobile phone network and she has received calls and made calls to eight unregistered mobile numbers. None of them traceable. There seems to be a pattern. Every month, sometimes

217

less, that mobile number changes. Some are made from Eastern Europe. Mainly Romania and Lithuania and then . . .' Brady said.

The word 'Lithuania' had jolted Brady when he had first seen it on the list of logged calls. It had immediately made him think of the two Eastern European men caught on the surveillance tape at Rake Lane Hospital. And the black Mercedes with the Lithuanian licence plate. If he hadn't noticed the small "LT" in the corner of the licence plate he would have never made the connection. But the image he still couldn't shake from his head was that of his brother Nick, the driver of the black Merc.

'. . . the UK. The calls are predominately located in the London region but in the past month they've been traced to the North East,' Brady explained. 'It seems that this Marijuis character travels backwards and forwards between the UK and Eastern Europe. Maybe they've found a new business partner in the North East, which would explain why they've branched out up here.'

Brady noticed the interest in Claudia's face and had already second-guessed what she was thinking: Marijuis was a sex trafficker. Someone who picked up pretty young girls, promising them the world.

The question was, if the gang did have a North East connection, who was it?

Claudia would be wondering exactly what he was wondering: did Marijuis have a brother? And if so, were they working together? And what was the link to the North East?

'Harvey and Kodovesky, I want you to interview all of Melissa Ryecroft's friends and classmates to see if she mentioned Marijuis to any of them. What we crucially need is some information on this character. And on the guy who left a message on her Facebook wall offering to take her to London for a meeting with the Models 1 agency. His Facebook account was fake, as we expected, much as the appointment with the model agency was too.' Brady paused as he took another drink.

The way the day was going he needed more than just lukewarm water to get rid of the bad taste in his mouth.

'Melissa Ryecroft got handpicked by this Marijuis character in Budapest. He chose her because she was sixteen and stunning looking. Model material . . . like your Russian girl,' Brady said. His eyes rested briefly on the bloodsoaked bed where the Russian had lain while she had been sexually assaulted and butchered.

Claudia followed Brady's eyes as he turned to the images of Melissa Ryecroft's decapitated head and body.

'How and why Melissa Ryecroft ended up in this condition is what we're here to find out, people,' Brady said as he looked back around the table. 'As of yet, nothing's come back from the lab. Wolfe said that he didn't find traces of sperm in the victim's vagina and rectum as condoms were used. And industrial bleach was used after the victim's death in an attempt to destroy any DNA evidence. I'm not holding out much hope, and neither is Wolfe, but we'll see what comes back from the lab.'

Brady turned his eyes on Daniels and Kenny.

'I need you two to check Newcastle Airport security cameras for Thursday. Both inside the airport and any footage by the pick-up point outside. Also, look at the Metro surveillance footage. If she did go to the airport I imagine she would have taken the Metro there.'

Kenny and Daniels nodded.

'Right, any questions?' Brady asked, keen to get moving. No one said anything.

'Alright, you know what you've got to do,' Brady said.

He watched as they pushed their chairs back and stood up.

Brady looked at Claudia who had remained seated. 'My office?' he said.

'Alright, but I haven't got long,' she said. 'There are some details on Melissa Ryecroft that I want to cross-reference and to do that, I need to be at Pilgrim Street to access it.'

'Why don't you tell me exactly what you're cross-referencing?' Brady asked.

Claudia looked at Brady. 'Perhaps we should continue this in your office.'

Chapter Thirty

Brady sat down at his desk and watched as Claudia closed the office door and then took a seat opposite him.

He was worried that Claudia had found out about Nick somehow. That she and her team had been watching him. That they had made the connection that he had come up from London with the two Lithuanian brothers and was working for them. But even worse than that was the thought that she had somehow figured out that he was Brady's brother.

'Jack? I need to tell you something about Simone . . .' Claudia delicately began as she met his eyes.

'What about Simone?' Brady interrupted, surprised.

'She was one of the detectives involved in investigating the murder of the Russian girl, Katya. The one that took place a few weeks back in the London hotel.'

'Go on,' ordered Brady, aware of the adrenalin beginning to course through his body.

'She was the one who got the information out of the Russian victim before she died . . .' Claudia paused, as she tried to gauge his reaction.

Something in her voice made him uneasy. Then it hit him.

'Simone's father thought it was *me* . . .' Brady began, shaking his head in disbelief.

'Jack? Look . . .' Claudia attempted to explain.

'No. Let me think!' snapped Brady. 'Frank Henderson said that Simone had come back up to the North East to talk to me. She had told her flatmate that she had a meeting up here with someone who worked in the Northumbrian force, named Brady.'

Claudia didn't say anything.

'It was *you* . . . wasn't it? You're the Brady she was meeting. Of course, Claudia Brady. You're the head of a major sex trafficking unit. The biggest in the country. So who else would she share the information she had with, if it wasn't you?' demanded Brady, raising his voice.

Claudia remained silent.

'Did you meet with her?' he shouted, angry at her refusal to answer him.

He stared at her. His dark brown eyes cold.

'Of course you did, otherwise you wouldn't know what you know,' he muttered quietly. He frowned. 'Don't you think it's crossing a line? The woman you caught me in bed with contacting you?'

Distressed by the suggestion, Claudia looked away.

'So . . . what happened?' demanded Brady. He wasn't going to let her off that easy. 'Did you send her into Madley's, is that it? Did you know they were going to be in there that night and so you sent her in as bait? Is that it? See if they bite and take her to wherever they're holding the other trafficked girls? Was that it?'

'Jack! Please . . . you've got it all wrong,' Claudia desperately insisted.

'Have I? Have I really?' questioned Brady harshly, unable

to disguise the contempt he felt. 'If it had all worked out, imagine where you'd be now. Not sat in my office with a mutilated copper fighting for her life.'

She shook her head, her eyes now looking at him. They were filled with tears.

He stared back at her. It was a cold, hard look. One that Claudia didn't recognise.

She shook her head. A spark of anger firing within.

'I *didn't* send her to Madley's nightclub. Alright? She did this off her own back.'

Brady narrowed his eyes at her, clearly not believing her.

'Don't you dare turn this on me, Jack! This was a malleable – gullible even – rookie who was desperate to impress you. And what did you do? You took her to bed!'

Brady clenched his fists trying not to react.

'You shared with her your paranoid, delusional suspicions about Mayor Macmillan and his drug-dealing brother, Ronnie Macmillan, who you claimed procured prostitutes for his politician brother. Young girls, like the ones we try to help off the streets in the West End and down by the quayside in Newcastle. Girls as young as eleven being worked by pimps. But the problem is, Jack, it was all hearsay. Nothing has ever been substantiated against Mayor Macmillan. He has no connection with his brother. Nothing. You should be more careful when it comes to listening to idle gossip. Politics is filled with lies and rumours, all aimed at bringing a man down for the sake of the opposition. Mayor Macmillan has made it very clear that he's not responsible for his background or the family associated with it. He's a man who has made good for himself, regardless of the odds stacked against him—'

Brady interrupted her furiously. 'What the hell has this

got to do with Simone being attacked? You've already suggested that you think she was targeted by this Nietzschean Brotherhood you were talking about,' he pointed out accusingly, his eyes dark and threatening.

'I know exactly what I implied. And I still stand by that – it's why she's been branded with the "N". However, it was a combination of what you had told her about Ronnie Macmillan and the new information she had that he was branching out from drugs into the sex trade.'

'What new information?' demanded Brady.

'I got word from some of the women I deal with about what Ronnie Macmillan was up to. He's a nasty piece of work and gets a great deal of pleasure out of humiliating and beating up his girls. Likes them to "respect" him, allegedly. Anyway, he's creating quite a cartel for himself. He has other pimps and drug dealers working hand in hand with him. And he's buying up a lot of local businesses and unused land—'

'What for?' interrupted Brady.

He had no idea that Ronnie Macmillan was capable of running such an empire. Then again, thought Brady, was it really Ronnie Macmillan or was he just the front man? The target if it all went wrong. His brother, Mayor Macmillan, had the brains and the looks in the family, whereas Ronnie had always been the ugly one with a lot of muscle. Too much muscle by the sounds of it.

'I don't know,' answered Claudia uneasily.

She shook her head as she thought about it.

'It doesn't make any sense to me . . . but it's all kosher. We can't get him for anything. And believe me, we've tried. Which is what I told Simone. But . . .' Claudia faltered.

'What?' questioned Brady.

'Well . . . when Simone contacted me and told me about the Russian girl's murder and how she had heard talk that two of the men involved with the Brotherhood had moved up North, she wanted to know if I had heard anything.'

'And had you?'

Claudia nodded reluctantly.

'Macmillan . . . Ronnie Macmillan has seemingly got involved with some Eastern European gangsters who deal in sex trafficking.'

'Since when?' Brady asked, his mind reeling from the news.

'Fairly recently. From the intelligence I have, maybe the past two months, even three.'

'And Simone knew this?'

Claudia nodded.

'The problem was, Simone was too keen. Too eager. Had something to prove. Whether it was to her old colleagues here at Whitley Bay station or even you, I don't know. But she started doing some undercover work without my knowledge. She'd been up here on annual leave for three weeks before . . . before this happened to her. She made connections . . . connections that she didn't share with me which led to her arranging to meet with the two men that Carl, the Blue Lagoon bartender, described.'

Brady had been intending to catch up with One-Eyed Carl and find out what he'd seen. He now saw it as a priority.

'What did he say?'

Claudia shrugged.

'Not much. Just that she was stood at the bar with two guys. Well dressed, in suits, throwing their money around. He said that she looked like she was enjoying the attention.'

Brady thought back to last night when he'd seen her in the Blue Lagoon with the two men. And Carl was right, she didn't look as if she was out of her depth.

'I can only imagine that Simone was trying to sell herself as a high-class hooker who had come back home from the South and needed to re-establish her career in the North East, with the help of Ronnie Macmillan and his associates.'

Brady nodded. He hated to admit it, but it made sense. The problem was, where did they go with it?

'Have you told Gates all this?'

Claudia looked at him and shook her head.

'What do you take me for? A fool?'

'I don't know. I thought you and he were tight? More so since your new role.'

Claudia frowned at Brady.

'I'm careful, Jack. Always have been. If Gates believes I'm in his camp then fine by me. But the person I have loyalty to now . . . is myself.'

Brady knew that was intended for him. And it was intended to hurt.

'What does he know then?'

'That Simone came up here on some lead connected with the Russian girl's murder. That's it.'

Brady frowned.

'So, he doesn't know that she arranged to meet you?'

Claudia shook her head, causing some curls to fall over her face.

'No . . .' she replied.

'Why not?' questioned Brady.

'I've got too much to lose. If they think that I somehow set her up to infiltrate Ronnie Macmillan's goings-on then what do you think would happen? I'd be suspended while an internal investigation took place. If there's any suspicion that I sent her in without any backup, let alone authorisation, what do you think would happen? Christ, Jack! Ronnie Macmillan's a dangerous man. I may be career orientated but I would never sacrifice someone for my own gain. Especially another woman.'

Brady looked at her.

'Come on, Jack! You know how hard I worked to set this project up; how much I need to do it . . . Without me, it would . . .'

She didn't need to finish the sentence.

'You know what you're asking me to do, don't you?' asked Brady, taken aback.

'I know . . . but if I get suspended the cases that I'm working on would be affected,' she explained, trying to keep the desperation out of her voice. 'Jack, lives are involved here. Young girls' lives . . . it's not just about me.'

Brady sat perfectly still, thinking.

If he didn't speak up, it would be him in front of a firing squad. He'd be the one to be suspended; he could even lose his job.

But then there was Nick. Whatever was going on there was guaranteed to fuck up Brady's career anyway.

Brady thought about the message he'd received from Melissa Ryecroft's murderers.

A severed head left in a black bin liner in his car with the chilling words:

KEEP YOUR HEAD JACK OR YOU COULD BE NEXT – 'N'

Brady didn't exactly understand the meaning of the message. Apart from the obvious – that it was a threat. And he didn't know why they were targeting him. But it could easily be for the same reason that Frank Henderson had attacked him outside Simone's room – because they had found out that Simone had returned to the North East on police business connected with Brady. If Henderson had got the wrong Brady, why not them?

Brady had no proof that the two Eastern European brothers had put the note and severed head in his car. But the fact that they waited for him to leave the hospital and then followed him was evidence enough in his books. That and the fact that the note was signed with the same 'N' burnt into Simone's left breast and on the emblem of the signet ring they were both wearing.

The last thing Brady wanted was Claudia being targeted, or worse, ending up like Simone Henderson. He knew what he had to do. He had no choice and she knew it.

'Okay,' Brady conceded.

'Are you sure?' asked Claudia.

'I said so, didn't I?' replied Brady irritably.

He was angry with her. Furious that she had kept all this back from him and yet was now expecting him to take the blame.

'And you won't take any of this to Gates or Adamson?' uneasily questioned Claudia, needing to be certain.

'I said I wouldn't,' assured Brady, but his voice was hard.

'Thanks, Jack. I can't say how much I appreciate this . . .'

But it wasn't only Claudia he was protecting; he was also trying to protect his brother, Nick.

'I need you to pull everything you have on Ronnie Macmillan. Understand? I want more information on these Eastern European men he's gone into business with and I need it in the next hour or so.'

Claudia looked at him, about to shake her head and say it was an impossible task.

'Don't even try and tell me you can't do it. Because I know you can. You've got a hell of a lot of information back at your office that I don't have access to. You have informants and you have sex trafficked women that you've freed. Contact them. Interview them. Anything that leads us closer to these men, Claudia. And I mean anything.'

'Jack. Do you know how difficult that's going to be? It's a Saturday for God's sake! I've got no chance of getting all that you're asking together on my own. And, Christ, most of the women have returned to their countries of origin.'

'Ring them then,' suggested Brady.

'Do you fully understand what you're asking me to do for you?'

'Do you understand what you're asking me to do for you?' retaliated Brady, his face darkening.

He was in no mood to be messed with; and especially not by his ex-wife who was asking him to risk his career to bloody well protect her own.

Brady was under no illusions. Claudia and DCI Davidson, her new boyfriend, co headed a groundbreaking new Human Trafficking Centre in Newcastle equal to Sheffield's. It was clear that she would sacrifice Brady to keep her position, both professionally and personally.

'Why?' questioned Brady.

'Why, what?'

'Why keep my name? Brady. Is it just to piss me off? Or were you banking on there being a time like this one when you could use it to stitch me up?'

She looked away, refusing to answer him.

It was something that had been troubling him ever since

he had figured out that the Brady Simone had been talking about wasn't him.

'If you need help you can have Kenny and Daniels,' he stated, getting back to the real issue.

'Oh, you have to be kidding me. Bloody Laurel and Hardy? I don't think so!'

'Take it or leave it.'

'What about Anna Kodovesky? I'm sure she'd be more help in one hour than those two knuckleheads would be in a whole week working with me.'

Brady thought about it.

'Alright,' he conceded.

Kodovesky was good at her job and she kept her mouth shut.

Daniels and Kenny were responsible for most of the sick jokes that did the rounds at the station. Additionally, neither of them knew when to keep quiet. And in a case as delicate as this, Brady needed discretion.

'Thanks,' said Claudia.

'Yeah,' muttered Brady suddenly standing up and walking towards the door.

'Where are you going?' Claudia asked.

'Gates's office. He wants to see me,' he bluntly answered.

'Jack?' questioned Claudia, worried.

Brady walked out his office, slamming the door behind him.

Chapter Thirty-One

Brady breathed in deeply as he looked at himself in the mirror in the gents'.

He was still shaking from his run-in with his boss, DCI Gates. He had requested a meeting to supposedly get an update on the murder investigation. But it had soon become apparent that Gates was more interested in giving Brady a kicking to add to the one he had already had from Frank Henderson.

The upshot was Gates wanted a 'case management review' with Brady on Monday morning to decide what action he was going to take against him in relation to Henderson and Adamson's separate complaints. And also to discuss reassigning Conrad to Adamson.

Brady still felt winded. He and Conrad were a team. He couldn't imagine having another DS. Brady didn't work well with a partner. Everyone knew that. No one better than Gates. But somehow, he and Conrad had just managed to find a way of working together. Whether Conrad realised it or not, Brady couldn't imagine not having Conrad there. Conrad was irreplaceable.

And then there was the report that Gates had demanded by Monday. He wanted to know exactly how the murder victim's head had ended up in his car and what precisely he had been doing at St Mary's Lighthouse.

Brady bent over the washbasin and turned the cold tap on, trying to block out the image of what he had found in the black bin liner. He cupped his hands together and filled them with running water before dousing his throbbing face. It was still a mess. He didn't know how the hell he could give a press call to the public tomorrow looking as if he was the one who needed to spend a night in the cells. Another salient point made by Gates.

Brady suddenly straightened up when he heard the door open. He swung round, praying that it wasn't Adamson. Now wasn't the time to explain why Simone Henderson had mentioned to her flatmate that she was coming back up to the North East to meet with Brady. While he now knew that it had been his ex-wife Simone had been talking about, the information afforded him little consolation, given the fact he had no choice but to keep silent and accept the outcome.

'Bloody hell, bonnie lad! I've been hunting everywhere for you,' puffed Turner, out of breath.

Brady shot him a quizzical look. 'Aren't you meant to be clocking off? Your shift finished at 8pm, Charlie.'

Turner shook his scraggy head. He looked troubled. His small beady eyes barely visible beneath the sagging eyelids.

'What? What's wrong?' he asked as he walked over to his old friend.

'Just left the station and was about to get in my car and this kid came at me out of nowhere. Thrust this at me. Said it was for you and it was urgent,' he said, holding his trembling hand out.

Brady took it. It was a blank envelope but he could feel something inside.

'Where did he go?' asked Brady, trying to keep his voice level despite the rising panic.

'Disappeared before I could say anything,' answered Turner, his voice still shaky. 'Legged it down the back lane behind the station.'

'What did he look like?'

'I dunno . . . short, scrawny kid with a hoodie pulled down so I couldn't make out his face. Said he'd been paid a tenner to take it into the station but didn't have the nerve so waited for someone to come out . . .' Turner faltered and sighed as he looked at Brady.

Brady didn't say a word.

'I'm too old for this game, Jack. Too bloody old,' muttered Turner.

Brady rested a hand on his shoulder. 'Come on, Charlie. You'll still be here when I'm long gone,' he consoled.

Turner looked up at Brady, doubting his words.

It was then that Brady realised how frail and old Turner actually was without the protection of his uniform and front desk.

'Charlie . . . don't mention this to anyone. Let's keep this between us, yeah?'

Turner nodded.

Brady gripped Turner's shoulder, surprised that this kid had shaken Turner to this extent. He had been a copper for over thirty years and had dealt with more than his fair share of crime. Brady put his loss of nerve down to Simone's attack. Everyone at the station was feeling jittery. Watching their back. Nobody more so than Brady, he mused bitterly.

'He did what he was paid to do. Trust me, he's not coming back,' he reassured.

Turner's shoulders suddenly slumped forward. He raised his eyes up to meet Brady's.

'What are you involved in, Jack?' Turner asked as he nervously licked the spit from his thin lips.

He'd been in the game too long not to know that kids wearing hoodies didn't make a point of hanging around police stations waiting to hand a note over to a copper.

Brady shook his head.

'It's nothing,' he answered.

Turner sighed heavily and walked out, leaving Brady with his own troubles.

*

Brady closed his office door and automatically went over to the window and looked out. It was approaching 9pm and it was already dark. The hazy orange glow of the street lights cast shadows up and down the street.

Was he still being watched? He wasn't sure.

'Shit!' he cursed to himself, angry at his own paranoia.

But who could blame him? He had seen the irrefutable proof on the hospital grounds security tape that he had been followed. And then they had watched and waited for an opportune moment to dump the victim's head in the back of his car along with a note. A message clearly meant for him.

He walked away from the window and resignedly sat down at his desk. He steeled himself before opening the envelope. Inside was a handwritten note. Immediately, he recognised the distinctive swirling letters.

It was from Nick. It had to be.

He held his breath as he read the words:

You're losing your head Jack. You're not thinking
straight. You need to see an old friend to find out about
N. You maybe need to look at their trademark – or TM
in short.
  N

Brady held his head in his hands as he tried to steady his breathing. His heart was racing as adrenalin coursed through his veins.

Then it hit him.

The note left with the severed head wasn't from the Eastern European brothers. Or the Nietzschean Brotherhood; it was also from Nick.

It was a warning, not a death threat.

Nick was warning him not to lose his head. Which was exactly what he was starting to do. And now his brother had sent a second note, stating the obvious. It meant he was watching him. Watching his every move.

Brady remembered that the 'N' had been printed in blood in the first note – the victim's blood, taken from a signet ring. Was that Nick's way of telling him that the Nietzschean Brotherhood were involved? That this was bigger than just some sex trafficked girl washed up on Whitley Bay beach?

'What do you want from me?' whispered Brady, desperation in his voice.

But he knew Nick too well. He wasn't playing a game with him; he was trying to help him.

Brady lifted his head up and slowly breathed out as he allowed relief to flood through him.

Nick may have been embroiled in some covert, sick sex trafficking operation but he wasn't a willing part of it. He was trying his damnedest to lead Brady towards the central players.

He reread the note, forcing himself to focus.

'Trademark . . . TM . . .' he muttered, shaking his head.

Then it hit him. The only old friend Nick had in the North East was Trina McGuire.

His gut feeling had been right when he had rung Trina earlier that day. But what he hadn't realised was that she had information on 'N', which he assumed could be the Nietzschean Brotherhood that Claudia had talked about. He thought back to the 'N' burnt into Simone's breast and the 'N' on the gold signet rings worn by the two men who had been captured on the hospital surveillance footage asking about the condition of the mutilated DC.

He took out his phone and rang Trina McGuire.

He had no choice. He had to make her talk.

He listened as the phone rang for a couple of seconds and then cut off.

It was clear that Trina had no intention of talking to him.

Deciding that there was nothing else for it, he grabbed his jacket off the back of his chair and stood up. He'd have to pay her a visit.

He shoved the handwritten note in his pocket for safe-keeping.

Suddenly there was a knock at his door.

'Christ!' muttered Brady, startled.

He had to get his head together otherwise he would be no use to anyone – especially Nick.

Before he had a chance to call out the door opened and Conrad walked in.

'Thought you might need something to eat, sir? The rest of the team ordered in Chinese so I thought I'd salvage some for you before it disappeared,' explained Conrad.

It took the younger man a second to realise Brady was going somewhere. He shot him a questioning look.

'Thanks, Conrad. Just put it down on my desk. I'll get it later. There's something I need to do first, and I need your help,' answered Brady.

'Sir?'

'Get your car keys, Conrad. We're going for a drive.'

Chapter Thirty-Two

Brady waited by the station's heavy wooden double doors. He drew heavily on the cigarette he'd rolled as he uneasily looked up and down the dark street. Even though it was deserted he couldn't shake the feeling he was being watched.

Conrad pulled round the corner in his dark silver Saab.

Relieved, Brady threw his cigarette away and walked over and climbed in.

'Where to, sir?'

'Gainers Terrace, Wallsend,' answered Brady.

'Sir?' questioned Conrad, worried.

'Know it?' asked Brady.

'Not personally, sir. But I have heard enough about it to know that we won't be welcome.'

Brady didn't answer him. Instead, he distractedly glanced in the passenger wing mirror as Conrad reluctantly pulled out left past the Northern Rock bank hitting the traffic lights in the centre of Whitley Bay.

Brady looked over at the Town House pub where two scrawny men with tattooed bare arms and Toon shirts were stood outside tabbing. He watched them uneasily, realising that right now he didn't trust anyone.

He turned his head away and looked across at St Paul's Anglican Church, on the corner of the traffic lights opposite the Fat Ox. It was a beautiful church built out of slabs of sandstone, surrounded by old trees. Headstones dating back a couple of hundred years still stood, despite the decades of lashing rain coupled with the hard, biting northerly wind that would sweep in from the North Sea.

It passed Brady in a shadowy, ghostly blur as Conrad put his foot down and headed up the small incline towards the roundabout which led out of Whitley Bay.

*

'Wait here, will you, Conrad?' instructed Brady as he made a move to get out the car.

Conrad cast a glance over at the Ship Inn and the ruins and the ominous, unlit flat lands surrounding them.

'Are you sure about this, sir?' asked Conrad.

Brady could understand Conrad's reticence. He felt exactly the same way.

The Ship Inn – or the Hole, as it was known locally, for obvious reasons – stood alone against a backdrop of a shipping industry that had long gone. The house lights of the Hole cast the only bit of warmth in this black, bleak, evacuated landscape.

The place was deserted. A no-man's land. The River Tyne and docklands, once crammed with ships and twisting sky-high cranes, were empty. All that was left behind were the shadowy, iron-crusted bones of what looked to be part of a helicopter landing platform and the weather-beaten base of an oil rig.

The Hole, a solitary, run-down, whitewashed Victorian

building had been left to rack and ruin now that the ship-yard workers had evaporated to become part of the North East's ever-increasing dole figures. But it still ran a business. One that involved strippers and sex. And, despite the dubious surroundings, the punters still came. Guaranteed anonymity given the Hole's unique location. No housing estate overlooked it, no grassland for dog walkers, only the bleak river and empty warehouses and flattened wasteland that spoke of an industrial era that had been sold down the Tyne.

Brady turned and looked behind them at the dark embankment that led down to this pit of despair. Again, deserted.

He thought about Conrad's question. Was he sure about what he was doing?

He shook his head as he turned and looked at Conrad.

'No,' Brady replied. 'But I've got no choice.'

'Tell me this is connected to our investigation into Melissa Ryecroft's murder, sir,' said Conrad, needing the reassurance that whatever Brady was about to do wasn't going to bring him more trouble than he was already in.

Brady knew he needed his deputy on side. And crucially, needed him to watch his back.

'I have information that someone in there knows about this Brotherhood that Claudia discussed,' he explained as he uneasily looked over at the Hole.

'Surely you want me in there with you, then?' asked Conrad.

'No,' firmly answered Brady. He turned and looked at Conrad. 'Firstly, two coppers going in there will get us nothing but trouble. Secondly, I need you out here watching who comes and goes.'

Conrad reluctantly nodded. He knew that arguing with Brady was pointless.

'Look, Conrad . . . I know the person in there that I need to talk to, alright? And I know for a fact that she wouldn't come near me if you were there. She hates coppers. I'm not sure she'll even give me a chance . . .' Brady stopped and sighed.

He was tired. Too tired for all this. He wanted to go home and take a long hot shower, followed by a couple of glasses of the full-bodied bottle of Rioja he had in his wine rack, accompanied by some blues music playing in the background. He knew he couldn't eat though: he had lost his appetite when he had found the victim's head in his car, along with a note that he was now certain was from his brother.

All he wanted to do was forget this day had ever happened. Instead, his guts told him it was just getting started.

'Keep your eyes open, Conrad,' Brady warned before getting out the car. 'You see anything, you radio it in. Understand?'

Brady was more worried about leaving Conrad out here in the middle of nowhere in darkness with no assistance than he was about facing whatever lay ahead of him in the Hole.

He had noted, as had Conrad, the three other cars parked up. One was a flash white Range Rover Sport, another, a beaten-up blue Volvo estate, and the third, a silver 1.9 Vauxhall Vectra.

Brady hazarded a guess the owners would be inside the Hole. Given the desolate location it was the obvious conclusion. Nobody in their right mind would stray down here and if they did, they sure as hell would turn straight back up the embankment to the main road.

Brady nodded as he approached the lumbering, thick-necked, shaven-headed man in his early thirties standing outside the front door of the Hole smoking.

'It's shit! muttered the man, staring straight ahead at Conrad's car.

'Thanks for the warning,' replied Brady as he pulled open the door.

'Just trying to save you money, mate. Better coming back after eleven. That's when the good acts are on. Got in some fucking gorgeous young tight-arsed girls with big tits. Don't speak much English but who's interested in talking? Better than the old trollops that are in there just now!'

The man scowled at the silver Saab as he drew heavily on his cigarette. He then threw it on the ground and turned to go back in.

Brady held the door open for him.

'It's your money!' the man grunted by way of thanks.

Brady let the door swing shut behind them.

The large room was dark. It took him a moment for his eyes to adjust. And his sense of smell.

The place was rancid.

It stank of men. The worst kind of men.

Wankers that would come here and throw not only their money around. Forcing girls to do things that their mothers had never taught them.

The smell of stale piss, stale beer and sex – dirty, passionless, perfunctory sex – clung to the air.

Brady watched as the thick-necked critic made his way to the bar. A bartender pushed a coffee towards him.

He grunted in appreciation, sat down and picked up a

folded paper and started doing what Brady presumed was a crossword.

It was obvious that he was the club's hired muscle.

Brady looked around the place. It was virtually empty. It didn't surprise him. It was just after nine-thirty on a Saturday evening, which was early for this place.

A bleached-blonde, long-haired woman was contorting her body provocatively as she danced in a cage suspended from the ceiling. A glazed look in her eye as she smiled and moaned, head back, mouth open, at the only man watching her.

Towards the back of the room he could make out four men who were drinking and laughing while a lap dancer did what she could to earn money.

'Black coffee,' Brady ordered as the bartender raised an eyebrow at him.

The man poured Brady some scalding, stewed coffee into a white cup and saucer and brought it over to him.

Brady took out his wallet.

'On the house,' the bartender said.

Before Brady had a chance to object the man had turned and was busying himself unloading the glasses from the dishwasher.

It was clear to the barman that Brady was a copper: he wasn't a regular and he wasn't interested in watching the girl dancing provocatively on the stage to the left of the bar or the young girl with the four men.

'Trina?' Brady called over. 'Trina McGuire. Has she started work yet?'

The bartender looked at Brady.

'What's it to you?' he asked.

'She's a friend.'

The bartender gave him a sceptical look.

'That's what they all say, mate,' he replied flatly.

He gestured towards the hired muscle that Brady had met at the door to get rid of him.

Brady realised he was bad for business. A copper questioning one of their girls wouldn't look good. It would be enough to scare off punters.

'Look, I'll make this easy,' he said, holding up his hand. 'Where's her dressing room? I'll talk to her there.'

'You having a laugh or what?' replied the bartender. 'Toilets is the best they get here! Try the fucking Moulin Rouge if you want dressing rooms, pal!'

Brady quickly scanned the dark room.

'Hey! Where do you think you're going?' asked the hired muscle as he pushed his crossword away and stood up, making sure that his imposing, steroid bulk was felt.

'I need the toilet,' answered Brady.

'I don't fucking think so. You need a piss, you take one outside like the fucking rest of us! And then you can fucking clear off!'

'Sure. I'll disappear but then I'll be back here with our Narcotics Unit and before you know it this place will be shut down. And that's before we get onto the illegal trade in sex here,' Brady said as he made a point of jerking his head towards the four men who were now whooping and cheering the lap dancer.

'Fuck you and your fucking threats. This place is clean!' answered the hired muscle.

'What about the foreign workers? All legal, are they?'

Brady was well aware that, like farm labouring and other crap jobs, cheap Eastern European labour would have been brought in. The sex industry was no different.

'I don't know what the fuck you mean.'

Out of the corner of his eye, Brady watched as the bartender made a call.

All he could make out was 'Trina'. Or was that 'Trouble'?

The hired muscle, no doubt paid the minimum wage to keep trouble out, made a point of readying his fists. Brady caught sight of the classic, fading bluish-black-ink tattoos of 'Love' and 'Hate' across the knuckles of each of his large hands.

'Look, I'm not here to cause trouble. Alright? I need to talk to Trina. So back off, mate,' Brady said as the hired muscle started to loom in close. Too close.

A second later and Brady heard her voice. Despite the lurid music playing in the background, Brady would recognise her voice anywhere.

A sense of relief flooded through his body. This was a place where he'd be lucky to get out alive if things turned nasty. His beaten-up body would be taken out the back. Shoved into the boot of a car and unceremoniously dumped with a bullet through his head into the cold, murky grey waters of the Tyne.

'What the hell are you doing here, eh? Looking for sexual favours like your pal, Adamson, are you?' scornfully demanded Trina McGuire as she strutted over in implausibly high killer heels.

Her scorn for DI Adamson came as no surprise. Brady had heard talk that Adamson liked to exert his status as a copper over women like Trina McGuire.

She shot Brady a look that told him he'd over-stepped the mark coming into her place of work.

'Davy man, fucking put your fists down, will you?' Trina ordered as she shook her head at the hired muscle. 'You'll

245

get Ronnie pissed off if he hears you knocked out a copper. And a mate of Adamson's at that!'

Trina's threat worked.

Davy sulkily skulked off back to his *Sun* crossword puzzle.

Brady couldn't blame him.

Trina might have only been five foot four and six stone if that, but she was dangerous. And she had one hell of a temper. Brady had been witness to it once too often when she'd come from work to pick up her street-hardened son from the holding cells at the station.

For such a petite woman she had an amazing power to reduce a grown man to tears. Which effectively is what she used to do to her foul-mouthed, 'couldn't give a fuck' son, Shane McGuire. Shane, a regular at the station, was a hard nut. He'd even landed a blow on Brady once when he'd been arresting the scrawny, sneering juvenile who had been high as a kite on amphetamines and had fought Brady and Conrad with superhuman strength due to the effect of the drug coursing through his cold, sweating body.

Trina McGuire caught Brady's eye. It was evident that she was unimpressed that he was there. She had the same sneer on her face that her son wore. She threw back her long glossy blonde hair as she scowled at him.

This was Nick's ex-girlfriend. And half of North Tyneside's if the local rumours were to be believed. Trina had never forgiven Brady for Nick clearing off to London. But given what had been kicking off in the Ridges at the time of Nick's youth, Brady had been relieved to see him go and not arrested, condemned to a life in and out of prison like his mates.

Brady had always had a thing for Trina. When she was

younger that was – not the woman she had become. Social determinism at its worst, he thought sadly.

She'd been a real beauty then. Like Brady, Nick and Madley, Trina had grown up in the ugly harshness of the Ridges; a run-down housing estate which was a no-go area for police and non-residents. Infamous for the riots in 1991 when community buildings had been burnt to the ground and shops looted in protest at the deaths of two local youths killed while driving a stolen car pursued by police. Suggestions by the boys' friends that the police had forced the vehicle off the road triggered the spark that saw the riots go up against a prolific background of social deprivation and crippling poverty. Riot police and the fire services had gone in, backed up by the police helicopter, only to be pelted by stones as a stronghold of at least 400 people held together as a community, fighting the shit lives they'd been dealt through the reign of middle- and upper-class terror meted out by Thatcher and her henchmen.

Brady looked at Trina McGuire. She had lost that delicate, remarkable beauty that had so set her apart in the Ridges. But years later, she epitomised everything about the sorry place. She might have still had that 'heroin chic' beauty about her, but even with the heavy black eyeliner and mascara, it was fading fast. A poverty-stricken, desperate junkie, who didn't have a hope in hell of getting out.

'You're bloody lucky your brother's not still around, Jack,' Trina warned him.

'That's the point,' replied Brady softly. 'He's back.'

'I told you, I've got nothing to say,' hissed Trina, not wanting to bring attention to herself.

'Look, the last place I want to be is here on a Saturday

night hassling you, alright? But Nick told me to come,' explained Brady.

'You having a laugh or what?' she scornfully replied.

Brady shook his head. The look on his face deadly serious.

'How do I know you're not lying then?' she cynically questioned.

Brady reluctantly took the note out from his inside jacket pocket and handed it to her.

Brady knew she instantly recognised the handwriting from the look on her face.

She quickly composed herself and handed the note back.

'I've got no idea what you're talking about,' she said. But her eyes betrayed her. She looked scared . . . very scared.

Brady replaced the note in his pocket and tried not to let his imagination run away with him. He had never seen Trina McGuire fazed, let alone scared. Clearly, she knew something about Nick and realised that he must be in deep trouble to have sent Brady here.

He suddenly caught sight of the bartender out of the corner of his eye. He was on the phone again. Observing Brady and talking quietly.

Too quietly for Brady's liking.

The name 'Ronnie' had rung alarm bells.

How many Ronnies were there in Wallsend who had a hand in the sex industry?

Only one, thought Brady. It could only be Ronnie Macmillan.

Brady turned his attention back to Trina McGuire who had obviously carefully considered the contents of the note. She didn't look too happy with the situation.

'Right, you . . . five minutes, but it'll cost you!' she ordered, hand stretched out.

Brady knew her well enough to know that it was an act to cover herself.

'Take it out your expenses! I have a job to do and bills to pay. But you pull any stunts like that sick bastard Adamson and I'll make sure Davy takes care of you good and proper like!'

Brady knew from Dr Amelia Jenkins that DCI Gates' 'golden boy' Adamson had allegedly compromised his status as a copper on an earlier investigation by attempting to force Trina McGuire to perform a sexual act on him. He had threatened to bring her in for questioning if she didn't follow through with his demands. Amelia, who had been assigned the same investigation, had walked in and found Adamson in a compromising position with Trina McGuire pinned against the wall. Since Adamson had been thwarted before his demands had been met, Amelia hadn't reported the incident. She had confided in Brady, unsure of what to do about what she had witnessed. But Brady had heard enough rumours about Adamson not to have been surprised by Amelia's disclosure.

Brady had heard nothing more about it, and had assumed that Amelia had decided to keep quiet, ultimately realising that corruption in a male-dominated force, aligned with deep-rooted sexism, was a powerful institution to single-handedly fight. He also knew that Trina would not have substantiated Amelia's story. Trina McGuire had her own way of getting even with creeps like Adamson; ones that didn't involve the police.

'I'm nothing like Adamson. You of all people should know that!' Brady replied sharply.

Trina looked at him.

'You're a copper aren't you? All the same as far as I'm concerned,' she scornfully replied.

Brady didn't bother retaliating. In her eyes he was a traitor; always would be.

He watched as she nervously glanced over at the bartender. He was obviously the look-out guy. Watching all the comings and goings. Anything odd, or not quite right got reported to the boss who was no doubt sitting upstairs in his office wanking over porn. Or his bank statement. Same difference, thought Brady.

'Yeah, yeah. I'm good for it,' Brady said as he took out his wallet.

He handed over three £20 notes.

She snatched them, counted and gestured for more.

He gave her two more.

'I expect some private time for that,' Brady said.

'Like I said, five minutes,' repeated Trina.

She then looked at the bartender who had just finished with the call.

'Bacardi and Coke. Make it a double and he's paying,' Trina said as she gestured at Brady.

Trina's eyes darted over towards the bottom booth. Three of the men were now clapping and shouting at something the lap dancer was doing to their friend.

'And one for Nicoletta. She'll need it after they're through with her,' Trina commented ruefully.

Brady was about to object but decided to keep quiet; he was just relieved that Trina hadn't had him thrown out.

'Twenty quid,' said the bartender placing both drinks down on the bar.

'*How* much?' queried Brady sceptically.

'You heard. Twenty quid or I call security.'

'Yeah, yeah,' answered Brady as Davy, the hired muscle shot him a look. He threw a twenty onto the bar. 'Keep the change,' he muttered as he picked up the drinks and walked over to the booth where Trina had sat down.

'Five minutes, starting now,' Trina said taking her drink.

'Nick,' Brady began. 'He's back.'

'So?'

'I can't get hold of him,' Brady answered. 'And for some reason he's pointed me to you.'

She didn't reply.

'Listen, Trina, this is serious. Alright? It's not a game!' Brady hissed at her, keeping his voice low.

She made a point of casually checking out her long, polished nails.

'Look . . . I don't know if you've heard but we've got a copper critically ill in hospital and a sixteen-year-old girl is lying sadistically murdered in the morgue.'

'What's that got to do with me?'

'Everything. Because I reckon Nick's been to see you.'

Trina visibly flinched, losing the hard edge that she needed to survive in the underworld she inhabited.

'For Christ's sake, Trina, he's in trouble! Understand? It's his brother you're talking to now, not a copper. And by the end of today I reckon I'll be out of a job anyway.'

She took a long, slow drink as she deliberated whether to talk.

'Come on, Trina! Do you think I want to be here? You read the note. You know as well as I do that he wrote it. I need to know what it means,' insisted Brady, trying, but failing to keep the desperation out of his voice.

'Alright,' she whispered. 'I honestly don't know what's

going on, Jack. Okay? All I know is he turned up here yesterday looking for a girl.'

'*Nick* did?' questioned Brady, stunned.

'Yeah . . . but not the way you're thinking,' she said correcting him. 'One of their girls had gone missing and they wanted her found.'

'Who's they?' demanded Brady.

'The men he works for . . . two brothers named Dabkunas. Marijuis and Mykolas . . .' Trina paused as she looked around nervously.

'How do you know their names?' Brady questioned as he realised that the initials on Melissa Ryecroft's body now made sense.

If Melissa Ryecroft had been taken by these men and branded then 'MD' would stand for Marijuis and Mykolas Dabkunas. And Marijuis was the name of her Eastern European boyfriend.

It all made sense now.

'How the hell do you think?' lowly hissed Trina as she shot Brady a hard look.

She was clearly pissed off and Brady couldn't figure it out.

'Nick!'

'What's he done, Trina? What the fuck has Nick done?'

If there was one person who was always in Nick's camp, that was Trina. Even when he dumped her to start a fresh life in London, she wouldn't have a word said against him.

Brady had always wondered about Trina's allegiance to Nick. And vice-versa. He knew that if Nick ever came up to the North East, he always made a point of visiting her. He had often wondered what the connection was between them.

'Nick's working for them, isn't he? These men are evil, Jack. You have no idea. I wouldn't even spit on them. They're bringing girls like Nicoletta into the country and taking their passports from them and forcing them to work.'

'What? Sex?'

'Fuck me! You're quick!' she replied, her voice thick with scorn.

She looked at Brady and shook her head.

Brady was certain he could see tears welling up in her eyes.

'Anyway, Nick's caught up with them. I don't know why . . . it's not like him, you know?'

Brady knew alright.

'What's he working as?' he asked.

But he already knew the answer. He just needed it confirming.

'He's working as their driver and bodyguard,' Trina muttered reluctantly.

She looked at him. Her eyes filled with fear.

'Jack? You've got to stop him,' Trina begged. 'Talk to him. Make him see what kind of men he's working for.'

'That's why I'm here. I knew he was caught up in some real bad shit.'

'He's not just involved with the Dabkunas brothers though. It's bigger than that. Much bigger . . .'

'What do you mean? Who else is involved?'

'Nick said . . . he said he was working for a very powerful man . . . an ambassador . . .'

Brady raised his eyebrows. 'Come on, Trina. This is bloody Wallsend, not London!'

'You think I don't know that? Makes no difference though . . . The Dabkunas brothers are just part of a chain of command, Jack. From what Nick said, he answers directly to an ambassador . . . the Lithuanian Ambassador. As do the Dabkunas brothers.'

Brady stared at her. He couldn't believe what he was hearing.

He suddenly remembered that Gates had mentioned that he was attending some fancy presentation talk at the Civic Centre tomorrow afternoon. The main speaker was the Lithuanian Ambassador, up on business from London.

But what business?

'I'm scared, Jack. From what I've heard these brothers own their girls and if they don't do as they're told, then they get punished. They'd have no qualms about putting a bullet in Nick . . . or worse.'

Brady tried not to focus on what the Dabkunas brothers would do to Nick.

'What do they do to their girls? How do they punish them?' Brady asked, thinking of how Melissa Ryecroft had been murdered.

'Ask Nicoletta,' Trina said, her eyes on the booth in the corner. 'Looks like she's finished.'

Brady turned and watched as she walked towards them. With each step she was trying to rebuild the self-esteem and self-worth that the four businessmen had stripped bare.

'It'll cost you though,' warned Trina. 'Same amount.'

'Fuck me!' muttered Brady as he took his wallet out.

'Cost you double if we were to do that,' Trina said with a wry smile.

Brady ignored her and counted out the money.

'No?' she questioned with mock surprise, enjoying his embarrassment.

'No,' replied Brady, as he handed the cash over.

Luckily he had had £250 on him. He'd been to the cash-point yesterday and had withdrawn £300; part of which he'd spent that night. And seemingly the rest was going on expenses today. He knew she was fleecing him. But he had no choice but to pay.

Nicoletta quietly watched the transaction before sitting down.

Trina pushed the drink Brady had bought in front of her.

'He wants to know about the Dabkunas brothers,' Trina said.

'Know nothing,' Nicoletta replied in an Eastern European accent.

Brady looked at her. She was young, pretty and very, very scared. He hazarded a guess that she was about eighteen, nineteen, if that.

'It's okay,' Trina said, taking her hand. 'He's a friend of mine, Nicoletta. Nothing's going to happen.'

Brady saw her discreetly press some of the notes he'd just handed over into Nicoletta's hand. Trina then tightly squeezed it.

Nicoletta looked at Trina. Her big brown eyes wide with terror.

'No . . . they do . . .' she mumbled, shaking her head.

'Trust me. He can help you, I promise,' reassured Trina.

Brady watched Trina, surprised by her gentleness.

Nicoletta nodded. But it was clear she wasn't convinced.

'Where are you from?' Brady asked her.

She shot Trina a nervous look. Trina nodded for her to continue.

The girl gestured towards the ceiling and he realised that she must live in the apartment above the club.

'I work . . . sleep . . . work . . .' she answered, shrugging.

'Do you live with anyone else upstairs?' asked Brady.

'Ronnie Macmillan, that's who,' angrily interrupted Trina.

'What?'

'Yeah . . . He owns this place and half of Wallsend by all accounts,' answered Trina. 'And he owns Nicoletta. Bought her from the Dabkunas brothers.'

'Why did they sell you?' Brady asked, curious.

'I gift,' Nicoletta quietly explained.

'A gift?' Brady asked, incredulous.

She nodded, making her long light brown hair fall into her face.

'Why? Why would they make you a gift?'

'Business . . . I . . .' She shrugged, turning to Trina for help.

'Macmillan took a liking to her and they handed her over to seal whatever deal it is they have going on,' explained Trina.

Nicoletta nodded.

'Why don't you go home?' asked Brady. 'Back to your country?'

She looked at Brady, incredulous.

'How?' she questioned, an edge of anger to her voice. 'No nothing . . . no money . . . nothing. They take . . . take everything,' she said resignedly.

Brady thought of Claudia and her team.

'I know people who can get you out of here. Who can get you back home,' Brady offered.

'They kill me,' she coldly stated. 'They cut sister's hands and feet off . . . if . . . if . . .'

She dropped her eyes and played with the ice in her glass as she thought about her options.

'I no go . . .' she said with a tone of finality.

Brady didn't like what he was hearing. Didn't like what he saw – the bruising on her bare arms, on her shoulders and, he noticed, in the centre of her bare back, as if she'd been kicked. He also noted the recent purplish discolouring on her right cheek.

But what startled him more than anything was her eyes. They were cold. She had given up hope. She was living a nightmarish existence. Pimped by Macmillan but also expected to service him after she'd finished in the club. And if he felt pissed off, he kicked her around as if she were a dog.

Every part of Brady's body screamed at him to just grab her and take her out of the place. Get into Conrad's car and drive. Drive her as far away as possible from Ronnie Macmillan and his club. But he knew that wasn't the answer. It was simple; she wouldn't come without a fight. And that would result in getting them both killed. Fear was her captor. Fear that the men who had taken her would stop at nothing to hurt her. And if they couldn't get her, then the next best thing would be her family back home.

The only way he could convince her that no harm would come to her or those she loved was by stopping these men once and for all.

'Nicoletta?'

She looked at him. Her eyes distrustful. He was a man after all. Why should she trust him? As far as she was concerned, he was no doubt out to use her just as much as the other men in her life.

'Have you been branded?' Brady asked, not wanting to, but he had no choice. He needed to know.

Nicoletta looked from him to Trina, confused.

'Show him your back. The bottom of your back,' instructed Trina.

Nicoletta did as she was told. She turned in the seat so he could see the bottom of her back.

Brady noted that she had the identical 'MD' initials positioned below a scorpion.

This was much bigger than even he had imagined.

'Do you know where they are? Where they stay? The brothers who did this to you?' Brady questioned.

He looked from Nicoletta to Trina.

Trina shook her head, as did Nicoletta.

'No . . . we watched . . . we . . .' Nicoletta looked to the older woman for help as she gestured towards her eyes. 'When move us.'

'They blindfold you?'

She nodded at him.

Brady inwardly sighed. He knew it wouldn't be that easy.

'How do they transport you?'

'Van,' she answered simply.

'Can you tell me anything about it?'

She shook her head.

'I've seen it . . .' interrupted Trina.

She edged forward towards Brady, looking around first to make sure no one could overhear her.

'It's a black Mercedes they drive. That's what Nick was driving yesterday. I was having a tab out the back and it was parked up.'

Brady realised that Nicoletta was crying. Silent, restrained tears.

'What is it, Nicoletta?' asked Brady gently. 'What are you not telling me?'

She looked at him, scared.

'Go on,' prompted Trina. 'Tell him. Tell him about your friend, Edita.'

'We friends. She Lithuanian like me,' Nicoletta said, her eyes downcast as she stared at her untouched drink.

'Her name? What's her full name?'

'Edita . . . Edita Aginatas . . .'

'What happened to her?' asked Brady recognising the name as that of the missing girl from Claudia's briefing.

Nicoletta shook her head. She couldn't speak.

Trina squeezed her hand tightly and nodded at her.

'She's disappeared, Jack . . . . That's what they do. They punish them if they try to escape. She has a six-month-old baby back home in . . .' She paused and looked at Nicoletta.

'Raseiniai,' Nicoletta whispered as tears slid down her face.

'Her mother looked after her baby so she could come to England to work. To send money back home.'

'No money . . . we no money send home,' corrected Nicoletta.

'Who took Edita, Nicoletta?' asked Brady.

'Dabkunas brothers. Marijuis Dabkunas . . . He Edita's . . .' She turned to Trina to help her explain.

'Marijuis was her boyfriend. Convinced Edita to come here. Turns out he was only out to pimp her. She tried to escape, to get back to her baby. From what I know she tried to persuade a punter from the club Edita and Nicoletta worked in before here to help get her out.'

Brady turned from Trina to Nicoletta and watched as tears continued down her pale, haunted face. Trina's words cutting her to the core.

He felt sick enough as it was without needing to hear any more. He knew it could only get worse.

'What happened to her, Nicoletta?' he prompted.

But she shook her head.

He turned to the other woman. 'Trina?'

'She got a package a few days ago from home. A punishment for talking to a punter and a warning of what could happen if she did it again,' explained Trina.

'What? What was in the package?' asked Brady looking at Nicoletta.

She anxiously chewed her lip as she thought about it.

'Baby. Photograph.'

Brady frowned. 'I don't understand.'

Trina cut in. 'Marijuis Dabkunas is in the photograph holding Edita's baby with his arm around her eleven year old sister.'

Brady shook his head. It didn't make sense.

'He has her baby and sister?' asked Brady.

'She doesn't know . . . nobody knows. Come on, Jack . . . You're the bloody copper! That's why she tried to get away. To get a chance to contact her mother, somehow to warn her not to trust Marijuis. That they had to leave and go someplace where he couldn't find them. But they found her before she managed to call them . . .'

'If this Marijuis hasn't already taken them,' Brady quietly pointed out.

Trina looked at Brady.

'I know . . . and now it's all gone horribly wrong.'

Nobody said anything. 'What happened to Edita?' Brady questioned, breaking the heavy silence.

'You tell us,' Trina replied.

'Only you can tell me that,' answered Brady.

'She just disappeared . . . Who do you think Nick was looking for? Edita!'

'Was she here, Nicoletta? Was she hiding here?' Brady asked.

The girl nodded, surprised that he had guessed.

Brady understood now why Nick would have turned up here looking for her.

'What happened to her then?'

Nicoletta remained silent, refusing to look at him.

'Trina? What happened to her? What did they do with Edita?' demanded Brady, turning to her.

Trina looked at Nicoletta.

'Tell him,' she insisted.

'She no stay . . . she flat . . . with others. Come here work. Dabkunas bring her. Wanted escape . . . warn family . . . I . . . help . . . I hide her,' she reluctantly told him, pointing to the back of the club.

Brady looked confused.

'I don't understand. Where?'

'There's a cellar downstairs, Jack. For the beer barrels. That's where Edita hid waiting for an opportunity to get out but they found her last night . . . and took her,' explained Trina.

Brady nodded at Trina, grateful that she was prepared to take the risk of telling him.

'Nicoletta?' he said gently.

'Dabkunas brothers . . . man . . . took Edita.'

'What did the other man look like?' asked Brady. 'Can you remember?'

Trina shot Brady a look but he ignored her.

'What did he look like?' he repeated.

Nicoletta shrugged.

'Scar . . . here,' she said pointing to her cheek.

Brady didn't say anything. But inside he felt sick.

He glanced across at Trina but she had her eyes cast down, refusing to look at him. They both knew it was Nick. There was no question that he was the driver of the van.

'What? What did they do?' he forced himself to ask.

'They . . . they . . . in van. Edita . . . took me. I . . . see cut fingers off . . .' She paused, unable to continue as she looked down at her own fingers.

'Who? Who did that to her?' Brady asked.

'Marijuis and Mykolas Dabkunas.'

'What about the man with the scar?' asked Brady trying to keep the desperation out of his voice. 'What did he do?'

'He not see. In front. Drive,' answered Nicoletta, not understanding the full implication of her answer for Brady.

'Did he know?'

Nicoletta frowned unsure of the question and then shook her head as tears uncontrollably slid down her face.

'Music . . . loud . . . in back . . .'

Brady nodded, in some small way relieved.

'They bring back me . . . Edita keep . . . but . . .' She suddenly hid her hands as she recalled what had happened to her friend.

Brady resisted the urge to reach out and try and comfort her, realising that words were futile.

He sat back and waited. As he did he couldn't help noticing that the bartender appeared too interested in what they were discussing.

Brady leaned forward, realising he was running out of time.

'These brothers, the Dabkunas brothers, were they wearing gold signet rings with the letter "N" on them?'

She looked at him, surprised that he knew.

In that one look he realised he had crossed the line. Asked one too many questions.

Her eyes were filled with horror.

'How? How know?' she whispered, her voice barely audible.

Brady realised that she was scared. Not of them, but of him. She feared that she had been tricked into talking and that he was one of them.

She suddenly stood up, knocking her drink over as she did.

'Nicoletta?' Brady said softly, as if talking to a frightened child.

For that's all she was, some eighteen or nineteen-year-old child, afraid and emaciated through lack of food. Still scared of the bogeyman. But in her case the bogeyman was real. He had come one night and taken her. Delivering her into a nightmarish hell.

'No . . . no!' she cried out, backing away.

Brady grabbed hold of her arm, trying to make her sit down and listen.

'Nicoletta, I can help you . . . please.'

'No . . .' she cried out, wild-eyed. 'You . . . you?'

'No, Nicoletta,' assured Brady, realising that the situation was getting out of control. 'Listen to me, what happened to your friend won't happen to you. I promise you. I can help get you out of here,' he pleaded.

He attempted to reach out. Calm her down.

But she backed even further away from him.

'What the fuck's going on here, eh pet?' snarled a male voice. 'Swapping fucking life stories, are we?'

Caught unaware, Brady looked up.

In that split second, Nicoletta legged it. As far away from him as possible.

Then suddenly the club's hired muscle, Davy, was in the frame. The bartender was standing behind him.

'Come on, lads . . . we're just having a friendly drink. Nothing to get hot and bothered about,' replied Brady.

But he didn't have a chance to say another word.

In one swift action Davy dragged him out of the booth to his feet. Brady might have been 6'2" but Davy was easily 6'7".

'Get out!' ordered Davy close to Brady's face.

Too close.

Brady could smell the sour stench of tobacco and coffee, coupled with the beer and curry he'd gorged on the night before Friday night traditionally being beer and curry night for the hardcore locals.

'If I see your fucking ugly mug back in here again, those cuts and bruises on your face will be nothing compared to the pasting I'll give you!'

'Davy man!' interrupted Trina. 'Will ye hadaway and shite! Bloody bloke's going now. Alright. No harm done like!'

'Ronnie wants to know what you three have been fucking chatting about,' Davy the bouncer fired back.

Trina shot the bartender a dangerous look. He'd fucked her over. And there was one thing that Trina McGuire took exception to, and that was betrayal.

The bartender ignored her, making it quite clear he didn't give a shit. His loyalty was with his boss, Ronnie Macmillan and not some has-been lap dancer-cum-prostitute.

'Talking about his copper mate Adamson,' snapped Trina. 'Alright? Wanker's trying to close us down. He's doing undercover work. That's why he's in here every other day. Or were you too dumb to realise that?'

Brady tried hard not to react.

The thought of Adamson turning up at the strip club straight into Davy's 'Love/Hate' fists quite appealed to him. It definitely wouldn't be the kind of hand action that Adamson would be expecting.

'Now let him go, will ye?' Trina demanded.

Davy did as he was told while the bartender walked back to behind the bar.

'You, out!' Trina then ordered as she stared at Brady.

'I'm going . . . I'm going, alright?' Brady said, putting his hands up to show there was no resistance.

'Too right you are! Turning up here causing trouble for me and my mate!' shouted Trina.

Brady was sure it was more for the benefit of Davy and the bartender than for him.

He walked to the door and left before Davy had second thoughts.

'And don't come back!' Trina shouted after him.

He turned to look at Trina as she stood in the open doorway and spoke quickly and quietly. 'Listen, if Nick gets in touch with you, let me know. You've got my number. Give it to Nicoletta and let her know that I can help her get away from this. There's a woman called Claudia who works with sex trafficked girls. She could get her into a safe-house. Yeah?'

'Fuck off, will you?' Trina shouted.

'You're better than this.'

'Save it, Jack,' she replied bitterly. 'We both know you don't mean it.'

Brady shook his head as he looked at her.

'And you tell that little shit Adamson that he's going to get his soon enough!'

'Do you want me to do something about him?' asked Brady.

'What?' sneered Trina. 'You're going to investigate one of your own for beating up girls from a strip club and forcing us to perform sexual acts on him for free? He thinks he can haul us in because of what we do for a living. Don't think your lot would be interested, do you, Jack? We're seen as no better than shit on your shoes! Whose word would they believe? A detective inspector or a lap dancer-cum-prossie?'

Brady didn't answer her. She was right. Unless he had strong evidence that Adamson was abusing his power as a copper then he couldn't do anything about it. Simply put, he was a copper who liked to exert his power – especially when it came to women.

'Anyway, once Davy's finished with him, the wanker won't be able to wipe his own arse again!' Trina stated.

'I mean it, Trina, you're too good for this . . .'

'Yeah? Tell my landlord that!' Trina snapped.

If Brady wasn't mistaken there were tears in her eyes.

Before he could say another word she angrily spun around and walked back into the club.

Helpless, Brady watched her disappear.

Brady made his way out to the Saab. Conrad had already turned the car around ready to head towards the embankment. As he walked towards the car his mind was reeling with thoughts of how he could get Nicoletta away from Ronnie Macmillan and the hell she was living in.

He got in the car as Conrad thrust it into gear. It was pulling away before he'd even had a chance to shut the passenger door.

Brady turned and looked back at the club. There was a reason why Conrad was so eager to get moving.

Two well-dressed, dark-haired men were now standing by the front door. They looked sharp. Expensive suits, well groomed. But trouble none the less.

As Conrad drove off towards the embankment Brady realised that there was something worryingly familiar about them.

'Conrad, turn the car round!'

'Sir?'

'Turn the car around!'

The tyres squealed as Conrad slammed on the brakes and threw the car into a three-point turn.

'Shit!' cursed Brady.

The men had gone.

'Who were they?' asked Conrad.

'They were the men with Simone last night in Madley's nightclub. I saw them . . .' Brady explained without thinking.

Conrad looked at him, surprised.

'Sir?'

'I was there. I walked into the Blue Lagoon for a drink after the Fat Ox. That's all, and there she was, stood drinking with them at the bar.'

'What did you do?' questioned Conrad.

'What do you think?'

Conrad shook his head.

'I walked out . . . I walked out and left her there. With them. The two suits who were stood there just now watching us,' Brady said. 'Wait here,' he instructed as he got out the car. 'And call back-up if I don't come back out in five minutes.'

Without waiting for a response he slammed the door and crossed the road over to the club.

Before he got to the door it was thrown open.

Davy the hired muscle was in his face.

'Fuck off, pal,' shouted the bouncer as he shoved Brady in the chest.

Brady pushed back hard, throwing him against the door. 'Where are they?' he bellowed. 'Where the hell are they?'

'Don't fucking push me, pal. Or you'll lose that pretty face of yours!' Davy threatened.

'The two men. The suits. Where are they?' repeated Brady as he tried to force his way past him.

'I mean it, pal, fuck off if you know what's good for you!' snarled the hired muscle.

Before Brady had a chance the bouncer aggressively pushed Brady backwards, forcing him out the way of the door.

Brady stumbled, losing his balance.

It gave Davy enough time to disappear inside.

Brady lunged for the door, but he was too late. It was locked.

He stood outside, pounding on the door. It was useless. He'd have to come back with back-up and a warrant to search the premises. But by then it would be too late. His other option was to sit and wait for them to leave.

He walked back to the Saab.

'Did you get a look at them?' asked Brady as he climbed in.

'No sir,' replied Conrad. 'I vaguely saw two well-dressed young men in suits, but that was it. It was too dark to make anything else out. Did you, sir?'

Defeated, Brady shook his head. That was all he had seen himself. It wasn't enough to put together a photofit. He was certain about that.

And he was certain that they weren't the Dabkunas

brothers, the ones caught on the hospital surveillance cameras. These boys weren't Eastern European – they looked more like locals.

'What do we do now, sir?' questioned Conrad.

Before he had a chance to answer he heard a crunch of gravel as a low-slung, sleek black Jaguar glided past them, headlights off. Brady realised the car had quietly made its way from behind the lane that led round to the rear of the club. It drove straight past Conrad's Saab heading for the only way out: the embankment.

Brady was certain that the shadowy figures in the front were the two suits who had been watching him and Conrad. In the back were two more figures: one a petite, long-haired female and the other a taller, bulky shadow, presumably male. Brady panicked; he was sure it was Nicoletta in the back.

Brady caught the shadowy outline of the other face. It looked like Ronnie Macmillan. But he couldn't be sure. He couldn't be fucking sure. It was too dark.

'*Shit!*' he cursed.

Before Brady had a chance to instruct Conrad to go after them his deputy was already swinging the car around. But before he managed to turn, two cars sped out from the lane behind the club and blocked him in.

'*Turn the car!*' yelled Brady.

'I can't, sir,' replied Conrad through gritted teeth. 'I can't move.'

Brady turned round to see if he could make out the licence plate. But they were gone. Disappeared up the embankment. They had two routes, either turning right onto Buddle Street which would take them to North Shields, or Neptune Road which was the back route leading to Newcastle.

'Conrad, knock those cars out of the way before I do some real damage!'

'I can't sir,' answered Conrad. 'We're completely blocked in.'

'Then get out the car and get them to move! Just do something! And call that Jag in. They're holding a girl against her will,' shouted Brady, realising it was no doubt futile as there were only two routes out of the place, one to town and one to the coast. Add in the obvious – that he had no details on the car, or even the occupants.

Realising he had no other option he got out the car, leaving the door wide open.

He legged it across the road towards the embankment, ignoring the painful spasms in his thigh and the burning in his ribs.

The unlit Jag had gone. And he had no idea which route it had taken. And it was too dark to see the licence plate.

His stomach twisted as he stood there with the realisation that something was about to happen to Nicoletta. Something bad.

If they thought she'd talked to a copper, then she was done for; once and for all.

He watched as the two cars that had blocked them in now sped up the embankment, one disappearing right, the other left towards Newcastle.

He took out his BlackBerry. Hand shaking, he somehow found Trina McGuire's number and pressed call.

'Trina?' Brady said when she answered.

She didn't reply.

'Trina, they've got Nicoletta. They've driven off with her. I reckon it was Ronnie Macmillan in the back with her and his two suits were in the front of the car.'

Again, Trina said nothing.

'Where, Trina? Where would he take her?' Brady asked, desperate.

'Don't you understand?' Trina hissed. 'I've done this to her. I told her she'd be safe talking to you.'

'Trina . . . I had no idea that she would react like that . . .' answered Brady.

'What did you expect with all those questions? Eh? You just kept pushing her!'

Brady didn't reply. He couldn't. He'd known he'd blown it when he asked her about the signet ring.

'Fuck you and your job!' hissed Trina in response to his silence.

'Give me Nicoletta's surname. Please, Trina! So I can try and get some details on her.'

He listened, desperate, but the line clicked off.

Chapter Thirty-Three

'Claudia?' Brady said.

Conrad turned expectantly to Brady. He was as anxious as Brady to get some news on the Jag and the missing girl.

After Brady had talked to Trina McGuire he'd immediately called Claudia. But all he'd got was her voicemail. He didn't know what else he had expected. It was after 10:40 on a Saturday night when he tried contacting her. He was surprised that she had rung him back given the fact it was nearly midnight.

Conrad, who was as demoralised and exhausted as Brady, was now driving them back to the station. They'd been on a frantic goose chase for the past hour trying to locate the whereabouts of the black Jag. But the car had simply disappeared.

Conrad had immediately radioed details of the car in as instructed. But none of the other patrol cars in Newcastle or North Tyneside had located its whereabouts. Even the police helicopter had been issued with details of the Jag and the direction it had been heading. But again, nothing.

It was Conrad who had persuaded Brady that it was

time to call it a day. And Brady was forced to agree that the search was now futile. They had gone – taking Nicoletta with them.

'You got my message about the girl, Nicoletta? Does her description match anything on your records?'

'I'm sorry, Jack,' Claudia said. 'But no. Didn't you get a surname? That might have made a difference.'

'No . . . I didn't get one,' answered Brady as he despondently shook his head at Conrad to let him know Claudia had nothing.

'Pity . . .' replied Claudia. 'They'll no doubt move her somewhere else.'

'Tell me something I don't know!'

'What I did do when I got your voice message was check out the veracity of Nicoletta's story about Edita Aginatas having a baby.'

'And?' questioned Brady.

'It seems that Nicoletta was right. We've verified Edita Aginatas' identity. Same girl that the punter from the West End described. And she does have a six-month-old baby girl living with her mother and younger sister in a village in Lithuania.'

'Christ!' muttered Brady.

Claudia picked up the worry in his voice.

'Jack?'

'Are they alright?' quickly questioned Brady.

'Yes, the police there have moved them to a safe house for protection.'

'Have they had any contact from her in the past twenty-four hours?'

'No . . . they haven't heard from her since she landed at Heathrow four months ago.'

273

'What about her so-called boyfriend, Marijuis Dabkunas?'

'He paid them a visit a few weeks ago. Claimed he was looking for Edita. That she'd left him and taken off somewhere.'

'Very clever!' muttered Brady. 'Do they have any contact details for this Marijuis Dabkunas?'

'No . . . nothing. I wish I could tell you more, but—'

'But nothing . . . We have nothing. All we have is two missing Lithuanian girls, one whose identity we can verify. As for Nicoletta . . .' His voice faltered.

'Jack? Why are you taking all this so personally?'

'Because I'm responsible for whatever they're doing to Nicoletta right now! She was seen talking to a copper for Christ's sake! Who knows what kind of sadistic punishment they're meting out and there's nothing I can do about it because I have no idea where they've taken her.'

'Don't you think you're jumping the gun here?' Claudia pointed out.

'Have you forgotten what happened to Simone?' demanded Brady.

He closed his eyes, blocking out the blur of the bright headlights as Conrad drove them back to the station.

He felt as if he was going to be sick. He couldn't let go of the image of Nicoletta's face when she described the brothers cutting off Edita's fingers. And there was Simone lying in Rake Lane Hospital, mutilated and left . . . He couldn't bring himself to think about what the future held for her now.

'What has Simone Henderson's attack got to do with this girl, Nicoletta, Jack?'

He breathed in deeply.

'Those two suits,' he began, trying to sound calm. 'The

ones I saw outside Macmillan's club just now and then driving the Jag with Nicoletta in the back were the ones who were in the Blue Lagoon with Simone. I'm certain of it.'

'Christ, Jack! Why didn't you mention this before?'

'Because I walked into the Blue Lagoon last night and saw Simone with two guys and walked straight back out. That's why. That and I didn't get a good enough look at their faces to work on a photofit of them. And . . . and I wasn't sure . . . I wasn't sure what the hell was going on. Alright? I wasn't sure . . .'

Brady sighed. He couldn't remember a worse day than the one he was having now.

He opened his eyes and stared straight ahead as Conrad sped down the coast road towards Whitley Bay.

'Look, Jack, from what I've found out about these brothers, they're not to be messed with. They have contacts in areas you couldn't even begin to second-guess. Who do you think buys these girls from them?'

Brady didn't answer her.

He was thinking about Melissa Ryecroft. How someone had bought the right to fuck her up to the point of her death.

'These are men in power. And they have money. It takes money to be able to choose a girl, buy her and have the reassurance that you can do whatever you want with her,' Claudia stated.

'What about those Eastern European brothers?' questioned Brady, needing to move the conversation along.

He'd already spent enough time going round in circles about Nicoletta's whereabouts. And the fact that he had promised her that nothing would happen to her.

'The Dabkunas brothers?' asked Claudia.

'Yeah, them. What did you find out about them?'

'They're ex-military. Until a year ago they were part of the Lithuanian army's Special Operation Forces, Aitvaras. Last known to be working as hired bodyguards. In other words, a euphemism for hired killers,' stated Claudia.

'Christ!' muttered Brady.

'I know,' sighed Claudia.

Brady knew there was no way he would let Claudia's name get caught up with men like the Dabkunas brothers or Ronnie Macmillan and his suits. Claudia would be easy meat. And he didn't want to think of her lying in the same mutilated state, if not worse than Simone Henderson. And if that meant taking whatever crap Gates was going to throw at him for his name being connected to the reason Simone was up in the North East, it was a given.

'Look, if it's any consolation I'll apply for a warrant for my team to search Ronnie Macmillan's club. If there's any evidence of sex trafficking or women being held against their will as sex slaves, we'll find it.'

'Make sure you search the cellar and his private quarters above the club. Nicoletta said that Edita hid in the cellar and that she was held upstairs.'

'I'll contact you as soon as I get any more information,' Claudia concluded.

Brady knew that she didn't like anyone telling her how to do her job. But he had to be sure that her team missed nothing. Nicoletta's life was at stake – as was Edita's. That was, if she was still alive.

'Claudia? Be careful. Alright?' warned Brady.

'I know what I'm dealing with, Jack. Remember, this is my job,' said Claudia evenly.

'Yeah, thanks,' answered Brady before she disconnected the line.

He didn't expect to hear any more from Claudia tonight. Hopefully she would get back to him tomorrow with something concrete. Anything that could help them find Nicoletta.

Brady leaned back and closed his eyes.

He was worried.

Worried that Ronnie Macmillan was involved in Simone Henderson's savage attack. He was certain that it had been him in the back of the Jag with Nicoletta.

If it was Ronnie, then word would get back to Mayor Macmillan that Brady was causing trouble for them, again. Brady was certain that Ronnie Macmillan, notorious drug dealer that he was before he diversified into the sex trade, had shot him in the thigh when Brady had been staking out a drugs deal. He was also sure that his brother Mayor Macmillan had ordered Ronnie to get rid of Brady because he was starting to ask too many questions about the Mayor's nefarious lifestyle.

Brady wondered whether him showing up at Ronnie Macmillan's newly acquired lap dancing club would reach Chief Superintendent O'Donnell's ears. He and Mayor Macmillan had sealed a friendship over rounds of golf at Tynemouth Golf Club followed by gin and tonics in the clubhouse. Macmillan had O'Donnell's ear, and not in a good way. Even O'Donnell seemed taken in by the politician; or was it that men of a certain rank looked out for one another, mused Brady. If the mayor complained privately to O'Donnell about Brady, he would certainly know about it through Gates.

O'Donnell had always been good to Brady. Looked out

for him, so to speak. He'd always been in his corner, having known him since he was a kid. O'Donnell, a newly recruited PC at the time, had worked on Brady's mother's murder. So he knew Brady's history. And O'Donnell knew what it was like to be different, to be seen as the outsider.

He was of African-Caribbean descent and had suffered intolerable racism in the force. But despite this, he had risen through the ranks and proved himself to be a formidable Chief Superintendent; respected by all under his command for his unerring sense of fairness, but also for his cut-throat attitude when one of his own crossed the line.

If DC O'Donnell, as he had been then, hadn't cornered the teenage Brady one night on the hardened streets of the Ridges about the brutal murder of a young male from Wallsend, then Brady would have ended up like Madley. Somehow, O'Donnell had got through to him. Brady had never talked about who had killed the kid, but O'Donnell still stood by him. Aware that his silence wasn't about protecting his neck, but someone else's. Admittedly, it didn't happen overnight, but O'Donnell had seen something in Brady as a teenager, enough to put his career on the line to risk helping him get out, never knowing whether Brady had in fact been involved in the murder. But the sudden disappearance of Brady's brother from the North East at the age of fifteen, shortly after the killing, was evidence enough for O'Donnell that Brady hadn't been involved. His brother's disappearance made him look guilty, but Brady knew Nick had been set up and had had no choice but to leave. And O'Donnell saw a trait that he admired – loyalty. Loyalty even at the cost of sacrificing yourself. But Brady's unquestionable loyalty to his brother was based on Nick's innocence.

But now . . . Brady didn't want to think about it.

He started to roll a tab as Conrad pulled up outside the station.

Brady's mind was twisting and turning like an animal caught in a snare trap.

He couldn't get rid of the thought of Nicoletta being driven away in the Jag. He was praying that Nick wasn't somehow involved with Ronnie Macmillan. If Macmillan was now in business with the Eastern European Dabkunas brothers, as Trina and Nicoletta had claimed, he was hoping against the odds that Nick wasn't involved. But he already knew, by Trina's own admission, that his brother had been at the lap dancing club looking for the missing Lithuanian girl, Edita Aginatas. And then there was the information Nicoletta had given him about the man with the scar down his cheek who was working with the Dabkunas brothers. The man who had helped find Edita and drove her to her fate.

The one thing he was certain of, he had to talk to Madley. The nightclub owner had contacts with all the criminal elements throughout the North East, including Ronnie Macmillan. If anyone knew what was going on, it would be Madley. Maybe he would have an idea about where Ronnie Macmillan would take Nicoletta.

However, all that would have to wait. Brady had already tried Madley's mobile and it was switched off. He had then rung the Blue Lagoon to see if he was there, but no one knew his whereabouts; or at least they weren't prepared to tell him. Brady decided that he would pay him a surprise visit tomorrow. Hopefully, then he might get some much needed answers about Madley's criminal nemesis, Ronnie Macmillan.

First thing in the morning he would also have to call Jimmy Matthews. Matthews had made it quite clear that Ronnie Macmillan and his boys had been in to pay him a visit. Brady needed to know exactly what Matthews knew and what game he was playing.

Chapter Thirty-Four

Exhausted, Brady collapsed on the beaten-up leather couch in his office. He rested his head in his hands as he thought over the events of that day.

Conrad cleared his throat.

Brady opened his bloodshot eyes and looked up at him.

His deputy was standing in front of him holding two mugs. He offered Brady the red and white Che Guevara one.

'You look like you need it, sir,' Conrad said.

Brady gratefully took it and watched as Conrad slowly sat down next to him.

'Any sign of that Jag yet?' asked Brady, already knowing the answer.

'No, sir. It's just disappeared. And as of yet, it hasn't returned back to The Ship.'

Brady nodded.

'It won't,' he muttered, accepting that would be the last thing the men would do.

He took a slow mouthful of the Talisker single malt, savouring the burning sensation. He sat back and waited for it to kick in.

'Go home, Conrad,' Brady muttered, as he rested his

head back and closed his eyes. 'The rest of the team have left. You should too. Get some sleep and be back for 7am.'

Brady had relieved the rest of the team. It was late and they wouldn't be much use to him sleep-deprived. He just hoped that this new day would bring them closer to apprehending Melissa Ryecroft's killers. But Brady had nothing concrete.

His mind kept replaying the image of the Jag as it stealthily pulled past them. The only question going through his mind was whether it really had been Macmillan in the back with Nicoletta. He couldn't be certain, but he couldn't ignore his gut feeling. Why, he mused, would Macmillan have a copper brutally butchered? It didn't add up.

Conrad didn't say a word. Instead he looked at the shallow contents of his mug.

'Conrad?' Brady questioned, opening his eyes and turning to him.

'I reckon you could do with some company, sir,' he quietly suggested.

'I'm not good company right now,' answered Brady honestly, sighing.

Conrad looked at his boss. He looked desperate. He didn't know what it was that was troubling him, aside from the obvious.

'Sir?' carefully began Conrad.

Brady took another much needed drink. It rasped the back of his throat as it slid down.

'Who is your informant?'

Brady dejectedly shook his head.

'You see, I can't quite figure out how you knew to go The Ship.'

'Better that way, Conrad,' answered Brady flatly.

'And I don't understand why the Dabkunas brothers – if it is them – left Melissa Ryecroft's head in your car.'

Brady didn't answer him.

'Sir? Why are they targeting you? Why the note? It doesn't make sense.' quizzed Conrad as he leaned forward.

'You and me both,' hoarsely whispered Brady.

His eyes were stinging. He put it down to the burning malt and not the fact that his whole body was ravaged with fear. Dread at what could be happening to Nicoletta. And horror at the knowledge that his own brother was a part of it; willing or not, he was still involved.

'Go home, Conrad,' instructed Brady. 'Things will be clearer in the morning. For both of us.'

He needed to be alone. He couldn't think straight, least of all with Conrad beside him, worry lines etched across his face.

'If you want to talk, you know where I am,' offered Conrad, standing up.

He walked over and placed his untouched mug of malt on Brady's crowded desk. He noticed the uneaten Chinese food that been left from earlier and hoped that Brady would see sense and eat something. Conrad didn't like leaving him in this state, but he knew he had no alternative. Brady was right, he needed to get his head down. And hopefully his boss would do the same. He was certain that they would have a long day ahead of them tomorrow.

Before leaving, he glanced back at Brady once more. His head was back and his eyes were closed. But the last thing he looked was peaceful. His countenance was that of a tortured man. Tortured by what?

Brady breathed a sigh of relief when he heard Conrad leave, gently closing his office door behind him. He stood up and walked over to the filing cabinet. Instead of pouring himself another measure of malt, he carried the bottle back over to the couch. Before sitting down, he looked out the window. The street was dark. Nobody was about. It didn't make him feel any easier. He still felt as if he was being watched; his every move scrutinised.

He let go of the dusty Venetian blind and lay down on the couch. He brought the bottle of Talisker to his lips and swallowed; anything to get rid of the torment he was feeling.

He then sighed heavily as he rested the bottle on his chest. He was scared, and he was even more scared to admit it.

All that kept going through his head was, why St Mary's Lighthouse? Why plant the victim's head with a note in his car there of all places? Nick knew him, and he knew that if he was planning on talking to Madley that would be where he'd do it. All three of them played there as kids. Nick, four years his and Madley's junior, would wildly run around, jumping in between the rocks, or just sit, mesmerised by the white Victorian lighthouse against the backdrop of the violent, brooding North Sea. The lighthouse had been Nick's favourite haunt as a kid. And even as an adult. If Nick ever returned, it would be the second place he would visit after their mother's grave at Whitley Bay cemetery positioned just off the top of the access road to the lighthouse.

Brady knew Nick was trying to tell him something by leaving the black bin liner with Melissa Ryecroft's remains inside. But the question was what?

Brady forced back the tears that were starting to burn his eyes. He refused to believe his brother was willingly involved with such a heinous crime. He knew in all probability that Edita was already dead. He had been a copper too long and knew the statistics too well to convince himself that they would find her alive. He closed his eyes, tormented by the knowledge that he had unwittingly endangered Nicoletta's life and that she might suffer the same fate as her friend Edita because he had made her talk.

Brady couldn't get rid of the thought that had been plaguing him since the briefing when Claudia had shown the team a photograph of Edita Aginatas. There was no denying it. The resemblance to the murdered teenager Melissa Ryecroft was startling. Exceptionally pretty with large brown eyes and long, straight, dark brown hair. It was no coincidence. The girls fitted a type.

The two girls had suffered the same sadistic torture; both had had their fingers cut off. One was lying in Rake Lane morgue and the other victim?

Brady couldn't shake the doubt torturing him.

It wasn't possible . . . was it?

Chapter Thirty-Five

Brady's phone continued to buzz.

Half-asleep, he stretched his hand out and fumbled around on the floor, knocking the empty whisky bottle over.

'Fuck!' he cursed.

Eventually he found it. He picked it up and looked at who was calling him at 6:10 on a Sunday morning.

He didn't recognise the number.

'Yeah? he warily answered.

Nothing.

'Who is this?' he demanded, suddenly sitting up.

He winced from the exertion.

The other person hung up.

Brady sighed heavily. He nervously dragged his hand back through his hair.

He looked at the number. It was a mobile number, one he definitely didn't recognise.

He stood up and squinted through the office window trying not to move the blinds. If anyone was out there, he didn't want them to know he was looking for them.

No one. It was early on a Sunday morning and the street was typically deserted.

He shook his head at his own paranoia. It was just a

wrong number. Nothing more. He decided it wasn't worth having the call traced. He had better things to do than chase shadows.

He breathed in deeply. He felt like crap. His ribs and face ached from the beating he'd received yesterday and his head pounded from too much malt.

He decided he had better straighten himself out before the team returned. He needed a shower and a black coffee to clear his head. He thought about going home but didn't want to waste time. That, and he couldn't shake the feeling that he was being watched. Under the circumstances, the station was the safest place to lie low. Which was why he had spent the early hours of the morning in a restless slumber on his office couch, haunted by dreams of Nick and his old man.

He had no choice but to use the station's antiquated shower room and risk the cafeteria's coffee and a bacon stottie in the vain hope it would clear his hangover.

*

Brady decided to call Claudia before Conrad arrived with an update from the team.

In recognition of the fact that it was Sunday morning, and she'd been up late last night working on any leads that might help, he'd waited until after 10:00am to make the call.

However, she answered her mobile immediately, as if she had anticipated it.

'Listen, I hate hasselling you . . .' Brady said, his voice filled with urgency '. . . I just need to know whether you got that warrant to search Ronnie Macmillan's club in

Wallsend to check out whether the women employed there as sex workers are legal? By the way I do use the term "employed" loosely,' he added.

'The team and I are just waiting for the warrant to be authorised as we speak.'

'Good . . . that's something,' replied Brady, impressed by her initiative. 'When you say your team, who are you taking?' he asked as an afterthought.

'Do you mean am I taking James Davidson? What do you think? These men are dangerous, Jack. He's trained in armed response. You do the maths.'

Brady didn't answer her. But if he was honest, he was relieved that she had Davidson with her.

'Keep me updated,' Brady said.

'Sure,' replied Claudia. She paused for a second before continuing. 'Jack? I'm doing everything I can to find that girl.'

'Nicoletta,' muttered Brady.

'Yes, Nicoletta. I've looked into all of Ronnie Macmillan's business affairs. The disused land he's been buying up around North Tyneside. All the abandoned buildings, including two warehouses down by North Shields quayside he's bought, allegedly with the intention of renovating them into luxury apartments.'

Brady waited, hoping she had more.

He'd already done the same thing. He'd got Conrad on to it as soon as his deputy had turned up. But they hadn't been able to find anything dirty. The money Macmillan had used was kosher and the building and land bought seemed innocuous enough.

Brady had also sent Daniels and Kenny down to check out Macmillan's latest acquisitions and was still waiting for word back. Not that he expected anything: Macmillan was too clever for that. Or at least, thought Brady, his brother, the politician, was too clever.

'I've also put in warrants to search those premises,' Claudia added. 'Just to be sure.'

'Appreciate that, Claudia,' Brady said.

And he meant it.

'Before you go . . . have you told Adamson any of this about Ronnie Macmillan and the two suits I recognised from the Blue Lagoon?'

'No . . . not yet. Not until we have something concrete,' answered Claudia. 'This operation is going to be tricky enough as it is, so the fewer people who know the better. Anyway, didn't you say that's his local haunt?'

'Yeah, that's what one of the lap dancers told me. He's Mr Regular there, which I'd say suggests a conflict of interest,' answered Brady.

'You could be right,' replied Claudia. 'I'll keep you informed.'

He was relieved that Claudia was keeping this from Adamson. How long before he found out was anyone's guess. But at least they had a head start.

Always at the back of his mind was Nick. Where was he and how could Brady get to him first?

'Claudia?' Brady said, stopping her from hanging up.

'Go on,' she said.

'My informant said that the Lithuanian Ambassador is tied up with the Dabkunas brothers. Do you know anything about this ambassador?' Brady questioned.

He had no choice but to ask. They had taken a girl in front of his eyes, there was one lying murdered in a hospital refrigerator and another, a copper, fighting for her life.

Brady heard Claudia take an intake of breath.

'What?' he questioned. 'What do you know?' he repeated when she didn't answer.

'I . . . I've had some contact with him. Not personally, but with his PA and secretary. I'm supposed to be at a speech he's giving at the Civic Centre this afternoon in fact, but obviously I'm prioritising this case.' Claudia's voice faltered as she tried to get her thoughts together.

'Go on.'

'There's a big formal dinner tonight at 8:30pm being held at the Grand Hotel in Tynemouth. I have to be there, as does James . . . I mean DCI Davidson. You see, the ambassador's over here supporting our sex trafficking unit because it's the first of its kind in the North East. And, given that a lot of Eastern European girls are trafficked and held as sex slaves in the UK, he's doing as much as he can to highlight the plight of the women who've gone missing from his country.'

There was a long silence.

'Jack?' Claudia said, an edge of panic in her voice when he didn't say anything. 'Whatever you do, keep what you've just told me to yourself, will you? You go around making allegations like that, then you'll be kicked off the force without a pension. With nothing.'

'I only asked if you knew anything about him,' Brady replied. 'I'm not going to take it to O'Donnell. I'm not that stupid.'

'Good,' answered Claudia. 'Because from what I've gathered, Chief Superintendent O'Donnell has worked very hard to get the Ambassador's support. You know, good publicity and everything. Especially for my unit. And O'Donnell isn't the only one involved here, I know that Mayor Macmillan is hosting this dinner tonight. And that he has had quite a few dealings with the Ambassador over the past six months trying to set up some business between Lithuania and the North East.'

'I *bet* he's trying to go in to business with him,' muttered Brady.

'For God's sake, Jack! Don't be ridiculous. You have the word of a snitch – a questionable one at that – against that of someone like Mayor Macmillan. I know who I'd choose.'

'That's what makes us so different,' replied Brady.

His phone started to beep.

'Look, get back to me if anything comes up,' Brady said before disconnecting Claudia.

He expected more of her.

He answered the new call. 'Brady.'

Rubenfeld's irritated voice came over the line. 'Why didn't you get back to me, Jack? I've got better things to do than chasing you up on a Sunday.'

'Look, yesterday was one hell of a day,' Brady explained by way of an apology.

'Save your breath and meet me. This is for your benefit, not mine.'

'Can't you just save time and tell me now? I'm up to my neck in it, Rubenfeld.'

'You and me both,' answered Rubenfeld. 'And no, what I have to tell you has to be in person.'

'Where?' asked Brady.

He knew that the hardened hack must have some crucial information to be insisting on meeting him.

'The Cluny at 2:00pm,' instructed Rubenfeld. 'Alright?'

'It'll have to bloody be alright, won't it!' He took a deep breath. 'Why the Cluny?'

The Cluny was a pub located off the beaten track down under Byker Bridge. It was one of those pubs that you had to know about, which made Brady curious as to why Rubenfeld wanted to meet there.

'Out the bloody way of prying eyes and ears,' answered Rubenfeld.

'What's this connected with?' asked Brady, starting to feel uneasy.

'Everything! Just get your arse in gear!'

Chapter Thirty-Six

Brady dragged heavily on his cigarette as Conrad parked up next to the Cluny in full view of the overhead Byker Bridge. The morning had gone slowly; too slowly. No new developments, nothing. He felt as if the team were chasing their own tails and getting nowhere fast.

Brady stared over at the pub wondering exactly what it was that Rubenfeld had for him. The Cluny was located in the Ouseburn area of Newcastle where it shared a former flax spinning mill with local artists, offices and recording studios.

It was well known locally and internationally, and often listed as one of the top 100 world's best bars. It was a live music venue as well as a pub and a café. Brady couldn't fault the place. Great music, good beer and appetising food. On an average day, he couldn't ask for more from life. However, today wasn't a typical day; it was far from it.

Brady turned to Conrad. 'Can you chase up Daniels and Kenny? We should know by now whether they've found any evidence of anything suspicious around the land and buildings that Ronnie Macmillan's bought up. And remind them that they've to keep their eyes out for a black Jaguar.'

'Yes, sir,' nodded Conrad.

'Any word back on Adamson's case?' Brady asked, knowing even as he spoke that it was a dumb question. He knew that he would be the last person to hear of any developments on Simone Henderson's attack.

'No, sir,' Conrad confirmed coolly.

Conrad had talked to Amelia earlier, but if the team had any new information she wasn't sharing it. Whether it was because she was worried Conrad would report it straight back to his boss, he wasn't sure. Conrad didn't like Brady's unhealthy interest in Adamson's investigation. Even less so as it was becoming clear that Brady's mind was torn between his own murder case and something else. Not that Brady would ever admit it, but it was obvious that something or someone had got to him. And Conrad presumed that was why they were parked up outside the Cluny for a meeting with an informant of Brady's. But whatever information Brady would glean, Conrad was pretty sure he wouldn't be party to it.

'And can you get an update from Harvey?' asked Brady. 'We should have heard by now whether any of Melissa Ryecroft's friends have any information on this Marijuis character. And Conrad, I need you to personally run a check on him and his brother, starting with the Lithuanian authorities. I want to know everything you can find out about them. Exactly what it is they do now, who they work for and why they're in the North East.'

He was certain that if Harvey had gleaned anything, he would have been in touch immediately. But it was still worth putting a bit of pressure on him.

'While you're waiting for me I need you to analyse the CCTV footage that Daniels and Kenny sent us.'

'Yes, sir,' answered Conrad leaning over and picking up his laptop.

He tried to keep his expression neutral but the last place he wanted to be doing this kind of work was sitting in his car while he multitasked as Brady's chauffeur. Yet he knew his boss had no choice: forensics were still searching for any traces of evidence left behind with the black bin liner containing the victim's head. And Brady had made it quite clear that he didn't trust anyone else to drive him around – something which only increased Conrad's concern about how far the note left in Brady's car was causing his boss to spiral to the point where he couldn't think straight.

'We're looking for two Eastern European-looking men being driven around in a black Mercedes with a Lithuanian licence plate,' stated Brady.

'Yes, sir,' replied Conrad, his brain racing as he tried to keep track of Brady's demands.

Brady thought of Daniels and Kenny. They had spent the past morning and early afternoon laboriously going over the airport footage. Neither one had spotted anything unusual. But Brady didn't accept their findings, which was why Conrad would now have to redo their job.

'Thanks, Conrad,' Brady said as he got out the car.

'The press call, sir? It's scheduled for 5:00pm,' questioned Conrad. 'And it's now 2:15pm. We've still got a lot to do before then.'

'I need to do this first, Conrad,' Brady calmly pointed out.

Given the state of his face, Brady had decided that Conrad would be better suited to give the press call about Melissa Ryecroft with Gates.

He shut the car door, putting Conrad's uptight attitude

down to the impossible workload he had just given him. But he'd had no choice. His team were under-funded and under-staffed and, unfortunately for him, Conrad was by far the best officer on his team.

Brady breathed out slowly, trying to get rid of the mounting pressure he felt and looked around for Rubenfeld. He couldn't see him amongst the smokers tabbing outside. Then he spotted the short, shabby figure standing alone, smoking. He would recognise that ugly mottled face anywhere. The nose in particular which was becoming more bulbous and purple every time he saw him. Rubenfeld was a journalist through and through; he liked to drink and his drinker's nose was a testament to that.

Not that Rubenfeld cared. All he cared about was his next story and next shot, and not necessarily in that order.

Rubenfeld always wore his shabby black raincoat, regardless of the weather, or the location. Brady couldn't imagine Rubenfeld without it. Underneath he wore a black linen suit; equally scruffy and in constant need of dry cleaning, mainly because of liquor spills when he'd had one too many. Which in Rubenfeld's case, was every night. But Rubenfeld had the tolerance of a rhinoceros. The man could drink the hardest men under the table and still remain standing.

Brady watched as Rubenfeld pulled the collar of his raincoat up around his neck. Rubenfeld had never quite acclimatised to the bitter North East weather after coming back from the South and had compromised on a heavy raincoat. Brady admired his pragmatism; this was the North East of England after all, where the temperature rarely rose above 60 degrees during the summer and the rest of the year was spent under a miserable, disgruntled drizzle.

Brady couldn't remember a time when Rubenfeld hadn't been around. As far as Brady could remember Rubenfeld had always worked for *The Northern Echo*. It was the bestselling newspaper in the North East and a lot of its sales were down to Rubenfeld. If there was a story to uncover, Rubenfeld was guaranteed to be the first one there. Brady didn't know how he did it, but he had an uncanny knack of turning up when he was least wanted. But if Brady was honest, he needed Rubenfeld as much Rubenfeld needed him.

Brady watched as Rubenfeld threw his cigarette butt away and started to make his way through the crowd.

'Leaving already?' asked Brady as he walked towards him.

'Nah! Looking for you, you tight bastard. You owe me a drink,' said Rubenfeld as he narrowed his eyes and scratched at his two days' worth of dark stubble.

'You call me tight? When was the last time you stood a round?'

'I've heard something that might interest you,' Rubenfeld began, deliberately ignoring Brady's question.

'How about we go somewhere a bit more private then?'

'Good idea, Jack. I suggest the bar.'

*

Brady watched as Rubenfeld knocked back his second whisky chaser.

He knew it always took a couple of drinks to loosen Rubenfeld's tongue.

They were sitting at a round table by the window. From there Brady could see the bar and watch as people came and went while he waited for Rubenfeld to talk.

'Another?' asked Brady.

'Aye, why not?' answered Rubenfeld.

Brady expected as much.

He took his wallet out and walked over to the bar.

'Another pint of Peroni and a double whisky,' ordered Brady. 'Throw in a bag of salted nuts as well, would you?'

Brady returned to the table, handing Rubenfeld his drinks and chucking the peanuts his way.

'Don't say I never buy you lunch!'

'Like I said, you're one tight bastard!' scorned Rubenfeld as he ripped open the packet.

He took a handful and threw them into his mouth as he looked at Brady.

'There's some sinister shit going on, Jack,' Rubenfeld said as he chewed.

'Like what?' asked Brady, pushing his black coffee out the way as he leaned in towards Rubenfeld.

'Name first,' demanded Rubenfeld.

'You're a shit, do you know that?' said Brady.

'*Quid pro quo*, Jack. You know the score. I've a story to finish and it's missing a couple of details. You tell me, I ring it in so it can go to print, and everyone's happy. Including my bloody editor – which would make a change!'

'Melissa Ryecroft,' answered Brady, knowing that the news was going to be released later that afternoon anyway. He knew the way to loosen Rubenfeld's tongue and that was to offer him scraps ahead of any press release.

'And?' questioned Rubenfeld.

'Sixteen-year-old local girl. Parents live on the Broadway, Tynemouth end. She went to King's School sixth form before someone decided to murder her.'

'Is it right she was decapitated?'

Brady looked surprised.

'I hear things,' muttered Rubenfeld through another mouthful of nuts.

Brady nodded.

'Amongst other things. But at this point that can't go to print. Understand?'

Rubenfeld ignored Brady.

'What else?' he asked.

'Savagely raped and . . . and she had a captive bolt pistol shot through her forehead.'

'Bloody hell, Jack. That's a first in my book! I thought that kind of shit only happened in films, not for bloody real.'

'I know . . .' muttered Brady.

He was right though, mused Brady. That kind of weird, sadistic shit wasn't what he expected to find happening in Whitley Bay of all places.

'Any leads?' Rubenfeld asked.

'Do you really think I'm going to tell you?' Brady said, shaking his head.

Rubenfeld gave out a deep, gurgling laugh.

'One day, Jack. You just might, one day.'

'How much have you had to drink?' mocked Brady.

'Never enough!' answered Rubenfeld as he drained his pint of Peroni.

'What do you reckon it is? A copycat-style murderer?' questioned Rubenfeld.

'What do you mean?' asked Brady.

'You know that adaptation of Cormac McCarthy's book? That film *No Country For Old Men* with Javier Bardem as the psychopathic hitman playing havoc with a cattle stun gun?'

Brady nodded. It was an obvious connection. One he had already made.

'A captive bolt pistol to be precise,' Brady said as he thought about the hole in Melissa Ryecroft's severed head.

'So is it some nutter who watched the film and decided to copy it?'

'No,' replied Brady simply.

'How can you be so sure?' quizzed Rubenfeld.

Brady shot him a look which said it all.

'Alright, alright I was just asking, that's all,' stated Rubenfeld.

'You want more details, wait for the press call at 5pm like the rest of the scavengers.'

Rubenfeld contemplated Brady as he picked up the small tumbler of whisky. He swirled the contents around before knocking it back in one.

'I've got a story to write up,' he said, thumping the glass back down.

'Not so fast,' Brady replied.

Rubenfeld sighed heavily.

'Alright . . . I'm hearing some crazy shit about Macmillan. The Mayor that is,' Rubenfeld began.

Brady moved closer to Rubenfeld's foul-smelling body, resisting the urge to ask him when he'd last had a shower, knowing the answer wouldn't be pleasant. There was a reason why Rubenfeld was permanently single.

'Seems he wants to expand. Go into business with this Lithuanian Ambassador who's up at the minute from London. Our paper's running a feature on his public address at the Civic Centre this afternoon. Load of cods-wallop if you ask me, but this guy has a lot of power and money. He's highly influential, so consequently everywhere you look, Macmillan's with him,' Rubenfeld said as he raised his eyebrows at Brady.

'That's it?' questioned Brady.

'Alright, you tell me why a Lithuanian Ambassador is walking around with armed security in the bloody North East.'

Brady shook his head, not wanting Rubenfeld to realise that he already had his own suspicions after his chat with Trina McGuire.

'For fuck's sake, Jack. Are your brains in your arse or what? Armed security guards who look like Dolph Lundgren for bloody hell's sake. It's the North East of England not Beirut!'

Rubenfeld shook his head before taking another slug of whisky. 'He owns a shipping company. Controls cargo ships that ship all across the world. I've heard word from a source that Macmillan wants to be part of it. Wants to be shipping containers between Eastern Europe, and the North East.'

'Shipping what for fuck's sake?' asked Brady.

Rubenfeld raised his eyebrows. 'You tell me.'

Brady shrugged. 'Given what his brother Ronnie Macmillan's involved in, and his taste for jail bait, I'd say it's either drugs or human trafficking.'

Rubenfeld nodded. 'Polish food is what Macmillan's intending on shipping in. Doing a big publicity stunt supporting multi-culturalism and the growing ethnic minority of Polish people in the North East. Polish sausages, pickled cabbage and flat soda bread, supplied at cut-throat prices for all the local supermarkets from Redcar up to Berwick-upon-Tweed.'

'What else?' asked Brady, hoping that Rubenfeld had brought more than Polish sausages to the table.

'How does a Lithuanian ambassador build up a shipping empire that's worth millions? What's he shipping, Jack? Because I bet it's not just Polish bloody sausages!'

'Why do you say that?' quizzed Brady, wanting more than Rubenfeld was obviously prepared to give.

'Because if your shipping line is strictly legal, why walk around with half the Lithuanian military watching your back?'

Brady didn't reply. The answer was obvious.

'You want proof, Jack?' questioned Rubenfeld. 'Go see for yourself. The Ambassador is guest of honour at a big, swanky dinner hosted by Macmillan tonight at the Grand Hotel. Press are going to be there because from what my source has said, they're going to launch this new business partnership linking Eastern Europe and the North East of England. Then you'll see what I mean. Bloody Lithuanian military will be crawling all over the place.'

Brady didn't say a word.

'Question is why, Jack?' Rubenfeld said as he looked him in the eye.

'What's this Ambassador's name?' asked Brady.

'Nykantas Vydunas,' answered Rubenfeld. 'And from what my source has told me, he has two very dangerous Lithuanian ex-military men involved with him.'

'Go on.'

'The Dabkunas brothers. Evil bastards, they are . . . but no matter what I do, I can't get anything on them. All you hear is rumours and anecdotal crap. Nothing substantial. At least nothing that I could put into print. And let's just say that the Dabkunas brothers aren't interested in providing an armed guard to a container full of pickled cabbage.'

'Can I talk to your source – off the record, obviously?' asked Brady.

He needed to get more information on the Dabkunas brothers. And Rubenfeld's source seemed to know a hell of lot more than Brady or his team could lay their hands on.

Rubenfeld looked Brady straight in the eye. It was a cold, hard look.

'You look after your affairs and I look after mine. You haven't talked to me. Understand? I hear things . . . and that's the way I want to keep it. I don't want your lot fishing me out of the Tyne.'

Brady looked at Rubenfeld. If he wasn't mistaken, despite his hard appearance, the hack looked worried for his personal safety.

Chapter Thirty-Seven

Brady looked up at his office door as Conrad walked in.

They'd been back for under an hour and by Brady's reckoning, Conrad was due at the press call in less than thirty minutes.

'Have something here that might interest you, sir,' said Conrad as he walked over to his desk.

Brady felt his stomach knot as Conrad laid his laptop down and opened it up in front of him. He did his best to hide it.

'Aren't you supposed to be preparing for the press call?' he asked.

'Yes, but I thought you'd want to see this first,' Conrad said as he pointed at the freeze-framed image that he had brought up on the screen. 'This is the best Jed could do, but I think you can see their faces clearly enough to be able to release them to the public.'

'Let's see,' replied Brady as he took Conrad's laptop.

He hoped to God he wasn't going to see Nick's face caught on there.

He looked at the image on the screen. It had been taken from the airport CCTV footage at midday on Thursday. Two Eastern European-looking men, identical to those who had been at Rake Lane Hospital, were captured in grainy but inevitable realism, walking with a young girl between them. There was no mistaking it, thought Brady. This was the victim: Melissa Ryecroft.

'Good work, Conrad,' Brady said.

'That's not all, sir,' Conrad said. 'We got an image of the victim getting in their car.'

Brady held his breath as he moved on to the next image. He was hoping against all the odds that he wouldn't see a grainy shot of Nick caught on Newcastle Airport's surveillance tape. The last thing he wanted was a picture of his brother plastered across local and national papers and the news.

'See? It's clear that it's Melissa Ryecroft getting into the back of the black Mercedes while one of the men holds the door open for her. Next shot shows both men getting in on either side of her in the back. And then the final one of the car pulling away. Jed has tried his best to get a better shot of the driver but this is as good as it gets,' explained Conrad as he moved the digitally enhanced, freeze-framed images on until he came to the last one.

Brady clenched his fist under his desk while he tried to look as casual as possible.

If he believed in God, he realised now would be a good time to pray.

The problem was, he didn't.

He watched as the image on the computer screen jumped to show a blurred shot of the driver.

Brady sighed. Relief.

Conrad interpreted it as disappointment.

'It was the best shot we could get of him, sir. All that we can make out from his side profile is what looks to be a scar down his left cheek,' Conrad said as he pointed to the gnarled line inflicted on the driver's face.

'You could be right,' replied Brady. 'But like you said, it's hard to make anything out with this shot. Pity it's so blurred.'

Conrad looked at Brady, frowning slightly.

'Couldn't we release it using the scar as an identifiable trait, sir?' asked Conrad.

'If it *is* a scar,' replied Brady. 'It's such a poor image, I'd hate to commit myself to something that I'm not 100 percent sure about.'

Brady studied the freeze-framed image. There was no doubting it. The face on the digitally enhanced picture was definitely that of his brother, Nick. He was equally certain that the other two men had to be the Dabkunas brothers, Marijuis and Mykolas.

'Alright, release the images we have of these two. But discount the one of the driver,' ordered Brady.

'Yes, sir,' answered Conrad, surprised.

Brady made a point of ignoring Conrad's questioning tone.

Conrad realised he had overstepped the mark by tacitly questioning his superior's decision. 'What do you think, sir?' he asked, attempting to fill in the awkward silence. 'That one of them is this Marijuis boyfriend that Melissa Ryecroft was seeing?'

He changed the screen to a close-up image of the two men getting in the car. 'They fit the profile of looking Eastern European, don't you think?'

Brady didn't say a word. At this point he wasn't prepared to share what he knew about the Dabkunas brothers or the Lithuanian Ambassador for fear of endangering Nick.

Conrad turned and gave him a quizzical look.

Brady shrugged.

'You could be right. But I think we need a bit more proof than assuming they're Eastern European just because they're dark, don't you?' questioned Brady.

'Yes, sir,' dutifully answered Conrad.

'Look, Conrad, I have to make a call so why don't you get prepared for the press call? Gates will want those images to be released as well so make sure they're ready.'

*

'Jimmy?' greeted Brady when Matthews answered.

'Tell me you're stood in the visiting room with 200 grams of baccy on you,' said Matthews.

'Look . . . Jimmy, I can't make it. Too much shit flying around here for me to get over Durham way,' explained Brady.

'You're fucking having a laugh!' hissed Matthews.

'Jimmy, you have no idea. Believe me. I'm up against it with this murder investigation. I have Gates wanting to nail my testicles to the wall, followed by bloody Adamson.'

Matthews didn't reply.

'Oh for fuck's sake, Jimmy. At least I'm calling you.'

'Yeah? Only 'cos you're shit-scared about what I've got on you and Madley,' answered Matthews.

Brady didn't need to see Matthews to know that he looked dreadful. He would be unshaven, unkempt and edgy as fuck. He could hear it in his voice. Brady knew that Matthews was close to breaking point, which made him a very dangerous man. Both to himself and to others. Brady in particular.

'You know what, Jimmy? Right now I've got better things to be doing than listen to you threaten me,' stated Brady.

He was running out of time.

It was 4:45pm and he had two appointments that he needed to keep.

The first was with Madley. Not that Madley knew they had an appointment.

The second place he had to be was at the Grand Hotel. He wanted to be parked up, watching the guests arrive for the dinner that Claudia and her professional partner and boyfriend were attending, along with half the dignitaries from across the North East. But it was the Lithuanian Ambassador that Brady was interested in. And the Dabkunas brothers.

Brady knew he had no choice but to go alone. Nick was a good enough incentive not to involve anyone – including Conrad.

Matthews' snarling voice brought him back to the present. 'Yeah? Well, what if I say that Ronnie Macmillan's been trying to dig up some shit on you and Madley. Interested now?'

Brady held his breath.

'Got time to talk to me now, have you?' asked Matthews.

'Go on,' said Brady.

'I want out, Jack,' Matthews said.

'That's impossible,' replied Brady.

'Look, either I talk to you or I talk to Adamson. I don't give a shit any more. My loyalty is to myself now.'

'Wasn't that why you ended up inside?' pointed out Brady.

'You're a bastard, Jack!'

'Takes one to know one,' answered Brady.

He was too tired for all this shit. His head ached as much

as his leg hurt. He needed some painkillers to ease the dull throb in his ribs and swollen face that reminded him that he had spent the past two days chasing ghosts.

'What exactly do you think I can do?' asked Brady.

'Claudia,' answered Matthews simply. 'She's a fuck-off lawyer and she now works for the Home Office. Get her to represent me for free. Get her to strike a deal with the Home Office to release me early in exchange for crucial information concerning Macmillan and the copper who got knifed.'

'Come on, Jimmy,' Brady said. 'You're asking the impossible.'

'Then I hang up and I talk to Adamson and I throw in the part about you getting Madley to set your old man up for murder.'

Brady felt as if Matthews had just punched him in the guts. He thought for a moment he was going to throw up.

He breathed out slowly, trying to steady himself.

He couldn't think straight. None of it made sense. Admittedly he had asked Madley to make his dad disappear. He had no choice at the time. But he knew Madley wouldn't have murdered another man in the process. Not that Brady hadn't silently questioned whether Madley had had a hand in it. But as soon as he thought it he discounted it. Madley had done some dark shit, but he wouldn't take another man's life for no reason.

'Yeah? Truth hurts, doesn't it?' Matthews snapped when Brady didn't respond.

Brady was trying to figure out exactly how Matthews had managed to talk to his old man. Then again, he accepted, Matthews was banged up in a secure wing with the old bastard.

'You forget, Jack. We're the same, you and I,' he added.

'Fuck you!' replied Brady.

'What? Is that a guilty conscience that I hear?' goaded Matthews.

'Don't know what you're talking about.'

'Sure you do. But I'll remind you anyway. I'm talking about the homeless man, the sixty-three year old who was found dead by the library in North Shields. The man who had petrol doused over him and then was set alight. He burnt to death. All for a bottle of cheap Scotch. At least that's the evidence that was planted on your old man when he was asleep between two garbage bins in the back lane of Nile Street.'

'He did it,' answered Brady, his expression darkening.

Matthews didn't need to see Brady's face to know that he had crossed the line. He could hear it in Brady's voice.

'The CCTV footage in Shields clearly shows him arguing with the homeless man over a bottle of liquor,' stated Brady. 'He clears off after being landed with a couple of punches and comes back a couple of hours later with petrol that he's siphoned off a car. Footage shows him pouring it over the other man's head and body as he lay sleeping and then setting fire to him.'

'Yeah? But it was all a set-up. Your old man, with the help of Ronnie Macmillan, is going to prove that the man who goes back and cold-bloodedly murders the tramp wasn't him. That he got plied with drink. Bought by two of Madley's men. And when he fell asleep drunk, his clothes were removed. Then one of Madley's men puts his clothes on and, impersonating him, sets the tramp alight. They then put the clothes which are covered in petrol splashes back on your old man and leave the bottle of

Scotch clutched in his hands and the matches and petrol container beside him.'

'Is that the best you've got?' questioned Brady, trying to sound calm despite the fact his heart was racing so fast he thought it would explode.

Maybe it was the guilt he was feeling for asking Madley to sort the old bastard out once and for all. Maybe that was why he was sweating? His old man had spent twenty years inside for the brutal rape and murder of his mother. It should have been a minimum of thirty, but then some parole board decided to release him on good behaviour. Times had changed though. Nowadays a life sentence was seven years. Brady realised he should have been thankful that his old man had spent so long inside. But in his mind, the old bastard should have spent the rest of his life banged up.

'Who the fuck in their right mind would torch someone alive and leave the evidence on them?' questioned Matthews.

'He's a fucking drunk, Jimmy. I don't give a shit who he tells that story to because no one would believe him. Have you forgotten that he's already served time for murder?'

Brady steadied himself. He knew that his old man was capable of cold-blooded murder. Had already proved that once before. So why not this time? And anyway, he reasoned, his father had been tried and convicted by a jury. If there was a shadow of a doubt, surely his defence lawyer would have exploited it.

Matthews had nothing on him or Madley.

Matthews spoke again. 'I know you got Madley to arrange it.'

'Do you?' asked Brady, a hard edge to his voice.

'I've got better things to do with my time, Jimmy, than listen to your crap!'

'Wait!' shouted Matthews with an edge of desperation.

'Give me one good reason why,' demanded Brady.

'Because I've heard something that might interest you.'

'Like what?' Brady asked, feeling nothing but disgust for Matthews.

'Alright, your old man wants to settle a score with you and Madley. Convinced himself you set him up. But he's not the only one. Two of Macmillan's henchmen showed up about a week ago. Visa and bloody Delta they're called. Reckon their names are something to do with them being Macmillan's debt collectors,' Matthews stated.

'His men, Visa and Delta, where are they from?' asked Brady.

'What's it to you?'

'Just tell me, Jimmy!'

'From their accents I'd say London. Why?'

Brady ignored his question and moved on.

'And they wanted to talk to you?' Brady was starting to get a real bad feeling about what Matthews was going to say next.

'Who the fuck do you think? Nelson fucking Mandela? Of course me!'

'Why?' questioned Brady.

'They heard that I was a copper who also worked for Madley. They wanted some dirt on Madley to stitch him up.'

'What's Macmillan's problem with Madley?' asked Brady. This was news to him.

'I don't know if you've noticed but Ronnie Macmillan is buying up everything he can in North Tyneside. He bought that lap dancing club down by Wallsend docks off Benton Way.'

'The Ship Inn, better known as the Hole,' muttered Brady. 'In Gainers Terrace.'

'Yeah, that's the place. But then again, "bought" is another word for going in and just taking it over. The owner of the place got pushed out by Macmillan and his men. Or pushed into the Tyne depending on who you listen to, because the guy just disappeared. And no sooner, Ronnie Macmillan's taken the place over.'

'What's that got to do with Madley?' asked Brady.

'Because they've been leaning on him. Ronnie Macmillan's got himself a lucrative trade going on in the sex business. His new partners are Eastern European by all accounts, and dangerous fuckers. But Macmillan's got big plans. He wants to expand out to Whitley Bay. And that means buying Madley out. He wants the Blue Lagoon and the Royal Hotel because they're located right on the sea front. What do they say? Location, location, location? He could do a great trade there with an upmarket lap dancing club and a hotel right next door for punters to book in with one of the girls. Imagine the bookings he'd get from stag parties alone,' stated Matthews.

Brady breathed in deeply. Why the hell hadn't Madley told him any of this?

'But that's crazy,' he replied. 'The council wouldn't sanction a lap dancing club on the sea front.'

'How dumb are you, Jack? Fuck me! Do I have to spell it out for you? Ronnie Macmillan's only the puppet. The puppet master is his brother, Mayor Macmillan. He's the guy pulling all the strings and he's the one who would pull any string it took to license a strip club in Whitley Bay,' answered Matthews. 'Anyway, from what I remember there's quite a few lap dancing bars up and down South Parade so it shouldn't be that hard for Macmillan to get the council to agree. Greedy bastards that they are. What do you reckon, Jack? What would they choose? Revenue or protecting the local residents' interests?'

Brady didn't answer him. There was no point given the fact it was a rhetorical question.

'Exactly!' spat Matthews.

'And from what Visa and Delta implied, Ronnie Macmillan's one pissed-off boss. I never saw him, which was a good thing. It was bad enough to know he was waiting in the car outside.'

Brady listened. He could hear the fear in Matthews' voice.

'Why's Ronnie Macmillan pissed off then?' questioned Brady.

'He offered to bring Madley on board. Business partners, like,' explained Matthews.

'What? Sex trafficking and sex slavery and all that shit?'

'Yeah, that's about the sum of it. But Madley's refused. Doesn't want to get his hands dirty through using women's bodies. Moral man, he said. Fucking Catholic raised.'

Brady sighed. Relieved to hear it. Even though he already knew it, it was good to have it verified. And good that it was coming from Matthews who had previously been adamant that Madley was caught up in sex trafficking.

'And then the stupid bastard won't sell up. Won't go in to business with Macmillan and won't sell to him. No wonder Macmillan's pissed off. The guy's been more than fair. So . . .' Matthews paused.

Brady felt his stomach contract. He knew why now.

Why Simone Henderson's body had been dumped in Madley's nightclub. And then why the three-nines call to the emergency services had been made, bringing the police to Madley's door. It was a warning to Madley to get out. That if he didn't go, this was just the start of it.

'Why did Ronnie Macmillan's men come to you?' asked Brady, feeling sick. 'What did they want?'

Matthews went quiet.

Too quiet, thought Brady.

'What the fuck did they want from you?' he repeated insistently.

'I'm sorry, Jack . . .' Matthews stuttered. 'I honestly didn't know it would end up like this . . .'

'What the fuck did they want from you?' Brady was shouting now. 'What did you do?'

'They brought in a photograph when they visited. They wanted me to ID it. That's what they wanted,' muttered Matthews. 'They knew I was involved with Madley. That I spent a lot of time at the Blue Lagoon and so they thought I might recognise her.'

'Tell me it wasn't Simone? Tell me you didn't tell them she was a copper?'

'I had to . . . one word from them and I'm dead. For fuck's sake, Jack! You have no idea what it's like in here! No idea! It's killing me . . . fucking killing me! They threatened me with Kate. Said if I refused to co-operate they'd go after her and they would . . . they would hurt her so bad . . .' Matthews faltered, unable to articulate the details of what they said they would do to his estranged wife.

'Anyway,' he muttered. 'If they hadn't got the information from me, they would have got it from someone else.

You see, Simone Henderson made herself too obvious. Too keen to get close to Ronnie Macmillan. Women like her don't work as hookers; even high-class hookers. She's the one who got too confident. Careless even. She should have stayed in London, Jack. This was her call.'

'You bastard!' shouted Brady.

'No . . . Jack? Come on. You've got to understand. I . . . I'm not responsible . . . I'm the one who's in shit up to my fucking neck! Having to watch my back twenty-four-seven. I had no choice! I had no fucking choice!'

'Everyone has a choice, Jimmy,' stated Brady. 'Even a shit like you!'

'Yeah? And my choice now is to get out. You strike a deal for me and I'll talk.'

'They won't let you out, Jimmy. Don't you get that?'

'Fucking try, will you? That's all I'm asking!'

Brady was silent. He knew that if he got Matthews to make a statement against Ronnie Macmillan then he'd end up dead. Regardless of whether Macmillan was banged up or not.

He shook his head. He didn't know what to do. The problem of Nick was still ever present. If the police got hold of Ronnie Macmillan and his men then Nick would also go down.

'Let me think about it, Jimmy,' answered Brady.

'Don't take too long. I can always go to Gates with this and I'll make a point of telling him that I told you first. That and your old man's accusation that you and Madley set him up. Wouldn't look good now, would it?' threatened Matthews.

Brady listened as Matthews hung up on him.

He breathed out as he looked up and stared at the dusty

grey slats of fading daylight stabbing through the off-white Venetian blinds.

What the fuck could he do now?

A loud rap on the door broke him from his thoughts. 'What?'

The door swung open and Conrad walked in.

'Sir, Wolfe's been trying to get hold of you. He said it's urgent,' stated Conrad.

That explained the irritating beeping on the line while he had been talking to Matthews.

'Aren't you meant to be at a press call now?'

'On my way now. Call Wolfe, sir. Whatever it is, he wouldn't say to me. All I know is that it's to do with Melissa Ryecroft's body.'

Chapter Thirty-Eight

'Wolfe, what's wrong?' asked Brady when Wolfe answered.

Brady massaged his forehead, trying to ease the mounting tension.

'I got it wrong,' confessed Wolfe.

'You got what wrong?' nervously questioned Brady.

'The body . . . the autopsy. I made a mistake,' wheezed Wolfe.

'You don't make fucking mistakes, Wolfe!' hissed Brady. 'Don't do this to me. Don't fucking do this!'

He'd never heard Wolfe sound like this: defeated. And it was scaring the hell out of him. But what was scaring him more was the hunch he had, the one he had ignored. He had pushed it to the back of his mind not believing it could be possible.

'When I examined the uterus and the reproductive system I found the victim to be suffering from severe endometriosis.'

'I know, you already said. So what's the problem?' demanded Brady.

A deathly wheezing silence.

'Wolfe?' Brady shouted.

'I . . . didn't notice because of all the damage from the

318

gang-rape. Add to that the severe scarring from the endometriosis she suffered made it really difficult to tell. But
when I had a closer examination I realised . . . I had a
feeling I'd missed something, you see.'

'What the fuck did you miss?' Brady spat as his body
broke out into a sweat.

'Endometriosis makes it very difficult to get pregnant . . .'

'You said she'd had an abortion. That, despite trauma
you could make out that she had had a botched abortion.
So what are you saying?' questioned Brady angrily.

Wolfe didn't answer him.

'What? She'd never had an abortion, is that it?' demanded
Brady, trying to get a grip on the situation.

'No, Jack. She'd had an abortion alright. But that wasn't
the first time she'd been pregnant. Her uterus shows
evidence that she'd already carried a foetus to full-term.'

'Wolfe? God no . . .' muttered Brady.

'I know . . .' he conceded.

'Fuck!' cursed Brady as he tried to think through the
implications of what Wolfe had just told him

'But it could still be her, surely?'

'I'm sorry, Jack. No. It's not possible,' answered Wolfe.

'Why not?' insisted Brady. 'Who knows what the
Ryecrofts are covering up about their daughter?'

Silence.

'Wolfe?'

'I've already contacted Melissa Ryecroft's GP surgery
and requested her medical records. I had to be sure. She
isn't the victim . . . Melissa Ryecroft has had an abortion.
But . . . she has never given birth.'

'What happened if she gave birth without telling anyone?
Some pregnant teenage girls have been known to hide their

pregnancy and then give birth alone, without medical intervention,' pleaded Brady, desperation breaking into his voice

The only thought going through his mind was that Brian Ryecroft had positively identified the body as that of his missing daughter.

'Listen to me, Jack. The body that I carried out the autopsy on is not Melissa Ryecroft,' answered Wolfe. His tone was reluctant but definitive.

'But her father positively identified the body,' stated Brady.

'Jack, you saw the state of the victim's head. The amount of knife wounds to the victim's face made it difficult to tell.'

Brady sighed heavily, wondering if the weekend could get any worse.

'Tell me the head definitely belongs to the body.'

'I already confirmed that earlier. What kind of an idiot do you take me for, Jack?'

Brady didn't know, but he was certain he was about to find out.

'Go on,' he finally conceded, accepting the worst. They – or should he say Wolfe – had fucked up big style.

He already knew who it was lying decapitated in the morgue. The missing fingers . . . the evidence the victim had had a baby. His hunch had been right.

'I rang the clinic in Budapest and demanded to talk to Dr Sabinas Bugas, the director of the clinic. I didn't believe that they couldn't keep a record of their patients and the serial numbers on the silicone implants they use. By law they have to, and if they don't they can get closed down. By all accounts that clinic runs a highly lucrative trade in plastic surgery. Their main clients are UK women looking for a cheap, quick fix and a holiday. But they also get Eastern Europeans paying for plastic surgery. Wanting to buy into the Hollywood ideal,' explained Wolfe. He paused for a moment to get his breath.

Brady waited.

It was like waiting to be punched in the guts. You know the blow's coming and you know no matter how much you prepare yourself, it's still going to hurt.

'Anyway,' continued Wolfe. 'I threatened Dr Bugas that we'd take court proceedings against them for withholding evidence. I didn't need to explain that the public image of the clinic would be so damaged that they'd end up losing most of their business. You know why they say they don't have the records, don't you?'

'No,' answered Brady in a muted voice.

He wasn't interested in the reasons behind the clinic withholding a patient's details. He was more interested in the identity of the patient.

'They're scared of litigation from their UK patients because of poor quality surgery and secondary infections. That kind of thing.'

Brady was silent for a moment.

Then he struck. His patience gone.

'Wolfe, just tell me!'

Silence.

Brady waited.

'The serial number in the silicone implants that I removed were implanted in an seventeen-year-old female named Edita Aginatas from a village in Lithuania called Raseiniai.'

Brady tried to steady himself.

He thought of Nicoletta.

He then thought of Edita Aginatas' baby and what would

happen to her now. And then of what had been done to Edita. Exactly as Nicoletta had said, she had disappeared. Her body savagely and sadistically raped and mutilated and a captive bolt pistol put to her head.

Brady swallowed. His eyes burning.

Tiredness, he thought. That's all. He didn't have the luxury to get emotional.

So Melissa Ryecroft was still missing.

And now Nicoletta.

That had to be the focus now.

He knew exactly who had Nicoletta: the Dabkunas brothers.

And Nick.

Brady had to contact Conrad before the press call went ahead. That was, if it already hadn't started.

He needed Melissa Ryecroft's details released. He needed the digitally enhanced images of her getting into the black Mercedes with the Dabkunas brothers shown on local and national television. And he needed to call Rubenfeld before his leading story went to print. And the worst part of all, the part that was really needling his spinal cord, was that he needed to make that call to Melissa Ryecroft's parents. He needed to tell them that he had fucked up. He had really fucked up big time.

*

Brady was anxiously waiting for Claudia to answer her phone and hoped that she hadn't already left for the Lithuanian Ambassador's swanky dinner at the Grand Hotel. It was now 6:17pm and there was a good chance she would be too preoccupied to talk to him.

He slowly breathed out, trying to steady himself.

In the event the press call had gone ahead at 6:00pm instead of 5:00pm, thus giving Gates enough time to collate the new information. Allegedly Gates was impressed that Brady had managed to forewarn them before they had gone public with the incorrect details on the investigation.

Brady wondered what would happen to Wolfe. It was a huge fuck-up. The first of its kind. Brady was worried: worried that Wolfe's liquid breakfasts and lunches were starting to take their toll on the Home Office pathologist. There would be an investigation and questions would have to be answered. Hopefully, Wolfe would get away with it this time. But what about the next time? Because Brady was certain there was going to be a next time. And if not, a time in the future would no doubt be waiting for him in the flat-bottomed transparent base of an empty bottle of Scotch. Reality had a way of catching up with you; a truth all too apparent to Brady at this particular moment in time.

'Claudia?' Brady said with relief when she eventually picked up her phone.

'Sorry, Jack. I'm really sorry. We found nothing. The girls that were in the club were all UK citizens and they were kosher.'

'What about the other premises that he owns?'

But he knew the answer would be the same. Daniels and Kenny had already reported back to him that there was nothing suspect about any of the properties or land that Ronnie Macmillan had acquired.

'Same deal – nothing,' answered Claudia. 'He's clean, Jack.'

Brady sighed. He had expecting as much but still hadn't wanted to hear it.

'Okay, thanks,' he said. 'I appreciate it.'

'The victim?' Claudia questioned.

'It's not Melissa Ryecroft. She's still missing. Whether that's giving her parents any comfort, who knows? They've seen the footage of her being led into a black Mercedes and being driven off.'

Brady didn't want to think back to the conversation he had with Brian Ryecroft after Wolfe's admission.

'I know . . . I can't imagine what they're going through,' said Claudia.

'No . . . neither can I,' answered Brady.

'The two men? Are they the Dabkunas brothers?' questioned Claudia.

'Your guess is as good as mine.'

He had too much to lose by sharing the information he had gleaned. He knew at this stage of the investigation, Claudia would take it to Gates and Adamson. She would have no choice given the fact that the two men seen abducting Melissa Ryecroft in the CCTV footage were the same two caught on surveillance camera at Rake Lane Hospital asking after Simone Henderson, and then later following Brady and Conrad as they left the hospital car park.

'Jack?' questioned Claudia. 'What's wrong?'

'Everything,' he answered quietly.

He hung up.

Brady stood up and put his jacket on. He'd had a call from Ainsworth saying that his car was ready to be collected. And given what he was going to be doing later that evening, he would need it. He needed to make sure that Conrad was busy – too busy to come looking for him. He knew from the way Conrad had been acting around him, questioning his judgement calls, that he had to do this alone. That, and the fact that he needed to make damn sure that no one knew about Nick. He was determined to bring down the Dabkunas brothers and their sick, twisted, lucrative enterprise.

And he would make damned sure that Nick was as far away from the North East as possible when it happened.

Chapter Thirty-Nine

Brady parked down a side street next to the abandoned eyesore that was the Avenue Pub. He looked across at the calm North Sea. It was a dirty grey colour. Reminiscent of the sky overhead. He rolled a cigarette as he steeled himself for what was to come next.

He had got out the station just in time. Turner, the desk sergeant, had rung him to tell him to watch out, that Adamson was searching the station for him in relation to Simone Henderson's attack.

'Reckons there are questions need answering, Jack,' Turner had said. 'Told him you were tied up on a joint murder and missing person investigation. Wasn't interested. Reckoned it would be the last case you'd ever work on. Arrogant bugger that he is!'

Brady appreciated Turner's loyalty. He had been around for years. But that didn't buy him any respect from the young blood coming through. They saw him as an old fool, too close to retiring age to be of any use to anybody. But Brady knew better than that.

He had left Conrad at the station researching Nykantas Vydunas, the Lithuanian Ambassador. Conrad wasn't overly impressed; not least because Brady wouldn't tell him why he was so interested in him. Brady had kept it to the point and stated, 'Mayor Macmillan.'

He had also left Conrad the job of finding out what they didn't already know about Ronnie Macmillan. The local drugs dealer-cum-gangster was becoming too powerful, too fast. And Brady wanted to know why. Brady was certain that his politician brother was pulling the strings, but he needed proof, and quickly.

He also needed to make sure that Conrad's hands were full. Too full for him to bother Brady tonight.

Kenny and Daniels were now chasing up various leads from Melissa Ryecroft's friends on Marijuis Dabkunas, her boyfriend. Including re-examining her Facebook page, her blog and her Twitter account for anything that would give them a lead on Marijuis and his brother. Whether anything would come of it, Brady seriously doubted.

And as for Harvey and Kodovesky, Brady had them staked out by the Hole. Just on the off-chance that Macmillan and his suits, Visa and Delta, turned up. Hopefully, he thought, with Nicoletta.

And then there was Claudia to think about. She would be attending the dinner at the Grand Hotel in honour of the Lithuanian Ambassador. As would Chief Superintendent O'Donnell and maybe even DCI Gates. Brady knew he would have to keep a low profile when he turned up there. The last thing he wanted was Claudia getting involved. Or his superiors. At least not until he got Nick out of the frame.

Brady put the cigarette in his mouth and lit it with his red refillable lighter. It reminded him of Claudia's hair.

He dragged heavily. He knew he had to kick the habit before the habit kicked him hard; hard enough to land him in the morgue.

He exited the car and looked up and down the street before locking the door. He had every right to be paranoid after what had happened to him over the past few days. He walked across Brook Street, heading for the Promenade.

Loud raucous shouts and laddish banter greeted him before he turned the corner onto East Parade.

'Bloody stag parties,' he muttered, dragging on his cigarette.

Business was looking good for Madley, noted Brady. He could see why it was such an attractive prospect for Ronnie Macmillan. Coachloads of young men with a disposable income on a weekend away. Weighed down with cash and a burning desire to spend it on a good time: alcohol, coke and a ride between the sheets. If Ronnie Macmillan opened up a lap dancing club adjacent to a hotel, he could cater for every stag party's needs and desires in one place.

Brady ignored the jeers as the lads, ranging from their early twenties to thirties, playfully jostled one another as a mobile phone showing some lewd footage was passed around. Brady knew that the emergency services would have their hands full later on. Faces glassed, broken noses and bust ribs . . . as the night progressed the list of injuries would go on.

He walked past them and up to the Blue Lagoon. The doors were locked, as expected. The place didn't open until 10:00pm. Brady banged on the doors.

He could see the barman, One-Eyed Carl, sorting out the bar. He looked up and saw Brady. He then picked up the phone and made a call.

Brady knew who he was calling; Carl was loyal to Madley. Always watching his back. Brady could see Carl's mouth move as he spoke to his boss. Then he hung up the phone, picked up the keys from behind the bar and walked over.

'You're early,' stated Carl as he locked the doors behind Brady.

He had his eye on the two coachloads of trouble parked up next door. The last thing he needed was them thinking this place was already open.

He followed Brady back to the bar.

'Can I get you something?' he asked as he picked up a tea towel and started polishing a perfectly clean pint glass.

'Coffee would be good,' answered Brady. 'Black, no sugar.'

What he would give for a pint or a shot of Scotch. But he knew that he needed a clear head. Especially later on.

Carl gave him a look of disbelief. He knew Brady liked to drink. Served him most weekends.

'Still at work,' explained Brady. 'And I've fucked off my boss enough today without him having another reason to sack me.'

Carl nodded and went over to the coffee filter machine. He poured Brady a steaming black coffee and brought it over.

'Thanks,' said Brady.

Carl gave him a questioning look.

'Madley's waiting for you,' he reminded.

'Let me drink my coffee first. Madley won't be going anywhere.'

He could now understand why Madley had brought in armed help from London. He had put Weasel Face's profile into the central database and come up with some unsavoury details. Madley's new henchman had unnerved him when he had seen him at the lighthouse yesterday. Enough for Brady to want to do some digging.

He'd discovered that the guy was a hired killer. No surprise there. He had only been out of prison for four months after executing (it was the only word to describe the killing) a client of Johnny Slaughter's who hadn't paid his debts. Brady shuddered at the details he had read about the way the bad debtor had been tortured before a gun was put to his right eye and the back of his head blown off. Weasel Face had spent eight years inside and was now out on remand because of good behaviour. Gone were the days, Brady bitterly mused, when life meant life. Instead, scum like Weasel Face could be released back into society in his late thirties with a prosperous career ahead of him in the world of violence and brutality.

'Where's Gibbs and the new boy?' asked Brady, making polite conversation.

Carl gestured towards the ceiling, indicating that they were upstairs with Madley.

Brady was surprised. This wasn't like Madley. He wasn't easily scared.

He took a mouthful of coffee realising that this was bigger and nastier than he'd first realised.

Brady then looked at Carl who was still polishing the same glass. But all the time he was watching Brady's every move. As well as keeping an eye on the doors.

'Carl? I need to ask some questions.'

Without looking at Brady, the barman stopped polishing and put down the glass. He turned and walked off to the kitchen, returning with fresh limes and a dangerous-looking knife and cutting board.

Brady watched. And waited.

Carl then threw the knife in the air, caught it by the handle and in one fast, furious movement swiftly chopped the limes. Finished, he aggressively stuck the knife's blade into the board and then looked at Brady.

Brady liked Carl. He just had a way.

Carl shot him a dangerous smile. 'What do you want to know?'

'What did Adamson ask you?'

'Shit is what!'

'What did you tell him?'

'Why?'

'Because your boss is in it up to his neck. That's why.'

Carl didn't react.

He never did. That was part of what Brady liked about him. He just got on with whatever crap was thrown at him. Including having his eyeball ripped out by a clenched hand punching him with a car key.

'I told him shit. He asked shit. I told him more shit.'

Brady looked at him and nodded. He expected as much. Carl saw everything that was going on around him. And he would have known that when Weasel Face showed up, things were going to start getting nasty. For all of them.

'Who was she talking to at the bar, Carl?' asked Brady.

'I told him I didn't see anything,' Carl replied with a laconic smile. 'Find it hard enough to keep my eye on the job as it is.'

'Yeah? But I'm not Adamson,' replied Brady.

'I may only have one eye but I'm not blind. You're still a copper,' answered Carl, losing the smile.

'Not tonight I'm not. And not where Madley's concerned either.'

Carl studied him.

He was only in his early twenties but he had an air about him. One that said that he had seen it all. Even with one eye he was a handsome guy. Never short of female attention. Tall, with tousled curly dark blond hair and an unshaven look to match. Always sharply dressed though. Smart black suit, white open-neck shirt and sharp shoes.

Barman, receptionist and prime look-out – he did it all. Without effort.

Brady watched as he picked up a new, equally clean glass and began methodically polishing it. Without looking Brady in the eye, he started to talk.

'Visa and Delta were in. Throwing money around. Acting like they owned the place.'

'Ronnie Macmillan's boys?' asked Brady.

'Yeah, the Macmillan boys. Nasty shits. Think the designer suits and sunglasses and the black Jag mean something. Means shit. They're still ugly, hired thugs, regardless of the Armani name tag.'

'Then what happened?' asked Brady.

'She comes in. The copper. Stunning looking. Too fucking good for those suited gorillas. Joins them at the bar. They know who she is and it seems that she already knows them. Macmillan's boys buy a bottle of champagne but they never touch a drop. She drinks maybe four glasses, if that. Then an hour and a half later I notice that her speech has started to slur and her eyes . . . you know that look? Pupils dilated? Can't stand up. She wasn't pissed though. But she was wasted. I reckon when she went to the loos they slipped something in her drink. I see it happening all the time in here.'

Brady knew that Carl's assumption was right. The lab

had found significant traces of Rohypnol, the date rape drug, in Simone's blood and urine.

'Why didn't you do something if you thought she'd been drugged?' asked Brady, an edge to his voice.

'I'm paid to serve people not to fucking babysit!'

Brady could hardly get in Carl's face about this; he was no better. He had seen Simone talking to Macmillan's suits and walked out. If he had only gone over and asked her what the fuck she was doing with them, then she might not be in intensive care.

'Did she leave with them?' he asked.

'Visa made a call and then ten minutes later they leave. Literally carrying the copper. They walked off down East Parade towards Brook Street.'

Brady shot him a questioning look.

'I was having a tab break out front,' Carl explained.

'Since when has Madley allowed his staff to have breaks? Let alone allow tab out front?'

'When Madley wants me to keep an eye on a situation. Visa and Delta chucking money around in his club to impress a copper is a situation.'

Brady nodded. He could see that.

'How did you know she was a copper?' asked Brady.

'Just did. Been around you too long. Anyway, I have a thing for faces. Remembered her being in here with you a couple of times.'

Brady winced. That was over a year ago when he had last been in the Blue Lagoon with Simone, then a DC and his junior colleague.

'What happened next?' he asked.

'A black panel van, Mercedes I think, is parked up in the back lane of the Avenue pub. Visa and Delta and the copper approach it and are met by two evil-looking shits dressed in black suits. Ex-military, I'd say.'

Brady frowned. 'Why do you say that?'

'You can just tell. They had this edge about them. Real nasty edge.'

'Did they look Eastern European?' asked Brady.

'Yeah . . . foreign. Dark, dangerous, with a fucking glint in their eye which told you they'd slit you from ear to ear if you looked at them the wrong way.'

The Dabkunas brothers, thought Brady.

'What about the driver?'

Carl shook his head. 'Couldn't see the driver from where I was stood. The van was parked facing the other way.'

'How did you see all this stood out front?'

'I was having a tab break. I'm allowed to stretch my legs,' slowly answered Carl as he started polishing again.

'What made you follow them?'

'Madley asks me to do something, I do it. No questions asked.'

'Can you describe the van?' asked Brady.

'Yeah, cost a lot of money. New. Mercedes-Benz black panel van. Tinted windows. You know the type used for carrying cargo?'

'Yeah,' Brady replied, getting the idea of what kind of cargo they'd be carrying. 'Did you get the licence plate at all?' he asked hopefully.

'No,' answered Carl.

Brady raised his eyebrow.

'It was dark. You do the maths,' answered Carl, giving Brady a look.

Brady wasn't sure whether the barman had actually seen the licence plate. But he knew not to push him.

'Why did they do that to her? Simone?'

'Your guess is as good as mine,' Carl shrugged.

'Come on, Carl. You don't expect me to believe that?'

'Look, this goes nowhere. Alright? The shit that's going on now is dangerous. For me . . . for Madley . . . Even you.'

'Who? Who are you scared of?'

Carl stared at Brady. 'Who do you think?'

'Ronnie Macmillan.'

Carl's reaction told Brady he was right.

'Why? What's Ronnie got to do with this?'

'Everything,' answered Carl as he stared hard at Brady.

'Go on.'

Carl shook his head. 'Alright, but I'm only telling you because he's leaning really heavily on Madley. Understand? He needs sorting and if that means banging him up to get him off Madley's back then so be it.' Carl paused for a moment, looking down the corridor which led to the entrance upstairs to Madley's office.

'A black Jaguar turns up Brook Street and then pulls into the Avenue car park at the bottom of the back lane. Right by the Merc van.'

'What happened next?' asked Brady.

'Visa and Delta had hold of the copper. She was completely wasted by now. Whatever they had given her had kicked in. Couldn't stand up. They were arguing with the two Eastern European guys. It looked as if it was about to get nasty. Looked like the two ex-military-looking guys wanted to put her in the back of the van, but Macmillan's boys weren't letting her go. Then Ronnie Macmillan gets out the back of the Jaguar and steps in. He said something to the Eastern Europeans. Whatever he said calmed the situation down.'

'Who took her then?'

'Who do you think? Ronnie Macmillan. He opened the boot of his Jaguar and she got dumped in there. Visa and Delta got in the front, Ronnie Macmillan got back in the back and they drove off, followed by the Merc van.'

'Did you see the driver of the van?' asked Brady, trying to keep his voice level. He needed to know. To know whether it was Nick.

Carl looked at him and shook his head.

'No, like I've already said, it was dark.'

'Which direction?' asked Brady.

He was already thinking that he'd get Conrad to check out the CCTV footage they had along the Promenade. He knew that where they'd parked up there were no cameras, which was why Adamson wouldn't have seen either the black Jaguar or the Mercedes van. Let alone Ronnie Macmillan's boys dumping Simone Henderson's drugged body into the boot of Macmillan's car.

'They drove along the Promenade and turned up Marine Drive.'

Brady had a feeling that Macmillan might have taken her back to his club in Wallsend. After all, he did have private rooms there which guaranteed his clientele anonymity. It was the kind of place where no one would ask questions. A perfect front for whatever Ronnie Macmillan and the Eastern European brothers were involved in. And then there were the abandoned warehouses and buildings that Ronnie Macmillan had been buying up. He could have taken Simone Henderson to any of those locations and mutilated her. Then again, Brady had to trust the fact that Claudia and her team and Kenny and Daniels had found nothing suspicious at any of Macmillan's premises.

And, given the gravity of Simone's attack, Brady couldn't imagine that she had been taken far. Otherwise, Ronnie Macmillan and the Dabkunas brothers ran the risk of her dying in transit. And from the game that Macmillan was playing with Madley, he wanted the police to raid Madley's club on a tip-off that a copper was lying with near fatal injuries in the gents'. Brady didn't want to think of Nick. He didn't want to think that his own brother could have had a hand in anything so heinous.

'Why didn't you contact the police when you saw her being abducted?' asked Brady.

Carl looked at Brady.

'I do what Madley tells me to do. I reported exactly what I saw to him. It's then up to Madley what he does with that information.'

Brady simply nodded. 'Thanks, Carl.'

'This goes nowhere. Understand?' demanded Carl.

'Trust me.'

'You're a copper, what's there to trust?' replied Carl.

Brady nodded. He understood Carl's point.

'Right now being a copper is the furthest thing from my mind,' he replied quietly. 'And right now, I reckon I'm the only person Madley can trust. And with Ronnie Macmillan prepared to do anything to get him out, I'd say he needs me. Wouldn't you?' His voice was heavy with concern.

Carl didn't say a word. He didn't need to: they both knew that Brady was right.

No surprise then that Madley was shitting himself, thought Brady as he watched Carl start to get the bar ready for the crowd that would be in soon enough. He had every right to be. Mayor Macmillan was clever. A new threat had come to the North East: Eastern European gangsters. And

Macmillan had made sure that he was aligned with them. After all, they were a breed apart from the likes of Madley and Johnny Slaughter and even his own brother, Ronnie. At least they had some kind of morality code, thought Brady. Whereas these Eastern European gangsters had no morals. And that's precisely what made them so dangerous; that and the fact that they were ex-military.

Chapter Forty

He'd gone out for a tab first, before going up to see Madley. He needed an excuse to get out and make a call. One that had to be made in private without Carl overhearing.

He sucked hard on his cigarette to keep it alight as he stared up at the sky. It had been a dark, dismal grey day but now that evening had come there was a change in the air. The sky was lightening as the mute, overcast blanket that had covered it started to lift.

Brady could just make out a blood red sun, burning on the horizon. An omen if ever there was one.

'Conrad?'

'Yes, sir?' answered Conrad.

'What have you got?'

'Not much, sir. I did get some background on Nykantas Vydunas, the Lithuanian Ambassador, and he's on his third marriage to some French ex-model. He has one child, a nineteen-year-old daughter from his first marriage, currently studying at Oxford. From all accounts a bit of party girl. Spends more of her time in London clubbing it than she does at university.'

'Did you get anything connecting him and Macmillan?' Brady asked.

'No, sir. Whatever business deal is going on between the Ambassador and Mayor Macmillan appears to be kosher. Vydunas is a multi-millionaire, old money. His business is shipping. Runs a highly successful cargo shipping company. And that's the only connection I can make with Mayor Macmillan. He wants to use Vydunas' cargo company to ship over Polish provisions to the North East. It's all to do with some multi-cultural push between the North East of England and Eastern Europe, in particular Poland.'

'Anything else?' asked Brady.

'That's it, sir. Apart from . . .'

'Yes?'

'Well, it seems that there's a lot of activity around him just now. He's called in extra security. Whether he's expecting trouble in the North East, I can't say but he has got an unusual amount of armed personnel surrounding him. He's also booked in at the Hotel du Vin, close to Newcastle quayside. Ideal location given it's off the beaten track. He's booked the whole hotel for a week. The staff there have intimated that he seems obsessed about privacy and security. Especially when he's holding business meetings or has clients visit.'

'Like who?' asked Brady.

'I don't know, sir. I couldn't find that out.'

'When you say clients do you mean women?' asked Brady.

'I honestly can't say. The staff said that he's extremely cautious and demands absolute privacy for his visiting guests.'

Brady knew the Hotel du Vin. He had taken Claudia there once for dinner to sample the delights of its noted wine cellar. It had commanding views of the River Tyne and the quayside. It had formerly been a shipping head-quarters and had been renovated, as had most of the old buildings down that part of the quayside.

'Conrad, you wouldn't know if a black Mercedes panel van has been making visits to the Ambassador's hotel, would you?' Brady thought back to his conversation with Carl, Madley's bartender, and Nicoletta's description of the black Mercedes van used to transport the Dabkunas' girls around.

'No, sir,' answered Conrad sounding confused. 'But I can make enquiries.'

'Can you also go over the CCTV footage of the Promenade in Whitley Bay from last night? A black Mercedes-Benz panel van pulled out from Brook Street and headed down the Promenade turning up Marine Avenue. The Mercedes was tailing the black Jaguar that we saw Macmillan and his boys in earlier. I want to know where they go. See if you can trace their movements at all. I have a gut feeling that they were heading for Macmillan's club or maybe one of the disused properties that he's bought up.'

'Sir?' questioned Conrad, realising the job he was being asked to do.

'Contact me when you have something,' answered Brady.

'If this is to do with Simone Henderson's attack, shouldn't we take this information to Adamson and Gates, sir?'

'What do you think, Conrad?'

'Sir?' repeated Conrad, unsure.

'I wouldn't piss on Adamson if he was on fire. Does that answer your question?'

'Yes, sir,' replied Conrad.

'The murder of the Lithuanian girl, Melissa Ryecroft's abduction and Simone's attack are all connected, Conrad.

Trust me on this. Which makes it our investigation now. We've just got to prove it and I'll be dammed if I hand anything over to that bastard and then watch him take the glory.'

'How do you know, sir? How can you be so certain?'

'I just know, Conrad.'

Brady hung up.

He drew heavily on his cigarette as he listened to the pulsating music coming from further down East Parade, in the direction of South Parade. The back of the Blue Lagoon nightclub. It was a miserable sight. Bricked walls on either side, beer crates and overflowing bins blocked Brady in. In front of him were two cars. The gleaming, new Bentley was Madley's and the three-year-old silver BMW was Gibbs'.

Brady drew again on his cigarette. The air was suffocating. Filled with intoxicating smells. The Pizza Cottage, the Indian restaurants and the two Italian restaurants along East Parade were in full battle when it came to the heady aromas spewing from their kitchen extractor fans. Brady's stomach growled. He realised he hadn't eaten anything since the bacon stottie he'd had for breakfast that morning. But all he had to do was think of the shit that Nick was caught up in to quell his appetite.

He took one last drag on his cigarette before throwing the smouldering stub away. He had to call Claudia. He needed to make sure that they had searched all of the rooms at Macmillan's club. Including the cellar and those on the first floor and the attic rooms. He just needed reassurance that nothing had been missed. That there were no traces of blood anywhere, or weapons hidden. In particular the hunting/survival knife that was used to decapitate Edita Aginatas.

And that they had definitely found nothing incriminating at the buildings and wasteland that Macmillan now owned. He knew Claudia would be getting ready for the dinner in honour of the Lithuanian Ambassador, held by Mayor Macmillan. But Brady had no choice. He had to be sure.

He scrolled down, found her name and pressed call.

As he did so, he shoved his free hand in his trouser pocket, absent-mindedly fingering his wedding ring.

'Claudia?' he questioned when the phone picked up.

'No,' came the answer. Simple and to the point.

'Can I talk to her?'

'She's busy.'

Before Brady had a chance to answer the phone went dead. He knew it was Davidson. Recognised the voice. And Davidson clearly knew it was Brady.

Brady stood for a moment holding his BlackBerry. He felt as if he had been kicked in the guts. And if the truth be known, he had. DCI Davidson had made it very clear that Claudia was off-bounds to him.

*

'Jack,' greeted Madley as Brady walked into his spacious first-floor office.

Brady knew straight away that he was pissed off. Who with, he didn't yet know, but he was certain he was about to find out.

He cast his eye over the huge room. Madley was standing with his back to Brady, staring out of the impressive ceiling-to-floor window. Weasel Face was behind the door, watching Brady's every move while Gibbs waited by Madley's side.

The tension in the room was palpable. Brady wasn't sure

what he had walked into, but he knew he didn't like it. There was an edge, a desperation to hold onto power regardless of the consequences, that Brady could feel clinging to the air. Ronnie Macmillan had gone one step too far with Madley and Brady presumed Madley was now in the throes of working out how to get the bastard back.

Brady should have been worried, but he knew Madley could look after himself. He, after all, had been raised on the hardened streets of the Ridges, just as Brady had. A childhood that set you up for anything that life would throw at you; Ronnie Macmillan and his politician brother being two of them. Even ex-military SAS types like the Dabkunas brothers.

'Problem?' questioned Madley, still with his back to Brady.

'You tell me,' answered Brady as he walked over to the window trying his best not to limp.

The last thing he wanted was Weasel Face spotting a weakness.

Madley didn't answer.

'Boys. Leave us alone,' ordered Madley.

Madley waited until the door was firmly closed.

'Matthews . . .' Brady began.

Madley looked at him and waited.

'Ronnie Macmillan's boys went to see him inside. Wanted a word. They knew he worked for you.' He watched Madley's reaction.

Madley's glinting brown eyes narrowed suspiciously.

They stood in silence for a few moments watching through the window the blood-red explosion that lit up the horizon.

'Bastard,' Madley finally said.

There was a tone of finality in that one word. Enough for a cold shiver to go down Brady's spine.

'Exactly what did he say?' Madley questioned.

Brady shrugged.

'Exactly what?' repeated Madley.

'Reckons that my old man was stitched up by two of your boys.'

'And that's what Matthews told Macmillan's boys?'

Brady nodded.

'Visa and Delta are their names. Seems they took the shit my old man's been saying seriously.'

'Fucking bastard. Deserves everything he got.' There was a malevolent menace in Madley's voice.

Brady couldn't disagree with him.

'And what? Matthews is listening to that piece of snivelling shit?'

'Matthews wants out,' answered Brady.

'Heart fucking bleeds. Bent copper and all, he won't last long inside.'

Again, a chill went down Brady's spine.

'Not only that, Matthews identified a photograph they had of Simone Henderson. The copper found in your toilets early yesterday this morning,' he added.

Madley's eyes dangerously narrowed as he absorbed this new information.

'Martin?'

'What?'

Brady noted that Madley still wouldn't look at him. His glinting brown eyes were studying the drunken, high-spirited revellers below with predatory interest. He had the look of a man who was out for the kill. And Brady knew that Nick, amongst others, was a target.

'Why didn't you say what's been going on with Ronnie Macmillan?' ventured Brady.

Madley's jaw tightened.

'Because I can sort this out myself,' he answered.

'Doesn't seem that way to me,' replied Brady.

'I wouldn't worry about me, Jack. I'd say you already have your hands full trying to stop that brother of yours. He's got himself involved with some bad company. Just like before, but this time he can't come running to me to sort it.'

'I'll stop him.'

'I hope for his sake that you do. If you don't, then I will. With the help of Johnny and his brother Billy.'

Brady knew the kind of help Johnny Slaughter and his brother, Billy, more notoriously known as 'Billy Slash Slaughter', would give Madley.

Madley slowly turned and looked at Brady.

'Stop him. Because believe me, Jack, I don't want to hurt him. But if I have to, then that's what I'll do.'

Brady knew the score. He couldn't argue with Madley. Nick had crossed the line, not only with Madley, but also with his own brother. It was now only a matter of time before either Brady or Madley tracked him down. Brady was just hoping that Weasel Face didn't get to him first. Brady knew that Weasel Face had a penchant for putting the barrel of his gun to his victim's right eye and blowing their brains out.

'What do you know about Macmillan and these Eastern European brothers that he's working with?' Brady questioned.

Madley turned back to the window, his face suddenly darkening.

'I know that this is bigger than you imagine.'

'I already know who they are,' Brady replied. 'Ex-military until a year ago. Dangerous fuckers who were in the Lithuanian army's Special Operation Forces. Last known to be working as bodyguards. From what I heard they're working for the Lithuanian Ambassador who's up here just now.'

Madley shook his head. 'You're not listening. This is bigger than you can imagine, Jack. Let it go. Find Nick and get him the fuck out of my town. That's all you have to do.'

Madley turned and held Brady's eye. The look was hard and dangerous.

'And leave me to deal with Macmillan and those Dabkunas bastards. Because believe me, those sick fuckers won't know what's hit them when I'm done.'

Brady didn't argue with Madley. It was pointless.

He turned and walked towards the door.

'And Jack?'

Brady stopped and turned to look at Madley. He had his back to him as he looked out the window.

'Tell Nick from me that I never want to see his fucking face around here again.'

Chapter Forty-One

Brady limped back to his car, kicking a vodka bottle out of his way. He turned back instinctively, checking that no one was following him. He realised that his paranoia was getting the better of him. He was starting to see things that weren't there.

'*Come on, Jack!*' he angrily muttered to himself.

He needed to get his head together. And fast. But he couldn't get rid of the feeling that he was being watched from every shadowy corner. Ghosts from his past coming back to haunt him.

He took his phone out. It was now 7:48pm and he had two missed calls.

One from Conrad and the other from Claudia.

He unlocked the Granada and climbed in, making a point of checking the back seat and floor first for any more surprises. Nothing.

Despite Ainsworth and his forensics team's meticulous search, whoever had had left the severed head in a black bin liner on the back seat had been very careful not to leave any other incriminating evidence behind.

Brady tried to block the image of the black bag's contents

from his mind. He shakily breathed out, trying to steady himself.

'*Come on . . . get a grip . . .*'

He held his head in his hands trying to rid himself of the panic he was feeling.

He had to focus. He needed to call Conrad. To get back on track.

He forced himself to look at his mobile. He pressed call and waited.

'What did you find?' he quickly questioned, as soon as Conrad picked up.

'They didn't turn up Marine Avenue. They continued along the Promenade to the Links, sir,' answered Conrad. 'The CCTV camera on the Siam Restaurant on the corner of Marine Avenue shows them continuing along the Links Road towards Whitley Bay cemetery. That was at approximately 1:19am.'

'Both of them?'

'Yes sir, the Jaguar followed by the Mercedes van.'

'Where were they heading?'

'I don't know, sir,' answered Conrad. 'I know that they don't get as far as Seaton Sluice or even Old Hartley. So they've stopped somewhere along the Links. Either Feathers caravan park or by Whitley Bay cemetery.'

'Or by St Mary's Lighthouse,' muttered Brady.

He thought back to the victim's head and note left by his brother in his car and the significance of the location – the lighthouse. Brady already had a gut feeling what it was his brother was trying to tell him. But he didn't want to believe it.

'Sir?' questioned Conrad.

'Think about it, Conrad. Why do you think the van followed Macmillan's car?'

'If it is his car, sir?'

'It's his bloody car alright! Check the licence plate,' hissed Brady.

'Couldn't get a shot of the licence plate from the angle of the camera, sir.'

'Moot point. It's him alright,' muttered Brady darkly.

'I have checked and there's no black Jaguar registered in Ronnie Macmillan's name, sir.'

'I wouldn't expect it to be registered in his name. He's too clever for that, Conrad. He uses the car for business and the kind of business he deals in he won't want anything that connects him to it.'

Brady sighed as he started up the engine, resisting the urge to put the car in first and drive. He felt too vulnerable sitting there.

'What those bastards did to Simone was carried out in that Mercedes van. They'd have the space and the privacy to carry out what they wanted with her. And you tell me where no one would question hearing a woman screaming?' demanded Brady, not taking his eyes off the street and road around him.

'I don't know, sir,' answered Conrad uneasily, worried by the fraught tension in his boss's voice.

Brady sighed irritably. 'What do you do with yourself when you're not at work, Conrad?'

Conrad didn't reply.

Brady already knew about his personal life. It was something they didn't talk about.

'Well, there's one place you obviously don't go and that's St Mary's Lighthouse. The two car parks there are used by doggers from all over the North East. So a woman screaming in a van with a couple of men might have raised something, but it wouldn't have been an eyebrow, that's for sure.'

Still Conrad remained silent.

'What about later on in the morning? We know that Simone was discovered by Carl, Madley's bartender, at approximately 3:15am so that means that they had to return to the Blue Lagoon to leave Simone in the gents' there.'

'I already checked the CCTV footage for around that time, sir,' answered Conrad.

'And?'

'No Jaguar but the same Mercedes van returns along the Links, continuing onto the Promenade at approximately 2:56am.'

'Which is in the direction of Madley's nightclub, the Blue Lagoon.'

Brady cursed under his breath as he thought about Nick and what he was trying to tell him.

'Look, Conrad,' he began, trying to steady his voice, 'I have a gut feeling that Edita Aginatas wasn't the first victim. I reckon that the Mercedes van is used to transport girls. Victims that have been murdered for sexual pleasure. Just as Claudia detailed when she talked about the Nietzschean Brotherhood.'

'You really believe it's happening here, sir?' queried Conrad incredulously. 'In Whitley Bay of all places?'

'You do the maths, Conrad. Edita Aginatas' body washes up on the shore of Whitley Bay beach. High tide last night was at 11:18pm BST and then low tide was 4:23am BST.'

'Sir?'

'I checked yesterday morning's tides with the coastguard,' Brady explained. 'Either they don't know their tides or she was deliberately dumped mid-tide position. Hell of a coincidence then don't you think that her body washes up around 4:00 in the morning? Same morning that Simone's butchered, drugged body is dumped in Madley's nightclub. I reckon it's the same van that was used to dump Edita Aginatas' body.'

'So how do they get the body out there so it gets washed up? If they do it by Whitley Bay or Cullercoats or even Tynemouth Beach surely someone would see them? And the van was heading in the opposite direction, sir,' Conrad pointed out.

'Wrong location, Conrad,' snapped Brady. 'I used to play around the lighthouse when I was a kid. There's a sandy beach down there hidden from view on the left-hand side. The other side is covered in rock pools and jagged rocks so a boat wouldn't be able to come in on that side to take the body out. And nor would they throw a body over the railings on that side as it would hit the rocks below. I reckon a small tugboat must have met them down there on that beach. It wouldn't make much noise so it wouldn't bring unwanted attention. Edita's body would have been taken out and dumped in between tides. If they wanted her to disappear they would have weighted her down, Conrad. And they didn't. After talking to Nicoletta I reckon that Edita was murdered and her body was intentionally dumped so it would wash up as a warning to the other girls like her not to attempt to make a run for it.'

Conrad's silence said it all.

'Get back to me as soon as you've got something,' he muttered thickly, realising that Conrad didn't quite trust him on this.

He sighed heavily as he cut the call. He couldn't blame

Conrad. None of it made sense; least of all to him. He had been certain from everything that Carl had said that Ronnie Macmillan and his boys Visa and Delta had attacked Simone. But now he wasn't so sure. The CCTV evidence showing the black Mercedes van heading back to the Blue Lagoon suggested that this was the work of the Dabkunas brothers. And he couldn't ignore the fact that Nick was in their employment. Trina McGuire had said as much. Nor could he ignore the fact that his brother had left Simone's body in the toilets before making the 999 call.

All Brady could think was that Ronnie Macmillan and his boys procured Simone for the Dabkunas brothers as some business deal. That possibility was made all the more likely by the fact that Simone, according to Claudia, was already investigating the Eastern European brothers who Brady now believed were operating an international sex trafficking operation using St Mary's Lighthouse as a drop-off point.

He agitatedly ran his hand over the dark stubble covering his face.

He had a small, over-stretched team doing everything in their power to find some information on the Dabkunas brothers, to lead them to Melissa Ryecroft's whereabouts. Appeals had been made to the public for any information regarding the abducted teenager. Brady had decided it was better to go armed with as much information as possible to throw at the public. Then, hopefully, they'd get some kosher calls connected to the murder rather than the crazies who wanted instant fame and notoriety, regardless of how they came by it. As of yet, nothing concrete had come back about either the car used for her abduction or the two men seen placing her in the back of it. Her friends had all been interviewed but there had been no contact from her since her disappearance. Nor did they have any information on the victim's boyfriend, Marijuis Dabkunas. Either from her friends, or from any other police authorities.

Brady reluctantly accepted that the Dabkunas brothers' military background gave them the skills and knowledge to cover their tracks and elude detection. He shuddered to think how large their operation actually was and how many girls had ended up like Edita Aginatas.

*

He looked at the other missed call: Claudia. Davidson had obviously told her that Brady had rung.

He pressed call and waited, hoping that he wouldn't hear DCI Davidson's voice.

'Claudia?' questioned Brady when the call was answered.

'I haven't got time to talk, Jack,' agitatedly stated Claudia.

Brady supported the phone against his hunched shoulder as he used his free hand to rub his eyes. He was tired and hungry and in need of a drink. But he knew his night was just beginning.

'Claudia,' Brady began, ignoring her exasperation, 'when you searched Macmillan's club did you thoroughly search all the rooms on the first and second floor?'

'Jack, Ronnie Macmillan has nothing. He's clean. Just like his brother, Mayor Macmillan. You've got to let this obsession of yours go before it costs you your job.'

'Answer the question.'

Claudia sighed wearily.

'No. Alright?'

'No,' repeated Brady. 'I thought you had a warrant? I

asked you specifically to search the cellar and all the rooms above the club.'

'To check out whether the girls he had employed there were legal. Yes. But we didn't have a warrant to go poking around in the disused rooms upstairs. There's only so much I can do, Jack. Unlike you, I play by the law. Remember that? You need a good reason to search his private premises. His work place is a different matter. We went in on the principle that we'd had reports that he was employing illegal immigrants. Nothing more.'

'Personal premises?' questioned Brady.

'That's what I said. Supposedly he occupies the upstairs rooms. Said he likes to live above the club to keep an eye on his business.'

'Shit, Claudia!'

'What?'

'You've given him ample warning to get rid of whatever women or evidence of sex trafficking and imprisonment he has there. Including Nicoletta,' Brady agitatedly pointed out.

'Come on, Jack. You can't lay this at my door!'

'Can't I?'

'You know you can't,' replied Claudia firmly. 'I did everything I possibly could within the constraints of the law.'

'Yeah? Tell that to Nicoletta's family and Melissa Ryecroft's parents. And God knows who else these bastards are holding.'

Claudia was silent.

'Look, I'm sorry. Alright? It's just . . .' Brady faltered.

'Don't you think I feel the same way? I deal with this kind of crime day in, day out. But unfortunately there are procedures to be followed whether we like it or not.'

'I know,' muttered Brady.

'Look, I've got to go. Keep me updated?'

'Sure,' answered Brady before the line was disconnected.

He started the engine up and pulled the Granada out from Brook Street and turned right into the Promenade.

He narrowed his eyes as he slowed down for the zebra crossing ahead. He looked to his right and watched as what looked to be a hen party staggered across the road, the scantily-clad women walking arm in arm, four-inch heels clattering as they went.

Brady double-checked the rear view mirror again, making sure he wasn't being followed. Despite his feeling that someone was tailing his every move, the road was clear. He pulled away, heading along the coast in the direction of the Grand Hotel in Tynemouth. Adrenalin was coursing through his veins at the thought of what was coming next.

He had two girls missing.

One Lithuanian sex slave who he only knew as Nicoletta, taken by Ronnie Macmillan, and the other, a sixteen-year-old sixth-form student who had been abducted by the Dabkunas brothers.

Chapter Forty-Two

Brady pulled up opposite the Grand Hotel. It was now 8:13pm. All he could do was wait. He switched the Granada's engine off and looked at the steps leading up to the hotel. Red lights burnt on either side of the imposing hotel. A doorman in gold braid and a top hat stood erect, looking official.

Mayor Macmillan was out to impress, noted Brady.

He took out his Golden Virginia tobacco and started to roll himself a cigarette.

He had too many thoughts going through his head.

Always there, weighing him down, was the thought of Nick and what his brother had become involved in.

Brady sat smoking cigarette after cigarette as he watched and waited.

What exactly for, he wasn't sure. All he knew was that the Lithuanian Ambassador would be here soon and that something was going on. From what Conrad had said, the Ambassador had hired extra armed security. So evidently he was expecting trouble in the North East. But from who, Brady had no idea. And then there were his connections with the Dabkunas brothers and Mayor Macmillan.

Brady sighed heavily and rubbed his eyes. He knew exactly why he was here. On the off-chance the Dabkunas brothers turned up in the capacity of ex-military body-guards, accompanied by Nick. He needed to get hold of Nick first. Give him time to disappear before calling in for backup. Brady knew that he was risking everything for his brother right now. But he had no choice. Nick, excluding Madley, was his only connection to his past. They were the only two people who really knew Brady. And he wasn't going to let that go. There was also the fact that Nick was the only family he had left. His old man in Durham Gaol didn't count as family.

Brady tried to ignore what had been troubling him. He had been pushing it to the back of his mind but now, as he sat outside the Grand Hotel waiting for Nick, it was torturing him. If Visa and Delta had heard his old man's accusation that Brady and Madley had set up him up, then it would come as no surprise that Nick had heard as well. Brady didn't want to think it but the thought kept coming back. What if Nick was intentionally trying to sabotage Madley as payback for the old man? After all, it had been Nick on the security camera, caught dumping Simone Henderson in the toilets. And it was Nick's voice on the 999 call reporting the mutilated body of a copper in Madley's nightclub, the Blue Lagoon.

Brady inhaled deeply as he tried to forget the CCTV image of Nick stood leaning against the black Lithuanian-plated Mercedes, waiting to tail him when he left Rake Lane Hospital with Conrad. Not long afterwards, the decapitated head of a Lithuanian girl had been left in his car. Along with a note, signed 'N', which Brady desperately wanted to believe was representative of the Nietzschean

Brotherhood – the Dabkunas brothers' ring with the 'N' emblem was the most palatable explanation.

But what was haunting Brady was the glaring possibility that the 'N' could mean 'Nick.' After all, that was how he always signed any correspondence between them. Whether it was an email or a text, Nick always signed it with an 'N'. Exactly as he had signed the handwritten note delivered to the desk sergeant, Turner.

He heard a car pull up and looked over at the Grand. Two black Mercedes were there with their engines idling, awaiting instruction. In between them was a black, ostentatious Russian limousine with diplomat's plates. Brady had never seen its kind before, but he knew it would have a reserved power beneath its bonnet.

Brady watched as the front and rear doors of both the Mercedes opened with quiet precision and eight black-suited, ex-militia killers got out.

A second later, the driver of the limousine got out and looked around. With a single nod he dispersed the eight others into a well rehearsed, tried and tested octagon of protection. Another look around and the driver walked over and opened the rear door of the limousine to let out the Ambassador. Brady noted that he was speaking into a hidden microphone. The driver, sunglasses on, regardless of the dusk settling in, suddenly stopped talking. He gave the Ambassador a brief nod of assurance, and then stood back.

Brady could see the hint of a shoulder holster under the driver's jacket as he stepped back from the limousine. Ex-military, assumed Brady. He had that look about him. The black suit, crisp white shirt and black tie didn't disguise the fact that his main job was as a bodyguard; the chauffeuring was a front. Throw into the mix his muscular, taut, 6′4″ build and the set jaw and determined, distrustful expression and there was proof enough. Without adding the bullet-hole scar on his cheek and the blonde, side-parted hair which revealed an earpiece. He was the central player and around him, strategically placed, were his team. No doubt his old comrades in war. It was clear he would have always been in charge; the highest ranking soldier. He wouldn't trust anyone.

Brady watched as the Ambassador got out. Alert, lean, with short, well-groomed sandy hair. His dark blue, hand-tailored suit fitted his 5′10″ frame perfectly. His moderately handsome face was tanned, accentuating his bright blue eyes. Overall he had the appearance of a man who had money – lots of it. Enough money not to have to worry about anything in life. Yet, Brady couldn't help noticing that the Ambassador, for all his power and money, looked troubled. It was etched across his face. He merely nodded at his driver, distracted it seemed by what lay ahead. His bright blue eyes looked up at the elegant entrance of the Grand Hotel where Brady realised Mayor Macmillan was now standing, proud and arrogant, with other councillors, waiting to greet him. Brady noticed that Chief Superintendent O'Donnell was one of the official dignitaries, dressed in his braided uniform ready to welcome the Lithuanian Ambassador.

Brady waited. Expecting the Dabkunas brothers to get out of the limousine. Accompanied by Nick.

It didn't happen.

The Ambassador, dignified and now composed, walked up the wide, sandstone steps towards his newfound business partner, Mayor Macmillan. Behind him, his driver shadowed his every move.

Brady watched them disappear into the hotel reception area.

Five minutes later he could see Mayor Macmillan standing at the window with the Lithuanian Ambassador by his side. Each had a tumbler in their hand as they seemingly discussed the view. But Brady knew better than that. It would be business they were discussing. Or at least the business front they would be using for their illegal imports.

*

Brady checked his phone. It was now 10:37pm.

He was expecting the Ambassador and his driver to be leaving soon. He could make out official-looking figures around in the bar. The dinner presumably over, the guests were now enjoying drinks. Claudia being one of them, mused Brady.

He lit the cigarette he had rolled, not wanting to count how many he had smoked while he had been sat waiting.

What for exactly, he was unclear of now. The Dabkunas brothers hadn't showed. Neither had Nick. He presumed the Ambassador would be returning to his hotel, along with his heavily armed entourage.

Maybe Rubenfeld had got it wrong?

But he would have been surprised if he had: Rubenfeld's contacts had never let him down. In as much as Rubenfeld had never let Brady down.

His phone suddenly rang.

Brady picked it up and answered it.

'Yeah?'

He realised his heart was racing.

'Jack?' It was DS Tom Harvey's voice.

Brady had assigned Harvey and his partner, DC Kodovesky, the job of stalking out the Hole. He needed Ronnie Macmillan's every move monitored on the off-chance it would led them to Nicoletta.

'What is it, Tom?'

'Ronnie Macmillan's on the move. Accompanied by his two suits. They returned about an hour ago to his club. Looked as if they went upstairs. Lights went on and what not. Then they left the club and got into a black Jag. Both suits in the front and Macmillan in the back.'

'Anyone with him in the back?' questioned Brady, thinking of Nicoletta.

He couldn't rid himself of the image of what had happened to her friend, Edita. Her punishment for talking out of turn with a punter had been rape of the most sadistic kind, and then murder.

'Nothing, boss,' answered Harvey.

'Shit!' muttered Brady.

'But a black Mercedes van pulled up when Macmillan and his men were inside. The driver made a call and then drove round the back of the club.'

'Go on,' instructed Brady when Harvey paused.

'I got out and followed. But I was too late. I didn't see what they were picking up. All I saw was two men throw some large black bundle into the back of the van. Then they jumped in and shut the doors. The van then sat with its engine idling. I walked back to the car and that's when Macmillan came down with his men. He got in and as he did the Mercedes transit van came out from the back of the club and Macmillan's Jaguar took off, tailing it.'

'Did you see the driver of the van?' asked Brady trying his best to keep his voice level.

'Yeah, as he drove the van around front I saw him. Looked different from the two men who were in the back of the van. But still the type you wouldn't want to mess with, if you get my drift.'

'Describe the driver,' ordered Brady as he clenched and unclenched his free hand.

'Blondish, cropped hair. Ex-military-looking sort. Three-inch, deep scar down his left cheek. He was wearing sunglasses so I couldn't see his eyes. The two other men had short, cropped hair as well but they were dark. Dark hair, eyes, skin. You know, as if they were Eastern European. You know that look I'm talking about?'

'Yeah, I know,' muttered Brady.

He knew all too well.

'The driver?' Brady began. 'Did you get a good enough look to be able to do a photofit?' He was hoping the answer would be a simple no.

'Not sure . . . maybe,' answered Harvey.

Brady winced. Harvey's words feeling like a punch to his gut.

'What about the other two Eastern European men?'

'Yeah, got a good look at them. I'd say they're the same men caught in footage at Newcastle Airport with Melissa Ryecroft.'

'Fuck,' muttered Brady, wondering why Harvey hadn't stated that crucial piece of information first. 'Did you get their licence plates?' he asked, trying to control the frustration in his voice.

'Kodovesky did,' answered Harvey. 'We've already radioed them in to see what comes up.'

'That's something.'

He looked over at the Grand Hotel. It was aglow with soft lighting.

He couldn't see the eight security guards anywhere. They were obviously doing their job, which was to disappear into the background and watch and wait.

Exactly the same game Brady was playing.

'Are you following them?' questioned Brady, frowning.

'What do you think?' answered Harvey flatly.

'Where are you now?' fired Brady.

'Joining the coast road.'

'Heading in which direction?'

'Let's see . . . yeah, not Newcastle. We've just joined the slip road towards the coast.'

'Don't lose them! Understand?'

'Yes, boss,' answered Harvey.

'Keep me updated. And call Daniels and Kenny. I want them on standby in case you need their backup.' Brady thought for a second. 'And notify Conrad,' he added.

He knew out of the lot of them, Conrad was the one he could trust.

Brady disconnected the call.

He looked over at the Grand Hotel. Suddenly there was activity.

Out of nowhere the eight ex-militia men reappeared.

Brady watched as Mayor Macmillan walked down the wide sandstone steps of the hotel with the Ambassador. Behind, the Ambassador's driver followed. The eight ex-militia flanked the two men on both sides, scanning in all directions.

Brady wasn't sure what was being discussed between the

two men, but the Ambassador looked distracted. In a hurry to get away. As did his men.

Brady watched as the Ambassador shot a look at his driver who stood directly behind discreetly talking into a hidden microphone.

The driver paused talking and waited for what seemed to be instruction.

Brady noted that whatever was unfolding in front of him hadn't gone unnoticed by Macmillan.

Brady was intrigued. Mayor Macmillan was calm, collected. Too collected, he thought.

The Ambassador distractedly shook Mayor Macmillan's hand.

On a nod from the driver, Brady watched as the team of eight men walked down the steps of the Grand to flank the Ambassador's car. The driver walked alongside the Ambassador as he headed towards the limo. He opened the rear door and waited for the Ambassador to climb in.

Brady was certain that the driver looked tense. On edge. Even though he looked as if he was patiently holding the door open, Brady could see that he was alert. Discreetly scanning the unfolding scene for signs of trouble.

Brady started the Granada into action. Ready to follow.

Before the Ambassador climbed into the limousine he did something that struck Brady as odd. He firmly placed his hand on the driver's shoulder and spoke quietly.

Brady watched, as Macmillan watched.

The driver nodded, his face terse. His jaw locked, his eyes burning with a murderous coldness.

He respectfully, albeit with some restraint, closed the door. He then walked to the driver's side, opened the door, looked briefly at his men. He barely moved his head but it was enough for them to return to their cars.

Brady watched as the limousine pulled out in the direction of Whitley Bay, leaving the two Mercedes behind.

He waited a couple of seconds for the two black Mercedes to follow. They didn't. He had no choice but to kick the Granada into action, otherwise he would lose the Ambassador. He swerved out, performing a 180-degree turn and headed in the same direction as the limousine.

Suddenly one of the Mercedes swung out, blocking his path.

'Fucking bastard!' shouted Brady as he braked hard.

He looked in the rear mirror to see what the other Mercedes was up to. As expected, it had strategically positioned himself behind Brady.

'Fuck you!' muttered Brady as he ground the gears furiously, throwing the car into reverse.

Foot to the floor he sped backwards, steering the car around the Mercedes.

He swung the car into the back lane further down from the Grand Hotel and reversed hard, avoiding the parked cars dotted on either side. He gunned the engine on the last stretch, hoping that there was no oncoming traffic on the quiet suburban road that the back lane fed onto. There wasn't. He turned hard right and slammed into first, and headed back down towards the coast, leaving behind the Grand to his right at some speed.

He looked to the right and saw one of the Mercedes lurch forward as the driver spotted him. In his rear view mirror he clocked the second Mercedes reversing out of the back lane behind him.

Turning left he put his foot down.

'*Bastards!*' cursed Brady as he threw the car across the roundabout the wrong way. Again, trusting to luck that there was no oncoming traffic.

Tyres screeching, he accelerated in an attempt to keep the limousine in sight.

Chapter Forty-Three

Brady sped over the zebra crossing and past Tynemouth boating lake, keeping his eyes straight ahead. He could see the limousine passing St George's church as it snaked its way along the coast.

His phone buzzed. He picked it up, one hand on the wheel. It was Conrad.

'Conrad?' distractedly answered Brady as he kept his eyes on the road.

He briefly looked down at his speed.

Sixty mph.

The limousine was disappearing from view.

'Fuck!' he muttered in frustration.

'Sir,' answered Conrad. 'I've got some news.'

'Go on,' ordered Brady.

'Simone Henderson . . . she's regained consciousness.'

Brady put his foot to the floor. His speed climbed dangerously as he tried to catch sight of the limousine.

In his rear view mirror he could see he was being tailed. Both Mercedes were driving hard to catch him.

'She managed to give us something . . . wrote it down.'

'Just fucking tell me!' shouted Brady as he swung the car round the bend in the road.

'Her handwriting's shaky but there's no mistaking who she's saying did this to her.'

Brady felt his stomach knot. He clenched the wheel. He couldn't get rid of the image of Nick carrying Simone Henderson's brutally mutilated, unconscious body, wrapped in a black bin liner into the toilets.

'Macmillan. Ronnie Macmillan.'

Brady aggressively pushed his foot to the floor, ignoring the speedometer.

'Fucking bastard!' hissed Brady.

'Adamson knows, sir. He's on this now,' informed Conrad. 'He's put out an all-unit alert on Macmillan.'

'Fuck him. Does he know that Harvey and Kodovesky are tailing Ronnie Macmillan?' demanded Brady.

'No . . . not yet. That's why I'm ringing you, sir,' answered Conrad. 'I do know they've got a warrant out for his arrest and that Adamson's on his way to Macmillan's club to get him. But obviously, he's not there.'

'Get in your car and help me before that snivelling bastard takes over. I need you to intercept those bloody bastards who are trying to stop me following their boss.'

'What's going on, sir?'

'I've got two fucking black Mercedes filled with eight ex-militia types determined to stop me following a Russian limousine that I reckon is going to take me somewhere interesting.'

'Where are you heading?'

'Along the coast, past Cullercoats heading towards Whitley Bay. After that, who knows!'

'Right, sir. On my way now,' quickly answered Conrad.

'And not a word to Adamson or Gates. Understand?'

'Yes, sir,' Conrad said. He was already running for his car.

'Fuck!' cursed Brady as he swung the Granada around another bend, wheels screeching.

He looked in his rear mirror and breathed out. He had momentarily lost sight of the two Mercs.

He disconnected the call.

He then put his foot down, forcing the speedometer up to 80mph.

He flicked a glance at his rear view mirror again and cursed. The first Mercedes was speeding round the bend in pursuit of him.

'Fuck!' muttered Brady again as he stepped on the accelerator.

He sped down the road. Up ahead a group of drunken men staggered across the tarmac, oblivious to the oncoming car.

'Get out the way!' shouted Brady as he slammed on his brakes.

The Granada skidded erratically before coming to a halt.

Brady thumped his horn in frustration.

'Get out the bloody way!' he screamed.

One of the men gave Brady the finger while others jeered obscenities.

Brady could see the Mercedes coming up from behind.

He had no choice. He was going to lose the limousine if he didn't do something.

He kicked the car into first and swung it to the left. Mounting the pavement, he drove past the group of men refusing to move.

He quickly looked in his rear mirror. The Mercedes that had caught up followed Brady's move, swinging off the road onto the pavement.

'Come on, Conrad! Where the fuck are you?' panicked Brady as he threw the car back onto the road.

Ahead of him, he could barely make out the tail lights of the limousine as it continued along the coast.

Suddenly he heard cars slamming their brakes and then furious beeping and shouting.

Conrad, thought Brady. It had to be. The station was less than a minute away by car. All he had to do was drive down one of the roads leading off the Promenade to block them.

He looked in his rear view mirror and right enough, there was Conrad's silver Saab obstructing the Promenade road. Relief flooded through him, relief that Conrad had stopped the two cars. But it was quickly replaced by cold dread as Brady saw six of the eight men get out the two cars and make a move towards Conrad.

Brady had no choice but to leave Conrad to deal with the situation alone. He put his foot to the floor, pushing up to 70mph, hoping to God that the roads were clear. He focused on his target: the limousine which was now within sight.

Brady already knew where the Ambassador was heading. The lighthouse.

His phone buzzed again.

Brady answered it, easing off the gas.

'Yeah?' agitatedly answered Brady.

'We lost Ronnie Macmillan, Jack,' came the answer.

'Fuck it, Tom!' shouted Brady. 'What did I tell you? *Don't fucking lose them!*'

'They got away from us at the traffic lights in Whitley Bay. We're blocked in!'

'Save it for someone who gives a damn! Right now I've got bigger problems thanks to you.'

'Come on, Jack! You can't blame us.'

'Get yourselves over to the lighthouse asap.'

'Yeah, will do as soon as these bastard lights change.'

'I don't care how you do it, just get there. Alright? Same applies to Kenny and Daniels,' ordered Brady.

'Sure,' answered Harvey.

'And whatever you do, do not let Adamson or Gates know where you're going. Understand?'

Before Harvey had a chance to say anything, Brady had already cut the line.

He watched as the limousine passed Whitley Bay cemetery on the left and the crazy golf course on the right. It suddenly indicated and then turned right, straight onto the road leading to St Mary's Lighthouse.

Chapter Forty-Four

Brady waited until the limousine disappeared from view, following the road round to the second car park that directly faced St Mary's lighthouse. He cut his lights as he pulled in and let the Granada idle slowly into the first car park. The area was deserted. But he knew something was about to happen in the further car park hidden from public view. He tried to get the Granada as close as he could to the bend ahead so that he could make a quick getaway if necessary.

He cut the engine as adrenalin coursed through him. He had no choice but to leave the Granada and follow on foot.

Sticking to the grass verge he stealthily made his way towards the bend in the road. As he turned he saw three vehicles parked up about forty feet away from him: a black Mercedes van, Ronnie Macmillan's Jag and the Ambassador's limousine. Crouching down from view, he made his way to the public toilets for cover, ignoring the painful spasms in his thigh.

His breathing was shallow and fast. He tried to steady his nerves for fear they would hear him. There was only one thing going through his head: his brother.

What would he do if Nick was there? And crucially, how

long did he have before backup arrived? Would there be time for Nick to disappear?

Steeling himself, he looked out from behind the brick wall of the toilet block.

He watched as the Ambassador got out of his car and walked over to the Jag accompanied by his driver. Brady watched as the rear door opened and the Ambassador climbed in and joined Ronnie Macmillan in the back. The Ambassador's driver stood on watch beside the rear of the Jag, constantly surveying the area for any unexpected trouble.

Brady deeply breathed in as he realised Rubenfeld had been right all along.

He quickly looked around for Visa and Delta. They were talking with someone.

His heart was pounding. He felt physically sick when he realised who it had to be. The darkness made it difficult for see, but he was certain it was him. There was no mistaking it: it was his brother, Nick, who was talking to them.

Trying to control the terror that consumed him, Brady dragged his eyes away and looked over at the Mercedes van. Two men were sitting in the front watching. But it was too dark and too far away for him to be sure that they were the Dabkunas brothers.

Brady couldn't believe it.

Ronnie Macmillan and the Dabkunas brothers were working together which meant . . . He thought about Simone.

He tried to steady himself, his mind racing as he realised the magnitude of what was taking place. He had swerved between believing Ronnie Macmillan and his henchmen,

Visa and Delta, were responsible for Simone's attack, then back to the Dabkunas. He now understood that they were in it together.

'Oh Christ!' he muttered under his breath.

He heard a noise and shifted his attention. Paralysed, he watched as Ronnie Macmillan buzzed down his window and barked an order at his men.

Whatever he said prompted Visa and Delta to walk over to the boot of the Jag.

Brady stood up and stealthily walked along the edge of the toilet wall trying to get as close as possible without being seen.

But before he knew it, they had spotted him

It was over with before he had a chance to react.

The black van screeched into reverse, swung itself around and sped past him at 60mph. Brady saw the same men in the front. The same men that had been filmed kidnapping Melissa Ryecroft. The Dabkunas brothers.

'Fuck!' he cursed.

He turned to get back to his car. He needed to radio for assistance. God knows where Harvey and Kodovesky were.

But before he had a chance to move a gunshot fired out.

Brady crouched down and watched as Nick came out from nowhere and floored the Lithuanian Ambassador, shielding him from the gunfire.

'Fucking bastard. You set us up with the fucking pigs! I said if there's any police we'll kill her!' threatened Ronnie Macmillan.

More gunshots rang out in Nick's direction.

The Ambassador's driver retaliated.

Suddenly, the Jag took off with Visa and Delta in the front. Tearing past Brady at breakneck speed.

Brady saw his chance and ran over to Nick.

'What took you so long, Jack?' demanded Nick as he looked up at Brady. 'I gave you enough fucking clues!'

Brady couldn't answer. He had too many questions.

'Move it, Jack,' ordered Nick. 'She's in the boot of the Jag.'

'I don't understand,' said Brady, searching his brother's contorted face for answers.

He could see that Nick had taken a bullet to his left arm. Otherwise he could tell from the anxious look on his brother's face that he would have taken the Ambassador's limousine and gone after Macmillan.

Everything was moving too fast. This wasn't what he had expected.

He stood, frozen to the spot.

He had no idea how many bullets his brother had taken for the Ambassador. Let alone what kind of undercover work he was doing for him.

He couldn't think straight. His mind had gone blank.

'Her name's Monika. She's the Ambassador's daughter!' Nick shouted at him in an attempt to make him move. 'She's been held for ransom, Jack. You don't get to Macmillan he'll kill her. Now fucking move it!' urged Nick desperately.

'I . . . I haven't heard about any ransom. Nothing's been reported to us?' frantically questioned Brady.

'Of course it fucking hasn't! Stop asking questions like some dumb fuck and go after him like I said!'

Without thinking, he did as he was instructed. He ran, not feeling the pain in his ribs and thigh, numbed by adrenalin.

Nothing mattered. Answers could come later.

He had to get to his car and catch Macmillan.

Brady sparked the ignition of the Granada. Sparks and the metal components of the V8 growled in perfect unity. He slammed the gears into reverse, and looked quickly around as the tyres carved a black scar into the fresh tarmac. He pushed the gears into first and felt the car's power thrust him back against the black leather seat.

He swung out onto the dual carriageway at about 80mph, his eyes glued to the red tail lights of the black Jag, speeding away from him. He threw the gears into third along the dual carriageway. The rear wheel drive almost slewed him into the grass bank. He managed to hold it and thrust his foot down hard.

'Fuck!' cursed Brady, narrowly missing a Nissan Micra as it pulled out on him from the Brierdene Pub, swinging out across the two lanes in a U-turn. He caught a glimpse of the oblivious grey-haired couple inside as he passed them at 98mph on the wrong side of the road.

He had no option. He'd spent too long doubting what the hell was going on instead of just trusting Nick and acting on it.

The Jag ahead dropped into a lower gear and pulled away. Brady breathed in heavily and put his foot down, aware that the Jag had forty years of improved tech. He somehow managed to reach for his phone to contact Conrad.

'Black Jag, southbound, Links past Brierdene Pub, at speed,' he shouted.

'On it, sir,' replied Conrad.

'Chopper,' ordered Brady. 'We're not going to lose this bastard.'

'Yes, sir.'

'Where are you?'

'Coming up towards the roundabout by Monkseaton Drive.'

'They're heading in your direction. You're going to have to block them off,' instructed Brady

Silence. Brady wasn't surprised: he knew the price Conrad had paid for the Saab.

'Conrad!' yelled Brady, as he watched the Jag approach the roundabout. 'They've got a fucking girl in the boot!'

'Yes, sir.'

Brady threw his phone down on the passenger seat and slammed his foot to the floor, thrusting the car even harder. He could see Conrad's Saab approaching the roundabout at the same time the Jag was approaching from the opposite direction. Brady reached the tail lights of the Jag as it braked before it swerved hard, taking the corner.

He watched as Conrad took an extreme right onto the wrong side of the road to block the Jag. He heard the furious collision of hot metal and then the squealing of tyres as the Jag tried to swerve to avoid the Saab. It hit the right-hand wing of Conrad's car with a heavy swing that sent it lurching across the kerb into the Rendezvous Café car park.

Brady looked at Conrad to make sure he was alright. His cold, steel-grey eyes confirmed that he wasn't injured. Or if he was, he hadn't noticed. They were narrowed, his jaw was set. He was determined that Macmillan and his suited thugs weren't going anywhere fast.

Brady thrust the Granada after the Saab and Jag, spinning it round so it blocked the exit.

In the distance sirens screamed full pelt. Lights flashed, closer and closer.

Brady wasn't sure whether they were coming to his

assistance or the Ambassador's. Not that it mattered right now. The only thing that concerned him was apprehending Ronnie Macmillan before he disappeared.

Brady could see steam coming from the front end of the Jag. Fluorescent green coolant was pissing all over the car park like a Newcastle fan after thirty minutes extra time.

The Jag was fucked. It was going nowhere. That much was clear. He watched as the driver attempted to turn the engine over, again and again. It was futile.

Ronnie Macmillan realised as much and bailed as the sound of sirens gained.

Brady watched as Ronnie pulled out a hand pistol.

'Fuck!' muttered Brady as he watched Macmillan make a run for it.

He had no choice but to go after him.

He threw himself out the car, rolling in a ball to protect himself from the shots being fired in his direction.

He looked up to see Conrad revving the Saab's engine.

'Conrad! Get the fuck down, will you?' ordered Brady as he saw his deputy throw his car into gear and swing it towards the Jag and into the direct line of fire.

Brady used the distraction and sprinted after Macmillan, ignoring the shots and the screaming grind of metal against metal. He heard one more shot before it was over. He didn't have time to turn back and make sure Conrad was alright. Breathing hard and fast, ignoring the crippling pain in his thigh, he sprinted after Macmillan. Before Ronnie knew it, Brady had rugby-tackled him, grabbing him by the legs. Macmillan went down with force. Face smashed hard into the jagged ground. Brady knew his nose was broken before he saw the blood.

With his full weight holding Macmillan down, Brady grabbed a handful of his hair and dragged his head back.

Macmillan screamed in agony.

'Ahhh! You bastard! You're breaking my fucking neck!' shouted Macmillan.

'Yeah? Tell you what. That's only the start of it you fucking bastard!' snarled Brady.

Without thinking he smashed Macmillan's head forward, hard into the ground.

'Where are they? Eh? Where the fuck are they, you sick bastard?'

Blood spurted everywhere covering the front of Macmillan's white shirt and black suit. The ground was splattered. Brady paid no attention. He yanked Macmillan's head back again.

'Didn't fucking hear you! Where are they? Nicoletta? Melissa Ryecroft? What the fuck have you done to them?'

'You bastard! I'll get you done for police brutality!'

'Yeah? Log it in the complaints book!'

Macmillan moaned through gritted teeth as Brady aggressively yanked his head back for the third time.

'This is for Simone!' Brady replied forcefully thrusting Macmillan's broken and bloodied face back into the hard, jagged, bloodied tarmac.

Macmillan spluttered and moaned in agony as blood gushed out through his broken teeth.

'I'll kill you if you don't fucking talk!' growled Brady.

Macmillan cried out in pain as Brady snapped his head back again.

He bent down to his ear.

'No witnesses see?' hissed Brady. 'Self-defence on my part. Already been shot at by your thugs. Didn't know if you had a loaded gun aimed for my chest when you came at me . . . Your fucking choice!'

He ignored the blood pouring down his hands from Macmillan's face.

He also ignored the sirens as they pulled up at the round-about and the shouts from the armed response team.

'One last fucking chance, you bastard!'

'Suck my cock! That's what I got your copper girlfriend to do. She's good, but then you'd know all about that, wouldn't you?' spat Macmillan.

Brady jerked his head back hard once more, ready to smash it into the ground again and again until he got rid of all his pent-up fury at what the bastard had done to Simone, Nicoletta and Christ knows who else.

But in that moment he suddenly realised what he was doing made him no better than the animal he was restraining.

'Go on, you bastard!' jeered Macmillan. 'What are you waiting for?'

Brady didn't react. Instead he fought every instinct coursing through his body to obliterate Macmillan's face so that, like Simone, he'd never be able to talk again.

'You and I are the same, Jack. We both have brothers who we have to protect. No matter what you fucking do I'll never talk. Loyalty comes first. Then again, you'd know all about that as well, wouldn't you?' sneered Macmillan.

'We're nothing alike, Macmillan,' stated Brady calmly, regaining his composure.

He released his hold on Macmillan's head, letting it fall forward. He then twisted Macmillan's arms even further behind his back, ignoring his cries of pain as he physically restrained him until the armed response team took charge.

'She's in the boot,' Conrad called out. 'I can't get her out. It's jammed . . . the boot lid's jammed . . .'

Brady turned round but before he had a chance to react, Conrad had collapsed to the ground.

'Conrad? *Conrad?*' shouted Brady as he jumped off Macmillan and ran towards his deputy.

Four armed officers immediately had Macmillan covered before he tried to get up and make a run for it.

Brady didn't notice. His attention was on Conrad.

His deputy lay in a heap on the ground. His eyes closed. His mouth open. His breathing erratic.

It was then that Brady noticed the blood pooling out from under Conrad. A small burn hole in his shirt told Brady that he had been shot in the shoulder.

'Paramedics! I need paramedics over here!' screamed Brady as he bent over Conrad.

Chapter Forty-Five

Brady ran to the Jag. He tried the boot but it wouldn't budge. The rear wing had buckled when the car had gone over the kerb and hit the low wall surrounding the car park.

He blocked out the noise of the armed response unit. They had already disarmed Ronnie Macmillan's suited henchmen, Visa and Delta. Not that they were going to give them much trouble. Not after Conrad had rammed the driver's door at speed. The glass on the driver's side was shattered from the impact.

Visa, injured from the collision, had crawled out of the Jag through the driver's side; the passenger door had been blocked tight against the low wall. Delta, the driver, was in a critical state. It was clear from the damage to his head that it had smashed with full force against the door pillar when the Saab had hit. Visa had climbed over his lifeless body, armed with a handgun, ready to take out Conrad. Then Brady.

Conrad had taken a hit to the shoulder. Straight through his windscreen.

Brady had been lucky. He had missed the couple of shots fired in his direction as he had run after Macmillan.

Conrad had reversed the Saab back and then put his foot to the floor and drove it straight at the armed henchman who, with deathly precision, had his gun aimed at the back of Brady's head.

His bones had snapped like twigs as, unable to react quickly enough, he was rammed between Conrad's bonnet and the driver's side of the car.

Silence had followed.

Brady by then had had his hands full questioning Macmillan while Conrad had pulled himself from the Saab, bleeding profusely. He had moved over to the boot only to find it jammed.

It was Brady who was standing there now, struggling to release the lid. His mind sped while the world around seemed to move in slow motion. Flashing lights blurred around him while muted, distorted voices yelled orders and commands.

Brady thought of the crowbar in his boot. He ran to the Granada.

Questions came at him from every angle.

Brady heard himself state the situation, barely realising it was him talking.

'She's in the boot. Lid's jammed.'

Grabbing the crowbar he ran back to the Jag, wincing in pain as the old gunshot wound in his leg kicked off.

He wedged the bar under the lip of the boot lid and somehow, with a strength he didn't know he possessed, he prised it open.

He heard gasps behind him. And realised that the armed response unit had followed him, as had the paramedics.

A girl with long dark hair lay naked in a foetal position. Arms and legs bound, mouth gagged.

For a moment, Brady thought she was dead. Her skin unnaturally pale. The torches shining into the black, industrial plastic lined boot showed an arsenal of torture implements. Varying lengths of knives neatly arranged in a leather holder. Ropes and black tape lay across the knives, ready and waiting. But in the corner of the boot, Brady immediately recognised a captive bolt pistol from the images Claudia had shown them at the briefing which now felt like a life-time ago.

He looked at the girl's chest, to see whether she was still breathing. To his relief he could see it move. Delicately and out of balance.

Brady bent down and as gently as he could tore off the black tape that gagged her mouth.

She gasped.

Eyes wide, terrified. She stared at him. Her large almond brown eyes screamed of the unimaginable horrors she had witnessed.

'Monika?' he quietly questioned. 'It's the police. You're alright. You're going to be alright.'

Brady stood back and let the paramedics get her out. He watched as she was wrapped in a blanket and then laid on a stretcher. He realised that her captors had drugged her: her eyes were wide open. Her mouth unmoving, her breathing like a bird with a broken wing struggling to fly.

Brady stared into her eyes. He knew she held the key to the whereabouts of both Melissa Ryecroft and Nicoletta.

'Monika?' he whispered, crouching down. 'Where's Melissa? Girl who looks just like you. They took her. The men that took you, they took her as well. And another girl, Nicoletta. Where are they?'

Monika stared at him, eyes wide with terror.

She somehow managed to shake her head.

'No . . . no . . .' she mumbled with a heavy Eastern European accent.

'What, Monika? What did they do?'

'They . . . they have her. Took her in the van . . .' she mumbled in shock.

Brady watched, feeling his stomach contract.

'Who? Monika? Took who?' he desperately demanded.

'Melissa . . .' she whispered.

'Nicoletta? What about Nicoletta?' pleaded Brady.

She looked at him terrified. She shook her head.

'I don't know . . . . I don't know . . .'

Brady felt sick. He realised she was telling the truth. She had no idea.

He then thought of Melissa. The black Mercedes van in which the Dabkunas brothers had sped off.

He didn't have time to think. He had to react.

He didn't realise it but he was shaking. Trembling uncontrollably.

A paramedic wrapped a blanket around him.

Brady threw it off.

He limped to his car just as the Ambassador's Russian-plated limousine pulled up.

The driver got out. But the Ambassador had already got out first. He pushed his way through the police towards Brady. His bright blue eyes mad with fear.

'Monika?' he questioned. 'My daughter? Monika?'

Brady touched the Ambassador on the shoulder to reassure him.

'She's going to be alright,' Brady said.

Tears flowed down the Ambassador's face as he lost all restraint.

He nodded in gratitude.

'Thank you,' he said. 'Thank you.'

Brady watched as he left him and moved through the officers and medics to get to his daughter.

He turned to make his way to the Granada, catching the Ambassador's driver's eye as he did so. The other man gave Brady a curt, stiff nod of respect before he took charge again.

Brady automatically checked the limousine as he passed it, but could see that Nick wasn't in the car. He expected no less.

He walked over and climbed in the Granada. He then picked up his phone.

He had four missed calls from DS Harvey.

'Tom?' he questioned. 'Where are you?'

'Wallsend docks, Jack.'

'Did you get them?'

'The bastards got away from us. They had another car waiting for them. Took off before we realised it. Daniels and Kenny tried to follow but they've just disappeared. The chopper's looking for them now but I wouldn't hold much hope. Didn't even see the make of the car. Looked like a black BMW saloon, but couldn't be sure. Didn't even get a partial on the licence plate. Between the two cars we managed to get the van off the road. But they were too quick. They'd had a car following. They'd obviously planned to dump the van.'

Brady sat back. His breathing shallow and low as he listened.

He didn't want to ask the inevitable question. But he had no choice.

'Are they there? In the van? Melissa Ryecroft? Nicoletta?'

'I'm sorry, Jack. I really am,' answered Harvey.

'For fuck's sake, Tom. Just give it to me straight will you?'

Brady noticed that his free hand was trembling.

'Melissa Ryecroft is in a bad way. She's been badly beaten and raped, but she's still alive. Paramedics are taking her to Rake Lane. But . . .' Harvey's voice faltered.

'What? What did they do to Nicoletta? What the fuck did they do?' demanded Brady.

'She's not there, Jack. We have no idea where she is,' answered Harvey quietly.

'What about Melissa Ryecroft? Does she know what's happened to Nicoletta?' asked Brady, unable to keep the desperation from his voice.

'I've questioned her about Nicoletta. And she's answered as well as she could under the circumstances. But she doesn't know her whereabouts or what happened to her.'

Brady hung up. There was nothing left to say.

He didn't have the time to fill Harvey in on all the details. Not that he knew, anyway. He would have to wait until the Ambassador made a formal statement to know whether or not his daughter had been kidnapped and held for ransom. And what part his own brother had played.

He needed to get as far away from the flashing blue lights and screeching sirens as he could. He would answer questions later. First he needed to find Nick. He needed to check he was alright. And then he needed answers.

He pulled back onto the Links dual carriage way and sped back towards the lighthouse, trying to block out the image of Conrad lying on the ground, unconscious. The paramedics had assured him he would be alright. That it was a superficial wound. The bullet had gone through his shoulder.

It could have been worse: it could have gone through a vital organ. Not that that made Brady feel any better.

He still felt as if he was going to throw up.

How could he have let this happen to Conrad?

Frustrated and angry with himself, he violently swung the car off the dual carriageway, turning as tyres protested onto the single-lane road towards the lighthouse. He sped past the first car park, forcing the car round the bend into the second one.

His headlights lit up the bleak, isolated spot. It was deserted.

He got out the car, leaving the engine running and walked over to where he had seen his brother fall. Blood covered the ground. Nick's blood.

Brady wildly looked about him. No one.

'Nick!' he frantically screamed at the top of his voice.

'Nick?' he repeated in all directions until his voice turned hoarse.

Nothing. He had gone.

Chapter Forty-Six

Brady looked up expectantly at Claudia as she walked out of Simone Henderson's room.

Despite the fact it was 2:47am she was still dressed for the Ambassador's function at the Grand Hotel in a long black dress. In her hand she carried a pair of designer three-inch heels.

Brady stood up, holding back a wince. His leg and ribs still throbbed from the exertion of running after Ronnie Macmillan.

Claudia walked over to him, her bare feet softly padding against the sterile floor.

She shook her head apologetically.

'I'm sorry . . . she's refusing to see you, Jack.'

Brady tried to swallow back his emotions.

'I . . . I understand . . .'

'She's just not ready to see anyone,' explained Claudia.

But he wasn't anyone, thought Brady.

He nodded. He would give her some time and then he would come back. He needed to talk to her. Reassure her that he would be there if she needed him. Brady accepted that it was irrational to feel responsible for what had happened to Simone, but it didn't lessen the overwhelming guilt he felt.

'What do you think she'll do when she recovers?' asked Brady.

'I know the force wouldn't turn their back on her. I'm sure they'd find a position for her when she's ready,' quietly answered Claudia.

'What? A desk job? That's not Simone. It would kill her . . .' Brady said, faltering.

'I don't know, Jack. I think the focus right now is on her recovery.'

Brady turned away from Claudia. He didn't want her to see how the thought of what lay ahead for Simone pained him.

'At least we have her evidence against Ronnie Macmillan and his men. And the Dabkunas brothers,' stated Claudia optimistically, in an attempt to change the subject.

But Brady knew it was false optimism. They might have evidence against the Dabkunas brothers. But that was all.

'I've got to go,' he muttered dejectedly.

'Are you okay?' asked Claudia, concerned.

She gently rested her hand on his arm.

He looked at her, not knowing what she expected him to say.

'I mean . . . I heard . . . about Conrad.'

'Yeah, I'm fine. Thanks to him. If he hadn't taken that bullet in his shoulder for me it would be a different story.'

'How is he?'

'Out of surgery. The doctors reckon he was lucky it was just his shoulder . . .' answered Brady, not wanting to think about what could have happened to his deputy.

He owed Conrad his life. Something he would never forget. He had paced the floor for the past two hours while a team of doctors and nurses had worked to remove the shattered pieces of bone. Only when he knew he was definitely going to be alright had Brady left his side. He still had a job to do. And he knew that was what Conrad would have wanted.

Claudia stared at him. Waiting.

'Jack?' she began.

Brady wasn't sure what she wanted. He wasn't sure about anything any more.

'There was nothing you could have done,' she said, as if reading his mind.

He looked at her.

'Nicoletta. The Dabkunas brothers have no doubt taken her. Look, if it's any help there's a nationwide search on to apprehend them. All airports, ports and docks have been informed. It won't be long before we get them. And hopefully Nicoletta,' reassured Claudia.

But her voice sounded as confident as Brady felt.

He knew the chances of catching them were slim. They were ex-militia with an international network behind them. And money. The Nietzschean Brotherhood had successfully eluded the authorities so far. And Brady couldn't see why that would change.

Claudia's phone suddenly buzzed. She took it out and looked at the message.

'Look, I've . . .' she faltered, unsure.

'I know. He's waiting for you outside.'

Her hand limply dropped back to her side.

'Give Conrad my best,' she said.

Brady nodded.

He watched as she disappeared through the ICU security doors.

He knew she'd be alright. After all, she had DCI Davidson waiting to take her home.

*

Brady sat still, very still beside Melissa Ryecroft's bed.

She had fallen asleep. Her breathing soft and relaxed.

The exertion of telling him what had happened had taken its toll.

As had the sadistic cruelty she had suffered.

At least she was heavily sedated. The drugs working to keep the nightmare of the past seventy-two hours at bay. For the time being, until she woke up. Then she would have to relive the horror of being raped, again and again.

But Brady still had questions he needed answering before her parents would be brought to her bedside.

Unfortunately, questions she couldn't answer.

She had no idea what had happened to Nicoletta. Didn't know whether she was alive or dead. The last time she had seen her was in the back of the black Mercedes van hours earlier when they had taken Monika out, leaving her and Nicoletta. They had then drugged them both and when she had come round she had been alone in the van.

The Dabkunas brothers had gone. Taking whatever personal belongings they needed before getting out of the North East – including the women they owned. Melissa had explained that Macmillan and the Dabkunas brothers had kept at least ten girls enslaved, hidden in some undisclosed apartment down by North Shields quayside.

It fitted exactly with what Nicoletta had told him.

But they were gone. Long gone. Dismantled their sick operation when Claudia's team had gone in, their investigation inadvertently warning the Dabkunas brothers and Macmillan that the police were watching them.

Brady couldn't help noticing the bruising on Melissa's pale thin arms where she had been held down. Her face was swollen and covered in cuts from where she had been hit. And hard, thought Brady.

He looked at the tell-tale mottled, purplish bruising around her neck where one of the Dabkunas brothers had choked her until she had passed out.

She had told him how she had tried to escape on the first night; the Thursday night after they had picked her up from the airport.

She had been taken, blindfolded, to the undisclosed apartment where the other girls were held. An apartment that they were still searching to no avail in a desperate bid to find Nicoletta.

Gates had ordered every officer in and had demanded backup from other area commands. But so far, Nicoletta hadn't been found.

Brady looked at Melissa. He didn't like to think of what she had suffered. Brutally raped into submission by both brothers. Then taken out of bed for a meeting in the early hours of Friday morning with a prospective punter. One with a distinctive feature – he had a finger missing. And he was part of the Nietzschean Brotherhood. The white platinum 'N' signet ring a giveaway.

Brady looked up from Melissa's resting body and across at Kodovesky. He had asked her to be part of the interview; given the nature of the crimes committed against Melissa he had needed a female copper there. A good copper at that.

Kodovesky caught his eye.

'She's a brave girl,' she observed quietly.

Brady nodded.

They had both listened to Melissa's account of how she had tried to escape, jumping from the car as it slowly drove along the Promenade. Heading for St Mary's Lighthouse had been Brady's guess. And his hunch had been proved right. After the Dabkunas brothers had finally caught her she had been taken, unconscious, in the boot of a black Mercedes, to the lighthouse car park. That was where she had been raped again and again by the passenger in the back of the black Mercedes.

Brady looked back at her as she slept peacefully. It was no doubt the first rest she had had since her abduction.

'Do you think she'll be alright?' asked Kodovesky.

'Yeah,' answered Brady. 'She's a survivor. She's already proven that. Come on, let's go. I think she's told us all she can remember. Best we let her sleep.'

He looked up at Kodovesky.

'And by the look of you I reckon you could do with catching up on some sleep as well.'

Kodovesky nodded.

'At least we got to her in time. It's not worth thinking about what would have happened to her if you hadn't been there, sir,' stated Kodovesky. 'If it hadn't been for you we wouldn't have found her.'

Brady didn't want to think about Nicoletta. If only they could have got to her sooner. If only . . .

He rubbed his face. He was tired. Too tired to cope with

the reality of what had happened to Nicoletta, let alone the rest of the missing girls.

'Sir? Are you alright?'

'Just knackered, that's all,' answered Brady as he stood up to leave.

Chapter Forty-Seven

Brady walked out the main reception's glass revolving doors. The cool, fresh May Monday morning air hit him. A welcome relief from the hospital's sterile air conditioning.

'Fuck you! You bastard!'

Adamson came out of nowhere and lunged for Brady. Within seconds he had him pinned up against the wall. He had taken Brady by surprise.

'Get off me!' hissed Brady.

Before he knew it Adamson had his hand wedged under Brady's chin, forcing his head back against the brick wall.

'I'll have you for this! Make sure you watch your back, Jack, because I'm onto you. If it's the last thing I do, I'm going to see you kicked off the job for good.'

'Not my problem if you can't fucking work your own investigation,' retaliated Brady.

Adamson pushed even harder against Brady's chin, tilting his head hard against the wall.

'Yeah? Well enjoy the glory, you bastard. Soon enough you'll fuck up again. And Gates and O'Donnell will see you for the waste of fucking space that you are!'

Brady attempted to push back. But Adamson had him good.

'Shame about Conrad. You want to fucking hope for his sake that the bullet he took in the shoulder hasn't permanently disabled his right arm. Because if it has, he's worse than useless on the job. Fucking career over with.'

Adamson might as well have punched Brady for the effect his words had. Brady stopped struggling.

Adamson heard someone coming out the revolving doors and automatically let Brady go.

'Watch your back. One day I'll get you for fucking me over on this.'

Brady shot him a 'fuck you' look.

'That's a promise!' Adamson growled. 'And keep the fuck away from Simone Henderson before I finish off what her father started!' he warned. 'I'm not the only one around here who thinks you're to blame for what happened to her. Fucking bastard.' He shoved Brady hard against the wall for effect.

Brady didn't retaliate. The words had hit as hard as punches.

He watched as Adamson straightened his tie and walked towards the hospital's main entrance.

There was nothing that Adamson had said that Brady could disagree with: ultimately he felt responsible for what had happened to Simone Henderson, just as much as he felt responsible for Nicoletta.

*

Brady went back to his car. He unlocked the Granada and climbed in. Five hours had now passed since the Dabkunas brothers had disappeared. Five, long, arduous hours of nothing. It was now 3:47am. Time was running out. That was, if she was still alive.

Before he had left the hospital he had checked with DCI Gates to see whether there were any developments only to find that they had hit a brick wall. It was as if Nicoletta had just disappeared. And it seemed that Claudia wasn't the only one who believed that the Dabkunas brothers had taken her with them.

But it didn't rest easy with Brady. If they had taken Nicoletta, then why not Melissa Ryecroft as well? It didn't make sense.

Brady had already tried to get Ronnie Macmillan to talk. Unsurprisingly, Macmillan was keeping his mouth firmly shut. Once he had been released from Rake Lane for the injuries he had sustained while resisting arrest, he had been put in the hands of Harvey, who was now waiting for Kodovesky to join him before he started interviewing Macmillan. Whether they would have more luck than Brady, he doubted.

He breathed out slowly as he started to roll a cigarette. He needed something, anything to calm him down. Sleep-deprived wasn't the word for it. It was now Monday morning and he hadn't slept properly since Thursday night. He was absolutely exhausted but he couldn't wind down. Couldn't switch off until he knew the whereabouts of Nicoletta.

He had tried calling Trina McGuire while waiting for Conrad to come through surgery. She hadn't answered. He had left repeated messages, anxious for her safety. He had then sent uniform round, worried that the Dabkunas brothers or Ronnie Macmillan had punished her for talking. And their kind of punishment meant she would never talk again. Thankfully, she was at home. Brady understood why she had ignored his urgent demands to call him. After all, it was him forcing Trina and Nicoletta to talk that had endangered Nicoletta's life and caused her to disappear without trace.

He had also called Nick's mobile number. Again, it had cut to voicemail, forcing him to leave a frantic message asking about the whereabouts of Nicoletta.

Again, nothing.

He lit his cigarette and sat staring at Rake Lane Hospital, thinking about the information Melissa Ryecroft had given him. She was certain that Nicoletta had remained in the Dabkunas' van when they had taken the Lithuanian Ambassador's daughter out. The Dabkunas brothers had then drugged both girls. The next thing Melissa had been aware of was coming round, alone. She had no idea when Nicoletta had been taken from the van or by whom.

Brady tried to remain calm. Panicking wouldn't get him anywhere. He had to think logically about that night's events. He knew the answer was there somewhere. He just couldn't see it.

He started with where he had seen the black Mercedes van: St Mary's Lighthouse. He wondered if Ronnie Macmillan had met the Dabkunas brothers there and if Monika had been removed from the van and dumped into the boot of his Jag at the same spot, ready for the ransom exchange with the Lithuanian Ambassador. That left Nicoletta and Melissa drugged and presumably unconscious in the van.

Brady replayed in his head when he turned up at the lighthouse. As soon as the Dabkunas brothers had seen him, they had taken off. Shortly after that, their van had been apprehended by Harvey and Kodovesky and another police car in Wallsend. The only victim inside was Melissa Ryecroft. At some point, mused Brady, they had dumped Nicoletta. But when? And crucially where?

They wouldn't have had the chance once they had fled from the car park. That much was clear from the fact that they had left Melissa in the back of the van after the police car chase and made a run for it.

The only obvious place was St Mary's Lighthouse.

But Brady had already revisited the lighthouse car park looking for Nick and found nobody.

He closed his eyes.

He thought back to the lighthouse ... to Nick ... to when they were kids ...

What was it about the lighthouse that Nick was trying to tell him by leaving Edita Aginatas' severed head in his car there? And what was the meeting Brady had witnessed hours earlier with the Ambassador and Mayor Macmillan about? Additionally there was the CCTV footage that Conrad had found of the Dabkunas' black Mercedes van following Ronnie Macmillan's Jag heading towards the lighthouse after they had drugged, then abducted Simone Henderson.

Brady thought back to Nick as he had once been – a four year old playing on the small, sandy beach positioned directly below the twenty foot, sloping cliff where the second car park was positioned. The rocky beach lay hidden from view. The perfect location.

But the perfect location for what?

Then Brady remembered what he had explained to Conrad. That he believed Edita Aginatas' body was taken by a small boat and dumped at sea. The perfect access to the boat would be via the sandy beach and causeway, hidden from prying eyes, that led to the lighthouse. A causeway ruled by the tides. When the tide was in, the lighthouse was inaccessible, as was the sandy beach. The beach was a dangerous place to be if you didn't know the tides. Within minutes it could disappear when the tide changed. And there was no way back.

'Jacky, watch our Nick will you? The tide's coming in quick and if the two of you aren't careful you'll vanish. Taken out to sea!'

Brady jolted forward at the memory of his mother's voice warning him against the furious incoming tide. He suddenly knew why Nick was so attached to the lighthouse – it was the only time their mother had taken them there as boys. In fact, it was the only outing they had had before she died. Money had been short and a trip out to the lighthouse from the Ridges was a big deal in those days.

Brady could remember grabbing Nick's hand and scrambling with him up the rocks to safety as the tide rapidly moved in, devouring every inch of the beach. When he had looked back, the causeway had already gone. Access to the lighthouse disappearing with every inch of fast-moving water. And then, within seconds the small, rocky beach had gone, devoured by the ravishing tide.

Brady then thought of Nicoletta. Thought of the sloping drop that led to the rocks directly below the car park where the Dabkunas brothers and Macmillan had waited for the Ambassador to turn up. In that moment he realised what they had done with her.

They had thrown her over the cliff, to the rocks below and the tide that would inevitably take her body. Over five hours had gone by since he had seen the Dabkunas brothers at the Lighthouse. And in those long five hours the tide

402

could easily have taken her body out to sea, never to be found.

*

Brady aggressively threw the Granada off the dual carriageway into the turn for the lighthouse. He could see police cars already parked up. Blue lights flashing, sirens screeching alarm. Overhead the police helicopter's infrared light was already moving over the dark water searching for anything that resembled life. Gates had been true to his word and when Brady had radioed in with his suspicion he had called in every available resource he had to search the rocks and water directly below the cliff.

Brady ground the car to a halt. The second car park was full of officers with torch lights and tracking dogs howling at the thundering helicopter blades overhead.

Brady jumped out his car. He had to know whether he was too late; whether the tide was already in. He left the car park and ran down towards the small slipway that led to the causeway and beach below.

'Thank God!' muttered Brady.

The tide was only starting to come in.

'Fuck!' muttered Brady as he continued to run, jumping off the slipway onto the rocks.

They didn't have long to find her. Once the tide started, it would come in fast and furious.

He could see a group of officers huddled around something up ahead in the rocks directly below the cliff car park above.

'Is it her?' screamed Brady, trying to be heard above the noise of the rotating blades overhead. 'Is it Nicoletta?'

403

He jumped and scrambled desperately over the rocks towards the group. An officer turned and looked over at him. Brady didn't recognise him. His face was illuminated a ghostly white from the helicopter beam above.

'Is she alive?' Brady called out hoarsely.

But his voice was lost.

Taken by the North Sea wind that had suddenly picked up and the thunderous helicopter blades.

He reached the group. Forced his way through, panting and gasping.

And then he saw her. Nicoletta, wrapped in a black bin liner, black duct tape sealing her mouth. Her body lay contorted, bones broken from the twenty foot fall.

'Is she . . . is she?' Brady began, trembling.

She wasn't moving. Her ghostly illuminated, lifeless face was waxen.

He tried frantically to reach her but was pushed back by the paramedic team.

Chapter Forty-Eight

Brady got in his car and drove. Fast and hard. Speeding along the back roads from North Shields, following the Tyne River heading towards Newcastle quayside.

He was late.

He had just read the text that had been sent at 10:33am. It was now 11:03am.

He didn't recognise the number and knew it would be an unregistered phone that would be dumped once used.

The message had simply said:

'Tyne Bridge – 30 mins.'

Brady knew who it was from, which was why he was driving at breakneck speed.

He had tried calling the number. No answer. He had then texted 'on way' in the hope that they would wait.

He swung the car off City Road and down onto the quayside. He drove past Newcastle Court House and continued on towards the Tyne Bridge, pulled hard into Lombard Street and parked, wheels screeching as he did so.

He jumped out and looked around.

The place was starting to fill up. It was late on a Monday morning; Brady expected no less. He looked over at the screeching seagulls swooping down into the murky black waters of the Tyne.

He had reached his destination. Under the metallic, dark green curve of the Tyne Bridge right next to the red swing bridge.

No one. At least no one that he recognised.

He shakily got out his phone and checked. Nothing.

'Fuck!' he cursed as he dragged his hand back through his hair and scanned the car park in front of the swing bridge for any sign.

Then Brady heard the distinctive roar of a Ducati 848 sports bike as it raced down the quayside towards him.

He watched as the black Ducati and rider with matching black leathers and helmet pulled up in front of him.

For a moment Brady didn't know what to do.

The rider sat upright and lifted his black tinted visor and looked at Brady.

'What took you so long?' he asked.

'Tying up loose ends,' answered Brady.

'You're lucky I came back. They'll be looking for me now,' stated Nick.

'I know,' answered Brady. 'Your arm?'

Nick automatically looked down at his left arm.

'Sorted,' he answered simply.

'Who?' asked Brady, knowing full well that Nick couldn't have gone to hospital without questions being asked.

'You don't want to know.'

All Brady could see was Nick's blue eyes. Narrowed and dangerously dark.

He was on the run. Had to get out of the North East before they put a bullet through his head.

'The Ambassador's daughter?' asked Nick.

'She's fine. They hadn't touched her,' answered Brady knowing full well that wasn't the reason Nick had risked his neck to meet him.

'What about—'

Brady cut in. 'Found her minutes before the tide would have taken her out.'

'Is she alive?'

Brady nodded.

'She's a mess. Broken bones, hypothermia, but thankfully she'll live. She was there for over five and a half hours. If it hadn't been a warm May night she would have . . .' Brady faltered and shook his head.

They both knew that on any other night the cold, North East climes would have killed her. Or had her head hit one of rocks below on impact she would have been dead. Luck had been on her side. And Brady's.

'If they hadn't been in such a rush to get away they would have made sure that she didn't survive that drop. They must have quickly pushed her over the edge which was fortunate for her as it seems that she rolled down the cliff's slope, landing up against the rocks below. They didn't realise we would find her. Let alone alive. They no doubt thought that if the drop didn't kill her, then the tide soon would.'

Nick sighed, relieved.

He then looked Brady in the eye.

'I wish we could talk but . . .' Nick turned his head to the overhead bridge towards the dull sound of morning traffic.

Brady knew he had to cross the bridge heading south. Putting as much distance between him and the North East as physically possible.

'The Dabkunas brothers?' asked Brady.

'Your guess is as good as mine,' answered Nick.

'The Ambassador?'

'Contracted me to find his daughter,' Nick replied. 'Unofficial of course.'

Brady waited.

'A month back she was drugged and kidnapped from a nightclub in London. Held for ransom. No police involvement or she ends up dead. Small mercy given what the Brotherhood would have done to her first,' stated Nick.

'Why? For money?' questioned Brady.

He knew from Conrad's research into the Lithuanian Ambassador that he was a multi-millionaire.

Nick narrowed his eyes as he studied Brady.

'You call yourself a copper, Jack?'

Brady looked puzzled.

'The Dabkunas brothers and whoever it was that was controlling them wanted a piece of his container line.'

Brady remembered that Conrad had said he had an international cargo business. One now contracted to the North East shipping Polish goods in. But Brady now realised what kind of cargo the Dabkunas brothers had intended on shipping.

'Skin traders?' questioned Brady.

Nick didn't answer. There was no need. His eyes said it all.

'Mayor Macmillan?' Brady asked, all too aware that he had gone into partnership with the Ambassador. 'What's his involvement?'

Nick shook his head. 'I've done my job. Like you said, yours is to tie up the loose ends.'

He pulled out a brown package from his jacket.

'This might help,' he said, handing it over to Brady.

He then opened the throttle.

'Be careful, this Brotherhood is more powerful than you know,' he warned.

Brady didn't need the warning. He had witnessed what they were capable of doing.

'Tell Madley I didn't mean to fuck him over. It was simply a means to an end.'

Brady nodded.

Nick stretched out his hand and touched Brady's shoulder.

He in turn grabbed Nick's arm and held it tight, not knowing when he'd see his brother again.

'Nick?' Brady said staring into his brother's determined eyes.

'No . . .' answered Nick.

He then let go of Brady's shoulder, pulled his visor down and revved the engine.

Brady stood back and watched as Nick sped off. No turning back.

He waited under the bridge. Waited to hear the roar of the Ducati as it took the Tyne Bridge out of Newcastle.

Brady closed his eyes as he heard the sports bike disappear. Where Nick was going, Brady had no idea. Better that way, he thought.

Chapter Forty-Nine

Brady had tried his best to avoid people when he made his way to his office. The station was buzzing. It was Monday, late afternoon, and the news of Nicoletta being found in time had gotten round. She was currently in Rake Lane Hospital receiving medical attention. Much to everyone's relief she hadn't suffered any serious complications from her injuries. She had various broken bones, hypothermia, but nothing more. Shock seemed to be the main concern. But with time, and the right people helping her, Brady was certain she'd recover.

Claudia and her team were already working with Nicoletta. Trying to piece together the events that had led to her being sex trafficked by the Dabkunas brothers.

Macmillan's boys, Visa and Delta, had both suffered fatal injuries. The only injuries Ronnie Macmillan had suffered were to his face after Brady had apprehended him.

At least, that's what Brady had told Gates.

It was enough.

Nobody was going to question how much force it took to restrain him.

Rubenfeld had already been in touch. Brady had filled him in on the events. He had to keep him sweet. After all,

410

he was one of his best snitches. And anyway, they had both agreed this was a huge coup for Northumbria Police.

The problem was Ronnie Macmillan had already told him he would never talk. And Brady believed him. He would go down with a damming sentence and still never utter one word in his defence or against his politician brother. No deal would be brokered for information. He would, out of family loyalty, serve without question whatever the courts threw at him. And given what they had, he'd be put away indefinitely.

Gates or O'Donnell weren't overly concerned by Ronnie Macmillan's silence. They were more than happy with the outcome. Brady and his team had intercepted a sex trafficking and slavery operation right under everyone's noses. And then there was the Lithuanian Ambassador who only had the highest accolades for the Chief Superintendent's force.

Ainsworth and his team were already forensically examining the Jag and the abandoned Mercedes van. Brady was certain that there would be forensic evidence linking the van to Macmillan and the Dabkunas brothers. And then there was the Ambassador's daughter's testimony. Not that Brady had been there to take her statement. DCI Gates had dealt with that, along with Chief Superintendent O'Donnell in some disclosed location. After all, this was the Lithuanian Ambassador who had diplomatic immunity. Right now, Brady was certain that his daughter, accompanied by the Ambassador and his armed security, would be flying home in a private jet.

They also had Melissa Ryecroft's statement detailing how she had been kidnapped by the Dabkunas brothers for the Nietzschean Brotherhood's nefarious purposes.

Brady swallowed hard. He didn't want to think about

411

Edita's decapitated body washed up on the beach. Had the Lithuanian girl been sold to the highest bidder in the Nietzschean Brotherhood? Brady didn't know and had to accept the chances of ever finding out were slim. He knew that Claudia's team would be working all hours to find the Dabkunas brothers and the other members of the Nietzschean Brotherhood. But whether they would was another matter entirely.

Brady was certain others were involved. There was a covert brotherhood out there, but he knew that he wouldn't find out. Not yet, anyway. With some time and investigation he might just add some names.

Nick's name of course was never mentioned. He hadn't officially been on the Ambassador's payroll. In fact, he officially didn't exist. Job over with, and he had disappeared. The Ambassador would have had money paid in hard, untraceable cash.

Brady didn't want to think about the Dabkunas brothers. They were still at large. And he knew they would have a price on Nick's head.

He picked up the brown envelope that Nick had given him.

An unlabelled DVD was inside.

He opened his laptop and put the DVD in.

He watched as it started to play.

A masked man could be seen holding a pistol to a girl's head. Brady recognised her as Edita, the decapitated Lithuanian girl.

Brady watched, feeling sick as the masked man, ignoring Edita's pleas, pulled the trigger, firing the captive bolt into her brain. He turned away, unable to watch as her brutalised, heavily bleeding body began to spasm and convulse.

He had seen enough. He had seen what Nick had wanted him to see.

The masked man had no identifiable traits apart from on his right hand. The hand that put the pistol to the victim's head. He was wearing a gold signet ring with the emblem 'N'. And his pinky finger had been mutilated, cut off at the joint. Exactly like the man Melissa Ryecroft had described.

Brady picked up his phone and called the number logged from the text Nick had sent him.

The phone had been disconnected. What more did he expect?

He picked up the brown envelope and shook it, hoping to find a note. But there was nothing.

No number. No contact email address. Nothing.

Brady sighed and placed his head in his hands wondering when he'd next see his brother. If ever.

He put the DVD back in the envelope, opened his drawer and filed it. He would get Jed, Northumbria's computer forensic officer, to analyse it later. Not that he expected to get much back. But he would have to officially hand it over, claiming it had been handed to him anonymously.

First, there was something he needed to do.

He pulled out the bottle of Scotch that he kept for moments like this one. Not that he ever thought this day would come. He slowly unscrewed the lid and poured himself a liberal measure into his Che Guevara mug.

He then placed the open bottle on his desk.

'To you, Nick,' sighed Brady.

He then knocked it back. In one swift move. His throat rasped as the whisky, a Talisker bought by Madley, burnt its way down.

He could feel his eyes stinging. They weren't smarting from the twelve-year-old single malt. Nor was it because of the note on his desk.

It was the note from Charlie Turner that he had read first, before opening up the package from Nick.

Turner had taken a call from Kate Matthews, Jimmy Matthews' estranged wife, on Brady's behalf. The call had come into the station thirty minutes ago at 8:33am.

The note simply stated that Matthews had been found at 6:45am by a prison guard in his cell with a ballpoint pen sticking out of his neck. He was now in a critical condition. Whether he would pull through was debatable.

Brady thought back to his conversation yesterday with Matthews. He had begged Brady to help him get out. Had blackmailed him and then tried to trade the information he had on Ronnie Macmillan. He was desperate. And rightly so, thought Brady. Whether the attack would have happened anyway, given he was a copper banged up with the very prisoners he'd helped put away, or whether word had got out that he'd talked was now a moot point. Either way, he was a dead man. Inside prison or outside. And Matthews had made himself a very dangerous enemy: Madley.

Brady sighed heavily. He hadn't slept for days. But he wasn't ready to go home; not yet. Still too pumped with adrenalin.

But he knew full well the reasons why.

It was watching a Lithuanian girl being brutally tortured to death. She had died a horrific, unimaginable death.

He raised the mug one more time.

'Edita . . . and to the others still out there,' Brady whispered.

His phone suddenly buzzed.

It was Amelia.

'Hi,' he quietly answered.

'I just wanted to check how Conrad was doing?' Amelia replied, her voice filled with concern.

'He's good. Or should I say as good as can be expected. It could have been a lot worse,' sighed Brady.

'How are you bearing up?'

'I'm OK,' Brady replied.

There was a heavy silence. They both knew he was lying.

'If you want someone to talk to you know where I am,' offered Amelia breaking the palpable awkwardness.

Brady didn't answer.

'Look, I've got to go. Let me know if you want to get together for a coffee or maybe a drink, yeah?' suggested Amelia.

'Yeah . . . Thanks,' muttered Brady.

There was nothing left to say so she hung up.

Brady sighed heavily. He wasn't ready yet.

But he recognised it was time to move on.

To let go of the past.

Read on for an extract of Danielle Ramsay's compulsive debut novel, *Broken Silence*, out now.

Chapter One

She felt sick, really sick.

She moaned as the ground started to swirl in front of her.

'Oh fuck!' she slurred as she drunkenly collapsed onto her hands and knees.

Trembling, she waited for the nausea to pass.

Finally certain that she wasn't going to puke she pulled her long blonde hair back from her face and looked around, but it was too dark to make sense of the rubble and half-fallen walls of the abandoned farmhouse. She suddenly realised that she was alone.

'You fucking shit!' she yelled out, angry that he had just left her there in the middle of nowhere.

She waited, but there was no response. The surrounding trees and bushes conspired against her, rustling and creaking, fooling her into believing that someone else was there.

'Fuck you and your fucking attitude! I hate you! You hear me? I fucking hate you!' she screamed defiantly. 'You're the one with the problem, not me!'

She slumped back onto her knees and stared up at the black starless sky. Everything seemed so pointless. She hated him. She hated him for using her and then just throwing her to one side. She would have to be stupid not to notice that he wasn't into her any more. She had heard the rumours. Who hadn't? She knew there were other girls, but she'd hoped that she had meant something to him. She had foolishly believed that he could take her away from her crap life; that he could somehow save her. But now that he had got what he had wanted, he wasn't interested any more.

She felt a cold wetness on her face and realised she was crying. She wiped her damp cheeks aggressively, angry with herself for feeling like this. Angry that she had let him get to her.

'I don't fucking care what you say. I'll tell whoever I want to about what you've done to me. Then you'll be sorry! You hear me? You'll be the fucking sorry one, you bastard!' she threatened, ignoring the tears as they continued to fall.

Exhausted, she attempted to get to her feet. Certain that she could stand she pulled out her mobile phone from the front pocket of her short black denim skirt. She tried to make out whether she had any new messages or calls.

'Bastard!' she muttered when she realised she didn't.

She started to scroll through her phone book looking for his number.

Suddenly she heard footsteps coming up behind her. She smiled, relieved that he'd come back.

She froze as the smile faded from her lips.

'I . . . I . . . didn't mean the things I said . . . yeah? I was just really mad with you, that's all . . .' she stuttered as she shook her head.

It took her a second to register what was about to happen.

Shocked, she dropped her phone as she numbly staggered backwards as she tried to get away.

In her panic she tripped over and fell to the ground. She grabbed her scarf which was lying beside her and rolled over onto her knees as she attempted to get up. But a hard kick to her back winded her, forcing her down again.

Suddenly the scarf was pulled from her hand.

'Ahh!' she cried out as her head was yanked back by her hair.

She felt something being slipped around her throat. She couldn't understand what was happening. And by the time she did, it was too late. The scarf was already securely knotted around her neck. She screamed as she clawed at the material. But the harder she fought, the tighter the scarf was twisted, silencing her.

She frantically tore at the scarf, desperate to breathe but she couldn't loosen its hold over her. Panicking, she scratched at her neck ferociously as the burning pain in her lungs intensified. Finally, she collapsed forward, unconscious of what was about to follow.

Chapter Two

The phone was ringing. It had to be bad. He could feel his heart pounding. He turned over and buried his head into the pillow but the ringing continued. He tried to ignore it but it was pointless. He opened his eyes and lay there for a moment drenched in sweat.

It was dark, still night. He looked down at the cluttered floor gingerly and squinted at the alarm clock, his head exploding with the effort. It took a few seconds before he could make out it was only 4.30 am. And another couple of seconds before he realised the phone was still ringing. He stretched out his trembling hand and groped around on the floor.

'Yeah?' he mumbled hoarsely.

'Detective Inspector Brady?'

Without answering, he disconnected the call and dropped the phone to the floor. His head was thumping. He had the mother of all hangovers, which wasn't surprising considering he'd been on a suicidal bender for the past couple of weeks. He had been downing a toxic mixture of whisky and beer to forget his wrecked life and block out the recurring nightmare he had had for as long as he could remember.

422

But lately nothing seemed to work. Even when he sank into a drunken sleep he always woke up sweating, heart racing.

He tried to recall the previous night. All he could remember was drinking too much and then . . .

He felt sick at the thought. He winced as the knot in his stomach tightened. He turned his pounding head tentatively. A young woman lay asleep on her stomach beside him, naked from the waist up, the duvet discreetly covering the rest of her body. Her thick, dark, shoulder-length hair was spread out over the pillow. He watched as she gently breathed in and out. He couldn't even recall her name let alone what she did for a living.

He swallowed hard, trying to dislodge the sour taste in his mouth. Never before had he plummeted to such a nadir. There hadn't been anyone since Claudia, his wife, had left. And now here he was with some young woman who he didn't even recognise lying naked beside him.

The drinking was supposed to distract him from who he was, not make him feel even worse about himself. He thought about getting some painkillers and decided that he couldn't be bothered to get up and rummage around in the dark. The last thing he wanted to do was wake up Sleeping Beauty.

The phone started to ring again. He froze as she started in her sleep.

'Fuck!' he muttered.

He stretched his right hand out and blindly searched amongst the months of debris scattered on the floor.

'What?' he answered in a thick Geordie voice, silencing the shrill ring.

He watched as she stirred briefly before slipping back into a restless slumber.

'Brady?' questioned a low, deep voice.

'Who wants to know?'

'DCI Gates.'

'Sir?' questioned Brady, thrown.

'You're a hard man to get hold of, Jack,' continued the dispassionate voice.

'With all due respect, sir, I'm not expected back until Monday.'

He regretted the words as soon as he had spoken them. Gates wasn't the kind of man that you wanted as an enemy.

'You have half an hour to get it together.'

'But . . .' he objected.

'I'll have a car waiting for you. Make sure you're ready,' Gates ordered, leaving him no choice.

By the time he had thought of a response the line was dead.

He stared blankly at the phone trying to figure out what was going on.

Moments later he was roused from his musings by a dull, heavy pain in the pit of his stomach. He needed to piss. He pulled the duvet back and swung his legs onto the floor.

A searing pain shot through his left inner thigh. He instinctively pressed down hard with both hands onto the knotted wound and held them there as he waited for the pain to subside.

He didn't know who he hated more; the bastard who had tried to blow his balls away or Claudia for leaving him while he lay fighting for his life. Admittedly he had given her a good enough reason, but even he hadn't expected to come round from surgery to the unwelcome news that she'd had enough. Not only had she left him, she had left the area. It didn't take him long to find out that she had gone to London and had no intention of coming back to the North East.

He hated his life, hated what he'd become without her. Not a single day had gone by since she'd left him when he hadn't considered finishing what the bastard who had shot him had intended. But that was over six months ago, and here he was, still drunk, still bitterly alive.

He could feel a clammy sweat building up on his forehead and wasn't sure whether it was because of the pain in his leg or alcohol poisoning.

He looked at the clock. 4.54 am, he thought, sighing heavily. He stood up shakily and waited a few moments, unsure of whether he was too drunk to stand. Finally certain that he could stay on his feet he slowly limped over to the bedroom door.

'Where . . . where are you going?' murmured a sleepy voice.

He paused.

What could he say? Sorry, I don't even remember fucking you last night, let alone your name?

He shook his head.

'Go back to sleep,' he muttered.

He watched her mumble her consent and turn over. He stood for a moment wishing that his life were that simple.

*

Bleary-eyed he blinked back at his reflection and ran his fingers through his long dark hair pulling it back from his face. He'd been meaning to get it cut but hadn't got around to doing it. He stared at his heavy hooded, dark brown bloodshot eyes.

He was six feet two and slender with some muscle. He was attractive; at least that's what his soon to be ex-wife had told him. Not that he could see it. But he knew there was something about him that women liked. Sleeping Beauty lying in his bed was testimony to that.

But throughout the five years he had been married he had never fooled around. Not once, not until that fateful night. And even then it was over before it had even started. But it was enough for Claudia to bail. He knew it was a convenient out for her. After months of Claudia working long hours in a blatant attempt to avoid him, Brady drunkenly and pitifully fell into the arms of a seductive new colleague – Detective Constable Simone Henderson. Claudia had walked in on them without Brady knowing. It wasn't until the following night when his balls were nearly blown away on an undercover drugs bust that he realised that Claudia knew about his indiscretion. She had rushed to the hospital as soon as she heard he had been shot, wanting the reassurance he was still breathing so she could have the satisfaction of handing him divorce papers.

Brady lifted a wet hand and tried to wipe clean the smeared blur that was his reflection. He looked rough, too rough to crawl into work. He ran his right hand over the dark stubble that covered his chin and crept up over his cheeks. In a last ditch attempt to straighten himself out he splashed icy cold water over his face. It made no difference; he still looked half-cut. There was only one thing that would sober him up and that was a hot shower followed by black, bitter coffee. He needed to at least appear sober if he was facing Gates. He knew that whatever had happened must have been serious enough for Gates to be calling.

Chapter Three

Brady heard the doorbell ring and looked at his watch: it was 5.25 am, bang on time. He dragged heavily on the cigarette in his hand before crushing it out. Already the third one of the day, he noted, acknowledging that he had failed to kick the habit before returning to work.

But at least he was starting to sober up. Add to that a shave and a change of clothes and he looked halfway decent.

Brady poured himself some hot black coffee and looked around at the chaos that had crept into the house after his wife had left. Row after row of empty Peroni bottles, half-eaten Chinese take-away cartons and empty pizza boxes pretty much summed up his life now. It stank.

He switched off the kitchen light and walked down the hallway, his heavy footsteps resonating on the wooden floor.

He looked around in disgust. A lamp was still on throwing a gloomy light over the mess his life had become. Overflowing ashtrays were scattered all over the room. Discarded whisky and beer bottles lay across the dusty wooden floor. Over six months' worth of weekend news-papers were dumped on an old leather armchair. Books lay in piles around the room, while others haphazardly lined the handmade wooden bookcases that covered two of the walls.

His office at the station, with its high, rattling windows and bulky, rust-stained, leaking radiators, felt more comfortable to him than his own home. More so now that he couldn't stomach living alone in a three-storey five-bedroomed Victorian house. The fact that Claudia had not only moved out, but had taken every scrap of furniture that wasn't nailed down didn't help. He had volunteered to be the one to leave, but Claudia had declined his offer. The fact that she had walked in on Brady in their bed with a young colleague had been incentive enough for her to pack up and go. And to be fair, he couldn't blame her. Between them there had always been one rule, never bring work home.

They had both worked for Northumbria Police. It was his job to lock the scum up who made decent people's lives a misery and it had been Claudia's job to support the same scum by offering them legal representation; regardless of the crime. She was a lawyer and also acted as the Duty Solicitor at his station. She was damned good at her job; so good that the law firm she worked for in Newcastle were preparing to offer her a partnership.

They had met through work and somehow had survived everything it had thrown at them until now. Brady knew that even his boss, the emotionally cold and unflappable DCI Gates, had a soft spot for Claudia. Who didn't? She was strikingly beautiful with a mane of long curly reddish hair and a fiery personality to match. But Brady hadn't married her for her good looks; it was her quick wit and stunning intelligence that had seduced him. And the fact that she was everything he wasn't; middle-class, educated and compassionate. She fought injustice because she believed in civilisation. He, on the other hand, didn't believe in a better society. Brady was a realist and to him, civilisation was just another false god that idealists liked to believe in. His job was to prevent the world from becoming the dark and dangerous place he knew it to be.

Brady looked at the two empty whisky tumblers sat side by side on the tiled hearth. He recalled bitterly how he and Claudia would often share a bottle of whisky in front of the fire while Tom Waits played in the background. In the early days they had passionately argued about anything and everything from politics to literature. He felt physically sick as he thought about what he had lost. She had meant everything to him. More than even she had realised.

Wincing, he bent down to retrieve his jacket from the floor. Pulling it on he turned to see who Gates had sent.

It was Harry Conrad. He looked half-frozen. As always, his blond hair was cropped short and neat. Clean-shaven, with the look of a man who took time over his appearance, Conrad wore a conservative charcoal-grey suit with a blue shirt and dark blue tie. Over this he wore a heavy dark grey woollen overcoat.

That was Conrad for you: always clean-cut, well-dressed, polite and ready to take orders, even at five in the morning. Conrad had the makings of a Detective Chief Superintendent. He was well-liked by his superiors because he was eager and always did as he was told. That guaranteed success, something Brady had found out the hard way.

'Fuck it,' Brady said under his breath.

Gates really was trying to mess with his head. It was cold, too cold and dark to be out of bed. And too early to be dealing with this.

'Gates sent me, sir,' Conrad eventually said. He looked uncomfortable; his five feet eleven body hunched over, head down.

Brady suddenly felt old as he stood looking at his thirty-year-old deputy. Brady may have only had eight years on Conrad, but for the first time he could really feel the age difference.

'Why?' Brady asked as he narrowed his dark brown eyes.

Conrad shoved his hands in his coat pockets uneasily while Brady continued to stare at him.

'I was just ordered to pick you up, sir.'

Brady didn't reply.

Conrad uncomfortably filled in the silence.

'We've got a murder victim, sir. A young woman.'

Brady didn't know what he had expected when he started back on Monday, but it definitely didn't involve any high-profile cases. He felt uneasy, something about this didn't feel quite right.

'What details do you have?'

'I've just been called in myself, sir. All I know is that the body was found in West Monkseaton, on some abandoned farmland near the Metro line.'

'Do we have an ID?'

Conrad shook his head.

If Conrad had said North Shields or even Shiremoor Brady would have understood but not West Monkseaton. It was classed as the upmarket part of Whitley Bay. Then again any place was better than Whitley Bay; to say the small seaside resort had seen better days was an understatement. The town was a testimony to the credit crunch, most of the retailers having closed up leaving behind a trail of depressing, musty-smelling charity shops and seedy pubs.

The only thing the rundown coastal town had going for it was that it was within commuter distance of Newcastle upon Tyne; a university city with a thriving student population and Goth culture. Newcastle was also known for the Bigg Market where punters would binge drink into the early hours, women staggering in their four-inch heels, and short, strapless dresses leered at by packs of thuggish men in sleeveless shirts – regardless of the North East's all-year sub-zero temperatures.

But Brady knew from first-hand experience as a copper that the seaside resort of Whitley Bay could also hold its own when it came to binge drinking and lewd behaviour. So much so, it came as no surprise to Brady that the small, shabby, seaside town had been rated as a weekend stag party destination equal to Amsterdam.

'Gates is waiting for you at the crime scene sir,' Conrad emphasised. He was under strict orders to collect Brady and get him to Gates ASAP.

'Let me grab my keys,' answered Brady as he rummaged through the unopened mail and other objects dumped on the ornate marble mantelpiece.

Conrad looked around uncomfortably at what had become of his boss over the past two months. He had known the place when Claudia had been around and found it difficult to accept that it had degenerated into this soulless squalor. The smell of decaying food and stale alcohol clung nauseatingly in the air, as did the overwhelming feeling of despair and loneliness.

The last time Conrad had seen his boss was when he had visited Brady in hospital, shortly after surgery.

Unfortunately, he had witnessed Brady losing it after Claudia had served him with divorce papers. That was over six months ago. Brady had refused to see him after what had happened. Wouldn't allow him in to visit and when he discharged himself, refused to answer his door or any of the phone or email messages Conrad had left. Conrad had been worried, but not surprised that Brady had gone to ground given his state of mind after Claudia had left him.

Clutching his keys Brady limped out to the hall. Conrad followed.

'Haven't seen you since the incident, sir,' Conrad offered, unsure whether he should mention it.

'Yeah, well I've been busy,' answered Brady.

They both knew he was a lousy liar.

Brady felt awkward. He had avoided Conrad for the past six months, deleting any messages Conrad had left without listening to them. So what? Brady thought. Conrad should be the one feeling guilty, not him. He had had word from an old colleague that Conrad was rumoured to have requested a transfer. Admittedly, it was only a rumour, but it still felt like a betrayal given everything they had been through. To make the situation worse, he had also heard that Conrad was scared that Brady would have some kind of breakdown. Even Brady had to admit that if he was in Conrad's place, the last person he'd want to be teamed up with was himself. Not after what Conrad had witnessed.

'So, put in for a transfer yet?' As soon as the words had slipped out Brady hated himself.

Conrad was thrown.

'No, sir. Why, should I have?'

'You tell me!'

'You've lost me, sir?' replied Conrad.

Brady could hear the hurt in Conrad's voice making him feel even more like a bastard.

'Forget it . . .' he muttered. 'Forget I said anything.'

'No, if you have something to say then say it,' demanded Conrad.

Brady looked at him, mildly surprised, but impressed at Conrad's ballsy outburst.

Brady shook his head.

'It doesn't matter.'

'I disagree. The fact that you could even think I'd put in for a transfer says it all,' Conrad stated.

'All right! You want me to tell you what really pissed me off?'

Conrad looked at him, locking his steel-grey eyes on Brady's.

'You of all people knew what Claudia did destroyed me. I mean fuck it, Conrad! You were there! She didn't even respect me enough to tell me in private. She insisted you stayed in the room so you could witness my humiliation. What the hell do you think that did to me, eh?'

Conrad steadily held his gaze without saying a word.

'So why then would you go to Gates? Why go over my head to my superior and tell him that I was a liability to myself and the job?'

'Because it was the truth,' answered Conrad simply.

Brady shook his head as he looked at his deputy.

'You left me no choice,' added Conrad.

Brady turned away. He couldn't look at Conrad. He didn't want him to see the pain in his eyes. He knew that Conrad was right; he had left him no choice.

Brady knew that what Conrad had seen in the hospital

that night had scared him. Brady had scared himself. But it had affected Conrad so much that he had gone to see Gates without a word to Brady. Conrad had suggested that Brady needed a psychologist to help him get over being shot. In reality what he needed was a bloody good solicitor to help him get over his wife.

He couldn't believe it when the police psychologist casually dropped by the hospital. Brady had the feeling that Gates had been secretly hoping that he had finally lost the plot and that the psychologist would recommend he should retire early from the force on medical grounds.

It didn't take long before Brady found out that Conrad was responsible for his shrink sessions. After that he refused to see him, knowing that he would do something to Conrad that he would later regret and then really would be in need of a shrink. When he finally discharged himself from hospital he ignored the barrage of phone messages and texts left by Conrad.

'You know why I couldn't tell you,' explained Conrad. 'You were in no state to hear reason, not after . . .' His voice trailed off, reluctant to bring up Claudia's part in Brady's self-destructive meltdown.

Brady knew Conrad was right. Nothing Conrad could have said would have stopped him that night. Nothing.

His memory of exactly what had happened that night after he had come round from surgery wasn't that clear. But what he did remember was Claudia coming in and handing him divorce papers and Conrad being forced to stand there, not knowing what to do. Then Claudia turned on her high heels and left without giving him a chance to absorb what she'd done. After that, he couldn't really be sure of what followed. He vaguely recalled pulling the wires from his body as he tried to get himself out of bed to go after her. And then Conrad perilously trying to stop him. Despite his condition he came at Conrad with a strength he didn't know he possessed.

It had taken two male nurses to get him off Conrad and to forcibly hold him down until a doctor came with an injection so strong that it knocked him out for the rest of the night. Conrad had dutifully stayed by his bed for the next twenty-four hours, despite Brady having broken two of Conrad's ribs in the struggle. But Brady had no memory of Conrad's vigil. Nor did he remember repeatedly calling out for Claudia, unaware of what had happened. The days following came and went in a painful, drug-induced blur until eventually he accepted that Claudia wasn't coming back.

Not that Conrad had told him that. It was his psychologist who had shared this information. Allegedly, Conrad had refused to even tell Gates how he had sustained the injuries, despite visibly having a broken nose and stitches zigzagging over his top lip and across his eyebrow. Add to that the medical report that had been filed on Brady's sudden insanity. Even a fool would have realised that Conrad had got caught in the crossfire. But Conrad was loyal and he had done his best under the circumstances to protect Brady. And even Brady had to acknowledge that Conrad was protecting him when he went to Gates.

'Look . . . Conrad, I understand. All right?' Brady quietly conceded.

It wasn't until now with Conrad stood in front of him that he realised he wasn't angry at Conrad. He was angry with himself for putting Conrad in that situation in the first place. And he knew the real reason Conrad went to

Gates wasn't because he wanted him to lose his job; it was the opposite, he wanted him to hold on to his job. And if that meant bringing in the police psychologist, then Conrad had no qualms in requesting that Gates did exactly that.

'Honestly, I understand,' he repeated.

Conrad nodded, grateful that they had finally cleared the air.

'Jack? Jack? What's going on?' interrupted a soft voice from the top of the stairs.

Brady felt as if somebody had stuck a knife in his stomach and twisted it. He'd completely forgotten about her.

They both turned and looked up. Sleeping Beauty was standing shivering in what appeared to be just her T-shirt and skimpy knickers. She pushed her dark tousled hair out of her sleepy face as she stared in bewilderment at the two men below her.

'It's nothing. Go back to bed,' Brady answered, embarrassed. His throat felt dry and tight. He didn't want anyone knowing his private business; especially Conrad.

Looking at her standing there, vulnerable and still drunk, he felt disgusted with himself. He realised in that moment that Claudia was right about him. He was a bastard. He would never change, not really. And here in front of his and Conrad's eyes was the evidence. He couldn't believe how low he had stooped. He could now see what had eluded him last night: her age. If she were twenty-one it would have surprised him.

'Come on,' he said as he turned to Conrad.

Conrad didn't say a word.

Brady knew what he would be thinking. And if he were in Conrad's shoes right now, he'd be thinking exactly the same thing; that he deserved to lose Claudia.

436

'Jack? Jack?' she called out in a tremulous voice.

He turned and looked up at her still standing there, shivering.

'I'll . . . I'll leave my number so you can call me about tonight . . . yeah?'

Brady nodded and then walked out into the black, empty night after Conrad. He knew for her sake the best thing to do was not call her back. Let it go and pretend it had never happened.

He could see nothing but blackness as he reached the path at the end of his long, front garden. But he could hear the thunderous crashing of the heavy waves as they beat against Brown's Bay below. He lived on Southcliff, an imposing and exclusive row of Victorian houses that lined the cliff, facing out towards the North Sea. Nestled on a tight bend between Cullercoats and Whitley Bay, Brady had never been sure whether the row of houses fell in the sought-after fishing village of Cullercoats or whether it marked the very edge of the shabby seaside resort of Whitley Bay.

Claudia had fallen in love with the place as soon as she had seen the bending cliff with its dramatic plunge to the waiting rocks below. On a good day the view from the first-floor living room and second-floor study were breath-taking; dazzling azure waters lay perfectly still as far as the eye could see. White sailing boats and small, brightly coloured fishing boats would serenely blend in against the backdrop of stunning blue. But when the sea mirrored the grey, blackening skies overhead, the brooding waves would thrash against one another as they threw themselves against the cliff, violent and furious. At times the waves would be so high they would crash against the path lining the cliff, covering the large windows of the house in a thick, salty sea spray. If one of the local fishing boats was unfortunate enough to be out collecting lobster nets during a storm, Brady would watch through the murky windows mesmerised, while the tiny boat would be mercilessly tossed from one black wave to another.

'Bugger me! It's cold!' he said as turned up his jacket collar against the cold, bitter air coming off the North Sea.

Conrad didn't reply as he made his way along the walkway towards his car parked on the tight bending road at the edge of the jutting cliff.

Brady knew Conrad wasn't impressed with what he'd seen. And Brady couldn't help but agree with him.

Danielle Ramsay's Writing Tips:

- Firstly, you will need determination, self belief and to be prepared for a tremendous amount of hard work. Competition is high (especially in the crime genre) and only a few manuscripts ever reach an agent or editor's desk. But don't give up. Keep motiviated by believing in your work and reminding yourself how badly you want to be a writer.

- Character, plot and location are the key ingredients to a successful novel. BUT you must know your genre first and then apply the above three key ingredients. How do you get to know your genre? Read . . . read and then read some more. The more you read, the better the writer you will become.

- Write about what you know. If you're interested in writing crime then follow everything crime related. Absorb yourself in it. Same applies to location – know your setting. Live it, feel it – walk it. For that crucial characterisation – people watch. Interview professionals in the related area you want to write in, if at all possible. This will give you ideas about who your main character is and how they operate. Understand the procedures they follow. And then, know your character inside out – what they think, feel and how they would act in any given situation. In other words, bring them to life!

• You've researched your genre, you have a plot, a character and you've found that ideal location to set it in, now all you need to do is start writing. The key to staying on track is writing everyday for an hour an half to three hours maximum – regardless. Writing everyday means that you will not get tied up in knots and loose the thread of your plot.

• Finally, be patient. Writing is a slow process. Very few writers publish their first draft – or even their first novel. So be prepared to re-write again and again. And don't be precious – be prepared to take well-meaning advice and criticism from someone you trust. And remember that 'those brick walls are not there to keep us out; the brick walls are there to give us a chance to show how badly we want something'. (Randy Pausch, 'The Last Lecture' 2007.)